What if Moses [illegible]

What if a small band of Israelites, accompanied by Moses, secretly returned to the wilderness looking for a very different Promised Land?

And what if there is much more to the man and the story than we have been told?

Community of Promise *is the untold story of Moses in the voice of Eliezer, his mystical second son. He offers it as a counter-balance to the "official" account, written by Gershom, Moses' concrete-thinking first son and stenographer of mystical experiences.*

Community of Promise *is fiction that behaves like non-fiction!*

While raising social, economic, political, theological/religious, and community issues, the story follows Moses and the fledgling community through their exploration of emerging identity and ultimate destination.

The study guide included at the end of the book makes Community of Promise a welcome resource for book study groups.

Moses' humanity discovered beneath the "Mantle of the Prophet" will touch you deeply.

Community of Promise

The Untold Story of Moses

A Novel

Love to Jennifer and Bruce!
– Mom

Wayne E. Gustafson

Entos Press

Entos Press
Ithaca, NY
www.entospress.com

This book is a work of fiction. The words and actions of all characters, including those named in the Biblical story, are products of the author's imagination.

Copyright 2010 © Wayne E. Gustafson

All rights reserved, including the right of reproduction in whole or in part in any form.

Cover design by Megan Pugh
BlinkDigitalGraphics.com

Manufactured in the United States of America

ISBN 978-0-9826338-0-9

For Jo Dunn
whose timely question to me about Moses' prohibition from the Promised Land inspired this story.
Happy 100th birthday, Jo!

Acknowledgments

If I were a highly organized person, I would have noted, in writing and at the time they gave their help, all of the people who have supported the writing, editing, and printing of *Community of Promise.*
But, I'm not that organized! Besides, I think there are perhaps hundreds who have contributed to this process.

Still, I want specifically to acknowledge a few people, while recognizing that however many names I include, I am sure to leave out other equally important people. To those not specifically named, I hope you know who you are and that you will accept my gratitude for your contributions to this book.

I want to thank my very first reader Alan Parrish who encouraged me to keep writing. Thanks also to Krishna Ramanujan who taught me the basic elements of self-editing. And thanks to Aileen Fitzke whose thoughtful critique provided the foundation for the first major rewrite of the story. Thanks to the book study group participants who were willing to try out the novel in that setting, and whose useful feedback about the novel and about their experience in the group laid the foundation for the Study Guide.

Finally, thanks to my wife, Phebe, and son, Luke who have put up with my frequent tendency to "disappear" while working on this project. Further thanks to Luke for creating the "interview with the author" video.

Wayne E. Gustafson
January 2010

Dramatis Personae

Characters from the Biblical Story of Moses

Moses—Son of Amram and Jocabed, and Brother of Aaron and Miriam.
Jethro the Midianite—Father-in-law of Moses
Zipporah – Daughter of Jethro the Midianite and Wife of Moses
Gershom—Elder Son of Moses and Zipporah
Eliezer—Younger Son of Moses and Zipporah
Milcah—Daughter of Zelophehad and Wife of Eliezer
Mahlah, Noah, Hoglah, and Tirzah—Daughters of Zelophehad
Joshua—Successor to Moses as Leader of the Israelites

Principal Fictional Characters

Jethro—Husband of Noah and Member of The Community of Promise
Sarah—Member of the Community Leadership Team
Asher— Husband of Sarah
Kenan—Member of the Community Leadership Team
Enosh—Soldier and Member of the Community Leadership Team

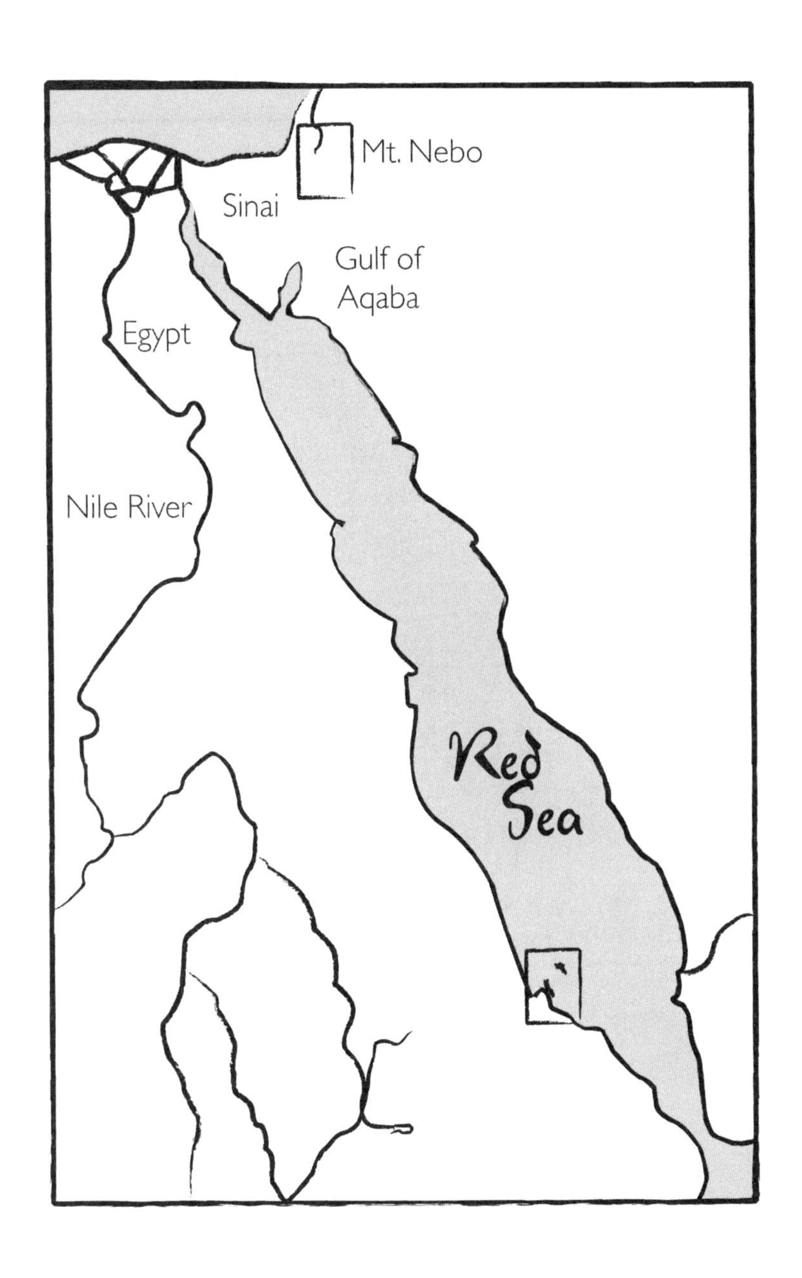
Mt. Nebo
Sinai
Gulf of
Aqaba
Egypt
Nile River
Red
Sea

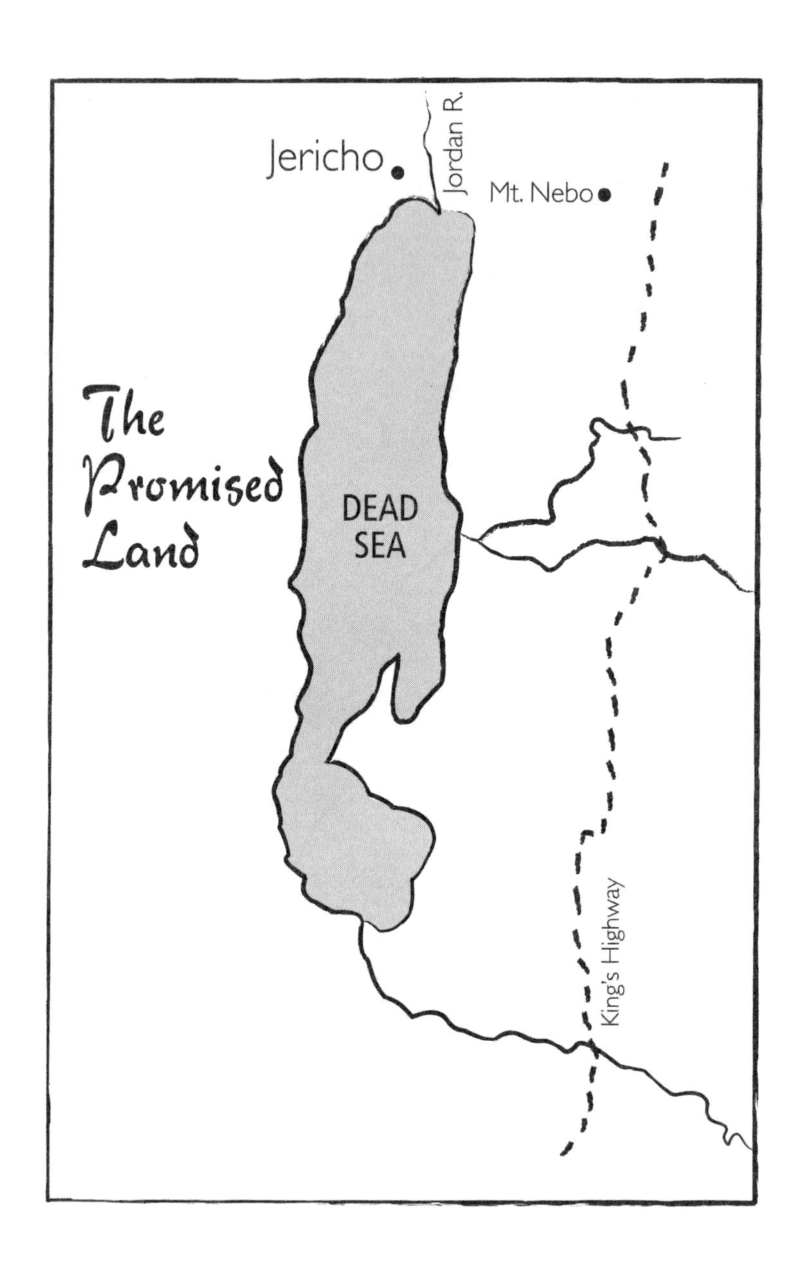
Jordan R.
Jericho
Mt. Nebo
The Promised Land
DEAD SEA
King's Highway

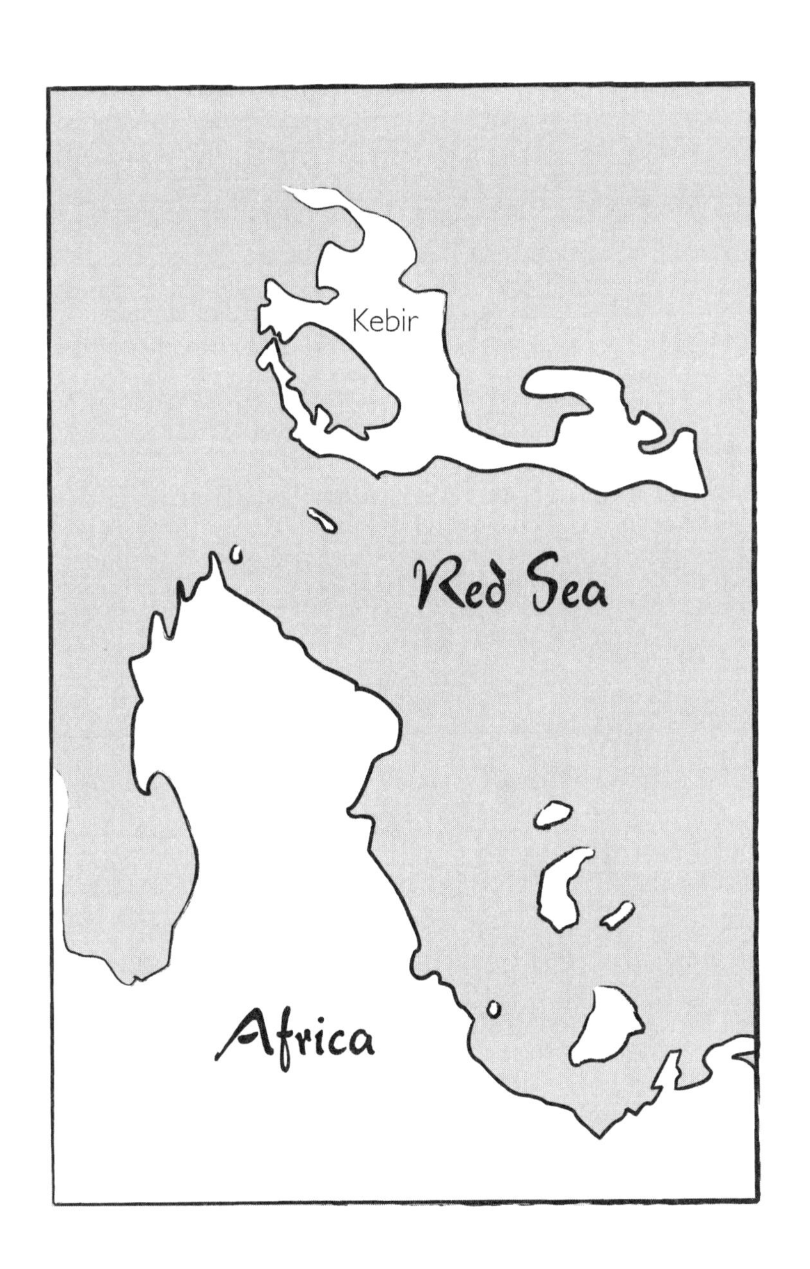
Kebir
Red Sea
Africa

Eliezer

Every person who ever met my father, even once, could tell immediately that he was an extraordinary person. I have always known that. Truthfully, I half-expected floods and earthquakes to trouble the world when he departed, but now I simply celebrate his life and his full passage into Divine Presence. I'm grateful that nothing will ever again interfere with his intimate relationship with the Holy One. I miss him already, but I'm sure I will adjust eventually to this emptiness where he once lived so boldly.

His rough, but beautifully carved walking stick sits across my lap. Moses cradled it in his arms during his last days. No, it's not the one that he used to find water for the Israelites or helped him impress Pharaoh so many years ago. That one passed into the hands of his successor, Joshua. The handle of this staff still has some roughness remaining, not like that other one that had been smoothed by more than forty years of Moses' touch. This one lacks the scars from hitting rocks or wadi beds to expose springs of water or from more than a generation of wilderness wear. Still, from the moment he received this new one, he cherished it. For Moses, the first staff symbolized holy power. This one represents the fulfillment of our other Promised Land, the one that we call The Community of Promise. By means of this staff, I will forever honor his rich life and the brave journey he made to join this community.

My memories of my father could by themselves have satisfied my heart forever if only my elder brother hadn't authored and systematically institutionalized the story of Moses, Prophet of God. Many will read "The Book" but, few, if any, will ever know who actually wrote it. I must admit that Gershom has written quite a story, and if I know my brother, he will promote it so that everyone throughout the generations will be acquainted with Moses. They will grow up reciting how Pharaoh's daughter rescued a little Hebrew boy named Moses from death or a lifetime of slavery, from drowning, and from the wrath of her own father, who would have killed him had he known the young boy's true identity. They will learn how she brought him up and surrounded him with the greatest luxury and power in the known world; how as a young man he had to flee to a far country; how he settled down to wife and family, only to meet the god of the mountain who sent him back to Egypt to save his people in dramatic fashion from their slavery; how he lead their ungrateful and recalcitrant selves for many years through the wilderness, right up to the brink of the ultimate prize – only to die without himself setting even one foot in the Land of Promise. Yes, it's quite a story that Gershom has pieced together[1].

As context for his story, let me tell you a few things about my brother. Gershom prefers to live his life at the center of the action, though he usually works in the background. Hence, readers will be convinced that Moses wrote his own book. But I know the truth. I know that Gershom crafted the words to record the tale for posterity, and I know that he transformed a mere, if dramatic story into the foundational document of Israelite identity and law.

Of course, Gershom's version presents more than the story of Moses. It also introduces Jehovah[2] (as Gershom refers to the Holy One), a god of power beyond imagining who, incredibly, has chosen this reluctant band of ex-slaves to become the one great nation by which all others will know the true God – if only the people will obey the rather detailed and specific divine law (as articulated by my brother, of course).

Believe me, I know him pretty well. His ingenuity and single-mindedness (however unimaginative) can propel him to any length necessary to attain his goals. Years of watching him have convinced me that he will surely find the means for his "holy" words to be known throughout the ages.

I ask myself why Gershom's version of the story doesn't satisfy me – a fair question that I feel compelled to answer, if only to put my own curiosity to rest. Any observer would readily agree that Gershom has his own particular bias. Still, I want to give him his due. My brother alone, while still new to manhood, dared to sit with a divinely transformed Moses immediately after he had descended from his encounter with I AM on the mountain. All the others, paralyzed by their fear, wouldn't come near him. Bravery and intelligence by themselves, however, cannot ensure accuracy or guarantee a comprehensive account. I know from my own observations that Gershom's written words don't quite tell the whole story.

But that's only part of my problem. My brother may have known "The Prophet of God" but he never really got to know his father. Of course, larger-than-life-prophets don't easily avail themselves in intimate relationships, even (especially?) with their own families.

Now that Gershom has written his book, I see no other option but to tell another version of the story according to my understanding and perspective. I will have my own bias, to be sure, but the world needs access to the whole story of Moses. And I want posterity to know the part of the story that transcends even Moses.

I am motivated by an additional sacred obligation to record the exploits of a small group of brave (some would call them foolish) people who chose to join Moses on a quest for a radically different Promised Land, one that forever lives within and among them. Moses spent his life trying to teach us to know the Holy One. I pray that this writing will honor and carry forth his work.

Just for the record, none of the latter part of my account can be found in Gershom's writings. There are two reasons for this. The more intimate story of Moses, the man, could never fit with my brother's picture of reality, so he wouldn't have written it down even if he had known about it. As far as he believes, (and here is the second reason) Moses died on Mt Nebo.

My brother was wrong.

Toward the end of his life, Moses told his story to his younger son, Eliezer (that would be me). When I put it together with my own experiences and with those of the others who journeyed with us, you will understand how we found a very different, but equally authentic Promised Land.

Prologue

Such a subtle change in the density of the darkness would have escaped his notice were the man not sleeping. Perhaps all darkness contains a heaviness that slips into the void, featherweight by featherweight, just barely hinting at the remote possibility of a new day. That infinitely minute photonic alteration, however, carried sufficient force to nudge the sleeper's sense toward his awakening.

Vague stirrings of questions slowly surfaced, floating just out of the mind's reach—specks in an ocean of sentience. Like a bubble of air burped out by a deep-sea creature, the thought floated up through the murky depths toward the much-filtered light of the nascent morning.

Somewhere in his memory lived an image—no idea where he picked it up—of human consciousness: a raft, often adrift, but buoyed up by an infinitely deep sea. And at the bottom, birthing, carrying, and animating all creation resides The One - I AM - I WAS - I WILL BE - I AM BECOMING - YHWH - The Holy One. The man pictured no substantial image of the divine, although somehow he knew that nothing could be more real.

This particular ephemeral bubble had many times before begun the journey from the divine depths, wending its way through denizens and detritus, as it rose through the sea of unconsciousness. Each time, it would break through the surface into consciousness, this tiny bubble of an idea, merely adding its small pop to the oceanic hiss of awakening thoughts. No one knows why some thoughts attract notice while others merely blend into the hiss, lost to consciousness forever.

But this time, front and center in his dawning awareness shone the divine message:

"The Promised Land is within you and among you."

Chapter 1

The feather of a thought tickled Moses awake. He yawned and shook his head as if to dislodge the tiny but intrusively authoritative idea like a sandy irritant to be smacked out of an old sleeping skin.

"Honored One, what is it? How may I serve you?"

"It's nothing… Go back to sleep, Zipporah."

The manservant chuckled softly, honored by Moses' sleepy mistake. He, too, missed the constant grounding presence of Moses' wife. "Was it that dream again, Honored One?"

Dream? No, he couldn't quite call it a dream, though certainly it came from the same place. "I just woke up with a strange thought, that's all. I'm fine. Go back to sleep. I'm going out for a walk."

He reached for his staff and used its stout length to cantilever his body off the sleeping mat. He ran his free hand through his thick hair, donned his outer coat, and picked his way through the dark tent toward the heavy tent flap. Moses stepped out to face the inky and still star-filled sky that stretched above the pinking dawn. Absent the moon, he could sense but not quite see where foot met sand. The cool air brushed his cheek like a chaste kiss that whispered the promise of sunny heat and enough passion to turn sand and rock into desert fire.

Moses loved his old companion, the wilderness, adorned in any outfit. Her satiny morning garb with its signature tang of cool air belied his age and convinced him that he could live forever.

The farther he walked away from the tents, the more the familiar immensity caressed him. Perhaps others found the wilderness to be harsh, but Moses had thrived here for the last forty years. And nothing calmed him or reminded him of the ever-present Holy One more than a walk in the glory of daybreak. As long as he attended to sacred dawning, he could avoid thinking about his band of Israelite nomads. Before long, they would come to life, certain to intrude into his early morning delight with their inevitable complaints, unrest, and chaos. All of the people he had rescued from Egypt were now dead, but their children, the ones who followed him now, were just as ornery and contentious as their parents had been.

Moses stretched to unkink the knots in his aging back. Holding the tribes together through their decades of wandering and journeying had almost broken it. He hoped, at least for the sake of his back, that the journey was finally at an end. He worried though about the good life they might lose when they stopped being simple wanderers. Nevertheless, they had finally arrived at the brink of their hope. Just across the river the Land of Promise stretched out before them.

Well, Divine One, he thought, I hope you know what you're doing.

The question brought back the stray (or was it?) thought that had so abruptly snatched him from sleep. "The Promised Land is within you and among you."

He wasn't sure what it meant, but somehow it echoed his concern about the soul-dangers that hid, waiting, across the river. Still, this new land was reported to be flowing with milk and honey. It was all the people could talk about.

Their impatience was understandable enough. The Promised Land shone out as their reward after all the hardship. They could hardly contain their joy. They were sure that Jehovah would never be stopped by the mere detail that Canaan was already occupied. They would just move in, kill them, kick them out, or enslave them. Nothing would stop them from taking possession of their god-given reward.

Well, Moses thought, at least that's what they expect. And then, like a shifting desert wind, the sadness flowed back into his breast.

He reached down to grab a handful of coarse sand and threw it in frustration. "What's wrong with me?" he said aloud. He wanted to be able to rejoice with them. He was trying, really he was. But the burdensome sadness filled his heart, and there, hidden in that neglected corner of his soul, was the pall of dread that turned his breath to sand and his bowels to water.

He had been so sure of himself, so filled with the Presence of the Holy One. Not even the might of Egypt had been able to prevail against that divine authority when Moses led the Children of Israel out of their generations of bondage. They still have their faith, he thought. I seem to be the one who's lost it. I hear them talking and planning all the time. "We're going to be a great nation. People from everywhere will flock to pay respect to Jehovah's chosen people. If Jehovah is for us, who can prevail against us?"

But something isn't right. Oh, why can't I just dream and celebrate with them. Maybe I've led them for so long that I can't avoid seeing danger behind every rock and bush. That's it. I'm just being a foolish old man who's lost his faith.

When did that happen? I think I had plenty of faith when we started, but all the worry and responsibility has gotten to me. Only the Holy One could have known how much responsibility I would end up taking on their behalf. Maybe I'm just tired.

Moses leaned on his staff and felt immediate comfort flow into his body through its smoothed grip. With a great sigh he turned to retrace his steps toward the tents and his ever-present responsibilities.

"May the Holy One bless you this day, father."

"Eliezer," a startled Moses replied. "I often come out here alone in the hour before dawn. But what brings you to life so early in the day?"

"Father, I had a dream..." And, as he spoke, the first direct ray of sunlight spilled over the horizon to envelop them in divine radiance.

Chapter 2

Throughout the day Moses went about his usual activities. He met with his deputies, heard their reports of countless adjudications, and went to pray in the Holy One's tent sanctuary. At least he tried to pray. Periodically, the conversation with Eliezer spilled into his routine, not unlike the dawn light over the horizon. Eliezer had dreamed of a city—not mud buildings or tents or temples—but a city, nonetheless. People at work and play, people who belonged to the earth, the sky, and one another, people who must be gods (or at least must know the gods), so serene and loving shone the looks on their faces. "I came as a stranger," Eliezer had told his father. "I asked to be presented to their leader. In obvious bewilderment they said, 'But you are the leader. Come! Lead with us!' And when I joined with them and looked into each face, I seemed to behold the very image of the Holy One. To my amazement, I felt the Holy Countenance looking back at them through me. Then I awoke, my face wet with tears and my heart yearning to hold onto the dream's experience as it slid away."

After completing his description, he had collapsed into Moses' arms and wept as if the world were ending.

Such a dream, thought Moses, and such holy tears from my son. Moses raised his hand to his face. His skin still burned under the place where Eliezer's tears had soaked his beard. He had never before seen his younger son so moved by anything. Moses supposed it made sense, though. Eliezer was a bit of a dreamer, not like his elder brother, Gershom, at all.

Moses emerged from the tent of the Presence and quickly ducked between two donkeys to avoid being seen by anyone and scurried off to his own tent.

Sometimes Moses wondered how Gershom and Eliezer could possibly have emerged from the same womb. Gershom was all business with a natural talent for order and organization. When Jethro, Zipporah's father and Gershom and Eliezer's grandfather, had recommended the creation of tribal judges to assist Moses, he appointed Gershom before even considering anyone else. Gershom surprised no one when he quickly succeeded in sorting out those judges. Then he organized the priesthood and trained his priests to allow the people no deviation from the letter of the Law.

Ah, The Law, Moses thought. As he remembered it, just a few simple statements of divine principle had come to him on the mountain, but Gershom insisted that they be applied to every possible exigency. A few broad statements inviting Moses and the people into relationship with I AM had multiplied into the six hundred and thirteen laws of Jehovah.

And then, when Gershom had learned about the great nations of the world and had discovered their dependence on religious codes of law, he set out to make Israel greater and more righteous than any of them.

"What else can it mean to be Jehovah's chosen people?" Gershom was heard to say as often as anyone would listen. "We have an obligation to take our rightful place in the world! We can expect nothing less of ourselves. Has Jehovah chosen us to be a light on a hill for all humanity or not?"

Moses' sons never saw anything the same. While Gershom was occupied with instructing the priests or figuring out the details for the construction of the temple, his younger brother was attending to the survivors of a family whose matriarch had died. Or he might be found in the desert with the children, delighting in their startling descriptions of the stark beauty around them.

Moses absently lifted a skin to his lips but forgot to drink any of the water in it. What should he make of Elie's dream? Why couldn't he simply dismiss it as just one more impractically fantastic product of his fertile mind? Of course, he would have been able to if not for his own dream. Even so, he was tempted to minimize the significance of the two events as mere coincidence. But try as he might, he knew that his only real choice was to take them both seriously.

Moses moved through the remainder of the day as one entranced. Without his staff he might have fallen on his face among the tents. Perhaps, he thought hopefully, still trying to escape from the divine voice, if nothing else happens, life will return to normal tomorrow.

Chapter 3

Joshua strode through the camp. His every step and the rhythmic flex of his muscles communicated power. Joshua was tall, ruddy, and he wore a permanent scowl, the legacy of an Amalekite sword that had sneaked through his defenses to split his cheek. The cheek had healed, but the scowl remained. He had small, black eyes, always intense, wary, set deep under furry and furrowed brows. His natural size, strength, and yes, even his grace made him a formidable soldier. Called to service early, he had spent a lifetime protecting the people.

With the right kind of guidance, perhaps from the right woman, his strength might have supported kindness. In the absence of such a feminine touch, however, his only suitable role always took him to the front lines of battle. He had a wife, of course, but would any General ever allow a woman's softness to penetrate his military bearing?

At first, Joshua had felt honored by Moses' attention and had welcomed his tacit selection as the next leader of the Israelites, but he couldn't shake his doubts. Moses couldn't live forever so he might soon be forced to take full leadership. The thought deeply troubled him. He was smart enough to know he wasn't very smart. He was a poor organizer and always had to be reminded of the larger purpose of their present campaign. Though brilliant with strategy and formidable in battle, he didn't really comprehend the politics of war.

His anxiety now propelled him through the collection of tents toward his meeting with Gershom. He was convinced that all things would be possible for him as long as Gershom could be at his side. Joshua drew a deep breath, released it, and then relaxed at the obvious value of Gershom's assistance. This alliance would surely enhance his status.

Had he known what Gershom's help was going to cost him though, he might have chosen to forget their appointment. But then, few people ever knew Gershom's price in time.

Unfortunately for Joshua, and as it turned out, for the Israelites, his straightforward belief in human goodness blinded him to the darker side of human motivation. Without Joshua's credulity, Gershom might never have gained sufficient power to shape Israel's vision of the Promised Land.

A hopeful Joshua arrived at Gershom's tent unaware that he was about to give Gershom the final piece to the "power-puzzle" he had been so carefully assembling. The Israelites might never recover from its completion.

Gershom enjoyed a significant following among the priests. They looked to him for leadership and for help in clarifying their sacerdotal function. They had tried going directly to Moses, but since his time on the mountain they had found him inarticulate, almost confused. It was as if he was forever trying to teach them about matters so far beyond words that all he could utter were grunts and groans. Gershom alone seemed to understand Moses. He always appeared to know what Moses meant, and by extension, what Jehovah required of the people.

Joshua felt no surprise then when he found Gershom surrounded by priest-attendants. One of them opened the tent flap at his approach. The only thing potentially surprising about his apparent station as the Administrative Leader of the Priests was that Gershom was not one himself.

"You are expected, General."

The tent had been designed to reflect Gershom's power and no one could avoid feeling overshadowed upon entering. By wilderness standards its sumptuous atmosphere bordered on the obscene. Priests by the dozen swarmed around this and several adjoining tents, attending to the administrative and religious duties on behalf of the Israelites. It would have been astounding to Joshua, had he thought about it, how many decisions were necessary to keep them all in some semblance of organization. The floor of the main tent was strewn with soft animal skins. In one corner Gershom sat with a scribe at his feet. Every bit of this priestly bustle could be attributed directly to his articulation of the social and religious requirements of the Israelites. While Moses experienced the connection with the divine, Gershom translated it into specifics. Though physically small and delicate, his growing authority and political power were beginning to tower over all others, even Joshua.

None of the Israelites could have known what Moses had actually experienced with I AM on the mountain, but Gershom, the practical one, insisted on their indoctrination into his concrete and detailed interpretation of Jehovah's expectations—for them and of them.

No one could deny Gershom's clarity of faith. He believed with his whole being that Jehovah desired Israel to be a great nation. They were Jehovah's chosen people, after all. In time, He would demonstrate their position of divine favor to the world. What a bargain—the small price of a little obedience to a few clearly articulated laws would secure international greatness. Gershom could never understand the unruly and contentious nature of the Israelites. They represented an affront to his inherent sense of clarity and order. If he could not depend on the people to be obedient toward the higher purpose that he alone saw so clearly, then he would just have to make it a requirement. They would behave—or else.

From Gershom's perspective, a few laws, a few priests to require compliance, and a few executions for minor infractions were worth the trouble to keep them in line. Dominion over the known world began just the width of a river away. Gershom was not about to allow any Israelite misbehavior to get in the way. When Joshua entered the tent, Gershom finished his dictation and dismissed all others from their presence except for the scribe seated at his feet, tablet and stylus at the ready.

Their decision to meet had arisen from an apparently chance encounter the day before. Gershom had overheard Joshua berating one of his lieutenants for not procuring a sufficient supply of armaments. It was clear to anyone listening carefully (and Gershom always listened carefully) that he had expected his lieutenant to accomplish what Joshua felt unable to accomplish himself.

"Hard to keep them all in line," Gershom had ventured.

"If I could just find someone who was able to organize things for me, I could keep my attention on strategy."

Gershom paused as if calculating the implications of Joshua's statement. Never one to miss an opportunity he said quietly, "This might be possible. Come to my tent tomorrow after you break your fast. We can talk then."

Now he was here. "Come in, Joshua, make yourself comfortable. There's food left from the morning's repast. You are welcome to any of it."

"Thank you, no." Joshua's stomach rumbled, but he ignored the food. Eating could wait. Gershom watched the immense General settle his bulk on a pile of animal skins.

"I trust the day finds you well, General."

Joshua chuckled. "Yes, revered one, I have not yet met with my officers so no incompetence has had occasion to present itself."

"Ah, so it is. As you can see, I have to deal with my own legions of minions. Every minute requires my vigilance over them. Hardly any seem capable of taking leadership or initiative. And not one of them seems capable of holding any larger vision. Of course, my scribe here is an exception."

The scribe showed no obvious reaction, though his cheeks flushed slightly at the compliment.

"You said you might be able to help me," Joshua ventured. "What did you mean?"

Gershom didn't answer right away. He took a long breath, stretched, rose to pour a goblet of goat's milk, moved slowly across the tent floor, and then sat back down. Joshua fidgeted in the silence. Finally Gershom said, "You have a difficult and precarious problem. You want your officers to be competent enough to do their jobs for you, but not so competent as to threaten yours."

Joshua sat up with a start. Obviously, the possibility had never occurred to him that his officers might be jealous of his power and position. "Do you really think I need to be concerned about their ambition?" the general asked uncertainly.

"It never hurts to be careful. I'm just looking out for your best interests, friend," Gershom waited before adding, "Perhaps we can help each other."

"So how is it that I can be of assistance, Honorable One?"

"Well, I'm not exactly the one who needs help."

"Who, then?"

"Moses."

"Moses? What on earth does Moses need that he can't ask me for himself?"

Gershom answered in a slow and precise voice. "As you well know, Moses is an extraordinary man: strong, courageous, and of course, uniquely able to commune with the God of our fathers. His place at the head of this challenging group during our forty-year sojourn in the wilderness has clearly established his brilliance. Who else could have accomplished what he has?

"But, that doesn't paint a complete picture of Moses. He is, as are we all, (how shall I put this?) ...Moses is a complicated man. As his son, I see things that others, blinded by their love, fear, or anger toward Moses, simply do not see."

"Careful, now, Gershom. Some might think that you were being disloyal, even seditious."

"I know, I know! But hear me out. I said: he needs our help. I have no interest in undermining Moses. I want to support him. In fact, and you must tell no one of this, I've been helping him for some time now in ways that no one sees. Remember what I said: Moses is a complicated man. When it comes to seeing the big picture, no one has greater vision. When it comes to decisiveness in the face of the uncertainties of the wilderness, no one stands on a firmer foundation. And when it comes to perceiving the presence and revealed truths from our Holy Lord, Moses stands beyond us all. No one else could go to the mountain to stand in the Holy Presence and return sane, perhaps even alive. So, Joshua, do not think that I am in any way being disrespectful to my father.

"It's just that, like all men, he has... shortcomings. He's blind to the practical application of his divinely-given revelations. And this is where I come in. Who do you think has translated his mystical conversations with Jehovah into a system that can be taught, administered, and judged? Moses may have talked with Jehovah, but I figured out how to translate Moses' inarticulate groanings into a system of laws, rites, and rituals.

"At this very moment, the priests, under my supervision of course, are even working out the precise specifications for the construction of a permanent tabernacle once we take possession of the land beyond the Jordan. Jehovah has led us to this land and Jehovah will deliver it into our hands. For our part, we must be prepared to follow God's law—precisely, and to every last detail—if we expect to succeed.

"Jehovah has made this much perfectly clear through Moses: If we do things His way, we thrive and become the preeminent nation of the world. But if we fall away from Jehovah's requirements, then He will turn against us and we will perish."

Joshua seemed not to be listening so carefully now. His eyes flicked toward the tent flap and he stifled a yawn.

Gershom stood up and walked across the tent to stand over the general. "Do you understand what I'm saying?"

Joshua didn't speak right away. Still glassy-eyed, he mumbled. "Yes, I understand. Moses has told us as much."

At first, Gershom looked angry, but then his countenance smoothed. He placed his hand firmly and fraternally on Joshua's shoulder, looked him straight in the eye and said, "Now, I suppose you're wondering where you come in."

Joshua's eyebrows shot up.

"I need you and your army to enforce Jehovah's laws!"

After Joshua left the tent, he congratulated himself on his cleverness with Gershom. How fortunate, he thought, that Gershom needs something from me. Now I'll have all the help I need to reinforce my place as Moses' successor. As long as Gershom needs me, I have him at a disadvantage. It's great to be a general who knows how to identify the weakness of an adversary and then exploit it. He fairly swaggered as he made his way though the camp.

Chapter 4

Normal? How could he think that anything could ever be normal? His last normal day must have happened when he still thought he was an Egyptian. No, not then either. Nothing was ever normal for the grandson of Pharaoh. Thinking that food might restore his balance, Moses stopped his unproductive musing and started looking for something to eat.

Forty years in the wilderness had created Moses' deep appreciation for food. He had learned how little food he actually needed. A few days here and there without any food actually fed his soul. In Pharaoh's court, food had always been abundant and its quality and taste would have been astonishing if it hadn't been so "normal." During his escape through the desert from Egypt to Midian, he had enjoyed his first-ever experience of even slight hunger. In those days he knew nothing about how the wilderness could sustain life, so he almost died for lack of nourishment during the crossing. The memory of those first bites of food that Zipporah served him in Jethro's tent still made his mouth water. Those simple, life-saving morsels—nothing at all like the sumptuous Egyptian meals—had given him lasting gastronomic appreciation. His mouth watered now as he gathered together his simple but elegant meal of flat bread, goat cheese, and a congealed stew from the night before.

In a way, the approaching end of wilderness fare saddened Moses. To hear the Israelites talk, the benefit of the Promised Land revolved mostly around food: milk, honey, grape-laden vines, and such. Was it really so bad not to worry about what you'd have for your next meal? For sure, the food promised to be rich and abundant enough. But what would happen to their deep sense of the Holy One's saving grace, or to the spiritual value of their thanksgiving prayer: "This bite of food going into my mouth right now keeps me alive. The Holy One provides just enough bread for the day (but it's still enough)."

Moses groaned. Even in the Promised Land, sooner or later Gershom would probably get his hands on the menu. That'd surely take all the fun out of eating. For his own part, Moses had made a long-standing pledge that he would always pause and give thanks before taking that first bite and then again after the last one. According to Gershom's understanding of the law, the people were required to say the blessing in order to please Jehovah, but Moses knew by experience that simply the awareness of appreciation and gratitude made the greatest difference. And that was enough reason for him.

He had just lifted a piece of bread dripping with goat cheese to his mouth and was about to take the first bite when Moses saw Eliezer making his way toward him. He loved looking at his second son. Anyone who had known her could see Zipporah's influence in the young man's stance and manner. Well, he was really not so young anymore, but Moses still looked at him through a father's eyes.

Moses had been looking forward to more conversation with Eliezer. He hadn't been able to stop thinking about the younger man's dream, or his own either. Perhaps some new thing was happening. If nothing else, Moses could always recognize Holy Presence. He didn't always welcome it, though, because it tended to affect radical changes, and too often it turned people against him in irrational anger. No matter, experiencing Holy Presence was always worth it.

Moses watched Eliezer's approach and marveled at his easy manner. He was short and dark with no particularly striking features. From a distance he was thoroughly unremarkable, but anyone who got close to him could never ignore his presence. To pass near Eliezer was like being blessed by the spirit of the Holy One. Whenever he stopped to talk, the recipient of his attention felt embraced by his gaze and elevated by his attentiveness. Everyone who entered his sphere of influence experienced a kind of adoption.

Eliezer would make a fine leader for this wilderness people, Moses thought. But Joshua (non-spiritual, unimaginative Joshua) had already been tapped as the heir-apparent Prophet of God. Joshua could lead soldiers into battle and he could inspire men to follow him, but Moses had observed that he couldn't carry the spirit of the Revelation or see through the eyes of the Holy One. Nothing to be done about it now, though. Joshua would lead. Besides, Gershom's political acumen left no doubt in Moses' mind that Eliezer would always be denied access to the highest ranks of leadership.

"Father, how does this day find you?" To Moses, Eliezer's words were as a spring fragrance, borne on the gentle breeze of a warm smile. If the younger man carried any concerns at all to Moses table, they would not become evident until he had communicated his respect and affection for his father.

"I'm about to partake. I was just anticipating the joy of the first morsel, but your presence outshines everything. Please, join me. There's more than enough."

Eliezer broke off a piece of the bread and covered it with goat cheese. "The excitement builds every day. I hope the land we're about to enter can deliver on its ambitious list of promises. It seems that the image of our final destination becomes more lush, green, and fecund with each telling."

"So it does. So it does."

When Moses brow furrowed, Eliezer asked, "Father, what is it? You seem troubled."

"Well, I have a lot on my mind. Do you have time to listen? It may take a while."

"I can't imagine anything I'd rather do. You talk and I'll eat and listen."

"Make yourself comfortable while I try to figure out what to say." Moses shifted to get more comfortable on the pile of skins and began. "Elie, although I was born in Egypt and came to my maturity in the household of the king, as you know I became a man of the wilderness. The more remote the land, the clearer I can hear the divine voice—and the more I know who I am. Lately though, as we've approached the Promised Land, the voice has become garbled and I hardly know myself. I have a hunch that others feel the change, too. I worry that they will lose the divine spirit."

"I know what you mean."

"If your brother has his way in the Promised Land, (and he probably will), the people will be "strongly encouraged" to live in obedience to the law. That's not necessarily bad, but I wonder, will their hearts still warm to I AM's love for them? Will they still tremble in awe when they perceive the Holy Presence? Over the years, I've seen their astonishment when they thought they would die of starvation but then learned to trust in the abundance of the wilderness.

"In those moments when their hunger came face-to-face with the remarkable sufficiency of the wilderness, they knew the Holy One. And they knew their own Holy selves, learning to revere both as they would a lover. They could never dominate the wilderness, so their only choice was to dance with it.

"I worry about what will happen when they find they have the power to dominate the Promised Land? Gershom will teach them to feel entitled to special prominence among men and nations, and I fear they'll lose what's most precious. Already, I grieve for them, though in their growing excitement, they're most likely to discount my grief as the foolish nostalgia of an old man."

"It's too bad they don't know how much you love them."

The two men went on eating in mutually compassionate silence for a time.

"Father, you were talking about hearing the Divine Voice. I've wondered about that for a long time."

"Oh? In what way?"

"Well, how do you do it?"

"How do I do what, son?"

"How do you hear the divine voice?"

Moses went quiet. He sat still with eyes closed, his fingers moving over the handle of his staff as if playing a song on a musical instrument. Eliezer waited. Finally, the older man opened his eyes. "You know," Moses whispered, "you're the first person who has ever asked me that question."

"Well, I can't speak for anyone else, but I've always assumed that you were special, that the Holy One had simply chosen you among all people to receive the revelation. It never occurred to me that there could be any more to it than that. But something tells me that it's not quite that simple. So, what do you do? What's your part in coming into the divine presence?"

Moses thought for a moment, his bushy eyebrows twitched and his mouth worked silently. "Lately, I've noticed that the closer we get to the Promised Land the more distant the possibility of hearing the divine voice seems to be." And then, after a long pause, Moses continued, "Perhaps I need to go back to the beginning..."

Eliezer

Moses seemed reluctant to begin his story. He sat with a faraway look gnawing on the crust of bread in his one hand while the other cradled his staff almost like an embrace. I wondered if my father was a bit scared as well as excited that he was about to share, apparently for the first time, his divinely intimate experiences.

I had already begun to glimpse the depth of my father's suffering, and I was shaken by it as I watched him collect his thoughts. It was beyond reason that he should love the people so much, I thought, and it was tragic that Moses had received so little love in return.

My heart ached for him, though I had never known Moses to complain about the lack of recognition for his leadership. From a son's perspective, the lion heart of a leader beat in his breast, one not encumbered by a demanding ego. His deepest concern was always reserved for the well-being of his followers, and he wore the pain of their struggle as if it were his own. Maybe they relied on him too much. While it appeared to him that he alone had experienced those awe-inspiring times of communion with the Holy One, I was beginning to understand my father's desire to share the experience with the people, not just have it on their behalf.

In that moment, I was granted a glimpse of the loneliness of the Prophet. And, I realized with regret, that I had joined with the rest of the people in allowing Moses to go into Divine Presence alone. Only Uncle Aaron, (and, in his own self-serving way, Gershom, of course) had been willing to stand with my father.

Perhaps the nature of my father's lonely suffering might look clearer in the light of his relationship with his brother.

Moses and Aaron did not grow up together, but they shared many years after their departure from Egypt. Sadly, even Moses' brother was only able to get just so close to the Prophet of God.

I feel a pang of sadness for my uncle, too. Under the surface, Aaron had been reserved – some people thought him "wooden." But he had always opened his tent and his arms for Moses' sons. I loved the attention and besides, he always provided a solid foundation like an anchor whenever I was confused by life (and, I must confess, that was quite often). Uncle Aaron was special in another way, too. He possessed that somewhat rare ability to learn from his experiences.

Late in his life he told me how the golden calf debacle had stood as a wall between the brothers ever since. Moses could never accept that Aaron was just trying to help. Eventually Moses got over his anger but he never trusted Aaron fully again.

Though he gave Moses all the love and support he could, Uncle Aaron never quite understood the nature of this God of Israel. Consequently, Moses carried the vision alone. My uncle has been dead for many years by now, but I still miss his consistent and supportive presence. I could tell that my father missed him, too. I felt empty when Uncle Aaron died, but I can only imagine how much more isolated my father became. With the exception of my brother and me and perhaps a few other "children of the exodus," everyone else that Moses had ever known from before, and everyone who had journeyed with him in those early wilderness years died some years before. Even my mother, who was closer to Moses than anyone, had been gone a long time.

In those moments of preparation just before he began to tell me his story, I wondered if Moses was most afraid that the Holy One would abandon him, too.

Whatever he was feeling, I was ready to listen. I didn't want him to carry the prophetic burden by himself any longer. I prepared myself to hear my father tell his own story.

Chapter 5

"Moses. Moses! Get back here. Your mother will feed us to the crocodiles if anything happens to you."

The royal stripling shot a glare over his shoulder at his minders, but then quickly looked back down at the coarse sand and rock flying under his running feet. Watch your step, Moses, he reminded himself. If I even appear to stumble, they'll take me home. So, with his lip clamped purposefully in his teeth he ran on toward the edge of the oasis.

The oasis sat like a jewel in the desert. Moses loved to come here whenever he could prevail on his caretakers to organize an expedition for a few days. True to form, they had packed enough food and supplies for a small army so they were well sustained. None of that was necessary, of course, because the oasis itself was a source of food and water for several nomadic tribes who camped here from time to time.

Moses loved the vast desert with its emerald oasis. This place was so different from the noisy, dirty, clamorous city. It felt marvelous to be out of its sweaty grasp. Moses had been aching for this moment for several days, now. It was a joy to run, albeit shadowed by his portly and out of shape minders. The sand crunched under his feet and the remarkably cool breeze wafting through the date grove kissed his face. He veered to the center of the oasis where the cool spring bubbled with fresh water. Still sandal-shod, he splashed through the edge of the water, then scooped up some dates that had fallen nearby. By the time he reached the edge of the oasis, where the openness of the wilderness exhilarated him, date juice and saliva were already sliding down his chin. What good was an oasis if you couldn't taste and feel it?

Later, he would sleep in the open with only the heavens for a blanket. Throughout his life, whenever the image of this place would come to mind, he would smile to himself, remembering the sticky sensation of date juice on his chin and chest. He was certain that after death's journey, his *ka* would surely reside in a place like this.

At the edge of the oasis stretched the vastness. Though he loved the cluster of trees at the center, even they made him feel almost as claustrophobic as the city did.

No longer running, he hollered with all the imperial authority he could pack into his ten-year-old voice: "Stay where you are. Don't worry, I won't go any farther."

Moses loved this game: feet flying across the scrabbly ground, his minders running after him, holding their long robes up away from their feet, hollering in futility for him to come back. And just when they thought he would run away from them into the desert, he would stop abruptly and collapse at the base of his favorite tree.

Though a certain amount of play-acting went into it each time, he turned serious, almost threatening, when he commanded them to keep their distance. He needed time to sit, to think, to stare, to soak up the holy magic of the place.

His actions had transformed into sacred ritual soon after his first visit here. One time, he found a branch leaning against his favorite tree. From then on, every time he came to the oasis, he would retrieve the branch from its hiding place on his way to sit at that same outermost tree. It was long, straight, and stout. His young fingers could just barely encircle it. He would have used it for a walking stick, but it stood a full head taller than him and he couldn't bring himself to break it. Sitting against that tree with his "scepter" across his lap he felt like Pharaoh ruling over his subjects. He found delight in the support of the warm sand under his legs and even in the scratch of the rough bark against his back.

Whenever his stare stretched out toward the horizon, he would watch the desert heat shimmer up from the expanse of overheated sand and rock to paint an inviting, almost compelling, impersonation of vast oceans. Moses loved to get lost in that shredded space between present and eternity; all the while his fingers automatically stripped the bark from the branch to smooth it.

After a time: the voice. He didn't recognize it, exactly, or try to identify it; and it certainly never occurred to him to associate it with the divine. It was just there for his enjoyment, like the nourishing blandishments of his childhood nurses. The experience gave him no special knowledge about the Holy One's name, concerns, or hopes, but a sacred bond began to form like that of an infant's intimate contact with the soft, warm, and nourishing insides of a mother's womb. The profound connection would always remain pre-conscious and beyond articulation. Afterward, Moses knew no more than before, but Holy Relationship had deepened.

His many trips to that timeless place generated no specific thoughts about the divine, but in subsequent days and years, images of the creation of the universe, of the foundations of all being, and of essential meanings hidden at the center of being under hard and spiky shells of fear, greed, arrogance and violence would populate his dreams.

Always, even before arriving back in the city, Moses would begin planning the next trip. He could never get enough of being out there.

In time, Moses came to wonder if "the voice" somehow belonged to the oasis and the wilderness, so he would go there as often as he could. Besides, life in Pharaoh's royal court, even for a grandson, could be oppressive; another good reason for an outing. Festivals, affairs of state, and the endless hours of tutoring left him with little time for himself. When he did have time, he indulged his latest fascination—the priests. He watched with interest and amazement whenever they conducted their rituals for Pharaoh, and over time, Moses discovered a deep curiosity about religion. So, whenever he was granted some precious free time, he would follow the priests around. He planned to discern the source of their power and importance. After all, they moved in circles of high regard, and they had to be conversant with the realm of gods and spirits. He found himself particularly drawn to that certain few among the priests who had the authority to speak on behalf of the gods.

Everyone knew that Pharaoh was a god, but his father's frequent reliance upon the priests to bring their omens and auguries before him, caused young Moses to esteem them even more. Day after day he hid in the throne room or in the temple where he could eavesdrop. Statues, altars, and arrases in abundance afforded plenty of safe-enough listening posts.

He wanted to see how the priests invoked the divine voice, but he was shocked to discover that if perchance they did hear it, they seldom, if ever, told the truth about it to Pharaoh... unless of course, the divine word was consistent with what they thought he wanted to hear.

On one particular occasion, while hidden in a ventilation duct, he overheard the priests arguing about how to present the results of their divinations to Pharaoh. After a while their endless arguments bored him and he started to get sleepy. The stale and incense-laden air created the perfect conditions for daydreaming and soon the distinction between the activity and conversation in the room and Moses' own daydream began to blur and shred.

The voice! At first Moses thought there was another person in the conversation, perhaps standing just out of his sight. Eventually, he figured out that the voice wasn't coming from any of the priests after all. It emanated from somewhere else, perhaps even from inside him. The voice held a running commentary on the words spoken by those others present. Though he didn't understand it then, in later years he would recognize the voice as none other than his human experience of Holy Perspective.

Moses suddenly jerked awake and just barely stifled a cry. The voice was speaking—to him, "Moses! Listen carefully to them, and learn." He remained in his hiding place until long after the priests had gone—until he trusted his legs to hold him up.

So, these priests were to be his teachers, then. Moses made a solemn vow to the voice that he would be a good student who would grow up to be a beneficial and powerful Egyptian. In later years, and upon reflection, he decided that the voice was not directing him to learn from them at all. He was supposed to learn about them.

He did.

Young Moses continued to learn and grow, but eventually the unavoidable demands on an Egyptian Prince left no room for him to attend to the voice. Even the occasional dream no longer found welcome space in Moses' busy life.

The young man had been dreaming when a pounding sound startled him awake. His mind's eye continued to hold the image of a man lying on the ground, blood pooling at his feet, oh, so much blood. Moses grabbed a cloth to wipe the rivers of sweat that poured off his body. Then he wrapped it around his nakedness and headed to the door to investigate.

"Moses. Open the door." It was his mother's voice.

"Keep it down, woman. I'm coming."

In a few long strides he reached the door, lifted the latch, and opened it to her radiance. Moses' mother was the most beautiful woman he had ever seen, and even at this early hour, she looked ready to attend an affair of state. Her black eyes matched the color of her hair that was pulled up and back, held in place by a scarab pin. Her demeanor, however, did not match the class of her dress. Those beautifully kohled eyes were wide with fright.

"What were you thinking? Even the grandson of Pharaoh has enemies and now they know what you did."[3]

Moses stomach dropped. The image in the dream—it was real. He hadn't meant to do it, but the prostrate man had died at his hand. "He was unjustly abusing one of the slaves..." he began to explain.

"It doesn't matter what he did. You have put yourself in grave jeopardy. They're on the way to arrest you even now. I've packed some things for you and there's a horse and chariot waiting at the West door. In a few years, send a messenger to me and I will let you know if it is safe to return."

Moses opened his mouth to argue, but she cut him off. "Your grandfather is furious. He refuses to protect you."

In shock, he could only stare at his mother. His mouth went dry as reality hit him and sunk in, breaking the spell. He ran back into his sleeping room, quickly packed a few prize possessions, dressed, and ran out. His mother reached out to brush his shoulder as he went by.

"I love you, Moses. Someday, you will be great in the land," she said to the chilly space her son had just vacated.

He sped out of town in his chariot, his mantle snapping in the wind, leaving only the cloud of dust that billowed out behind him. He reached the edge of the wilderness before the day was out. He abandoned the no longer practical chariot, released the horses, slung his pack over his shoulder, and set out on foot. He had hardly taken time to think about where to go, but then he started to recognize his surroundings and realized where he was. He had traveled this route so many times before on his way to the oasis. That would be a good place to begin. He'd get a good night's sleep next to his favorite tree in the oasis, and then he'd decide where to go next.

That night, the voice came to him as it often did, just at that tipping point between sleeping and waking, though he seldom if ever recalled exactly what it said. This time the words washed over his anxiety like a cooling balm and lodged in his heart: "We know each other. That is sufficient."

He went to the spring, splashed water on his face and ate a few dates. Before he could even ask himself about his plan for the day, he knew it already: the pull on his soul from the East was irresistible. And besides, there could be no safe place in Egypt for Pharaoh's fugitive grandson. He was about to depart when the outline of a leafy bush commanded his attention. The intensity of its presence seemed at first to prohibit his feet from leaving. He could only move in the direction of the bush. I have to get going, an internal voice insisted, but he just stared at the bush. It was larger than he remembered from years ago, but a glance at its base explained its draw. There at his feet he found a stout walking stick. His hand recognized it from the first touch. It had aged from the weather, but its peeled surface graced his hand. He would need such a staff in the wilderness. Apparently, this one insisted on accompanying him.

Though the wilderness turned a rough face to all who dared its transit, Moses had years before fallen in love with its silence and its sacred spaciousness. Gradually, the distinctions among walking and thinking, breathing and praying blurred thoroughly.

No future existed other than to point his feet toward each day's rising sun. Whether he picked his way through sandy desert, plodded over marsh, or waded across waters made no difference to him. He found enough to eat, though at times just barely. He learned to anticipate the location of oases, so he didn't die of thirst. He took one step after another after another after another. Eventually, he was welcomed by a small tribe in the land of Midian, took Zipporah as wife and became a shepherd. In such a short time, his life became so unrecognizable in its transformation that his royal station in Egypt occupied only a small corner of his memory. His life filled up with gloriously open space: to sit, to think, and to dream.

There came those times, particularly during lambing season, when work would inundate all his waking hours, but mostly, the shepherd's life afforded him delightfully long, uninterrupted periods of quiet—where he could simply be. And that was just fine with Moses.

One day it occurred to him that gradually he had fallen in love with The Mountain. Whenever they camped in its shadow he would sit daydreaming for countless hours at a stretch with the mountain as his only focus. His first act in each morning's ritual was to check in with the mountain. Though it was barren and rough, the mountain seemed to radiate life-energy. He would watch its personality change as the clouds passed over it, sometimes enveloping it so completely that a stranger to the land would perceive no mountain at all. At other times, he could see each crevasse and rock in such detail that he yearned to reach across the distance and touch it. The Mountain's personality included many different moods that slid from one to another with startling speed. Moses remained captivated by its beauty and majesty and intrigued by its mystery, its almost ephemeral quality.

Moses awoke to a glow. The rising sun had painted the mountain a fiery pink. Its stunning beauty took Moses' breath away. He wondered which of its faces would manifest as the day progressed. Most days he could feel the mountain's pulse of life, but on this day he sensed its intelligence.

Moses ate, relieved himself, made a head count of the sheep, and prepared to settle himself as usual. His awareness, if not his eyes, never left the mountain. The voice was strong today. He had a fleeting thought that the voice had been growing stronger for days in a row, but somehow he hadn't paid attention. This day, he did.

Moses heard another voice and realized it was his own, calling to his brother-in-law to look after his flocks. Then he began to move toward the mountain. His ears rang with sound, though only the baa of sheep and the crunch of his sandals on stubbly grass were audible to anyone else.

The voice grew louder as he approached the mountain, and he heard and understood it in a seldom-used corner of his being. There were no words in his meager vocabulary that could hold or communicate with any semblance of accuracy or thoroughness the fullness of the experience or its meaning.

Moses wondered if the Divine Presence actually emanated from the mountain. Perhaps proximity affected his reception. On this morning, though, he knew otherwise: his level of receptivity was the only variable. Today he was wide open.

At the foot of the mountain, the raw beauty around him stopped him in his tracks. He noticed the elegant pattern in the piles of rough rocks and sand. He could feel the life force in each tree whose roots gripped the earth with unwavering tenacity. He greeted each green shoot that had found sufficient bits of dirt and moisture to sustain its life. He even tried without much success to memorize every one of them and to catalogue each unique aroma. He looked to the sky trying to recognize the shape and texture of every cloud, from the merest wisp to the ones that promised to fill the heavens. He wanted to remember it all, because he knew already that from now on he would never see anything in life the same.

Moses began his ascent, compelled to go forward while he fought the urge to panic and run away. So much Holy Presence suffused him that he hardly existed as Moses anymore. The Holy one was around, above, below, and within him. Everything, within and without, became indistinguishable from Holy Presence. The surrounding atmosphere crackled with divine heat, consuming, as if with fire, every shred of superficial identity or existence[4].

Moses climbed higher into the incinerating heat. It promised, if not threatened, to leave no residue of the man who had awakened just a few hours before. Though his identity was blowing away like so much ash, in its stead, a truer, deeper, more authentic self emerged. When he looked around, expecting to find all creation charred and black, what he saw caused him to remove his sandals, to fall on his knees in wonder. His awareness held room enough only for the most magnificent appreciation. Nothing real was destroyed, only his illusions. The reality of the mountain, of each rock, bush, and blade of grass seemed to radiate Holy Identity. Absolute Reality assaulted his senses.

Moses would struggle in futility for the rest of his life to create a word-picture worthy of the experience. And whenever he would try to repeat what he heard using the words of his mouth, he would apologize for their rank inadequacy.

Moses beheld eternity—the power beyond all earthly power. No family god or cultural panoply of gods could ever approach its glorious majesty. He beheld the foundation of all creation and he knew with startling clarity (that at the time felt more like terror) how precious all life was. Should this foundational power ever withdraw, nothing would remain. Mountains, rivers, oceans, nations, religions, governments—everything in creation—rested on this infinite presence for its very existence. Could any revelation be more stunning or unnerving than the tiniest glimpse of the Holy?

Moses prepared himself to perish while he knelt there in the heat of the inferno. It seemed fitting. He could not imagine any part of him audacious enough to continue existing. There was no past, no future, only Holy Now.

But he didn't perish. The Revelation had just begun.

Moses began to tremble, momentarily aware of the scrape of mountain rock on his knees and the pounding of a heart that strained to burst out of his body. Any more Holy Presence and he would surely explode.

The voice: "It's all right. You're all right. I'm here. Now, listen."

The discomfort of knees and back vanished. Mind and heart expanded. Hands that had somehow clamped over ears relaxed and dropped. He felt more than willed his nod of assent for the voice to continue.

"You know I support and contain all life, all being, all creation. Life is in me and I inhabit all of life. It matters to me more than you will ever be able to imagine, much less comprehend, what happens to you: each of you, all of you, every one of you.

"You have been taught that gods concern themselves with more important matters than your little lives. You are mistaken. You matter to me.

"You have been taught that you must keep me happy with your rituals and your gifts. These matter to me not at all.

"You have been taught that I will only help you if you fear me and accede to my demands, no matter how cruel or obscene. You have it backwards. My desire is that you fall in love with me, but whether or not that comes to be, I will always love you."

Moses noticed that he was attempting to write in the dust with his staff. He had to record these words—the world needed them. He had to capture the meaning so people could worship correctly. Abruptly, the stick lost its stiffness. He might as well have been trying to write with a serpent. But, as long as he didn't try to scribe the holy words, the staff retained its heft and shape in his clenched hand.

Moses sat, reeling in the dust and smoke. The Holy One cares what is happening to us. His mind spun to make sense. But, everyone knows about the gods and how to deal with them. Gods never care just for the sake of caring. Gods have certain requirements. Humans simply discover what the gods require, do those things, and then believe (or at least hope) that the gods will continue to give faithful humans what they desire. Humans have never had the power to compel particular behaviors from the gods, but most people believe that their rituals, sacrifices, and ethical behavior can at least swing the odds in their favor.

And of course, people always try to associate with the strongest gods. They want gods who can produce an abundant harvest. They want gods who can compel the sun to shine or the river to rise. They want gods who can at least defend them from their enemies, or at best propel them to military victories, preferably accompanied by mountains of acquired riches. And people know that powerful gods necessarily demand great sacrifices: goods, wives, husbands, even children. The sacrifice of life itself is required to satisfy the gods.

That's what people believe, whatever their social status or religion. That's what Moses believed -used to believe—before this. But if we can't influence the gods...?

Weighed down by his confusion, Moses turned to face Reality and fell into the intimate embrace of The Mountain. The boundary between the man and divine presence utterly shredded. In that eternal moment he thrummed in the infinite vibration of the Divine Name. Being Itself, who could be known as "I AM," showed Moses the divine depth of caring, not just in general, but in very specific terms.

The actual lives of the lowest of humans actually matter to I AM. What other god ever took such notice? If the harvest was poor or the river didn't rise, if the queen failed to produce an heir or an army appeared at the borders, humans took the blame. They must have fallen short of ritual perfection. Surely, they had committed some catastrophically immoral act.

In a flash of Insight, Moses understood that people tended to see their gods as petty, arrogant, jealous, and arbitrary versions of humanity's own worst characteristics.

Suddenly awash in tears of grief, Moses saw the futility of so much human religious activity. Time and again, people attempted to perform the required rituals to perfection, or they would go on a crusade to right some moral wrong. Once they believed the balance had been restored and the disaster averted, they thanked the gods profusely and redoubled their efforts at keeping the gods pacified. Humans, however, were always afraid, and they could never afford the risk of putting any real trust in the gods. It was unthinkable that they could matter in any personal way. In horror, Moses understood the truth. Most people saw themselves as mere sources of tribute, and perhaps even amusement, for the gods. As for the gods, how could they be any more than arbitrary powers who required appeasement or bribery before affording humans what they craved.

Moses couldn't even begin to guess how long he knelt there on the mountain. All sense of time had vanished; only the eternal and infinite presence of I AM remained.

The pain hit him like a boulder rolling down the mountain. Then the pain gave way to a gray fog of meaningless boredom that congealed into a black pall of despair.

That sound, what is it? Voices—crying out for help. With excruciating intensity the supplications of a nation assaulted him. Who was in such pain that they would pray so fervently? And what could possibly generate so much suffering?

The pain didn't belong to Moses. That much he could tell. Then somehow he knew: the Holy One was allowing him to experience the pain of that enslaved nation in Egypt. It was a wondrous experience for Moses, though he already knew, at least in theory, that gods could give humans such experiences.

Moses fell prostrate. How could he have missed the point so totally? The Holy One was not making him feel the suffering of the Israelites. The suffering belonged to the Holy One. When the people suffered, the Holy One suffered, only the Holy One didn't want the people to suffer. The Holy One loved the people with an infinite love. Human beings (and all creation, for all Moses knew) apparently mattered deeply to this Holy Presence. With that, the incineration of Moses' last illusions about gods and life was accomplished.

Moses was trembling again, his body wracked with pain and despair. "Stop it. I can't do this. I don't want to hear the voice, or feel any of this." He lifted his staff over his head as if to ward off the blows of an enemy. Who wants to hear voices? Life is so much simpler without them. He tried desperately to make himself run away from it. But he found he couldn't run, he didn't run. Instead, he remembered—more...

A boy—he was a boy! And he was hiding in the throne room, eavesdropping on the priests and his father. They were talking about the Israelites. Moses could see every detail of the room he had visited so many times before. He could smell the fragrant oils emanating from Pharaoh's skin, and his nose detected just a hint of the spicy incense that clung to the priests' robes.

Priest: Divine One, the gods have taken note that you are a builder. If you are to reside in appropriate comfort when you join them (may Pharaoh live forever) the sumptuousness of your tomb must reflect your extraordinary gifts and talents. Without such a tomb, how are the gods to recognize you as equal to, even surpassing, their divinities? We know this to be the unquestionable truth, but as you have no doubt observed, the gods can be, how shall I say it, easily distracted. We have determined through weeks of ritual, prayer, and divination that the gods have provided the means for you to establish your awesome splendor for all time to come. They have delivered into your hands an entire nation, placed it at your disposal—for your personal use in building your magnificent tomb.

They are clever, hard-working craftsmen and their women are strong and biddable as well. This slave nation has lived on Egypt's beneficence for generations. Finally, they will pay their debt to you. The gods require you to extract, to the last ounce, the life and labor from every last one of them. Their sacrifice to you will become your eternal home, the monument to your Divine Excellence.

Pharaoh: What is this nation you speak of?

Priest: They are known as the descendants of Israel.

Pharaoh: Yes, of course. I know these people. Already we have them at work all across Egypt. We must never let them assume power. Their great numbers could be dangerous.

Priest: Certainly, All Knowing One, you make them work and keep them weak. The gods, however, show us a way that you can make a more efficacious sacrifice of this nation of slaves. Their sacrifice promises an Eternal benefit to you that is almost beyond imagining. The life energy of each Hebrew slave who dies in the construction of your eternal home will be added to yours. This life-energy will propel you to the highest conceivable (or beyond conceivable) plane. You will be Supreme among the gods for all eternity.

Silence settled around them after the priests' words no longer echoed in the throne room. Pharaoh said nothing. His eyes took on a far-away look as if he were consuming this glorious eternity with his Divine sight. The two priests remained deathly still. Under hooded eyes, they watched Pharaoh closely. Would he become enchanted (as they had obviously planned) by this wondrous vision?

Pharaoh's eyes suddenly snapped into focus and stabbed at the priests. They recoiled and gasped.

Pharaoh: I already make considerable use of them. They create for Egypt riches beyond measure. If they all die, Egypt will have lost its most useful and talented workforce.

Priest (after reclaiming his breath):

You are, as expected, correct, Divine One. We come to you, not to incite your godly anger, but to put before you a sacred vision of Egypt that you, among the gods, have been chosen to realize. It is true that the sacrifice of the whole nation of human slaves is more than has ever been contemplated throughout Egypt's royal and magnificent history. With all respect and honor, we have been sent by the gods simply to point to the door that leads to your eternal station as God to the gods. As the gods see it, the sacrifice of a nation of slaves is a bargain price in exchange for an eternity of Divine Rule.

Again, the priests fell quiet while Pharaoh took his time to consider this extraordinary offer.

Pharaoh (standing up):

The gods have spoken truly. It will be as they have foreseen. I will spend the rest of my earthly days demonstrating to the gods that they have chosen well.

Priest: Truly, you see as the gods see ... and beyond. We remain honored to assist you in any way your divinity requires.

After they had made obeisance to this earthly god, the priests then left the throne room, but the boy saw looks on their faces that combined enormous relief with ruthless triumph.

Moses came back to himself, at least as much as possible while kneeling on the mountain, locked in his embrace with Holy Love and Power. So that's what those priests had been doing to the Israelites. It was no accident that he had overheard their ecclesiastical plotting. The Holy One had led him there. He now knew that the priests had divined correctly (he had sensed years ago that some of them "heard" clearly, at least some of the time) the danger the Israelites might pose for Egypt. They had come to believe that "the gods" were planning to make some special use of this slave nation, but in their myopic hubris, they incorrectly assumed the foretold greatness of these Israelites would stand as a challenge to Egypt. How could they have imagined that Egypt would play such a minor role in a much larger story?

Those small-minded priests were only concerned for their lucrative status as the prime spiritual authority in the land, not about power and honor for Egypt. Pharaoh was divine, to be sure, but the priests enjoyed a monopoly in dispensing the means and accouterments of worship. They would do anything to maintain their power, even annihilate a nation.

At the time of Moses' birth, it had been the priests who had incited Pharaoh to kill the male children of the Hebrews. That time, too, the priests had been partially correct in predicting the birth of an Israelite national hero. They could see no other choice but to act quickly and ruthlessly to eliminate the threat. Each and every Pharaoh generally played into the hands of the priests, but they always made the same fatal mistake: to the degree that Pharaohs actually believed in their own divinity, they were easily manipulated. All the priests had to do was play to their aspirations for divine superiority.

Moses saw so much while he knelt on the mountain in the embrace of the Holy One. He now had a new perspective on those once meaningless childhood events. He saw that the Israelites suffered as the pawns of priests and Pharaoh alike.

The bigger surprise to Moses was to feel the response of the Holy One. It mattered to I AM that the Israelites were in bondage.

Moses discovered to his astonishment that it mattered to him, too.

In his altered state of consciousness, the divine perspective became his own. Beyond all human imagining, he saw and felt just how much all of life mattered to the Holy One. Moses' inner being was stretched so much that he could even feel the

Holy One's love for Pharaoh, and for those manipulative priests, too. Who could have predicted that by means of the liberation of the Israelites, the Holy One would save the priests from their short-sighted fear and lack of imagination? And Pharaoh, too, from his hubris?

The Holy One then reminded Moses how much value there was in Egyptian culture. But if the priests and Pharaoh were allowed to be successful in exterminating the Israelites, they would do irreparable damage to the development of the Egyptian Collective Soul. So, there on that mountain, the Holy One called upon Moses to be the instrument of Egypt's rescue, too, not just the deliverer of the Children of Israel.

There is no way to describe with any certainty what transpired next between the Holy One and Moses' shattered but re-quickening self. Somehow he found his way back down from the mountain, still a man, still Moses, but permanently transformed by an unthinkably intimate intersection with the divine. Somehow he had come to know The Divine Name: A Name not to be used as a form of address, but to be 'known' as the tangible emanation of the being and character of the Holy One.

And what was this name? An entire scroll couldn't exhaust its meanings. It began, I AM, BEING ITSELF, I AM WHATEVER I CHOOSE TO BE, THE ESSENCE OF ALL CREATION AND CREATIVITY... Moses had experienced THE LIVING ETERNAL MOMENT: the place where earthly particularity and divine infinity were indistinguishable. The Holy Name was suffused with a surprising, but definitive quality that distinguished the Holy One from any other notion of god. Through his direct experience of unity with I AM on that mountain, Moses grasped another facet of the divine name, a glorious name, not signifying power or greatness, but embodying relationship. "I LOVE" was that name!

After he stumbled down the mountain, he walked right through the flocks, past the men who tended them. He looked neither right nor left nor gave answer when they greeted him or asked him what had happened. At the tribal camp he began to prepare for a journey, though he moved as one in a trance.

In the evening, he retired to his tent alone. Since Moses' return to the camp a few hours before, his sixteen year old son,

Gershom had watched him with fascination. Something important had happened. First, he sought first-hand reports from each of his uncles. They told Gershom how long his father had stayed on the mountain, how the mountain groaned, rocked, and smoked until they feared for Moses' life. They described the glow on his face and the faraway look in his eyes when he came back down.

After dark, Gershom slipped into the tent where he saw his father sitting, glassy-eyed, muttering, his knuckles white from gripping his staff. He listened as Moses groaned about gods, slaves, and the wonders of creation, and about an impending journey to rescue an enslaved people. Gershom's clear and organized mind could see and anticipate the great story that was about to unfold and change the world. He heard Moses call the god of the mountain by a name: Now he even knew the name of God: Jehovah.

Gershom listened to his father all night, then slipped out of the tent before first light, grateful that years before, Moses had insisted on teaching him to fashion letters and words on a tablet. Some day he would write this story.

It wasn't until Moses emerged in the morning that he finally spoke to his wife. "Zipporah, call my sons to help you prepare for a journey. We must return to Egypt."

"Moses, what happened on the mountain? They told me you were there for days. When you came into the camp, you spoke to no one. I've been so worried about you. They said it was as if you did not inhabit your own body."

Moses' eyes rimmed with tears. "My people are enslaved in Egypt. The Holy One sends me to them."

When she saw the look on his face, she had no reservations. Zipporah bowed her head and said no more. Within a few days she, Moses, and their sons, Gershom and Eliezer, set out for Egypt.

Chapter 6

Moses stood alone, the blood choked Sea of Reeds to his back and the expanse of wilderness ahead. Finally free and safe, the people of Israel had danced and sung their hymns of joy and gratitude all night. Moses' nose wrinkled up from the heavy smell of blood and iron that obscured the anticipated freshness of the sea air. He was tired but exhilarated. They had made it.

Moses closed his eyes. When he felt the desert breeze on his cheek, he was infused with a sense of homecoming. The strains of the music had barely ceased and the pink light of the new day was just beginning to illuminate the road ahead.

So much had happened since Midian. He had, perhaps foolishly, expected the Israelites to welcome him as their liberator and follow him willingly out of Egypt into freedom. At first they were suspicious of this "grandson of Pharaoh." Then Pharaoh characteristically flexed his imperial muscle by increasing their bondage. "Moses, stop! You're just making things worse. Go away or we'll have to kill you," they cried.

"Don't you believe me? The Holy One cares about you. I have been sent to free you."

Later, during his private time of prayer, his own hidden confusion threatened to turn into fear and anger at the Holy One. "They're right, you know! You're making things worse with your plagues and the apparently useless threats you keep giving me to deliver. I don't know who's most likely to kill me first, Pharaoh or the Israelites. Do you want me to die before we can get them to safety? Is that what you want?"

In the silence that followed, Moses had to admit that he had no choice but to continue, so each day he shouldered the divine burden again, no matter how bleak the results might appear.

Miraculously, after darkness, blood, death, pillars of fire, and pursuing chariots, they had finally made it. They were on safe ground and the people were happy.[4]

The night of dancing and singing was over and soon the sun would rise on the first day of their new life. They were more than hopeful; they were elated. This god whom they had known only through ancient stories had somehow broken Pharaoh's grip on them. Free air filled their lungs, and no Egyptian, no power on earth for that matter, would ever again enslave them.

Moses was relieved to be back in this place again, even though the last time he had crossed over he had been running for his life. The wilderness was more home to him than Pharaoh's court could ever have been. He hoped that in time the Children of Israel would come to love it too.

Loud voices broke his reverie. "This is crazy! What's he done to us? There's nothing here but rocks and sand. How does he expect us to survive in this? What'll we eat? Do you see even one tree? And where's the water? At least in Egypt we didn't starve to death."

Moses' good mood shattered and his stomach began to roil.

"Joshua. Joshua! What's going on?"

A muscular young man appeared at Moses' side. "Honored One, now that it's getting light, the people can see where we are. Apparently they expected to be rescued into nicer surroundings."

Moses groaned. "So, freedom itself isn't enough."

Joshua hung his head and studied the pebbles at his feet. "They want to know how they're supposed to find enough to eat. Some are already talking about going back."

"Don't these people have any faith? Didn't they see how I AM forced Pharaoh to release them? I can understand that they were afraid over the last few days, what with the Sea in front of them and Pharaoh's army chasing them. But turn around and look. The army has been destroyed. They're safe. What is their problem?"

"Moses, this people has been enslaved for generations. They need you to take charge. Remember, they're used to taking orders," Joshua said.

"Very well. Tell the people to take inventory of the food they have brought and wrap it securely against the sand. Leave everything they don't absolutely need here. Tell them to be ready to move as soon as the sun begins to go down. We will travel in the cool of the night and sleep by day."

Joshua turned to stride away but Moses stopped him by touching his shoulder with his staff. "And Joshua," Moses said quietly, "Tell them that the Holy One who saved them commands this."

Joshua swallowed hard. "Yes, Honored One, I will."

For the first two nights the Israelites followed Moses into the wilderness with little complaint. They feared that the God who had rescued them might reconsider and turn against them. By the third night they had endured about all the sand, wind, and heat that they could stand. And they had found no fresh water at all yet. Their complaints grew from a distant rumbling into the full power of a storm whose fury was aimed directly at Moses. Just as the sun began to rise, shouting came from the front of the column. "Water! Water! Come quickly! We've found water!"

Moses came over the rise as the first Israelites entered the wadi where they began to scoop up the water from the pools that lay scattered about in its bottom.

"Don't drink it!" Moses hollered. "That water will make you sick." But his words were lost in the frenzied shouting.

When he reached the edge of the wadi, they rounded on him. "Are you trying to kill us, Moses? What are we supposed to do now? Our skins are empty and this water is awful."

"Get out of my way, you fools. Don't you ever pay attention? I told you not to drink it."

"But we'll soon die of thirst. We're going to die! We're going to die!"

Moses ignored their caterwauling and strode into the wadi where he picked up a tree limb that had washed down from the mountains. "Out of my way," he roared. Then, he began jamming the branch into the bed of the wadi over and over again to punch through its hardened crust. "Get over here," he ordered four men. "Start digging."

In a few moments sweet water from an underground spring bubbled up out of the sand.

"Now you can drink."

No one moved.

"It's all right, drink now and fill your skins.

One by one they approached the hole in the wadi bed, reached down with cupped hands, and then tasted, daintily at first, and then with abandon. "It's a miracle," the cry went up. "Moses has made the bitter water sweet."[5]

Moses grabbed Joshua by the arm and started to explain what he had done, but when he saw the look of awe and reverence on the younger man's face, he released his grip, spat on the ground and walked away. In the commotion, he didn't notice his son, Gershom, standing nearby. Nor did he notice later when the young man disappeared into his tent to write his account of how the Prophet of Jehovah threw a tree into the bitter water and turned it sweet. Gershom was a believer.

Eliezer

How can I describe my brother? He may be the most intelligent person I have ever known. For a long time, I looked up to him, but after a while I found him difficult, if not dangerous, to be around. Gershom is always right. One might say that his theology requires him to be right. And Gershom loves words, particularly those words he writes himself. In his mind, the words themselves become more real than the events or ideas they attempt to capture.

When he sat with our father after Moses' first mountaintop encounter with the Holy One, sixteen-year-old Gershom concluded that Jehovah (as he always referred to the Holy One) had a plan for the salvation of the world. And it was then that he learned, to his astonished delight, the identity of the people Jehovah was about to choose to become the Holy Nation.

Moses never trusted his own ability to put his experiences into words, though I have concluded he was unnecessarily hard on himself. So when Gershom offered his services as scribe and speech writer, Moses was thrilled. He trusted Gershom while minimizing his own facility. Many years passed before Moses ever noticed the particular bias in everything Gershom did for him. By the time he caught on, Gershom had become so powerful as the organizer of the priesthood that even the Prophet of God did not have sufficient influence to dislodge him from his position.

I don't harbor judgment against my brother. I have decided that he was a true believer who always acted in keeping with the way he saw reality. That his reality was not my reality and that two sons of the same Prophet of God could turn out so different will (if it hasn't already) become evident ...

Chapter 7

Sweetness in the mouth; coolness on the feet. What a glorious way to enter consciousness. In time, the word, "date," would become associated with that pleasant oral sensation, and he would soon learn that his feet were splashing in a muddy pool, central in location and importance to an oasis. From the beginning, Eliezer lived life with his whole body. In his earliest moments of awareness, he felt connected, supported, even embraced by life. The same wilderness that presented such a challenge to so many people felt like home to him, for he had inherited his father's patient attention to detail, whether he was on the lookout for sources of water or whether he was exploring the deep reservoirs of sweet creativity and life energy (or even danger) in the people around him.

Zipporah, his mother, had marveled at the intensity of Eliezer's physical connection with the world. On this day like so many others, she had watched him from a distance. Later in the evening when she thought about how different her two sons were from each other, she was moved to tell an old story about Eliezer's older brother, Gershom.

They had finished eating and the food had been removed. All of her father, Jethro's, small clan then anxiously gathered around, for they relished these evening story times.

"Gershom had only about four years, but he was already hard at work," Zipporah began.

"Moses and I watched as he gathered twigs, rocks, and piles of sand to build a city. I didn't know it was a city; I had never seen one. But Moses recognized it right away. Gershom had never seen one either, but he had this innate gift for seeing extraordinary possibilities in the ordinary stuff around him.

Though he had always lived in a tent made of animal skins, Gershom's imagination created a place where people lived in tents of stone and dried mud.

"Later, when his attention was drawn to a colony of small insects in the sand, he studied them with exquisite care. One got the feeling that he wanted to improve the organization and structure of the colony, to say nothing of the behavior of its inhabitants. I sometimes wonder how my two boys could have emerged from the same womb."

Gershom's name referred to Moses' status as a foreigner. But Eliezer often thought that Gershom was surely the one who came from another world. There was nothing Gershom could not create or replicate in his imagination, and no creation of his imagination could ever exist beyond his firm belief that he could organize and rule it.

Eliezer was no less creative than his brother, but his prime directive in life couldn't have been more different. He just wanted to be helpful.

Zipporah never ceased being amazed by her two sons. Later around the evening fire, she began talking about Eliezer's exploits: like the time three-year-old Eliezer had dumped over the skin stewpot, nearly scalding himself, because he wanted to help stir the soup. She never got angry with him. She just held him while he cried over the mess he had made. Many crooked seams in the tent skins or woven baskets with unusual designs could be attributed to Eliezer's "helpfulness." She also noticed with great pride how quickly he learned and how much his mere presence brought joy to the most irritable of her relatives. He didn't say much, but he always seemed to inveigle himself into the middle of any conflict, naturally diffusing any consternation and freeing up lines of communication.

She watched while he became an accomplished student of human nature. He excelled both at distilling out the commonalities among people and in appreciating the exquisitely fine distinctions that made each of them interesting and unique individuals. Knowing how people wanted or needed him to be made it possible for him to keep everyone happy, except for his brother. No one could keep Gershom happy.

It was not that her older son was difficult to figure out, at least in a superficial way. He just wanted (perhaps, needed) everyone around him to agree completely with his every view. When faced with any disagreement, he would grudgingly accept compliance as a poor substitute for complete assent to his position. The loving mother saw the danger that the elder brother represented for the younger. To satisfy Gershom, young Eliezer would be required to cede his very identity, but she thought (hoped? prayed?) that he would never go that far. And she suspected that under all his bravado, Gershom was ruled by fear, even of his little brother.

Gershom never gave Eliezer enough time to figure out what he needed to keep him happy. He simply expected Eliezer to comply instantly with any demand. The problem for Eliezer resided in his deep-seated abhorrence to taking orders. The demands of others (particularly from Gershom), in short, felt unnatural to him. Gershom was always physically stronger, so Eliezer had no choice but to be smarter and more inventive. Mostly, he learned to stay out of Gershom's way.

Zipporah had been relieved to observe Eliezer's ability to avoid his noisier and flashier older brother. Gershom manipulated the action from the center, so Eliezer established his arena on the periphery. When the younger son wasn't occupied with keeping the world happy, he spent time alone, naturally gravitating toward solitary activities.

When Eliezer was old enough, the invitation to go with the men to tend the ever-present flocks delighted him. The long hours in the sunny but empty expanses of wilderness were not tedious to him. He loved the vastness around him into which his inner being could expand. He began to experience hints of an inner self that promised to be deeper and purer than his people-pleasing persona might indicate.

During his emergence into manhood, Eliezer came to realize just how much good will his own personal warmth could generate. Even in his adolescence, his ready smile and open ear had served to improve his chances of survival. He had always known that he could not be, and did not wish to be like Gershom. If Gershom was destined to be the bright light of flame, then Eliezer would provide the warmth of the embers. Every time he smiled at anyone and listened respectfully, he discovered that he actually took a deep interest in what he was hearing. He was captivated by their experiences and thus learned that he could become fond of almost anyone once he got to know them. Like his brother, he became a student of humanity. Eliezer developed an acute curiosity about what mattered to people. He listened for what gave their lives meaning. And he had a sense that his listening was helpful, though he rarely, if ever, gave advice.

Gershom also listened carefully and observed others meticulously, though for a different purpose. He was obsessed with cataloging people's weaknesses. Even as a young man, he believed that human weakness could only endanger Israel's ability to honor its commitment to Jehovah, so he learned to use their weaknesses to maneuver them into doing what he thought they should do. Perhaps he believed he was saving people from their own fallibility, but many, including Eliezer, wondered if Gershom manipulated people for his own benefit. It seemed evident that he used the Holy Covenant as a threat to get them to behave.

As they grew, Eliezer melted into the invisible life of the shepherd while Gershom became more strident, demanding, exacting, and concrete. Most people would never know how much his inner life was ruled by a terror of personal inadequacy. When he was introduced to Jehovah, however, he immediately saw the possibilities for greatness. At the same time all his fears magnified and his insistence on everyone's compliance sharpened.

Take a man with that level of fear, add a large measure of genius and access to political power and the result can be disastrous, particularly for those who wish to promulgate any competing point of view.

As each of them approached adulthood, they never dared stop watching each other, though what they had between them could never quite be called a relationship.

Chapter 8

"Good morning, son. This time I'm not so surprised to meet you before the dawning."

Eliezer flinched at the sound of Moses' voice. In the pre-dawn darkness he had not seen Moses sitting on the rock a few feet in front of him. Eliezer breathed deeply, then relaxed as the cool and clean morning air received his exhalation. "And to you as well... So, you were expecting me?"

"I hoped you would come. It appears that we have much of mutual interest to share. I'm grateful for your company. A dark despair has been gathering around me. It envelops me so thoroughly that I find myself longing for death. For reasons that still elude me, though, when you approach the pall lifts. I think I find in you the source of what I can almost call hope."

Eliezer bowed slightly.

"When we talked last," Moses went on, "I knew that I wasn't directly answering your question about how I open myself to the Holy One. Perhaps I can try again."

"Father, I believe that without either of us knowing it, you did, in fact, answer the real question that was hiding underneath my curiosity and I deeply appreciate your candor. Right now, though, I'm wondering if you could help me."

"What would you like me to do?"

"You can listen to me. Perhaps you can help me make sense of my—what do I call them?—divine connections?"

"Ah, perhaps my heart can hope after all," Eliezer heard his father say in the darkness.

"Father, I must confess some anxiety about telling you these things."

"I would hope you could tell me anything," Moses said with pain in his voice.

"Let me explain," Eliezer said.

The younger man settled himself down on the rock beside his father. There was a slight breeze that carried upon it the complex bouquet of wilderness vegetation. The moonless pre-dawn sky was clear and still held the brightest of the stars. As Eliezer took a moment to organize his thoughts, he watched a shooting star that streaked towards the still black western sky.

Moses sat with his eyes closed, waiting for his son to begin.

"For as long as I have lived, you have been The Prophet, the leader of this people. You've shown courage in those times when all others sought cowering invisibility. I've seen you angry and forceful when others could do no more than complain. You've remained compassionate when others seemed ready to slink away from you, expecting to incur your wrath and judgment. And, to be more personal, I've seen you as the righteous father who blessed his firstborn with position, power, and responsibility."

Moses winced.

"I'm not jealous of Gershom's position. That's not the point. I've been glad to be a shepherd who could contribute by manning his post with the flocks. Without the support of "the god of the mountain," though, many times I feared I would just plummet into the depths of oblivion. But I never allowed myself to imagine that a god (or even a Prophet) would ever stoop to acknowledge a shepherd. Father, I'm grateful that you've never treated me badly. Nor has our god ever shaken the ground beneath my feet, or threatened to cast me off into the void. You and the Holy One have always been kind to me—in a mountain-to-shepherd kind of way.

"Until two days ago, I would never have expected to see you in any other way or to have you offer me such a precious gift. I'll always appreciate that you've granted me a glimpse of the nature of your relationship (dare I call it a direct connection) with the Holy One. I'm grateful that you told me. To be honest, I fully expected some kind of dispassionate and practical instruction in mystical experiences."

Moses reached out to grasp Eliezer's arm, presumably to shift to a more comfortable position on the rock. But his hand lingered in what could only be a father's gesture of affection. Then Moses said, "I have to say, I was a bit surprised myself. I've learned the hard way to be very careful not to divulge too much of my experience to anyone. I've had enough trouble with the way your brother takes possession of my encounters and then records them in terms much clearer and much more definite than the actual experience warrants. But because it has always been so difficult for me to find adequate words, what choice did I have but to accept Gershom's transcriptions? I'm ashamed to admit it, but I have even used Gershom's words in my addresses to the gathered people.

"Forgive me, I'm rambling (that tendency seems to get worse with age). I'm just trying to tell you that I experience no such peril with you. And yet, I surprised even myself with my candor. And now, perhaps I can return the favor. Perhaps something riding on your heart has been preparing to make its brave journey in the direction of my lonely soul."

"Father, it's starting to get light. Come, let's walk away from the camp for a while."

As if shepherding a child, Moses reflexively reached for his staff and used both hands on it to lift himself from the rock.

Father and son walked in silence for a time toward that wilderness place where Soul calls in clear voice to Soul, and where the splendor of the Holy One cannot be dulled by the noise and filth of the camp. They carefully picked their way through one of nature's rock-strewn paths that wound among ancient boulders. These stood like stone temples erected to honor the primal force of creation. The two men spoke no words at first, but a sense of mutual familiarity welled up between them. Two extraordinary souls, neither of whom had ever really belonged to the heart of the people, now reached out tentatively and tenderly toward each other.

The mere physical activity of walking together bound them deeply. They kept catching glimpses of the Holy One in each other's face, while intuiting hints of a journey toward a future that neither of them could ever have imagined. In the same instant, each man felt the brush of Eliezer's dream. The Holy One in their midst precipitated into a solid foundation of trust.

It was time. Eliezer began his confession. "Father, that dream I told you about—it's not my first. I've had dreams and intimations of the Holy One for many years. Maybe the wilderness helps. There are those among us, maybe most of us, to be honest, who think the wilderness is a punishment. I know Gershom sees it that way. But it's always been home to me.

"When Gershom refers to the Holy One and calls 'him', Jehovah, I get the picture of an infinitely powerful king, who actually lives far away, but who shows up every once in a while to impress us with his roaring power, demanding that we hold to the terms of his compelling contract. I never thought of the Holy One as male, or female for that matter, until I listened to Gershom talking about 'him.'

"Perhaps you already know these things, but I have to tell you anyway so you can see how I think about (and feel about) the Holy One. I've always believed that I saw things from an eccentric point of view.

"To hear Gershom tell it, your conversation on the mountain with the Holy One offered the people a deal that was impossible to refuse. Then, after we had wandered in the wilderness for a generation, this Jehovah came to check on us to see if we were finally ready to enter the Promised Land. We failed the test, so we had to wander in the wilderness for another forty years—until all those who had originally set off from Egypt had died. After that, apparently, it became possible for their children to cross the Jordan and take possession of this wonderful land that is laden with such rich possibilities.

"Maybe I'm strange, but I have never thought that the Promised Land was such a great prize. (If Gershom is right about who Jehovah is, I'm already in big trouble for even talking like this)."

"I know what you mean, son. He does it to me, too. Please, go on."

"When I was a young boy, I was thrilled to be included with the flock-tenders. As soon as I started to tend the flocks alone, the dreams began. 'Dream' may not be quite the right word to describe what happened. Truly, I don't know whether I slept or not when they came to me. Other people were in the dreams (as I will continue to call them). I knew some of the people, and others, (most of them, actually) were strangers, though they always looked vaguely familiar. You remember that I told you some of this a few days ago?"

Moses nodded then waited for Eliezer to continue.

"Everyone present was (it was evident to me) part of something larger. I suppose Gershom would say something like 'Jehovah, was in them'. But that description doesn't quite make it," Eliezer groaned. "Father, I, too, have a hard time finding words.

"It would be closer to the truth to say that the people resided in the Holy One. No, that sounds too much like being surrounded, like the water in the oasis pool around a swimmer." Eliezer blew out his breath. "When you described your experience on the mountain—when you knew the presence of I AM but couldn't discern whether it was in you, you in it, it in the mountain, or identical with the mountain—you said you couldn't find the right words. I knew what you meant, so I think you can understand how inadequate I feel right now in my rummaging around for adequate language. I'm not saying that our experiences were identical. Something tells me that's not possible. I just have a hunch that we've touched the same reality."

Moses nodded again.

"Of course, I had no idea what was happening, so I resolved to put such foolishness out of my mind. I certainly didn't tell anyone. I was sure that no one would believe such a crazy story. As I look at it now, though, the worst reaction that I expected was a reprimand for daydreaming instead of flock-watching. Still, I vowed that there would be no more visions. Even if I had known for sure that it was the Holy One, who would have believed me? After all, you were the one who had divine conversations, no one else, and certainly not me."

In the growing brightness, Moses sighed at those words. His brow furrowed and he opened his arms to Eliezer. "If I could have changed anything in the last forty years, it would have been that. Perhaps my pride has kept the Prophet's Mantle wrapped too tightly around my shoulders and my staff too firmly in my grasp... Well, some pride, and a desire to protect the people, I think, from a difficult experience. I can honestly say that incinerating contact with the Eternal Fire is unpleasant at best. There's no safety. The brilliance of the Holy Presence obliterates any inner quiet or dark sanctuaries for closely held beliefs, prejudgments, or failings. Nothing is hidden; all is revealed."

Moses pulled his cloak tighter. "I desperately wanted to hide myself, cover myself up, to obscure my shamefully tiny self. And there was never any telling how the experience might dismantle or reconstitute the core of my being. I tried to imagine others being able to survive even a slight touch of divine intimacy, and I found I couldn't. Aaron and Miriam were exceptions, of course, though we never talked with each other about divine encounters.

"So, I was the conduit, Gershom the interpreter, and the rest of the people merely followed along, or more often, resisted following. I was the one who decided to keep the others away from the mountain, not the Holy One. After years of reflection, I remember it that way. But back then, I was so overwhelmed in Holy Presence that I couldn't separate what might have been the direct transmissions of the Holy One and what I, myself, pieced together while in the grip of such bone-jarring fear and vulnerability. I believed I needed to protect the people from Divine annihilation, so I chose to carry the burden of Revelation myself. My overdeveloped hubris may have done Israel a grave disservice.

"My accumulation of years affords me crystal-clear hindsight. If I let them, those years also tempt me to pass harsh judgment on that younger Moses without the moderation of compassion and kindness. Lately, the Holy One has taken to reminding me to be more charitable, even to myself. Still, I wonder, would we be following this particular path toward the Promised Land if more of the people could know the power and then shoulder the responsibility of communicating with the divine?"

Eliezer closed his eyes and when they sprang open again, he said, "Perhaps there are others."

"Other what?"

"Others like us who've experienced the presence of the Holy One but think themselves condemned by it. It's likely that they keep it to themselves so Moses, "the Real Prophet" doesn't bring divine wrath down on their sorry heads. Remember, they were warned to stay away from the mountain. Wouldn't they feel as much peril if 'the mountain' came to them? Even I didn't dare tell my own father about my experiences of the divine one because it was so dangerous."

A rivulet of sweat rolled down from Moses' neck to flow between his shoulder blades, whether as a result of the gathering heat of the day or the exertion of his mind, who could say. "Perhaps it's not too late," Moses went on. "If there are others who can testify to their inner word of divine wisdom, maybe this nascent nation can avoid the disaster that may well await it on the other side of the river. My old bones vibrate with foreboding. My people—my children—will gain land, power, and nation, but will they lose that precious soul they found in the wilderness?"

Eliezer stopped walking and ran his hands through his thick hair. "Father, I am confused by something my dreams seem to leave out."

"What is that?"

"I've never seen Gershom. You've been there. My mother, your brother and sister, my wife, and many others of our kin and companions have been there, but never Gershom. What do you think that means?"

"Elie, my son, who can say if the Holy One, or you, or Gershom himself is responsible? Gershom is Gershom, and he will always serve the God of his understanding. What disturbs me more at this point is my growing recognition that I just can't go with him. When the Israelites cross the Jordan to take possession of the Promised Land, They'll have to go without me. I think it's time for me to die."

"What?! I don't get it, Father. You've spent half a lifetime bringing them to this place. You have to lead them into the Promised Land!"

"Elie, I'm sure that I don't understand either. But you're right about me. I've longed for this moment when we would finally be rewarded after all our tests and trials. Right now, though, when I hear these words coming out of my mouth, I have to confess that they don't belong to me anymore, if they ever did. Those are Gershom words. And the Promised Land across the river is the product of Gershom's vision, not mine."

A stunned, yet holy silence settled over them as the two men walked quietly. Finally, Moses looked over his shoulder and said, "We've come a long way. Maybe we should head back. I have a lot to consider. I think you do, too."

They didn't speak any more during their long walk back to the camp.

Later in the day they found themselves together again in Moses' tent drinking goat's milk and gnawing on strips of dried lamb. They were anxious to resume their conversation.

Moses began, "Eliezer, I am older than anyone has a right to be. I have no regrets about my life. It has been more interesting than any life I could have planned. But now I don't think I have any choice but to stay on this side of the river and die. Honestly, if I were to go across I believe my heart would break if I had to watch these children of Israel, my children, lose the use of the spiritual treasure they found out there. And I don't think I could contain my inevitable rage at them. I am afraid I would say or do something even more hurtful than they could ever do to themselves.

"It almost happened years ago in the wilderness. Perhaps you remember. We had been traveling for a long time without finding any available fresh water. What little was left in the aging water skins was tepid and it tasted terrible. They started complaining ... again. 'We're going to die. Why has God brought us out of bondage only to have us die of thirst?'

"I knew where we were going, and I knew we would find water there. I tried to reassure them, but no one would listen. I was so frustrated with their lack of faith after all we had been through that I had fantasies of breaking the next complainer in half. I restrained myself, but just barely. When we finally reached the spring in the hills, I pointed at it with my staff. 'There's your water,' but they were so angry and, I suppose, scared, that they couldn't see it. They just kept complaining and whining and I was mad enough to start knocking heads off shoulders. Instead, I ran to the spring where a small boulder sat across the opening.

"I screamed, 'Here is your water!' and I hit the rock so hard with my staff that my hands stung. Their complaining grew even louder, so I hit the rock harder a second time. As a result it rolled into a small pool and made a tiny splash. Finally, they saw the water and rushed over to drink it.

"Of course, by the next day the story had spread throughout the camp that I had called the water out of the rock.[6] So many times they thought I had performed some magic when I simply knew where to find what we needed.

"Even now, I feel sick in the pit of my stomach when I think about my murderous rage and remember how close I came to lashing out at those panicked and terrified people.

"I don't know what stopped me, but, I fear that in the future I might actually hurt somebody if I ever again see their tiny supply of faith overwhelmed by their greed or their fear. It is better for them and for me if I stay here and die."

Tears came to Eliezer's eyes as father opened his life to son. He waited for several minutes before he was able to get words to move past the lump that had formed in his throat. Finally he stood up, walked across the tent, took his father's shoulders in his hands, looked deeply into his eyes, as if into his soul, and said quietly, "Father, I can see clearly why you would choose not to go across the river. But, before you decide to lay down your life, I ask one favor of you."

"What is it?"

"Father, would you journey with me for a few days back into the wilderness where we can hear the voice of the Holy One more clearly? We can fast and then open ourselves to receive some sacred communication. I think, too often, we automatically avoid the full force of Holy Presence. As you've told me, and as I've experienced myself, sacred encounters can be uncomfortable and disorienting. In this case, however, something in me wants to pursue rather than avoid the Holy One. I think we should go together to examine this emerging vision more clearly. Will you do this thing with me?"

Moses' closed his eyes as if peering down into the deepest places of his soul. When he opened them, he smiled warmly, a tear scampering into the thicket of his beard. "You are a son to make a father proud and humble at the same time. Of course, I'll go with you."

Chapter 9

It had taken Moses and Eliezer three days to prepare for the trip. How easy it had been to think up a plausible cover story. They knew that Gershom would immediately get suspicious if there were any talk of seeking Divine Encounters, so Moses merely said that Jehovah had come to him in a dream to express divine displeasure at the Israelites' lack of proper appreciation. The tribe had left their last semi-permanent camp in a hurry to avoid crossing paths with a large troop of Edomite soldiers who had been heading in their direction. Father and younger son had then reported to Gershom that Moses had been divinely chastised for not trusting Jehovah to protect them. The God of the Mountain had expected them to perform their required worship and then to take the time, demonstrating sufficient reverence all the while, to pack up the tabernacle for transport. According to Jehovah, the Israelites had betrayed their woeful lack of faith by being in such a hurry.

Predictably, Gershom ate this stuff up. He always required perfection in worship, lest the Israelites fail to honor their god properly. According to Gershom, Jehovah expected, make that demanded, such perfection. So, as their alibi went, the Holy one had specifically commanded Moses and Eliezer to go back there, make sacrifice, and erect an altar so no one else would be tempted to commit such a foolish mistake on that spot again. They would be gone for about ten days. The only reaction they got from anyone, including Gershom, was relief that Moses and Eliezer had been tapped to go, so they didn't have to interrupt their preparations for the crossing.

They left camp without fanfare, accompanied by a small train of donkeys to carry their provisions. A blemish-free goat for the "sacrifice" trailed behind. Both men appreciated the quiet that had descended on them as soon as the camp had receded sufficiently into the distance. At times they spoke, but for long stretches each man remained lost in an inner world of thoughts, questions, dreams, and visions. The only sounds to reach their ears were the crunches of human sandals and animal hooves against the gravelly ground, rhythmic breathing, and the occasional creak of a shifting bundle on the back of a donkey.

Moses was remarkably fit for a man of such advanced years. When he settled into an easy stride, he could walk for countless hours without fatigue. His life force was potent and focused. Although now, given that he had begun to question his life-long drive toward the Promised Land, he didn't know exactly where he was supposed to aim all that power.

Though their plan was to go out into the wilderness, their ultimate objective remained undetermined. With a very few notable exceptions, mostly for Moses, their direct experiences of the Holy One had always come unbidden and without conscious intent. Those times of Holy Communion usually included a disturbing depth of intimacy so no one in his right mind would seek it on purpose. And, just as with any experience of true intimacy, they always came away changed by it in some unpredictable or even undesired way. The Holy One was always present, of course, but only manifest when their human consciousness wasn't focused on something else. Daydreams functioned as an open invitation and the foggy consciousness between sleep and wakefulness often attracted something like divine footprints in the dew of awakening. Perhaps they usually chose to avoid direct contact because it took so much work afterwards to decipher the shards of divine connection that inevitably found their way into consciousness despite their human defenses.

This time, however, their expectations were different. Father and son had confirmed one another's growing belief that the time had come for direct connection. But while they hungered for it, they were also terrified of what this god, I AM, would require of them. Moses and Eliezer understood, especially now, the more popular human preference either for gods who could be bought off with rituals and sacrifice or gods who regarded humans as beneath notice. The gods who were known to have stringent or utilitarian requirements were at least consistent. The Holy One of the Israelites appeared to have requirements, to be sure, but these were relational, not behavioral; covenantal, not contractual. Most of the Israelites, and Gershom for sure, still strove to fit this new god into the old images.

For Gershom, the only differences between the old gods and Jehovah were two: This god was stronger than all the others put together; and this god had taken the initiative to select the Children of Israel for greatness. All Israel had to do was obey a few (well, perhaps, more than a few) rules and remain faithful to Jehovah, rejecting all other gods. The rewards promised to be well worth the inconvenience.

The chasm between Gershom's written interpretations and the Holy messages coming to Moses and Eliezer had grown increasingly precipitous the nearer they had come to the Promised Land. Father and second son had already determined that they would not, could not, follow Gershom's path. But, where then were they to go? Was Moses' right that they should escape by dying?

Eliezer didn't think so. That's why he had suggested that they risk the intimacy of divine presence. After he had learned of his father's re-developing vision, he proposed that it made the most sense for them to seek a dual mystical experience. They would make themselves spiritually vulnerable and, in so doing, be able to challenge or validate their respective glimpses of divine purpose. I AM was speaking and at least these two Israelites perceived the necessity to listen.

So, as they walked in the quiet of the desert, each began the gradual process of opening up. It was not that difficult to experience altered states of consciousness while traveling in the desert. Not much changed from step to step. The wind blew, the beasts grunted, the human feet kept up a rhythmic slap, slap, slap against the hard packed ground.

After they left the main camp, the two men easily followed the route the Israelites had trodden just a short time before. But now, a day and a night into the journey, they found themselves straying a bit off the track to their left. They moved toward what looked like an outcropping of rock on the horizon. Neither had said out loud, "Let's go that way." They were just drawn that way as if those low hills visibly beckoned to them. That the hills grew from their approach was just barely perceptible. Little by little they noticed that the closer they came, one hill among the cluster rose up to dominate the center of their awareness.

They had not consciously decided to fast, but the pilgrim pair had not eaten since leaving the Israelite's camp. Apparently the journey itself was their fast. Even with empty stomachs, no hunger pangs intruded on their awareness. Occasionally one or the other would absent-mindedly lift the water skin for a small sip. On they walked; their attention so fixed on the one hill that they were reduced to nothing more than four staring eyes and four rhythmically plodding feet.

Without conscious choice, they had, hours before, dropped the reins to their donkeys; but the beasts, to avoid being left alone in the desert, followed along at a respectful distance behind the two men. It was as if they were all being led—and perhaps they were.

The four eyes and four feet watched and moved in such unity that Moses and Eliezer, had they even cared to, could not have determined where one of them ended and the other began. But such a mundane question could find no hearing. The universe was reduced to staring eyes, plodding feet, and the one hill slowly growing into a mountain with a small oasis nestled at its base. The seeking pair walked right past the oasis and began their ascent. The donkeys stopped where there was enough rough grass and water to keep them during their vigil.

When the men finally came down from the mountain heights, there was nothing to say. No words could come close to describing their sacred experience. Even if they could find the words, how could they relate the story to anyone who had not actually been there? Neither man had any recollection of the descent. They just walked to the center of the oasis and collapsed side by side where they instantly fell into deep sleep.

The nuzzling of cold donkey noses and the intrusion of the bright sun after its own overnight sacred journey to the eastern horizon brought them to consciousness the next morning. At first, father and son startled each other with their proximity, but soon they remembered where they were. They were desperate to connect and share, particularly Eliezer.

"Father," Eliezer croaked, then fell silent as he groped for any word at all from the paltry supply in his brain that might dare volunteer to begin describing where, how, and even who he had been on the mountain.

In the silence stretching between the seekers, rich images of a unique and shared spiritual encounter danced from mind to mind. Finally, it was Moses who found his tongue. "Son, the words will come to you, but you must be patient. I learned this from other mountain excursions with the Holy One. For me also, the first words and images I tried to employ seemed so shallow that they could barely narrow the breadth and depth of what had happened. I've needed many years to reflect more fully on those earlier times. Your brother 'helped' me after my forty days of being washed over by the Holy one's love and intimate communication at Mount Sinai. As always, his scribe was with him, and Gershom instructed the scribe to record, not my words, but the words he chose to describe the mountain's events. I was trying in every way I knew to give a complete picture, but there was so much ambiguity in it that Gershom took upon himself the responsibility to clarify my inchoate mumblings. I thought he was being helpful, anyway. After all, we needed to find a way to communicate those Divine Ideas to the people. He was very good at getting to the heart of the matter while pruning away whatever didn't fit—for him. For all these years I haven't known what to make of my growing awareness that Gershom only recorded a carefully chosen portion of what happened to me.

"This time it's different, I want to tell the whole story, even though it may not make much sense right away. I'm prepared for the inevitable contradictions. So, take your time—let the images emerge more fully before you attempt to speak them. I'll do the same. When it is time for us to talk, we'll know it, because it will simply happen."

For the rest of the day, Moses and Eliezer occupied themselves by setting up a rudimentary camp with the few provisions they had brought. At various times they ate, walked, or slept. The memories of divine experience emerged, sometimes glorious, sometimes painful, sometimes stunning. They felt like women in the throes of labor.

It was most difficult to set aside the influence of past experiences and presuppositions so that new life and awareness could be born into their collective consciousness. So they thought, felt, and intuited. They laughed, cried, sweated, and shivered with chills. An observer might have thought they were dying. Perhaps something of the world is required to die to make room for the newly born. More than once, each, in turn, had swooned and fallen into a heap, then to awaken grasping a new piece of the mystical puzzle. They carried on like this until the third morning when they both awoke with words in their mouths that, at long last, didn't threaten to annihilate the world if spoken. When Eliezer looked at Moses that morning, he could see that Moses was ready, too. He was so sure that Moses would relate his experiences with gravity and profundity that he was shocked, then amused and delighted at his father's words: "I'm starving! Let's eat. Then we can talk." While they ate, they carried on as if nothing special had happened.

Moses: My mouth has never appreciated such poor fare more. This is better than all the rich food I ever tasted in Pharaoh's court.

Eliezer: Mmmm ...

Moses: I couldn't have said it better myself.

Eliezer: Cheese, flat bread, and a few plant roots. Pharaoh must envy our excellent fortune.

Moses: Mmmm ...

Eliezer: And you tried to tell me you have difficulty articulating your thoughts!

And so it went until they had eaten their fill. Then Moses stood up and looked around. "Let's walk a bit. My poor old bones will become forever rigid if I don't move."

They walked with their backs to the mountain in the direction of a tumble of boulders that poked up out of the desert floor some distance away.

"May I begin, Father?"

"Of course, son. I suspect that none of your previous connections with the divine have been anything like this one. Go ahead, I'm listening."

Eliezer reached up with both hands to run his fingers through the tangles of his coarse hair and heaved a great sigh. Once the words started (and he could not have identified exactly when that happened) they painted a picture so surprising that even he was taken aback by his own description of events. "The last thing I remember in my usual way of being in this world was thinking that an oasis was going to be visible soon. I was ready to rest a while, but then I saw that hill. At first, it was just a small irregularity on the horizon, just a little bump, really. I was surprised, though, at how much that bump filled up my awareness. It was as if nothing else existed, not even me."

Moses nodded and grunted in recognition. Eliezer started at the noise. He was already hanging so passionately onto the sound of his own voice that he had entirely forgotten the father walking beside him. His quizzical look remained as he tried to work out just who this was walking with him. Finally he shrugged his shoulders. It couldn't be that important, so he went on.

"As I simply observed that hill for a time (it really is quite small, isn't it?), I found myself looking out from the center of all creation. I was moving toward it and was already there at the same time. I had no sense of walking, and honestly, no sense of being in this body at all. No, that's not quite right. My physical presence just didn't matter, though in a way I knew that every tiny bit of reality effervesced with significance. I could have counted every pebble under my feet, except that I already knew the count, and, even more, I knew each pebble as a lover. I have no idea if I was on the hill or still on my way to the hill when the visions began. As I try to picture it now, I can't say for sure if I ever even arrived there. It doesn't matter, though, because the Holy One was everywhere, was everything, and was so much more. I felt that I could see to the very edge of being itself." Eliezer paused, looking confused.

"I just don't understand how that could be, because I also knew, or maybe I saw, that no edge was even possible."

This time it was Moses' turn to be jolted from his reverie. He had been listening, recognizing most of Eliezer's words as adequate depictions of his own "myst." The boundary between them was so porous after their shared experience that Moses heard Eliezer's words almost as if they were his own. It had been the subtle shift in his son's voice, signaling that he was addressing his father that had startled Moses. He found a way to say, "Don't worry about anything that seems to contradict. It's like walking around a goat. The goat looks different from each position, while it remains the very same goat. The images will reveal a greater fullness and integrity as you carry them with you. I am still, more than forty years later, gaining new meanings from that fiery bush. You're doing fine. Keep going."

Eliezer experienced a deepened respect for his father. He could see as never before how much wisdom his father had accumulated. He found himself welling up with hot anger at Gershom, who had consistently strained out the wisdom and kept only the fearful dross.

"Gershom! Gershom was there!" Then more slowly, "I saw Gershom, really saw Gershom, for the first time." Again Eliezer paused, his brow wrinkling. "Father, Gershom has never been in my dreams before."

Moses looked intently at his son, waiting for him to continue. After a moment during which he seemed to be peering into a faraway truth, Eliezer whispered hoarsely, "I think he was always there, but I never saw him."

Eliezer's gaze turned so far inward that he forgot his father standing next to him. His head dropped so that his chin rested on his breast. Then he said, "You know, I've never really liked my brother, and I have always been certain that he had no use for me, either. Now I see that he wears—has always worn—a shroud of fear. I just couldn't see it. I was blinded by his brilliance. He can write better and faster even than his scribe. I've been in awe of him for my whole life, though I never liked that he bullied and controlled everyone. I just stayed out of his way.

"Anyway, in the vision I saw two events in which Gershom was the central character. I don't know if these things really happened or if I just saw him in a new way. When I first noticed him in the vision, he was standing next to you holding a large net. You were speaking, and your words looked like white mud bricks that dropped out of your mouth. Gershom picked up each brick, looked it all over, and then packed some of them into the net. Then I saw him experimenting with different ways to put your "words" into arrangements that made the most sense to him. He seemed not only pleased, but he fit these word-bricks together with growing confidence. At the same time, I saw him as a child though I wasn't even born then. According to mother's stories, he was always building things. The more he was able to build, the happier he was.

Gershom took these word-bricks and started to pile them up, fitting them together into a fortress. He was putting the last brick in place when a sound caused him to turn away from his work. The Holy One was coming toward him. I knew it was the Holy One, though I can't seem to describe what I saw. I looked at Gershom and I could tell he was terrified. He ran into this fortress he had built, then came back out with a pure white lamb, placed it on a flaming altar, cut its throat, and then ran back inside. I walked to the fortress and then all around it, but I couldn't find any door or window. And there was no sign of Gershom. He was gone."

Eliezer felt a cool breeze on his face and then felt the tears that had been running down his cheeks. "Gershom is gone," he wailed and then fell into Moses arms where he sobbed uncontrollably.

Moses held Eliezer for a time, and then guided him to a large rock nearby where they both sat down heavily. Moses examined a scar on his staff before saying, "If I thought for a moment that Gershom would ever really listen to me, much less to the Holy One, I would go to him right now. I would invite him to join us. But I already know that his understanding is based in his fear, so my older son relies only on intimidation and force to get his way. Besides, I've seen his eyes radiating with visions of the Promised Land and I can't imagine that he could ever let go of his exquisitely precise and concrete expectations for the future."

Eliezer sniffed, "But isn't it our duty to try? Can't the Holy One give him a different vision?"

"Eliezer, you're a fine man with a good heart. I know you would do anything to transform your brother's views. But, it saddens me to say, Gershom is Gershom. He has never in his life made room for views other than his own. He's convinced that there is one right way to look at the revelations of the Holy One and, from his perspective, any other interpretation is automatically wrong at best and evil at worst. If we were to confide in him, I believe he would feel obligated to destroy us one way or another. I am not so concerned about myself. My life will not last much longer no matter what happens. But what about you, Elie? What destiny does your revelation call you to live out in your life? And what freedom do you need from your brother's influence in order to follow the Holy One in a new direction?"

Eliezer had been sitting with his head in his hands, but at Moses' words, he abruptly raised it up to look at his father, looking both horrified and intrigued by what he had just heard. "What are you talking about, Father?"

"Don't be upset, Eliezer. I was there, remember? I'm pretty sure I know what you saw. And I suspect that you saw through my eyes as well."

The younger man wrapped his arms around himself as if suddenly chilled and said, "Let's talk about you first. I think I caught a glimpse of what you saw, but I'm not certain I saw it clearly."

"I need to walk some more. Come." Moses stood up, stretched, and resumed walking, in silence at first. After a short while, he began. He took his time and chose his words carefully. If nothing else, his many years of life had taught him a deeply trusting patience. Even though his life might be nearly over, he walked with the relaxed demeanor of a man with plenty of time left.

Eliezer listened intently to his father. "Your description of the approach to the mountain was very much like mine. I have always experienced that kind of disorientation with the Holy One. You now know how disconcerting it is to be fully here and fully there, actually fully everywhere at the same time.

"In my vision, once again I heard the words that recently have been leaking into my dreams and fantasies: 'The Promised Land is within you and among you.' I have felt sure for some time that these words originated with the Holy One, but they haven't made any sense to me. I think I was confused by the ambiguity of the word 'you.' It seems that I have been hearing that word in the wrong way. Perhaps I've spent too much time with Gershom. This time, however, it sounded more like 'us.' You know, you, me, others, even the Holy One: all of us. The Promised Land is within and among *us*.

"This may sound obvious, but the meaning of 'us' is very different from the meaning of 'you'. I had been confused because I thought the Holy One was referring to 'me' personally, or even the Israelites in general. It wasn't making any sense that way because I kept waiting for some clearer direction about what 'I' was (or perhaps, 'we' were) supposed to do."

Moses stopped talking again. Eliezer walked along beside him. He sensed that Moses was trying to decide what to say next, so he remained silent, open, waiting.

Abruptly, Moses gestured with his staff before resuming his discourse. "You see, I've been feeling for some time that the Promised Land might not actually be a place. You can certainly appreciate that I could never say that out loud. Gershom would strangle me with his own hands to prevent Jehovah from taking offense at my obvious blasphemy. This time, though, I heard and I understood.

"It turns out that my speculation was both right and wrong. The Promised Land can be located at a particular place, but that's not a necessary condition. This is difficult to explain." Moses shook his head in frustration, then closed his eyes for a few moments before starting again. "Here is how my view about the Promised Land was wrong. I came to see in the vision that it's actually possible for some people to find a place, a Promised Land, if you will, that will support a nation. Some among the Children of Israel will take that route and it is important for me to remember in all humility that Israel will always matter to the Holy One. That means that the Holy One will continue to participate in Israel's development. Whether the Holy One will punish them if they don't behave properly raises a more complex question. Think about it. Every choice has its benefits and costs. If the Israelites don't take responsibility for the dangerous consequences of their chosen path, they will have abundant opportunities to be surprised and to experience pain and suffering. Some might interpret that painful experience as punishment.

"But my speculation is also right in a way. There is more to the Promised Land than merely taking possession of a certain territory. In the wilderness, we have learned so much more than how to battle, how to govern, how to worship, or how to be obedient to the creator of the universe. We've had forty years to learn how connected we are to each other and to the land around us. When we first entered the wilderness, it seemed to be a hostile place, like an enemy. Whenever we have learned to respect its dangers and appreciate its opportunities, we have discovered it to be a land of abundance that has supported us sufficiently.

"We also discovered in the wilderness that we were more than a conglomeration of slaves who belonged to and were cared for by someone else. We became a people. We discovered who we were, not only as individual travelers, but also as a nation, a tribe, even a family. Another way to say it is this: we experienced 'mattering' to each other. Part of the experience of mattering came from getting to know each other. We spent time together. We took interest in what one another found meaningful. We discovered each other's talents. And in some strange way, we learned to find the presence of the Holy One embedded in the way we got along together.

"Come to think of it, there was one part of the law that Gershom got absolutely right. The Holy One wants us to employ every thought, feeling, talent, desire, question, gift, step, breath, and anything else we might possess to enter into loving connection with I AM and with each other. No other law can possibly serve any useful function except with respect to that law of love. Gershom, in his compulsion to be thorough, expanded the Holy One's 'message of mattering' to include many specific activities. He assumed that killing, stealing, coveting, and adulterating other people's relationships had to be spelled out so that people would never inadvertently disobey Jehovah."

Moses stopped walking and talking for a few minutes as if he were mulling over what he had just said. His eyebrows wrestled with an unseen adversary, his mouth worked as if gnawing a bone, his cheeks flushed as if they had come too close to the fire, and his hands wrung the handle of his staff. They resembled hands that were squeezing the last drop of water out of a freshly laundered garment. And, of course, Moses had completely forgotten about Eliezer.

For his part, Eliezer could only be fascinated with Moses' descriptions and explanations and so he waited patiently (he was learning!) for Moses to continue.

"I'm not exactly sure how I know these things," Moses said, finally, "but they've become permanently resident in my mind. It is just not so simple to articulate what I have come to know. But, then again, what else is new. Articulation has never been the sharpest spear in my arsenal." Moses said these things as though talking to himself, and then as if Eliezer wasn't there at all, he resumed walking… and talking.

"When I think about the laws Gershom has created, particularly 'The Ten', I'm reminded of something I saw on our hill." Moses was silent again while he strode along the desert floor with Eliezer practically having to run to keep up. Then he stopped and held out his arms in front of him cradling his staff like a baby. "Elie, look at my hands. Do you see the Ark?"

"I don't understand, Father. That's your staff."

Moses looked down at it and chuckled. "When a vision has ended and I'm trying to describe it, sometimes the curtain between the reality of the vision and the reality of the description becomes porous and I can't tell where I am at any given moment. Please forgive me. Let me try again.

"In the vision I saw the Ark that Gershom designed and fashioned to carry the stone tablets from the mountain. Well, it looked like that one anyway, but for some reason I don't think it was the same one. You were carrying it, surrounded by a hundred or so men and women of all ages. I found your carrying it very odd, because, as everyone knows, Gershom's priests are the only ones who ever perform that duty when the people move from place to place.

"For some reason I needed to see what you were carrying in the Ark. When I stooped over to look inside, I discovered, to my astonishment, that while it contained (as I expected) two stone tablets, they were not the same ones as those in Gershom's Ark. Instead of bearing the inscription of the Ten, there were only two. One carried a version of the Holy One's name, the very name I had received on the mountain years ago. "I LOVE" was inscribed there. I had to look at the second one several times before I could decipher the inscription on it. What I read there turned out to be the True Name and purpose of the people who were surrounding you and the Ark. It's a bit difficult to say clearly in words, but it was something like 'You are to love I AM; You are to love WE ARE LIKEWISE.'"

"I don't…"

"Don't even try right now, Elie. You'll have plenty of time to be discovered by the meaning. Anyway, there's more."

Again Moses walked on in silent meditation. It appeared he was searching for additional words as if he had misplaced them in his tent and needed them to perform some important task during the day. Then he shrugged and muttered something like "Oh well, these will have to do…"

He turned to face Eliezer. "There is something else in the vision, Elie. I don't know what it means yet, but I think it's important." His breathing grew ragged, eyes bright, ready to bring forth tears.

"What is it? Maybe I've already seen it."

"Perhaps so." Moses said, though it still took him several minutes before he could speak. "At first, I saw myself walking with you. At some point, the vision shifted. Apparently, the journey had been going on for some time. At least I think so, because the scene was slightly different. You were still walking, still carrying the Ark, you and your surrounding companions. But, in this scene, the place I had occupied beside you was empty. I was nowhere to be found. Naturally, I was confused, but mostly I was surprised not to feel troubled about my absence.

"For some unknown length of time these scenes came and went like mirages over the hot desert. Shortly before I 'woke up' I was granted one more holy glimpse that I can only assume was a depiction of the dream you have described to me. Like the previous scene, I could see what was happening, but I wasn't there.

"The journey had ended and your people had established some kind of communal home. I was moved by how much you each obviously mattered to one another. At the end, my vision was dimming and I heard those now familiar words. I think you all were singing them: 'The Promised Land is within us and among us!'"

"Father, I can hardly believe what I am hearing. I had forgotten the song, but you're right, it was in my dream, too. That other part can't be accurate though. You have to be with us. I can't imagine it any other way. I can live without my brother, but not without you."

"Elie, I don't know what it means, but I have to believe that in the end, it'll be all right."

"I hope so. Now that I've found you, I want some time for us to be together. I never imagined it could be like this. I can't go on…"

Eliezer abruptly stopped walking and dropped to his knees, his head in his hands.

Moses reached down and put a hand on Eliezer's head. "What is it, my son?"

"Father, if you have decided that it is time for you to die, then I want to die with you. I can't bear the thought of facing the future without you."

"Oh Elie, please. Let's not get ahead of ourselves here."

Eliezer looked up at him.

With great tenderness he said, "First of all, I have made no such decision. Though I had been considering it, I assure you now that I will not take my own life, nor does it seem likely that I will just lay myself down to die, either. The only thing I know for sure is that I cannot go with Gershom into the Promised Land. The fruits of our time with the Holy One seem to indicate that the journey is not over for us. But where it goes, and how the decision will be made to take it, that I haven't figured out yet.

"Now, what about your life? It appears that the Holy One still has something in store for you. I think you're the one who has a decision to make in response to the Holy one's leadings. It seems to me that my further journey will somehow follow yours."

Eliezer pondered his father's words. Then the vision came back to him so strongly that momentarily the boundary between the vision and where he stood in the wilderness shredded. Slowly the pieces of the vision knit together and the gaps in his understanding were gradually filled with new meaning. Bit by bit he remembered where he was standing. He looked up, acknowledged Moses, and then turned around very slowly in a full circle. He saw everything. Moses was watching his face while disorientation and confusion were replaced by comprehension and wonder.

Eliezer turned to his father. "I think I understand a bit more, perhaps a lot more."

"Yes, it appears you do. But tell me."

"Well, I finally understand why Gershom has never appeared in my dreams before. It's now clear to me that he and I are not going to the same Promised Land. It is as true to say that I don't belong to his vision of a holy nation, as it is to say that he doesn't appear in my vision of a holy community. I don't yet know exactly what this means for us, though now I'm certain that I, too, am not going to cross the river to enter the Promised Land with Gershom."

The two men walked on in silence, each caught up in thoughts that simultaneously exhilarated and terrified them. While neither of them could have described how it happened, they each moved into that sacred space between them and knew that the Holy One was present with them and moved with them. Their spirits now pointed in a new direction, though it was practically inconceivable to imagine a life that was not focused on getting to the Promised Land on the other side of the Jordan River. For the entire time that it took them to walk back to the oasis, they felt supported and guided by the divine presence.

When they reached the oasis they set about preparing for their trip back to the Israelites camp. It surprised Eliezer to find himself thinking about Moses' staff. His mind's eye captured its detailed history in mere seconds. It was so real that he could see the handle smoothing from Moses oily hands and the scars accumulating from wilderness use. A thought disturbed him: He's going to lose it! By the time they left the oasis, Eliezer had found the perfect replacement and secreted it on his beast. I'll know when to give it to him.

Before long they were on the road again. Along the way neither felt the need to say very much, because each was lost in wonder at this new Revelation. After many hours of walking in silence, Father and son were struck simultaneously with the same thought. They started speaking at the same moment, fell silent, and then Moses said, "What is it, son?"

"What about the others?"

"That was my thought exactly. We have to find out which of the other men think as we do. No doubt the Holy One is conversing with more hearts than just ours."

"Perhaps so, Father, but it's not just the men we need to consider in this."

"What are you saying?"

Eliezer pondered for a moment. Three times he started to speak, then stopped. Finally, he took a great breath and held it for a moment. "You have seen in my dream that there are as many women as men."

Eliezer looked warily at Moses, prepared for some reaction. Moses appeared to remain open. "And there was no distinction between them," Eliezer went on. "The women reflected the Holy presence as much as the men. There must be women among us who also feel no joy at the prospect of crossing that river."

Moses walked on in silence, brow furrowed, eyes on the ground before him. Eliezer followed along watching Moses' back. Had he said too much? Could their new relationship withstand this potential challenge of inclusivity? Should he clarify, take it back, or simply give his father some filial support. But then he remembered his newly found patience and contented himself with breathing deeply and rhythmically and contented himself by watching the small eddies of dust kicked up by Moses' heels from each ponderous step.

After a while, Moses suddenly stopped and turned to look at his son. He had a strange look on his face that Eliezer, with all his experience in reading people, could not discern.

"Don't worry, my son. For some reason, I had already assumed that you would not change the direction of your life without your family. They must, of course, decide with you and it will be important for you to stay together. I believe that will have to be true for any other man who happens to share our glimpse of a different future."

Again, Moses paused. His eyebrows worked furiously while his teeth chewed on his cheek. "Let me tell you how I have come to this similar conclusion. You're right to consider that there may be others. As you know, Eliezer, many men have served as judges and mediators over the conflicts brought to them by the people. They bring to me only those situations that are the most refractory to achieving acceptable agreement. In this way, I am able to maintain a full understanding of the deepest currents of struggle and discontent among the children of Israel. I believe I can trace much of my present discomfort with our drive toward the Promised Land to what I have discerned in this process.

"I believe it's true that many, if not most of us, tend to be fearful and grasping. When we left Egypt, the chaos made it possible for the people to bring quite a bit of gold and jewelry with them. Those earliest disputes after we entered the wilderness were always about questions of ownership. Only the promise of protection by that "calf of gold" had the power to separate their grasping hands from their baubles. After that, I began hearing disputes that were about food and water. The Israelites were constantly afraid of not having enough, so they fretted, and hoarded, and stole from each other. The more they attempted to assuage their insecurity in these ways, the more anxious and contentious they became.

"I came to the conclusion then, and have held it for some time, that those who survived the time of bondage in Egypt carried permanent wounds. Their gratitude to the Holy One for their liberation remained obscured by their fear of not having enough. They could receive divine gifts, but they could never let themselves trust the Holy One. I kept reminding them of the many times and ways that the Holy One had demonstrated faithfulness to their needs, but I could never get near the source of their anxiety. I prayed for them all the time and during each direct encounter with the Holy One I would, I am ashamed to say, communicate my own lack of faith. I feared that the Holy One would tire of their complaining and would abandon them to destruction.

"Fortunately for all of us, the Holy One is as far-sighted as I am short-sighted. It became clear in our communion that the hope for Israel to receive and embrace the divine promise would have to rest with the next generation: your generation, Eliezer. I tried to explain to the people why it would be necessary for us to remain a nomadic wilderness people for another generation, but, as was to be expected, they interpreted the decision as a punishment by Jehovah. Whenever one of the former slaves died, I led the people in grieving. But, deep in my heart, their deaths also signaled one more step toward the day when we could embrace the Promise. You've also seen how I lead the celebration at each birth, how I dance all day and night until my body finally reminds me of how many years I carry. Each child represents my hope for the future.

"In the wilderness I've seen this generation mature in so many ways. Young men, (and yes, Eliezer, young women, too) have demonstrated how wonderful this community can be. They've worked together. They've supported each other. They've learned to identify the hidden abundance in the apparent harshness and barrenness of the wilderness. They have come to affirm themselves as a people with integrity, people who know the Holy One to be alive at the center of their community.

"So, over the years in the wilderness when the old ones died off and the young ones took their places of leadership, I observed a decrease in their disputes over ownership. I concluded that they were maturing as a people and that they would be capable of taking their growing trust in the Holy One with them into the Promised Land. Their trusting relationships, honed and purified in the wilderness, would transform the Promised Land first. And then it would transform the world. The fundamentally manipulative worship of all other gods would melt away in the presence of our Holy One: the God who chooses to care for us.

"How could I have been so wrong, so foolish? I never dreamed that Gershom's wooden and exacting reports would skew the vision so much. It feels to me like the promise of a trusting, sacred community has been slipping away.

"Now lately, the mediators are once again plaguing me with property disputes. Many of them are not even about present conflicts. People have become drunk with visions of land and conquest and booty. They already covet what their neighbors might gain in the land across the Jordan. They quibble and quarrel over formulas governing distribution. Of course, Gershom and his priests are right in the middle of it, making sure that their riches will be ensured.

"What disturbs me the most are the disputes that so many men are bringing regarding their women. You'd think they were haggling over cattle. Wonderful, capable young women who have worked, fought, and suffered alongside the men are being treated as if they were slaves on the auction block. The Holy One brought the Israelites out of Egypt. Who would have believed that this people would choose to bring the worst of Egypt with them?

"Eliezer, we cannot let this happen. I doubt we can save them all, but I have no doubt that many of these wonderful women will wish to see a different manifestation of the Holy One's promise.

"So, inquire discreetly to find men... and women... who share our vision. But, beware your brother! If he finds out what we're doing, he will likely interpret it as disobedience to his version of the Holy One's plan. He could find many defensible reasons in his profusion of laws to neutralize or eliminate us. Kinship will not stand against Gershom's obsession with divinely authorized greatness for Israel and for himself.

"Reveal only what you must at this point. There is no need to convince people with extensive arguments. Those who are open to trusting the Holy One will be able to act on a large measure of faith and a small measure of detail, at least for now. There will be time for them to change their minds later, should they choose to, and still catch up with those who cross the river ahead of them."

"I will do as you say, Father. I've been observing people for long enough that I know already who is likely to be with us. We will be back in the Israelite camp tomorrow. Come then and share the evening meal with my family and we will talk more. You do, of course, understand that my first contact will be with my own wife."

"Milcah is a fine person..." Moses looked warily at his son. "...though I don't expect that she will readily trust me."

"Father, I believe in this case trust in Moses is not significant. Trust in the Holy One is—for us, as well as for Milcah."

Chapter 10

Eliezer and Milcah inhabited a small tent in the section of the camp near the other childless adults. They had one son, Rahabiah. Sadly the damage to Milcah's womb from his birth precluded their having any more children. Rahabiah, now twenty years old, had taken a wife two years before. Already they had brought one new Israelite into the world and a second was on the way. Living just with each other now, Eliezer and Milcah had decided that they actually liked and respected one another. The one bone of contention between them was Moses.

If one were to choose a single person most qualified to stand as the epitome of strength and intelligence, Milcah would be a fine choice. Any of her four sisters could competently qualify for that honor as well. What a family she came from! Their father, Zelophehad[7] had been amazed at his family of five daughters and no sons! His friends alternated between ribbing him and pitying him. He always went along with their joking, because to do otherwise would be to jeopardize his good standing and reputation of respect in the community. He was fair in his dealings with others, and no one of his daughters ever felt slighted by the attention he paid to any other. Their mother, like so many of the women coming into the wilderness, had found life there to be no more difficult, though infinitely more rewarding, than life in Egypt. The women had always known how to survive. Whether in Egypt or in the Sinai wilderness, they took careful notice of their surroundings and were always able to obtain at least barely enough to feed themselves and their families.

Milcah and her sisters had been born in the wilderness, and while life was often harsh and always hard, they learned all the lessons the wilderness had to teach. For them, the wilderness was home. They were all very bright and Milcah was the brightest of the lot.

In the structural patriarchy of Israel, daughters had no rights of inheritance. When their father, Zelophehad, died in the wilderness, they made the bold (some would say foolish or futile) decision to present a petition to Moses regarding their rights to inherit their portion in the Promised Land.

Imagine their astonished joy when Moses, after he consulted the Holy One, decided in their favor. The decision astonished Zelophehad's brothers just as much as it had the young women, but there was no joy in their astonishment. As they saw it, land would leave the family as each daughter wed. It pained them to think that they would lose more land to each husband's family. Because they had learned from the disastrous experience of other foolish ones who had directly challenged Moses, they surreptitiously brought their concerns to Moses through his son. Gershom was a staunch defender of the patriarchy. For him, Jehovah was a Divine male who delegated all authority to the most able men in the community. As Gershom and so many others believed, it was against the obvious designs of Jehovah for any woman or child to have authority—and everyone knew that ownership of land conferred authority.

So when the uncles brought their appeal to Gershom they found a receptive ear. He was already distressed at Moses' reckless decision anyway. Had Moses held to convention and consulted Gershom first, the decision would certainly have turned out to be different. Gershom had been livid not to be included in the deliberation, because Moses, left to his own counsel, never understood the Holy One properly. That was why it was necessary for Moses *always* to obtain clarification and the proper interpretation from Gershom first.

Armed with the appeal on behalf of the uncles, Gershom quickly found an opportunity to approach Moses. His intervention was quite simple. All Gershom had to do was acquaint Moses with the political and commercial implications of his precedent-setting ruling. Convinced by Gershom's expert consultation, Moses agreed to an amendment. He still allowed the sisters to inherit the land, but required them to marry only within their own tribe. In short, they would only be allowed to marry their cousins. Gershom had so twisted Moses' mind that he ended up believing that he had succeeded in keeping everyone happy. The daughters got their inheritance; the patriarchal tradition remained intact (and, of course, the uncles would retain the use and control of the land). Milcah, however, vowed that she would never forgive Moses for reneging on his decision and never again would she trust him.

The situation became much more complex when she met Eliezer. Milcah had begun observing Eliezer while he was occupied with his surreptitious surveillance of others. His apparent loneliness and inherent tenderness raised her interest, but when she finally caught his eye, she felt as if the Holy One looked upon her through him. The deepest places in Eliezer called to the deepest places in Milcah. In that instant, they were united for all time. Imagine her fury when she discovered his identity: Moses' son! Moses' son! She stomped; she cried; she cursed; and she vowed never to give him so much as one more thought. But it was all in vain.

After a few days of her moping and complaining about every little thing, her sisters quickly caught on to her plight. Tirzah, perhaps next to Milcah, the cleverest of the five, started to giggle. With her infectious laughter, it didn't take long before all five were a silly symphony of cackles, wheezes, tears, and peals upon peals of laughter. It was as if a disembodied spirit had been let loose to ply a feather upon the sisters' most ticklish places.

When the laughter began to subside, Tirzah was the first to get serious—and she got very serious. The tent grew deathly still as each in turn caught her look.

"What is it, Tirzah? What satanic plot have you cooked up now?" Milcah inquired carefully, still gasping from their bout of giggles.

"Well," she said slowly, drawing out every syllable to bring to exquisite intensity her sisters' curiosity. "I think our moon-eyed sister has unwittingly fallen into a brilliant solution. Listen carefully now.

"Milcah has found a way that we can each inherit our portion of our father's allotment. As it stands now, we can still inherit, but we are allowed only to marry our cousins. But, in that case, our uncles will always have authority over us, and our husbands will as well. That's a dreadful thought, on all counts." She added these last words in visceral distaste at the thought of her thoroughly unappealing cousins.

"However, our esteemed sister has fallen in love with one of the few men among the Israelites for whom an exception would have to be made. No one could challenge a marriage with Eliezer. The marriage can be seen as an appropriate offering to the House and lineage of Moses. Eliezer, as younger son, will be pleased to share your inheritance. He will be grateful; you will have your inheritance; and our uncles will have neither control of the land nor authority over us. What could be a better solution? The five young women looked around at each other. Who knows who snickered first, but in no time, they became once again a gasping, giggling heap.

When they stopped the second time, Noah piped up, "If we select carefully, perhaps we each could make such a marriage. With a bit of cleverness, I'm sure we could find an additional four acceptable exceptions."

"Just stay away from that snake, Gershom!" Tirzah had snapped to end their conversation.

So Milcah and Eliezer had married. Within a year their son had been born, and now they had been living together and growing in affection and respect for each other for another twenty. Milcah really didn't hate Moses. When they were with him, not that often really, he was pleasant enough. But she still felt betrayed by his blind accession to masculine privilege.

Eliezer and Milcah were both careful observers. This was not unusual. Many among the Israelites had developed strong powers of observation from all those years of surviving in the wilderness. Even the wilderness could be abundant enough if you knew where to look. So when Eliezer returned from his journey with Moses and entered their tent she sensed immediately that something out of the ordinary must have happened. She nodded to him and waited with growing curiosity while he dropped his cloak and pack and then settled back on his sleeping mat.

"Milcah, it's a blessing to me that I never have anything to hide from you. It seems at times that you think my thoughts and feel my feelings even before I do. A lesser man would feel compelled to write you a bill of divorce for the infraction of trespassing in his mind and heart. But I love it, and I love you for it. I have never once experienced even a moment of loneliness with you. In the rest of my dealings with people, I feel little else."

"I love you too, Eliezer. But enough with the fancy words. My reading of your inner being is a bit blurry at the moment."

"I have much to tell you. These may be the most significant words we will ever exchange. But, I fear your reaction to one vital element in my news. It involves my father."

"What's that wishy-washy cheat up to now?"

"Please hear me out before you judge. I know you have ample reason not to trust him, but what I have to tell you may modify your view somewhat."

"Very well, Eliezer, I do trust you, after all. Thank the Holy One you're a different man than your father, or that viper who presumes to be your brother. Anyway, I've waited long enough. Give me something to divert me from my tedium."

"I'll fill in the details in time, but the short version is that Moses plans not to go across into the Promised Land with the children of Israel."

"What? That's preposterous. Moses has led this tribe for forty years. How could he not continue to lead us into the Promised Land?"

"He doesn't want to go." Eliezer waited a long time and sighed deeply before going on. "And that's not all."

Milcah went still. Her heart tried repeatedly to leap into her throat. "What is it, Eliezer?"

"I plan not to go either!"

For several minutes the only sounds in the tent came from outside: the muffled sound of voices, the occasional high-pitched whoop from a youthful game, the scrape of feet on the sandy path that wove among the tents. Eliezer hardly breathed as he waited for Milcah to digest this news. He had supposed that he knew what her reaction would be, but here in this weighty silence he was sure that he had no idea at all.

Finally, Milcah stopped her intense examination of the animal skin at her feet, looked up at Eliezer, released a sigh, and said in the quietest, calmest voice imaginable, "You had better tell me the rest."

Eliezer caught the breath that he had been holding. He shifted his body so he could look directly at his wife and began to tell her everything.

Chapter 11

Milcah wept for a long time. The tears started while Eliezer was still telling her the story. Something about this new layer of communication with the Holy One was so moving to her that it brought a flood of tears, a flood that occasionally rode on deep racking sobs. Moses' story, and even his own for that matter, had affected him in the same way. Eliezer was thoroughly perplexed at Milcah's reaction, though. He thought he knew her so well, but this time he couldn't tell if she was moved, afraid, angry, sad, or relieved. Her sobbing slowly subsided while he waited expectantly. He wanted to find out what her tears meant but he was afraid of the answer. And he knew better than to press her before she was ready. (Apparently, Milcah was also teaching him to be patient.) He decided it would be worth the wait.

At last, Milcah dried her eyes, took Eliezer's hand in hers and said, "I knew when I first laid eyes on you I would find an extraordinary depth of soul in your being. I have always sensed the presence of the Holy One around us and between us. I have prayed for the day when the Holy One would lead us to the Promised Land. But, as hard as I tried, I couldn't embrace Gershom's (and, I thought, Moses') vision. I have believed that I was too stubborn to see it his way. I have had dreams of the Promised Land for years, but I kept them to myself because they never fit what everyone else was describing as the prize at the end of our journey.

"My tears were tears of recognition, of coming home. What you and Moses saw on the mountain represents my dream, too. For that reason at least, I can honor your father."

Milcah's words broke through the paralysis gripping Eliezer. He went to her and held her close. Here was another physical manifestation of the presence of the Holy One. While his arms were wrapped around her, he considered his own confusion at the way so many men treated their wives—it was as if they were cattle. He and Moses had both noted that during the time of wandering in the wilderness, as long as they had no immediate expectation of getting anywhere in particular, relationships between men and women had been more collegial and respectful. If the sounds he had heard in the night were any indication, their mutual equality and respect had engendered deep passion and profound satisfaction. In recent times, though, he seldom heard men or women cry out in ecstasy. Once the Israelites began heading toward the Promised Land, the night became filled instead with angry demanding voices and cries of pain. There was no doubt that men and women still had intercourse, because babies continued to be born. But the sounds in the night no longer expressed the sacred music of intimacy. Everything in relationship had degenerated into issues about property and ownership. Moses had provided more evidence of the change when he had told him about the men who now came to him to complain about their willful wives. What a waste—to turn a beautiful soul into an object. And what did they gain? Only the fear of unnamed others who threatened to violate their property rights.

When Eliezer had told Milcah about Moses' observations, she had snapped, "It's that brother of yours! Gershom has done this. He is so afraid of everything—especially Jehovah," she said, sheer disdain dripping from her voice. "Somehow he got the harebrained notion that human passion was an affront to the Holy One. He is so sure that if anything matters deeply to the people, it'll distract them from their obedience to the Holy One's (pardon me, Jehovah's) laws. He's taught all the men to see their wives, all women, really, as sources of danger. He's such a snake!"

Eliezer couldn't agree more. Gershom took everything that was freely, even lovingly, provided by the Holy One and turned it upside down. When Gershom looked at humans, he saw two groups: the men, who were all stupid so they had to be controlled by his laws; and the women, who were all evil so the men had to keep them under control, likewise by means of Gershom's laws. Eliezer decided, certain that Milcah would agree with him, that only one person epitomized both stupidity and evil: and that person was Gershom, himself.

Those judgmental thoughts about his brother brought on a strong twinge of conscience in Eliezer. He knew he was not being completely fair to Gershom. While it was true that Gershom was myopic, tried to control every aspect of Israelite life, and behaved in a destructive way toward the creation of community, Eliezer was convinced that, down deep, he was mostly afraid. Whatever had made his brother so fearful Eliezer couldn't say and probably would never know. Nevertheless he felt a sad compassion for Gershom. At the same time, he reminded himself that his brother was dangerous and, like the snake Milcah saw him to be, required very careful handling, indeed.

When Moses' arrived to meet with Eliezer and Milcah, he was surprised to find several other people there as well. Two of Milcah's sisters, Tirzah and Noah, had come with their husbands. Two other couples sat next to them. Moses was sure he had seen them before, but he didn't remember their names. Each of them had made their way to Eliezer and Milcah's tent separately to avoid raising suspicion. Their concern was probably not warranted. Families and friends often gathered to break bread together. But, with Gershom's spies all around, they couldn't be too careful.

Milcah rose and crossed over to Moses, invited him to shed his cloak and put down his staff, and embraced him warmly. Surprised at the gesture, Moses looked across the room at his son. His confusion showed in the height his eyebrows rose above his eyes. Eliezer just smiled back at him. "Welcome, Father. We have prepared a most intriguing meal. I hope you are prepared to be fed."

Moses' nodded a "thank you" and followed Milcah to the place that had been left vacant for him.

After they had passed around large portions of a savory stew, flat bread, and goat's milk, Eliezer began speaking. "Father, each person here believes that the activity and leading of the Holy One does not necessarily point to the other side of the Jordan. But forgive me. I forget my manners. Of course, you know Milcah's two sisters, Tirzaz and Noah, and their husbands. As you may remember, each of these men belongs to the tribe of Levi.

Eliezer then turned toward the other two couples and continued with the introductions. "By means of very careful inquiry, I've discovered that these two of my companion shepherds and their wives have also come to know the Holy One by means of their 'daydreaming.'" Eliezer chuckled, "It's a wonder we have any flocks left, what with shepherds falling into trances all over the place." At these words, the two men grinned sheepishly and edged closer to their respective wives.

Milcah then continued. She addressed her comments primarily to Moses, "My father-in-law, when Eliezer told me of your recent experiences on the mountain, I remembered that Tirzah, Noah, and I had shared some strange dreams with each other years ago. Mahlah and Hoglah, our other two sisters, were there too, but right away they got angry and demanded that we never talk such nonsense again. I don't know why they reacted so. I have wondered if they, too, might have had such dreams but felt it necessary to protect us from the danger those dreams could have caused us. It is equally possible that they have had no such experience so they would simply not understand. Either way, it was too risky to ask them about it now, so I just invited Tirzah and Noah to come here today."

"And here we are, accompanied by our husbands," Tirzah added. "Fortunately, we chose our husbands wisely after Milcah's example." She beamed at her sister who promptly and uncharacteristically blushed.

"Who chose?" Tirzah's husband barked. Each person in the room sat up to look at him, seemingly afraid that he was angry, but the twinkle in his eye betrayed his adoration and obvious approval of his wife's amorous initiative.

"Father," Eliezer explained, "Before you arrived, we described, as best we could, the events of the last few weeks. We also told them that Milcah and I plan to go with you."

Moses' growing surprise now gave way to astonishment, not so much about Eliezer's decision, but that Milcah would willingly accompany him. He opened his mouth to speak, but before he could, Noah rose, bowed slightly toward Moses out of habit, and spoke on behalf of the assembly, "We all want to stay with you if you choose to stay here, or go with you if your steps lead somewhere else."

Now Moses was completely undone. He looked around the tent at each of these brave people. His heart filled with appreciation and respect for the obvious risks they would be taking. Each one met his eyes in turn, nodding to validate personally Noah's statement of their collective intention. He could hardly speak. Suddenly, his heart began pounding in his ears as he remembered seeing each of these women and each of these men in the vision he had recently shared with Eliezer. He examined their faces carefully and saw, expressed in each one of them, the countenance of the Holy One whom he had come to know so well in the wilderness.

Whatever thoughts Moses might have had in the last few weeks about simply laying himself down to die, the hopeful and determined looks in these young faces removed any remaining trace. This time when he opened his mouth he was able to speak, at first almost to himself. "The Holy One made a good choice to reveal divine caring to these children of Israel. It is obvious that you carry the image of the Holy One. I am horrified to think that we almost missed this opportunity due to the misguided zeal of my other son. I know in my heart that the Holy One desires to be embodied in the kinds of relationships that you have created with each other. I was afraid that all those wonderful lessons from the wilderness would inevitably be lost once Israel crossed the Jordan River, but you have restored my hope.

"Because I am an old man, I know that I won't live to see the full flowering of the community that will grow from the seeds you plant. But I am awed to have seen this much. The fulfillment of my life's journey lives in this moment. I am so grateful." His emotion welled up in his throat so strongly that he could not continue.

"Father, you are the Prophet who has led us to this. We're the ones who are grateful to you." Eliezer sounded almost as choked up as his father, but he managed to continue, "For right now however, we have to figure out how to get from here to there, wherever there is."

Tirzah spoke next, "I am the most suspicious of all my sisters." Milcah and Noah nodded in agreement with her self-assessment. "I have watched Gershom for some time. I became convinced a long time ago that he was not to be trusted. I have noted several recent meetings between Gershom and Joshua. I don't know what they are up to, but whatever is, it cannot be good for us. I fear the consequences of any alliance between Gershom's priests and Joshua's soldiers. It is, therefore, my opinion that whatever we do, it must be done quickly."

"It is not at all clear to me what it is we are supposed to do," Noah's husband ventured. "Does anyone know?"

Eliezer stood up to face the group. "I believe I have a slight advantage over the rest of you, because I've been thinking about this for several days now. Allow me to review where we stand. My father has decided not to accompany the Israelites across the Jordan River and into the Promised Land. When I learned of his desire, I was prompted to take seriously a vision that has been visiting me for many, many years. In this vision, I observed and joined a group of people, men and women together, through whom the presence of the Holy One lived. In recent days, particularly when Moses and I went out to seek the vision together, I was able to see it in much greater detail. I saw that each of you was present in that group. The look on my father's face when he entered this tent today told me that he recognized all of you in the same way. It appears that we have been given a sacred opportunity to bring that vision to its own unique fulfillment.

"Our immediate challenge is how to affect our separation from the larger body of the Israelites without triggering a destructive response from Gershom and his powerful allies. We're faced with the additional challenge of recruiting those other people who may feel called by the Holy One to accompany us. And, if that's not difficult enough, I believe we must accomplish all this within the next twenty days."

Tirzah spoke again, "I still have a question that is troubling me. Moses, how can you not lead the Israelites into the Promised Land without your absence demoralizing them or sending a message to them that the Holy One no longer travels at the head of their company?"

Tirzah's husband followed up. "If you just stay here on this side of the river while the others cross over, I predict that many will abandon the Promised Land, because they believe that safety resides only in your presence. It doesn't matter in the slightest how much they have resisted your leadership in the past. You are still the Prophet. At the same time, you can expect them to be very angry with you. They will do anything to persuade you to change your mind. They desperately want to take possession of that land that they believe is flowing with milk and honey. Besides, I agree with my wife that Gershom would never allow it."

The assembled group sat quietly as they pondered this concern. It was clear to all what a serious problem faced them. Actually, none of them had yet put into words their deepest concern—until Noah's husband spoke up. "Apparently there's only one way to accomplish this thing. Moses must die!"

At those words, everyone began shouting at once. How foolish could he be? They were so angry that they were threatening to throw him and Noah out of the tent. One by one they noticed that he did not seem disturbed by their anger. He just sat there, smiling. At first just to himself and then so the rest could hear, Moses started to chuckle, and before long he was laughing so hard that tears were beginning to run down his cheeks.

The rest looked at him in astonishment while they waited for him to compose himself. They couldn't imagine what could possibly be so funny. Moses looked around with affection at each individual. "I choose to interpret your reaction as an expression of your love for me, and I appreciate it deeply. Nevertheless, our friend is absolutely correct."

"Father, how can you find such a horrible idea to be even the slightest bit funny?"

"Think of it this way, Elie. There is a difference, in fact a very big difference, between dying and being dead." Once again, Moses looked around to see if anyone was catching on. All he saw on their faces (with the exception of his new friend, of course) was a painful mixture of confusion and horror—so he went on. "Gershom and Joshua and all the people who will follow them across the river and into the Promised Land must see me die, or at least be convinced that I have died. But let me assure you, I have no intention of actually dying—at least not quite yet."

One by one, their faces showed the dawning of comprehension and astonishment that was quickly replaced by grins of recognition and delight. Before long they were laughing hysterically and slapping one another on the back.

Then Noah raised another question. "I like the sound of the concept, but does anyone have a plan to accomplish it?"

They each looked around from face to face until Moses said, "Perhaps my new friend, your husband (what did you say your name was, again?) might have a plan."

"My name is Jethro. I believe I have been named in honor of your esteemed father-in-law. He was very helpful in mediating a serious dispute between my parents and another family. It seems that they gave me the name hoping it would bring some of his wisdom along with it.

"But, in answer to your question, one of my brothers is an administrative priest in Gershom's employ. He tells me quite often how disturbed Gershom gets at what he calls Moses' emotionality. He is always afraid that Moses might get emotional in the wrong way towards Jehovah and that this could bring wrath and punishment on the Israelites. So, I am wondering, Moses, if there is an event in your past where your emotions might be seen as having caused some potential trouble between the Holy One and Israel."

"I think I see where you're going with this," Moses replied. "Perhaps we can convince Gershom that the Holy One is angry about some small thing so that I'll have to bargain with my life for Israel's good favor in the Holy One's eyes. Jethro, is this what you had in mind?"

Jethro thought for a moment, the smile never leaving his face, and said, "Moses, please forgive my boldness in saying so, but your wisdom is akin to that of your father-in-law. It should be very easy to convince Gershom that the Holy One is angry at you, not at Israel. You can report to Gershom that Jehovah is punishing you by not allowing you to cross the river. With your life's purpose taken away from you, what other choice can there be but for you to die?"

Eliezer had been sitting over in the corner listening carefully to this exchange of ideas between Moses and Jethro.

At last, he stood up, walked to the center of the circle, turned around one full time while looking at each person in the room, and said quietly, "I believe I have a plan..."

Chapter 12

After they completed their planning, the various couples drifted away from Eliezer and Milcah's tent. Each had work to do with precious little time to do it. Perhaps the most challenging task for the next few days would be the matter of recruitment. They felt the need to approach people with care. They wanted to offer people the option to choose to go with them without alarming any of them, and certainly, without making Gershom suspicious. They had decided on approximately one hundred families as the most manageable size for their group. Next to the task of recruitment, the rest should be easy.

Gershom and Moses had consulted with one another only on occasion over the last few months. Frankly, Gershom was fully occupied making his official plans and he didn't want Moses' woolly-headed thinking complicating matters. He had been pleased when Moses and Eliezer had gone off on their recent trip into the wilderness to repair matters with Jehovah. Their absence left him more room to organize the community the way he wanted it. At this point, Moses represented a thorn in his side. He was not at all sure what he was going to do with the Prophet of God once they crossed the river to begin appropriating the Promised Land in the name of Jehovah.

When his aide entered to inform him of Moses' request for a meeting, Gershom just barely managed keep from cursing at the intrusion. "What does the old goat want now? I really don't have time for this!"

"The messenger did not give any details, but apparently Moses has received another communication from Jehovah during his recent time in the wilderness. He needs your help in discerning its proper meaning," his aide explained.

Oh, Great! Just what I need. But, thankfully he still comes to me with his dreams and divine images. Though his inner thoughts were raging, he betrayed no sign to his aide. "Very well, tell the messenger that I will attend Moses shortly. Now, get out of here, all of you."

As soon as the priests and scribes had all gone, Gershom allowed himself to acknowledge the pool of dread that was beginning to spread in his stomach. He had tried so hard to keep everyone in line. He had written laws, trained priests, overseen religious courts, all the while maintaining his own perfect adherence to everything he believed Jehovah required. And now, here they were, on the threshold of greatness, ready to take their God-given place among the nations. He fell to his knees and began praying fervently out of his desperation for Jehovah's continued favor. He finished his prayer, rose, brushed off his knees, and went to meet with his father.

Gershom was surprised upon entering Moses' tent to discover his brother sitting in the corner. Before he had a chance to question Eliezer's presence, Moses said, "Because Eliezer was with me in the wilderness, it seemed important for him to be here, too."

Gershom made a rapid calculation in his head and decided that, if he handled the situation carefully, his introverted and somewhat dull brother would present no problem. "Greetings brother," he said smoothly. "Our paths have not crossed for some time. I trust Milcah is not being too demanding for your sensitive constitution."

Eliezer always found it to his advantage that his brother underestimated him so thoroughly. "And to you, my brother. I have observed that you are organizing things in your characteristically adept way."

Gershom snorted. "So," he snapped, "as pleased as I am to see you both, I have much that demands my attention. Nevertheless, I am always prepared to offer whatever humble assistance I can. I understand that you have (how shall I say it) *been with* Jehovah again."

Moses sat still. He wore a troubled look on his face. "It is true that the Holy One has communicated with me. I've been granted a glimpse of the future."

Gershom's stomach started to turn again, whether with hope or dread he couldn't say. Why can't the old man speak clearly and directly? Gershom continued to look at his father and waited for what would come next.

Moses, in turn, waited while Gershom's discomfort grew. Finally, he continued. "I saw the children of Israel. They were crossing the river and taking possession of the land that flows with milk and honey as the Holy One has promised."

Gershom relaxed a bit, a feeling of hope began to swell within him. Still he said nothing.

"What is most significant to me about this vision is that I did not observe my own presence in the company of the Israelites. Needless to say, I was confused. In answer to my confusion and my unspoken question, I felt something I could only describe as divine displeasure. This, as you know, is not the first time that the Holy One had expressed displeasure at the behavior of the Israelites. So I inquired about what they had done this time to offend him. I might add that this took place after Eliezer and I had already performed the worship and erected the altar as we had been instructed to do. I could tell that our offering had been accepted, so this divine displeasure had to be about something else. I was prepared to argue on behalf of the Israelites as I had done so many times before, but I received no inkling of what had gone wrong. The only conclusion I have been able to draw is that the displeasure of the Holy One must have to do with me."

Gershom listened to Moses' words with little, if any, emotion. He was calculating, trying to isolate the problem and limit the damage. When he spoke, he heard his own words as if they came from someone else. He sounded more tentative than he intended. "Father, you of all people must have been vigilant in keeping Jehovah's laws. Is it possible that you have omitted something from your religious practice?"

"I've thought long and hard about that, Gershom. I'm not aware of any lapses. The only other thing I remember feeling was an old recollection of frustration and anger. I can't always say how I know these things, but I have a sense that the Holy One's displeasure had something to do with my emotions."

Gershom groaned. "How many times have I warned you that your emotions would get you in trouble sooner or later?"

Moses hung his head. "I don't know what I am supposed to do. You have always been able to sort these things out. I think I need your help now."

From the corner of the tent, Eliezer spoke up. "Father, there is one other thing you told me. I think Gershom should know it."

"I don't remember anything else, Eliezer. If there is more, please remind me."

"When we were returning home, right out of the blue, you began telling me of an event that happened years ago. It didn't make any sense why you were telling me at the time. But, as I listen to you now, I think I see the connection."

"Well, what is it!" Gershom snapped at his brother.

Eliezer looked at Moses who nodded for Eliezer to continue. "You told me about one of the times you found water for the people. You were angry with them for not having faith, and, I think, angry with the Holy One for placing such difficult and endless tests on the people. I guess you were supposed to teach them about the wonders of a god who could bring water from stone. Instead, in your anger, you hit the rock with your staff, so the people thought you had brought the water from the rock yourself. After you had finished telling me, you fell silent for a long time."

Moses continued to sit with his head in his hands, his gaze fixed upon the tent floor between his feet. Without looking up, he mumbled, "Perhaps the fault is mine after all. Well, Gershom, what am I to do?"

Gershom's head was spinning. It had been so difficult to be clear and precise about the expectations of Jehovah while there were ever-new revelations from Moses. He had often hoped for the day when divine revelations would cease.

He also remembered with a feeling of relief that Joshua had been chosen as the heir-apparent to Moses. He knew that with Joshua as the titular head of the Israelites, he himself could be the real power, albeit behind the scenes. It would be so much easier to maintain Jehovah's required obedience by controlling

Joshua and using his armies as enforcers. The thought of having Moses out of the way was almost too much to hope for. He had to use all his powers of concentration to keep his growing sense of relief from showing in front of Moses and Eliezer.

Still, for some reason his sense of dread remained. Clearly, Jehovah was testing him just like he had tested his ancestor, Abraham. Abraham had to be prepared to sacrifice his son, Isaac, as a demonstration of his obedience to Jehovah. And now, this same God was testing him to see if he was willing to sacrifice his own father for the sake of Israel's divine purpose in the world. Once he realized it was a test, he knew what he had to do.

When he began speaking, the quiet in his voice was tinged with coldness. "Father, there is no one who has expressed a greater commitment to or love for this Israelite nation than you. Your whole life has been dedicated to Israel's journey to this place. It appears, from what you and Eliezer have told me, that there is one more challenge that Jehovah has laid before you on Israel's behalf. While it is unfortunate that you lost your temper and that the Children of Israel subsequently drew an erroneous conclusion, the event provides an opportunity for them to learn, once and for all, the importance of obedience to Jehovah. Perhaps to you, your lapse is a small one. But, the principle behind it is not small. How can we ever maintain our identity as the people Jehovah has chosen to be an example to the nations if we can't maintain our own obedience to Him?"

Moses lifted his head to look at Gershom. "Are you saying that I am not to go with the Israelites across the river when they take possession of the Promised Land?"

"Yes, I am saying that. You can tell the people that Jehovah won't let you accompany them."

Moses looked pained. "This has been my whole life. If I can't go with the people into the Promised Land, then I have no reason to remain among the living." For the briefest of moments, Moses looked across the tent and met Eliezer's eyes, then quickly looked down again.

Eliezer then addressed his brother. "How can you do this to him? How can you be so cold?"

Gershom stood up, his hands on his hips and his eyes flashing fire. "Not that I expect you to understand, brother, but this is not some sentimental game. We are talking about the destiny of a nation here. What are a few days or months subtracted from the life of an old man next to that? You're as bad as he is. You always let your feelings get in the way of your good sense and your obligations."

"Do what you have to, but I won't be any part of it!" And Eliezer stormed out of the tent.

Gershom was about to continue his criticism of his brother's behavior, but Moses cut him short. "He'll be all right. Let him go. He'll soon realize that there is no other choice. I know I have to stay on this side of the river."

Had Moses not prepared himself so well for this meeting, he might have offered the suggestion himself that he would rather die than be prohibited from occupying his place at the head of the Israelites. Instead he waited.

Gershom was turned away from Moses and was glaring at the tent flap that had closed behind Eliezer. When he had composed himself, he slowly turned around to face Moses. "What you said before: that you would have no reason to live without the Israelites, you do realize that it has to be that way."

Moses heaved a great sigh, shuddering as the breath went out of him. "You're right. I see that now." Gershom opened his mouth to say more, but Moses went on, "I guess you mean that the people have to see it happen. I agree. They have to see and accept my death so they know that the Holy One will continue to be with them.

"But, Gershom, I must insist on one thing. I will decide the manner of my death. I have a sense, though I can't explain how I know it, that the Holy One will provide me with the necessary and most appropriate means. As I think about it now, I realize that for many years I have had premonitions about the nature of my own death. Of course, I couldn't make any sense of those fuzzy images at the time. But now, I am coming closer to knowing the answer. I will go into the presence of the Holy One this very evening. By tomorrow I will know what must be done and we can begin planning."

Gershom was about to leave, but he surprised himself by addressing his father once more. "My father, I know we haven't always seen things the same way, but I think I will miss you."

"It's all right, son. I do understand that you carry yourself in the most correct way you know how. I only hope that from time to time, you'll remember that Jehovah has also given us a law of love. Without love, obedience degenerates into crass compliance." And then, placing his hand on Gershom's shoulder he said solemnly, "May the God of our fathers go with you always."

Gershom was so moved by his father's blessing that before the emotion was able to engulf him, he turned abruptly and went out into the noise of the camp.

Moses, now alone in the tent, fell back into his seat and wept.

Chapter 13

"How will we ever recruit a hundred families in just a few days?" Eliezer was pacing back and forth as much as the confines of the tent would allow. "Maybe if we had a year..."

Milcah sat while her worried husband paced. The more agitated he became, the calmer she appeared. Even though Eliezer was a much different person than his brother, she knew that he also wore the heavy mantle of leadership on his shoulders. He wore it like a new cloak, not yet softened and contoured to his body by sufficient wear. He had told her that leaders were supposed to have the wisdom and cleverness to make things happen. They both knew how fearful he was that the task would be too great for him to accomplish.

His noise and restless energy kept pulling her away from her own somewhat tenuous composure. "Sit down, Eliezer!"

Either he didn't hear her or he was ignoring everything but his own inner struggle.

"Sit down! Who can think with all your commotion?"

He stopped pacing and glared at her as if she had slapped him. His mouth opened to argue, but she met his eyes with such a look of determination and upset that he closed it again. A cloud of sandy dust kicked up from the sleeping mat when he sat down on it with a thump.

Milcah spoke to him as if he were a fussy infant. "Elie, it's going to be all right." Then, she walked over to stand behind him, took his rigid shoulders in her small but strong hands and began to knead the tension out of his muscles. "These shoulders feel like they're trying to carry the weight of a mountain—and they are not succeeding."

Eliezer nodded his head in agreement. "Don't move your head. Let me work."

After several minutes of grasping, pulling, kneading, and pounding on his neck and back, Milcah reported, "There, I wager that feels a bit better. You've got to carry the weight of these challenges more lightly. If you keep this up, you'll be no more useful than Gershom."

At the sound of his brother's name, Eliezer flinched and tried to get up to resume his pacing. Milcah was quicker, though, landing with all of her small self on his back. He was so taken by surprise that he fell over and for a moment they resembled a nest of writhing snakes. As soon as he felt her weight shift, he rolled abruptly and found himself on top of her. His weighty concerns momentarily obliterated by the warm and familiar touch of her body, his hands groped for the openings in her robe.

"Stop that! Any other time I would welcome your observant hands, to say nothing about other members of your scouting party, but there is no time for that."

Eliezer rolled off her and let go. "At least I'm not pacing," he said with a crooked grin.

Despite herself, she smiled back at her husband with comfortable familiarity, the product of their many years together. "It's an improvement, I grant you. But I need you to listen to me."

Eliezer had heard that tone of insistence in her voice before, but it was always accompanied by wisdom. He loved her as much for her wisdom as for any other of her many outstanding qualities. "I'll try to sit still. Tell me."

Milcah sat so they could face one another. "Elie, you know I love you and honor you." He nodded. "But I don't even recognize this wild thing that's been pacing around our tent. I have never seen you like this."

Eliezer shoulders slumped. He began to make some apology, but she silenced him with a wave. "Have you already forgotten where you've been and what you've seen in recent days? When you described it, I was transported. The Holy One, Elie, the Holy One is with you."

Eliezer blinked but did not speak.

"When you and Moses were on that mountain, were you at all afraid?"

He took the time to think carefully about her question and had to admit to her that, no, he had not been.

"In any of your dreams, while sleeping or awake, have you ever felt at all burdened by the presence of the Holy One: that unreasonable demands were being placed on you?"

"No, never."

"What did you experience, then?"

He thought for a few minutes, his eyes unfocused as if straining to see that now faraway mountain. "It was as if ... I felt ... I think I saw ... this is always the hardest part. The words I plan to speak keep falling so short of what I'm trying to say—to explain. Let me try again." After a bedtime-like sigh that was half way to a yawn, he brightened. "There's this something that I breathe. I can feel it, but I don't know what it is. I am comforted to know that it always seems to be available in exactly the measure I need, at least, so far. I don't know how I know this, but I know that without its capacity to fill my chest, I would die. Perhaps I learned that lesson when I fell into the pool of the oasis as a child, and my mother had to fish me out. Anyway, I know these things."

Milcah watched him as he scoured the memories of his lifetime for more. "Whenever I take a step, there's always the earth beneath my foot. I should expect to fall through into no place, but I never do. Whether my steps are lighted by sun or lamp or whether I feel my way in the dark, my step always meets solid ground." Then he reached out and laid his hands on Milcah's cheeks. "And when I look at you, I seem to know that we're connected somehow. No, it's more than our connection through our son. I just know that I will always know you. The knowing itself is eternal and holy."

They sat for some time, refreshed by the "holy knowing" that flowed as the sea between them. Whether it ebbed or flowed at any given moment, it always simply was.

"So, Eliezer..." Her voice pierced him as the first rays of the sun pierced and obliterated the darkness. "If we have learned nothing else during our years in the wilderness, we have surely learned to trust the Holy One. So, I've been wondering about your dream. You told me you could see the presence of the Holy One in the faces of the people. Have you seen that presence in the faces of people around you when you were not dreaming or in a trance?"

"Yes, in you and Moses, for sure..." He paused to think. "Of course!" he said. "When we asked those few people to gather to meet Moses, it was as if they already expected the invitation. At the very least, no one seemed very surprised."

"That's what I thought, too. And that gives me an idea." The well-known peaceful and grounded tone in Milcah's voice could always be counted on to blow away Eliezer's anxiety like dust before the desert winds. He settled down to listen.

"From what you told me of your visit with Gershom, he expects Moses to die, and he needs the people to see it. We can work out a plan for Moses to be 'taken up' so there won't have to be a dead body. He should have 'companions' around him right up to the end, people who will stay behind to attend to the rituals of mourning. Meanwhile, Joshua will be prepared to lead the rest of the people across the Jordan once they have received Moses' commission and blessing.

"Those who stay behind will be able to escape back into the wilderness where they will meet up with Moses. By the time Gershom catches on—if he even does—it will be too late for him to do anything about it. Besides, he'll be amply occupied with the challenges of the Promised Land."

"I like your plan, Milcah, but I still don't see how we can recruit all those families quickly enough."

"Elie, for an intelligent man, you can be rather unimaginative —and not very trusting of the Holy One for that matter." Then, after a pause, she went on, "Think about the faces in the dream. You said you could see the Holy One in their faces, so you already have a pretty good idea of those people who would choose to go with us. All you have to do is ask them one simple question, and then watch their faces.

Eliezer's confused countenance began to clear. "What would I do without you?"

Milcah started giggling. "You'd better leave that question alone. You might not like the answer."

Eliezer grimaced at her. "I think I've got it. Let's see. The question will have to be constructed carefully." He stood up, walked around the tent, then stopped and turned. "How about this? 'You are being invited to assist Moses as he takes leave of his long life as our leader and prophet. If you are willing, then you and your family will have to delay your departure to the Promised Land while you attend to the necessary rituals.'

"And then we watch their faces. Those who are open to the Holy One in the same way we are will immediately agree, while those whose fortune has already taken up residence across the Jordan will not want to wait. We can make it clear that the decision is completely up to them. Those who are 'called' will know it, and the rest will feel free to accompany Joshua and Gershom."

"I think that'll work," Milcah said. "Then, all that is left is for Moses to give his final address to the people in his role as the deliverer of the Israelites. Except this time, you, not Gershom, will assist Moses in figuring out what to say."

"I doubt he will need my advice. I think he's been working on this speech for years without even knowing it. Still, I will gladly offer my assistance."

Milcah hugged her husband. "No more pacing, I see."

Eliezer smiled. "I don't know where we will go, but I'm sure the Holy One will guide us. I'll go over our plan with Moses so he can do his part with Gershom. Then we'd better get our group together again. We have a lot of work to do."

The next day Moses met with Gershom again to inform him about the nature of his impending death. He played his part so perfectly that Gershom went away from their meeting believing that it was his idea to recruit those families who would remain behind to surround Moses' during last days as Prophet of God to the Israelites and mourn his death.

Asher and his wife, Sarah, had awakened to bright sunshine that promised to heat up another day, further scorching the desert. Asher held a minor administrative job as overseer to a group of herdsmen. He had grown up tending flocks and had become a competent shepherd.

As they broke their fast, they speculated about their impending life in the Promised Land. "I was talking with one of my shepherds yesterday. He had been recruited by Joshua to go across the river to get a better idea of what we can expect to face there." Asher still had the energy of a much younger man in his small but wiry body. He spoke with animation, his hands flying in accompaniment to his words.

"What did he see?" His wife looked worried.

"Naturally, he had an eye for the land. It seemed more than suitable to sustain our flocks, but he also saw many flocks already grazing. There were cities, too ... big cities with walls and armies."

Her frown deepened as she said, "The battles will rage for a long time. Is this truly the place chosen for our new home? How many will have to die, Israelites and Canaanites alike, before we can live and raise our families in peace?"

"I've been asking myself why we have to take this land by force. Does the God of the Mountain need our victory to demonstrate His superiority?" Asher then fell silent and joined his wife in deep concern about their future.

"Whenever I look across the river, all I can see is blood, theirs and ours. We will have to kill or be killed. Why must it be this way?" Hot tears sprang from Sarah's eyes.

"I've wondered why we couldn't enter into a peaceful cohabitation with the Canaanites. There's plenty of land for all." Asher scratched his beard. "The answer is obvious, now that I think about it. Religious practice—that's it! The priests are always railing about staying faithful to Jehovah. They're afraid we'll be tempted to worship some other god. They say that if we go to other gods, we will never become a great nation. I guess the obliteration of the Canaanites is the price to be paid for our promised greatness."

"That's disgusting!" Sarah spat on the floor. "Didn't we learn anything in the wilderness? The Holy One never stopped showing concern for us. If we're reduced to serving the god who gives the biggest prize, then we're no different than anyone else. We'll just keep killing each other in the name of our gods until none of us remain. Oh, Asher, I'm terribly afraid."

"Dear heart, as much as I agree with you, I find I can't give up hope just yet. There were so many times in the wilderness when it appeared we would all die of hunger and thirst. I'm sure you remember that many in our company prayed for death just to get it over with.

"But here we are. We didn't die and our trust in the Holy One was never misplaced. Perhaps now we have a new opportunity to trust that the Holy One still cares and will lead us to new life, though I can't imagine what could be different. I just know that the Holy One has brought us through before. I've come to believe that the divine presence continues to work in our midst."

"Husband, my soul is so thirsty for hope. Your wise words help to quench it." Sarah then embraced Asher and held him as if her life depended on it.

And they were not the only ones among the Israelites who faced such struggles.

Among those Eliezer planned to invite was this same Asher. Even though they hardly knew each other, he had a strong intuition about this man. Later that day Eliezer found an opportunity where he could talk to Asher alone.

Of course, Asher knew that Eliezer was Moses' son. Who didn't? Eliezer, for his part, was unsure why, beyond his trust in his intuition, he was approaching this relative stranger. Perhaps it was the occasional look in Asher's eye that Eliezer had recognized. Whatever he expected from Asher, he wasn't worried. Milcah's plan was a good one, designed to give people enough sacred space to choose for themselves.

"You are Asher, I believe?"

"I am, Honored One."

Eliezer chuckled. "Some may desire titles and honors, but I am not one of them. Anyway, I have a request to make of you. It involves your family as well."

"I'm intrigued."

"You may have heard the rumor that Moses will not be leading the people across the river."

"I have heard also that the Holy One is expected to take his life. I guess that means he will die. If it's true, I am sad to hear it." Asher's sadness reflected in his face.

Eliezer chose not to confirm Asher's version. "There will be a group who will remain with Moses while he takes leave of his long life as our prophet and leader. I am asking you to join that group. It will take some time to affect the necessary rituals, so the body of the Israelites will enter the Promised Land without you. Once the rituals of tending to Moses have been completed, then we can resume our journey."

When he had finished speaking, Eliezer watched Asher closely. The other man opened his mouth to speak, closed it again, and then stood looking at Eliezer with a strange look on his face. Eliezer simply waited.

"Let me see if I heard you correctly. You want my family and me to remain here with a few other people to attend Moses' death and then to perform the mourning rituals. While we are there, Joshua will be leading the rest of the Israelites across the river. When the rituals are completed, then we can rejoin them."

"That is substantially what I am asking of you."

"May I be permitted to ask one or two questions before giving my answer? This is no small thing you ask."

"Of course. I'll answer them as well as I can."

Asher took a moment to formulate his question. "How long do you plan to keep us here? And how many do you expect will stay there with you and Moses?"

"We need about a hundred families to remain here for a month, perhaps two. I've come to believe that the Holy One desires this homage to the Prophet. Divine involvement always makes it very difficult to be precise about the timing, though. I'm confident that the Holy One will lead us."

Asher appeared to be having trouble breathing. And it may have been that a tear snuck down Asher's cheek as if seeking a hiding place in his beard.

Asher bowed ever so slightly and then straightened up. Then he replied with a tone of gravity that matched Eliezer's own. "I have followed the Holy One and Moses, the chosen Prophet, all my life. I will follow them until they are no more. Thank you for providing this opportunity for my family and me. I feel certain that the Promised Land will still be there whenever we get to it."

At that moment, both men were suffused with the sense of divine vibration that was as potent as lightning. Eliezer came to himself first, and said, "When the Israelites break camp to move, prepare likewise. You'll then be directed to the place where you and the other families will assemble."

Asher nodded, turned to go, but then stopped and walked back to Eliezer. "I know you'll be busy with your preparations, but I want you to know that I admire you. Clearly, the Holy One attends you. When we have time, I'd welcome the opportunity to get to know you better."

Before he realized it, Eliezer blurted out, "I know we will have ample time to discover and then develop a friendship."

Asher smiled broadly in response. "Yes, we will find enough time, won't we." Then he turned again and headed for his tent, his heart full of hope and wonder. He knew that Sarah would be as amazed and pleased as he was at this remarkable turn of events.

Chapter 14

About a mile outside of the Israelites' camp, Jethro had located the perfect spot where Moses would step down from his position as leader and prophet and from which he would go up into the mountain to offer his life to the Holy One. This natural basin nestled in between two desert hills. At the point where the two hills overlapped, a trail-like defile wound up onto the hill known as Mount Nebo. Only a few people abreast could ascend using that path.

Jethro recommended that the thousands of Israelites be arranged along the slopes that surrounded the basin. Above the sitting area, the slope became so precipitous that the only way up the mountain was by way of the defile. Moses, surrounded by the one hundred chosen families, would stand on the floor of the basin where all could see and hear him as he addressed his people one last time. He would then ascend the hill, passing through the crowd followed by his mourners.

Moses would then lead the procession up Mount Nebo by way of the defile. Finally, the remaining Israelites would be dismissed to resume their preparations for crossing the river, while the one hundred families remained on Mount Nebo to mourn and honor Moses' life.

Those who were grouped around Moses were relieved to see that the dawn sky was washed with a thin overcast. The cloud cover was not enough to block the sun entirely, but its filtering action would likely keep the rising temperature at a moderate level.

The people had been gathering and finding places to sit since shortly after dawn. A few found sheltered places next to protruding rocks or overhanging cliffs. The one hundred families had camped next to the basin all night so they were already in place, prepared to protect the path Moses would traverse to the opening of the defile. Some of those who came early figured out where Moses would be likely to pass, so they sat as near to the path as they could. They wanted to get a good last look at him.

Moses waited nearby until everyone was seated. All but a few of the one hundred families (the rest remained to protect the path) came to stand behind Moses when they saw him emerge into the basin. Jethro and Eliezer helped him climb up on the large flat rock from which he would address the people. Gershom, Joshua, and a few senior priests stood in front of Moses' rock facing the multitude. A hush settled over the crowd as everyone's attention turned toward their revered and aged Prophet.

First, Moses looked over the crowd, then bowed his head for a moment. When he spoke, his voice boomed across the crowd with a strength that belied his advanced age. "My beloved children, I have danced as each of you were born during our journeys in the wilderness. I have grieved and mourned as each of your parents and grandparents came to the end of their days in that same place. None of you here, today, has ever felt the lash of the slave master or been forced to shoulder the burden of building palaces or tombs for the use of others like your parents did. None of you has ever been refused your life-portion of sustenance.

"When your forebears followed me out of Egypt, they knew of the Holy One (for the legendary God of Abraham, Isaac, and of Jacob had lived on in their stories). As a consequence of generations of slavery in civilized Egypt, the "god of the story" eventually replaced "the god of the heart." They lost intimate touch with their Creator and they lost intimate touch with their own holy selves as well as with their identity as a people. They forgot, or perhaps misplaced their knowledge of who they were.

"Still, they groaned out the pain of their enslavement to the god of their revered ancestors. The Holy One cared to hear their groans and called to my heart to care, too. I have spent many years trying to convince you how much you matter to the

Holy One and to me as well. Perhaps some of you have received that love and have found it to be as precious as I have.

"With my love for your parents awakened and burning in my heart, I came to them, commissioned by the Holy One, not only to lead them out of bondage, but even more to restore their identity as a people. For them and for you, I have been the matchmaker, introducing you to your most holy selves and introducing you to the most Holy One. In the wilderness, you rediscovered your identity and became a people. In the wilderness, you met your God face-to-face. You learned to relate to the Holy One directly, not just through your stories.

"Naturally, those who had known nothing other than the imposed security of bondage needed to learn the deeper security of freedom. When the Holy One led them to food to assuage their hunger and to water to quench their thirst, they had their first experiences of a god who took the initiative to care for them. But, even though they had been delivered from bondage, their bondage still lived within them. They did not dare be free!

"Though I resisted the implications, the Holy One convinced me they could not succeed in the Promised Land without divine freedom in the soul. It could only be in human freedom that the people could perceive the freedom intrinsic in the Holy One. Only in freedom can you appreciate deeply enough the essential difference between the Holy One and all other concepts of god. Without your freedom, you will insist on relating to the Holy One as just another divine slave master. The slave master says 'Work for me and I will sustain you so you can continue to work for me'. The Holy One says, 'It is my nature to love and sustain you. If you receive my gifts your life will overflow with blessings. But if you twist my freely-given gifts, attempting to manipulate them according to your own short-sighted and selfish ends, you will turn my Holy Image into just another god of wood and stone. My gifts will turn to poison, and your attempts at worship and obedience will destroy you.'

"Whenever you worship the Holy One, worship in love. And then hold to the promise that day by day and moment by moment, you will be granted an overwhelming abundance of opportunity to express your love for the Holy One through the ways you treat each other. I entreat you to remember when you come into the Promised Land always to carry the Holy One, the One you met in the wilderness, in your hearts and minds, just as the Holy One carries you always in infinite love.

"At present, the priests of Jehovah guide you with laws and obligations. They exist to support you as you grow into fullness of communion. But as much as you rely on them for structure and support, never forget that you have been made in the image of the Holy One of Love who created you in love."

Moses closed his eyes and appeared to slump. Eliezer and Jethro jumped up on the rock to steady him as murmurs ran through the multitude. When Moses opened his eyes again, even the smallest child who sat the farthest away could see and feel Holy Light radiating in his gaze. In that moment, all knew the Holy Presence.

After Eliezer and Jethro came back down from the rock, Moses continued. "I am certain that by now you have all heard rumors about me. Here is the truth: I am now a hundred and twenty years old, and I can no longer move about as I please. Moses paused. "And the Holy One has now informed me that I will not cross the Jordan."

The multitude sat in stunned silence as legions of tears streaked dusty cheeks.

"At the dawn of this day, I took Joshua into the Holy Presence to receive the commission that I freely laid down, for I honor the leading of the Holy One.

"Just as your parents could not cross the Jordan, because they carried too much bondage in their hearts[8], so I, too, being of their generation, am not fit to lead you on the next part of your journey. I confess that I have already lost faith with you too many times.

"So, as the Holy One directs, I will ascend this mountain, watch you depart across the river, and then go to join those whose flesh does not separate them from Holy Presence.

"I leave you these holy words, this rule of life, the same words that the Holy One used to bestow the commission on Joshua: 'Be strong, be resolute; for you shall bring the Israelites into the land which I swore to give them, and I will be with you always.'"

Moses raised his arms and stretched them out over his beloved people. With tears in his eyes and emotion in his voice, he intoned, "May I AM – I CREATE – I LOVE bless your community now and for all time."[9]

After Moses finished blessing the people, Eliezer and Jethro climbed once again to his side and helped him descend. He went to Joshua, embraced him, and then handed him the staff that he had carried for generations. Moses then placed his hands on Gershom's shoulders, pulled him close and appeared to whisper something in his son's ear. Gershom held his father's embrace while he surreptitiously wiped his moist eyes on Moses' shoulder.

Gershom and Joshua stepped aside as the procession toward Mount Nebo began. Moses leaned on Eliezer's arm for support, his prophet's staff now clutched in Joshua's hand. Father and son lead, followed by Milcah and the one hundred families. The multitudes stood and began edging toward the path that Moses trod. He walked upright, his eyes focused on some distant place on the mountain. Sobs and exclamations of "Father Moses," "Bless you Moses," and "Don't leave us, Moses" washed over him. If he even heard them, he gave no noticeable indication. He just kept walking up the path and then into the defile.

As expected, after the one hundred families had passed through the crowd, many in the multitude decided not to follow Gershom and Joshua back toward the Israelite camp, but turned to join the procession into the defile instead.

After Moses had led this procession for about two hours, the trail narrowed, doubling back on itself several times. Suddenly, a commotion broke out near the front of the line. It was accompanied by chaotic shouting. Those below surged forward to discern the cause, only to hear the confusing words, "He's gone!"

Little by little the story filtered its way back down the mountain. It went something like this: Jethro had relieved Eliezer as Moses' walking support. At the last switchback, the trail was partially blocked by a large boulder so only one person could pass at a time. Moses went first. As Jethro came around the boulder, he was nearly blinded by a white light. He recoiled backwards, stepped on Eliezer's foot, and the two men went down in a heap. When they disentangled themselves and came around the boulder, they were just in time to see Moses being taken by angels directly into the Presence of the Holy One. And by the time Milcah and the others arrived, he had completely disappeared. Jethro claimed he heard something like a voice emanating from the light. The voice said: "Moses shall not pass through death. My friend is with me now."[10]

How rumors can fly faster than a person can run is a mystery of the ages. In practically no time, the story had reached Joshua and Gershom, who then began to fight their way through the dense crowd of curious Israelites. Not only did they question Jethro and Eliezer, but they organized a thorough search of the area before they would be willing to conclude that Moses had in fact gone into the presence of the Holy One. Gershom hoped to confirm (or debunk) Moses' death as soon as possible by means of his cadre of priests and Joshua's soldiers. Then he would accelerate the preparations for the river crossing. He didn't want to give the people too much time to think about what had happened before focusing their attention on the demands of occupying their new land. He had readily agreed that the one hundred families should stay for their required month of mourning for Moses. They could catch up later.

Eliezer looked around at these loyal families whose grief and confusion were palpable. He was well aware that he and his small group of organizers had much to do, and not much time to do it. Before thirty days had passed, they would be long departed. Eliezer quieted his breathing and reminded himself to rely on the presence of the Holy One. An arm around his waist and Milcah's familiar smell completed his holy moment of peace.

"It's a new day," Milcah whispered. "I can't wait to see where the Holy One will lead us next." They stood quietly with their arms wrapped around each other, surrounded by the chaos and struggle of new birth. They looked across the clearing and saw that Asher and Sarah were also embracing. The simple nod and smile that was shared between the two couples said all that was necessary.

Chapter 15

The first day after Moses' "ascension" found the one hundred families moving about in silent astonishment while they relocated their temporary camp nearer to the top of Mount Nebo. Late in the afternoon, all of them climbed up through the defile to gather at the top of the mountain to begin their ritual of mourning.

Eliezer addressed them. "As I look around at your faces, I can see that each of you in your own way knows the Holy One. To the extent that you have opened yourselves up to the divine presence, you have perceived the activity of the Holy One in our collective midst. Just as in the wilderness, the discovery of what you require to survive often happens in surprising ways and places. If you had not come to trust the presence and workings of the Holy One, you would not have agreed to remain here while the main body of your Israelite kin crosses the river. Many of those who were given opportunity to be here chose, instead, to follow Joshua.

"You who are gathered here have perhaps guessed that there was some risk and that there might be more to these events than meets the eye. You are correct. For your own reasons, you chose to participate. Now, those of us who worked out this bold plan with Moses have determined to take another risk by revealing it to you. When you have heard it, some of you may disagree with it or not want to be associated with it. All we ask is that you remain here and not reveal the plan to Joshua or Gershom until the prescribed thirty days have passed. We have determined, in keeping with the principles of our plan, not to require your adherence, but to request it humbly in the name of the Holy One."

When the crowd heard these words, a murmur arose through which a range of questions and emotions tumbled. There was some confusion as the crowd strove to grasp the import and meaning of Eliezer's words. Most of the questions in their minds, though, were tinged with hope. Apparently more of these people than just Asher and Sarah had dared to hope for some divine "other way" to be revealed to them. Perhaps this was it, many of them thought.

Eliezer waited for the gathering to settle down again. "Moses revealed to me and then to these few others around me his discomfort at the Israelite plan to occupy the land beyond the Jordan. He feared that the challenges of occupation and nation-building would likely overshadow, if not negate, the values we have learned through our long sojourn in the wilderness. This is the real reason Moses and the Holy One determined that he would not cross the river. I am grateful for the Holy One's compassion for my father in that decision." Eliezer wiped at his eyes with his sleeve and many in the crowd seemed to mirror his emotion.

"Because for many years I, too, have been granted an alternate vision of a life in covenant with the Holy One, I told Moses and then told my wife, Milcah, that I, like Moses, had chosen not to accompany Joshua to the Promised Land across the river. We few, Milcah and I, Tirzah and Noah and their families, and these others standing with me here have decided to return in the direction of the wilderness. We hope to find a place where we can live in harmony with one another and with the Holy One. In whatever community we create, we intend not to forget the lessons of the wilderness."

Eliezer paused. These words represented such a radical departure from the generally accepted goal of the Israelite wanderings that he waited for the people to absorb them. Some of the people already knew what he would say next, while others remained shrouded in confusion.

Slowly, their attention drew back to him. "Any of you who choose to accompany us and help us establish this community are welcome. We hope all of you will say, 'yes', to this invitation. We will wait to leave this mountain until the attention of the main body of Israelites is fully occupied in crossing the river into Canaan. Then we will begin our own search for the land of promise by going in the opposite direction. We will depart as soon as it is safe."

Again Eliezer waited as the people took in this astounding idea. "Now, what else do you need to hear in order to make your decisions?"

A man rose to speak. "Where do you expect to go?"

Eliezer nodded to Jethro who then stood before the gathering to answer. "We'll begin our search to the East. Because it appears that many of you have had a good deal of practice opening yourselves to the leadings of the Holy One, as a community we will cooperate in seeking divine guidance as we go. We will travel until we find a suitable place."

Then a woman's voice rang out. "Where did Moses go?"

Eliezer answered. "Other than what you have already heard Moses say, he did not tell us where he was going."

Eliezer hoped that would suffice for now, but she pressed him. "Will we see him again?"

Eliezer really didn't know how to answer her so he invoked her faith and patience, "I wish I could give you a more satisfactory answer, but the truth is, we will all hope to learn more about the activities of the Holy One and Moses as time goes on. I ask you to accept that much of an answer for now."

The woman scrutinized Eliezer for a moment, then shrugged and sat down. After a time with no more questions, they appeared to be satisfied, but then not quite.

A small, wiry man stood to address Eliezer. "Your stated goal: to live in harmony with one another and with the Holy One, doesn't sound so different from what our Israelite tribe has always hoped for. Isn't that exactly what is supposed to happen in the land of Canaan across the Jordan? Tell us what makes your vision so different, so that we might be persuaded to take the considerable risk of going with you."

Eliezer looked around at Milcah, her sisters, Jethro, and the others in their small group. He wasn't sure exactly what he wanted from them, but their nods of encouragement seemed to be enough. After taking a moment to ponder the depth and breadth of the question, he opened his heart and vision to the assembly. "Much of what I am about to say, you may already have heard (or even thought, yourselves) before. The Israelites have always placed the highest value on how Moses, inspired and sent by the Holy One, rescued them from bondage in Egypt. Even while complaining about the challenges and rigors of the wilderness, they, and you, never gave any serious thought to going back to Egypt. As you know, Moses has led this people since before all of you were even born. You also know that Moses, from time to time, has been known to come into the presence of the Holy One. After each time he would then share the Divine Perspective with the rest of us.

"What you may not know, or perhaps only have come to suspect, is that Moses regularly consulted with my brother, Gershom, about how to put into words those experiences of the divine that, truth be told, were always beyond words. Gershom firmly believes that the more concrete and precise the record of these experiences can be, the more likely will be our faithful obedience to Jehovah (as he names the Holy One). So, Gershom has taken the revelations the Holy One gave to Moses and has put them into the form of laws, directives, and divine expectations. And he has instructed the priests to teach and enforce them. Many people who think like Gershom take comfort from holding a clear understanding of what Jehovah expects of them.

"I can't say that Gershom is wrong. I only know that his vision of obedience to Jehovah and the nature of the Promised Land don't fit with the vision that I hold."

More murmurings scurried through the assembly, so Eliezer opened his arms to his new community. "Yes, you heard correctly. As I indicated earlier, I have also come into the presence of the Holy One many times over the span of my life. I am guessing that many of you have had similar experiences, but I believed, as perhaps you believed, that only Moses was the chosen Prophet of the Holy One, so I kept my own counsel.

"Just recently I finally risked sharing my dreams with Moses. His attitude of affirmation and acceptance granted me a deeper look at the revelation he had received. I began to understand what he had been trying to teach us for all these years. Moses' greatest gift to the Israelites has been the least understood. He has tried to introduce us to the Holy One. And more than that, Moses has been trying to show us that we, each and all, could have direct and intimate communion with the Holy One. He tried to teach us that the Holy One, who considers Moses to be a friend, apparently wants us to know that we matter, and, I have come to believe, to accept the sacred covenant of embodying that spirit of "divine mattering" into every aspect of our community.

"Where Gershom sees a demanding, dangerous, and fear-inspiring god, we perceive a god whose very name, and by that I mean whose very identity, is the eternal embodiment of love in community.

"What our unique community will look like and where it will finally take root is yet to be discovered. We will journey from this place to find a suitable land, one that is not already inhabited, where we can establish our new home and where our community can flourish.

"We hope - no, we believe - that each of you has received and now holds a compatible vision in your heart. Together we have a sacred opportunity bring those visions to their fullest realization. Together we will experience the active presence of the Holy One in our midst."

The people sat looking around at one another, too stunned to speak or move. Then one by one at first, and then in larger numbers they rose, approached and embraced Eliezer, the small group, and then one another. Not one remained seated or chose to leave the company.

Eliezer

If I am to record this account with accuracy and integrity I need to make use of voices and perspectives other than my own. Although we created a community according to the emerging divine image of a Promised Land where every participant was of equal value, there were some individuals whose contributions turned out to be particularly essential to its eventual success. When I recruited Asher to join our new community, I had never met his wife, Sarah, so I could not have anticipated what an invaluable presence she would be among us.

I could simply relate her story to the degree that I know it, but I have decided to invite her to tell it in her own words. Her life stands as a personal testament to my father's mission of acquainting the people with the loving reality of the Holy One.

There are others who played significant roles in the development of the community. Her story includes several of theirs.

Sarah

That particular dawning could have been the beginning of just another day. The same early morning coolness already hinted at the stifling heat of mid-day that would soon envelop the camp. The same sun trumpeted its brilliant newness when it peeked over the horizon. And beginning at the base of the mountain, the same unrelenting landscape of rock, sand, and hills spoke of the home that all of us had known for our whole lives.

The familiarity ended abruptly right there, for truly nothing at all was the same. Though we still moved in the direction of the "Promised Land," our goal was no longer a particular place. Our Promised Land had become an unknown manifestation of the spirit and identity of the Holy One in the community. In a sense, we were already in the Promised Land. It would move and grow with us, but it was no longer primarily a destination to be reached. Rather, it had become an eternal direction: the Holy One, forever coming to fullness within each individual, relationship and in the community as a whole. Of course, it would take us a lifetime to understand this. While on the journey it was difficult for some of us to embrace the fundamental changes that always accompanied the intimate activity of the Holy One. But it wasn't difficult for me. Without knowing it, I had spent my whole life preparing for this day.

I had been pretty upset about the thought of the Promised Land for quite a while. I had not been able to shed the obscene image of all the people who were going to have to be eliminated so that my family and I could take our "rightful place" in the Promised Land. I had often wondered why the gods seemed always to pit groups of people against each other in life and death struggles for presumably holy land. But of course, before now there had never been place, nor opportunity, nor permission even to ask such a question. In this moment of awakening on Mount Nebo, I was just beginning to believe that the Holy One might have a different, and hopefully less bloody, agenda for us.

My horror at the impending destruction in Canaan had been irrationally offset by the consuming fear that my family would not be able to obtain its fair allotment of Promised Land. The internal contradiction had been killing me.

How crazy, I had thought. Not only were Canaanites about to be destroyed, but distrust and enmity had already started springing up, even among the Israelite tribes, over which of them Jehovah would favor with the best land.

I remembered that in the wilderness the idea of personal ownership of most forms of property was not only unnecessary, it was perfectly dangerous. Our survival had required communication, cooperation, and a shared concern for the well-being of the entire company. Yes, I knew how dangerous the wilderness could be, but at least its dangers were the kinds people could learn from. Surrounded by reliable neighbors, a person could still sleep at night. And the neighbors in turn could sleep well, comforted in the knowledge that they could rely on you, too. But without mutual trust among neighbors, what peace could there possibly be? In the very short time that we had been on Mount Nebo, I could already feel renewed trust beginning to grow.

Then I started to get anxious again. I found myself wondering if competition for land and other property would inevitably emerge to plague us when we finally got to our ultimate destination. I laughed when I caught myself at it. We had a new covenant and it was helping us feel more like a community already. In this new community, no question would be seen as disloyal and no concern would ever have to remain hidden. I decided that I would do anything in my power to encourage all of us to promote trust in this beloved community.

I couldn't help but marvel at the strange turn my life had taken. Such a short time had passed since we had decided to return to the wilderness. Until just a couple of days before I had been filled with dread all the time, although even then I hadn't lost hope entirely. Awareness of the Holy One had burned hot in me since I was a child. But my optimism had been wearing thin as we approached the Jordan. Persuaded by all the evidence around me, I had reluctantly begun to accept my inevitable demotion from valuable community member to little more than a piece of property belonging to a man. It was not that Asher would wish that upon me, or would ever see me like that.

Fortunately, I enjoy in Asher a kindred mind, maybe even a kindred heart. But I knew that once we became established in the Promised Land across the river, he wouldn't really have any choice abut how to treat me. Even now, I shudder to think of it.

On Mount Nebo I reminded myself that a new journey lay ahead for us. As I think of it now, perhaps my origins helped me find my place in the community.

Chapter 16

Throughout her short life, Sarah had always felt fortunate, even when her experience of life didn't jibe with what the adults said about it. She and Asher had both been born and raised in the wilderness where they had ample opportunity to experience the mostly subtle, but sometimes startling, workings of the Holy One. Along with the Israelite people, they learned about the Holy One in two very different ways: through their first-hand experience and by means of the official teachings.

Sarah was a very grown-up ten-year-old. It was evening and she was sitting with her parents and several other families around the fire. They had eaten well this night and she was happily satisfied. Even at ten years old, she knew that sometimes there was not enough for every meal, but tonight no one was starving. That was good.

A young priest had joined their gathering. When he had eaten his fill, he stood to retell the ancient stories and to instruct the people in the requirements of the religious life. Sarah loved hearing the stories so she listened very carefully and tried to imagine herself in them.

"...and they lived in a beautiful garden that Jehovah had created along with the rest of 'The Everything'. They always had enough to eat and drink and they didn't have to travel long distances, or eat the dust of the wilderness.

"But then, they disobeyed Jehovah and He made them leave the garden. And people ever since have had to work hard and travel long distances. They get hungry and thirsty, and eventually they die, all because Adam and Eve did not obey."

Sarah frowned and looked around to see if her closest friend, Asher, was frowning, too. When she caught his eye, she saw that he was gnawing on the same questions that roiled in her. They would talk later.

Some of the stories didn't bother her so much. She loved feeling the connection to the ancestors, like Abraham and his wife, Sarah, her own namesake. She was fascinated, if confused when the priests had told of the treachery between Jacob and his brother Esau that led to Jacob running off, only to come back with the children whose names now designated the twelve tribes. Of course, she yearned to hear more about Rachel and Leah and the other women who must have played an essential role in these ancient events. Sadly, the priests didn't seem to know much about the women, and Sarah quickly figured out that it was dangerous for her to press them too much. Clearly, the men were the starring characters in these priestly versions of the stories.

She tried to bring her questions to her parents, but that didn't work either. They would answer some of the simpler ones, but they couldn't, or wouldn't, address those that she held to be more important. They would send her on her way, but not until she promised not to ask anyone else. And that just left Asher. Yes, they would talk later.

Even with her myriad of questions, she was intrigued by the more mystical episodes that managed to leak into the stories. She wondered about the dreams of famine and plenty that seemed to make it unavoidable for the Israelites to end up in Egypt. Were her own dreams that important? And she was totally fascinated by the image of Jacob wrestling with God, coming away with a permanent wound, but still demanding to receive a blessing before he would release his hold on the Holy One. She suspected that some of the women in those ancient times must have had similar experiences but somehow, those stories did not find their way into the official lore that the priests insisted upon transmitting.

In her brief ten years, she had experienced enough first-hand encounters with the mystical realm to be convinced that many people, men and women alike, were always in some form of communication with the Holy One. Maybe when I get older, she thought, events in my life might become the stories the priests will tell to future generations.

Asher made a face at her across the circle. They both knew what was coming next. This was the most boring part. The priest droned on about their religious duties and their social obligations, because someday they would get to the Promised Land and would become a great nation.

She had heard this all before, and to say that she had mixed feelings about these teachings was an understatement. Some of them were OK, she thought. She loved the practice of setting aside the seventh day to be a Sabbath or Holy Day. Most of the time on the Sabbath, they didn't have to travel and they spent the day playing, singing, and telling stories. If she had her way, though, the line between the sacred and the worldly would be much more blurry than the priests drew it. To ten-year-old Sarah, every day was holy, no matter what activities required her attention. Even simple breathing felt like dancing with the Holy One. When Moses and the priests had erected altars of stone to designate specific places where God met humans, privately she had affirmed her personal experience of the Holy One's continual presence with her.

She and Asher talked most about what she called 'The Stuff Laws.' She had never seen the need to designate certain things as hers and other things as belonging to other people. The community simply had certain material needs. In the wilderness the more those resources were shared the better became their chances for survival. Perhaps it was the simplistic thinking of youth, but she thought that a Promised Land filled with such abundance should make 'the Stuff Laws' unnecessary; except that whenever the adults would talk about the Promised Land, they usually ended up arguing about who was going to own which part of it.

"Do you get that part about owning stuff in the Promised Land?' she asked Asher later.

"Maybe they don't really believe it when the priest says how wonderful it will be."

She shrugged, but then gave Asher a hug. She knew that if she could count on nothing else, she and Asher would always talk like this.

Another time, she said, "You know the Ten Laws that the priest is always talking about, Asher?"

"Yeah, what about 'em?"

"Well, I think that if adults were less concerned about stuff, maybe they'd only need about six."

For some reason, they found the idea delightfully funny. They laughed until they couldn't stand up.

From time to time over the years, they would ponder the question more seriously.

"Who needs to worry about Stealing and Coveting when the well-being of the whole community is at risk?" she would say. Asher would nod gravely while his growing love for Sarah filled him to overflowing.

While the priests taught that Moses was the primary conduit for the voice of the Holy One (using "Jehovah" as the god's name had never really worked for her), Sarah already understood that the accumulated experience of the whole people in the wilderness demonstrated divine reality, too. She had already encountered the Holy One first-hand many times before. She also knew that the Holy One had touched the Israelites in countless startling ways before she was even born.

While Sarah's mother never answered her thornier questions directly, she did pass on her wisdom through stories from her own experience. Sarah never tired of hearing her mother tell about the time Moses went up into the mountain to get the law from the Holy One.[11] Even in her young adulthood, she regularly prevailed upon her mother to tell it again and again. Something about that particular event was more important and stunning than any of the other stories of their exodus from Egypt or of their first weeks and months in the wilderness. Many Israelites found parts of the story to be embarrassing and disturbing, but from the very first time she heard it, Sarah saw the beauty and compassion in it.

Sarah loved the sound of her mother's voice and when she was still small enough, she loved to curl up in her lap to listen.

"Moses had been gone up into the mountain for so long," her mother would always begin, "that we fell into a most deadly terror. Here we were in a strange and inhospitable land, forever certain that we were about to perish. Somehow Moses always found the means to comfort us just enough so that we could continue the journey afresh each day. In Egypt, we had prayed to the God of our ancestors to free us from our slavery, but most of us (Moses' sister Miriam was a notable exception) had no direct knowledge of this strange and nameless god who seemed always to be surrounded by fire and smoke. Moses said that the god had told him to rescue us from Pharaoh in Egypt, but we still didn't understand how we could keep from being destroyed ourselves by the Holy One's enormous power. It was clear to us, though, that Moses stood between us and certain death.

"When we came to the holy mountain, we were all terrified by the noise and smoke and mystery of the place. We didn't know if maybe this god had rescued us for 'his' own purposes and was now going to destroy us. I know it sounds silly when I say it, but we didn't know, couldn't know, who this god was and what divine consequence might be in store for us. For sure, we were plenty suspicious seeing that our supposed rescuer had lead us to such a dangerous and dreary place.

"As if we weren't scared enough already, Moses warned us that we would perish if we got too close to the god of the mountain. He didn't have to try very hard to convince us, but imagine how confusing it was when he then told us he was going up into the holy mountain alone. Was he crazy? No one could face all that danger alone. Maybe Moses would be the first one sacrificed to repay this god for our rescue. I know it doesn't make sense now, but in the middle of the experience it seemed possible, if not likely, to us that we would probably be next.

"Now as I think back, even though I know how things worked out, I am still proud of how we responded. We could have simply cut and run in an attempt to get back to Egypt where life, difficult as it had been there, was at least somewhat predictable. But we didn't do that. We stayed to help instead.

"Though we were afraid that Moses had already been consumed by the fire of the Holy One, on the outside chance that he was still alive, we came up with a plan that might help him, and ourselves, too. We made use of the best we had available. We attempted to invoke the assistance of Hathor, the most benign and responsive of the gods we knew from Egypt. The only things we carried with us that had any value were our precious pieces of gold and jewelry that we had taken from the Egyptians. We chose to sacrifice it all; and let me tell you, this was no small sacrifice for a bunch of slaves who had never before possessed such riches. Our plan was to create a manifestation in gold of lovely, cow-eyed Hathor. This was a god we could see, touch, and understand, a god who didn't scare us nearly to death with smoke and thunder, a god whose sole purpose seemed to be responding to basic human requests for assistance.

"So, we melted all the gold in a great pot, and fashioned a calf. We had learned in Egypt that Hathor preferred to be seen in that form. We danced, we prayed, we wept, and most of all, we begged Hathor to protect our beloved Moses from the dangers of this strange wilderness god. After so many days of praying and dancing we were thoroughly exhausted and were beginning to lose heart. Then we saw him! Our prayers had been answered; Hathor had heard us and had rescued Moses. Praise Hathor! We began again to dance and celebrate with renewed energy. Our dances and songs were hymns of thanksgiving for Moses' rescue.

"Well, when the great prophet came close enough for us to see his face, the dancing and praying quickly stopped. Moses was furious. He yelled and screamed. He called us the vilest of names. He even threw the stone tablets at us. Suddenly, some of the sons of Levi, having snuck away to put on their swords, plunged into the crowd and began killing men, shouting that those now dead and dying men had been unfaithful to "Jehovah." I can tell you as one who was there that those sons of Levi were just as involved with the creation of the altar to Hathor as any other child of Israel, but Moses was so furious that he never thought to question their accusations or their violence. I guess he just assumed that they were motivated by their superior righteousness. I never once trusted those sons of Levi after that day, and I tell you I was horrified when Moses elevated them over us and made them into a tribe of priests."

At this point in the story, her eyes would always fill with tears as she said, "I will never forgive them for killing your father, to say nothing of the other three thousand good men who were slaughtered that day. We now know that Moses just wanted us to give our trust to this god of the mountain, but to be honest, I could never do anything else but tremble in fear before Jehovah."

Sarah could see why her mother hadn't been able to separate her abhorrence of those events from the presence of the Holy One. Until the day she died, she was never able to trust in this powerful, but (according to her experience) petty and dangerous god.

Eventually, Sarah saw and found it to be tragic, that Moses was unable to comprehend why that first generation of freed Israelites carried such a deep mistrust of the Holy One until the day of death.

Sarah, on the other hand, came to know the Holy One in a completely different way. She hoped that some day she would be able to tell her stories among her family and friends without fearing that any personal mystical experiences would be taken as threatening to the priests. It was sad. She and Asher figured out that anyone who had known the Holy One directly had no choice but to remain isolated and alone with their memories.

After they retired to their tent on the day Moses was taken up, Asher wanted to hear her tell one of the stories from her life. He never tired of hearing Sarah's first-hand accounts. She was such a good storyteller. Maybe someday she would become a priest who tells the stories of the tribe. She'd be a lot better than that boring priest we grew up with, Asher thought.

"Sarah, tell me again about how you came to know the Holy One. I love hearing you tell it." Sarah settled herself into a comfortable corner of their tent, a far away look came into her eyes and she began. Asher closed his eyes, ready to create vivid pictures of the story in his mind from Sarah's richly descriptive language.

After a long pause while Sarah internally reviewed her own remembered images, she said quietly, "I had learned at an early age that the wilderness was always dangerous and I knew along with everyone else that it didn't take much for our surroundings to turn deadly. We ate well whenever we camped at an oasis, but the distance between one and the next could be vast. We always hoped for uneventful journeys whenever we traveled through the most inhospitable areas because we could so easily be cut off from our sources of food.

To be sure, we always brought as much food as we could carry, but there was still a limit to it."

After a predictable pause and a deep sigh, she continued with her story.

"I remember a time when we were traveling between two oases across a long stretch of uninhabitable rock and sand. I had already made journeys like this several times before, so I was prepared for it to be difficult and I knew that by the end of it, I'd be pretty hungry.

"My ears would perk up whenever the adults around me would talk about the journey. I felt as involved and responsible as anyone else, so I wanted to know how things were going. From what I could tell we were making acceptable progress. Then, one day, a commotion arose at the center of our temporary encampment near Moses' tent. I ran there with the others and saw that the advanced scouts had returned to us to report the sighting of an enemy army directly in our path. We were too far along the route to go back to where we had started. Besides, the reason we left there was that we had depleted the food supply.

"It was clear that we were in trouble. We didn't have a large enough fighting force to engage this army and there were no other oases we knew of that we could get to before our food supplies ran out.

"After he had consulted with Joshua and the other military commanders, Moses announced to us that we had to change our direction in order to skirt around the danger. He called the people together and warned us that as a consequence of the detour the journey would take considerably longer. We were instructed to begin emergency rationing of food and water immediately. He also told us that we were to prepare to depart as soon as possible and that we would have to travel more and rest less each day.

"I don't know if I was more scared or excited. I do know that I felt very grown up. I was just as responsible for our survival as anyone else. I would do my part, walking more and eating less. At least for those next few days, I saw and heard very little bickering. We were afraid, but our fear translated into greater awareness of one another and of the larger company's needs. I felt myself to be part of a large integrated organism that required the healthy functioning of each of its parts if it were to escape annihilation.

"We managed to skirt around the enemy army without being detected but the detour through the worst part of the wilderness added about a week to our journey. As food ran out and water became scarce, a kind of numb determination settled on us. And then the food was gone. For three more days we walked (our beasts of burden could not carry our weight). I became aware of a light that seemed to be shining behind the dullness of the hungry eyes around me. At first I thought it was simply the glaring reflection of the murderous sun off the bleached sand, but the longer we walked, the more intensely it shone. As I remember it with my adult mind, I think that the prolonged hunger and thirst was incinerating personal self-interest and peeling away layers of fear-generated short-sightedness, thus exposing a deeper reality, a transcendent connectedness. At times, the life-giving light seemed to detach itself from the individuals, appearing to manifest between us and around us. Hour after hour passed as we felt ourselves carried by an unseen force across the emptiness.

"Not only did I see these 'light-forms' around others, but I knew that I, too, was being led or carried by a reality that was at the same time separate from me and residing deep within me. In those days I came to know a depth of power and compassion that I soon learned to recognize as my direct awareness of the Holy One.

"When Moses finally allowed the company to rest, I fell into a deep sleep. When I awoke, I was disoriented. The position of the sun in the sky told me it was mid-day, but the shredding heat and blinding light had been replaced by a soft, almost caressing glow, and the usually arid air was infused with a cooling mist. I was alone, but soon noticed others moving toward me. I didn't recognize their faces though they certainly were not strangers. I felt completely 'at home' in their presence. Though I could hear their conversation, it struck me as strange because when one spoke, the voice came from all of them. When I found myself surrounded, I heard my own voice coming out of me and at the same time addressing me. 'This is the heart of life. We are many; we are one. I am One in you and with you.'

"Asher, I don't think I can reproduce the rest of the words I heard, but I am convinced of the truth of what I came to know that day. It seemed as if the Holy One was speaking in my heart and if it were possible for me to put words to the meaning, they would be something like these:

> I am the God of Being and Loving. Nothing is more important than my connection to you and that connection necessarily unites you with one another and makes you One. I want you to learn about the risks of being human. I want you to learn that shortcuts will kill you, in body, in soul, in both. I want you to know that you will be tempted to create images of the Holy out of the personhood, power, or goods that you believe you possess. While you may be able to preserve your individual bodies that way, you will ultimately destroy the fullness of your being. Your friends will become enemies. Your surroundings, no matter how abundant they may appear, will threaten you. There will be voices among you that will even dare to elevate human words to replace the Living Presence. This is happening among you even now.

"Asher, I don't know if I thought it then, or if it has come to me little by little over the years, but I think the Holy One was warning us about 'graven images'. As you know well enough, we hear about the dangers of idolatry all the time. The priests never seem to get tired of holding up 'Golden Hathor' as the epitome of our evil tendencies. We're all right as long as we don't make 'pictures' of Jehovah or other gods to worship. But Asher, I think the words themselves are being used as graven images. The priests say that these are 'Jehovah's Words', but I don't think human thoughts are capable of wrapping all the way around the fullness those words contain. Besides, now we learn that the words were not even Moses' words. Gershom wrote them. Who knows if we will ever see Moses again, but if we do, I would love to hear his description of what he actually experienced on that mountain. But I am getting away from my story.

"Seeing and feeling the reality of 'the light' and experiencing my full participation in it taught me that the Holy One can never be known outside of us and our relationships. The problem with all images of gods (graven or otherwise) is that they're too easy to see as separate realities. To make matters worse, whatever forms, symbols, or language we use to describe divine reality inevitably contain elements of idolatry. While this is unavoidable, it only becomes problematic if we don't know it. We can use our forms, but we have to guard against allowing our forms to become replacements for the Underlying Reality.

"I learned—that is, we all learned—something else on that day years ago. I learned that anything we own or believe we are entitled to can become a 'graven image'. I am certain that I was able to 'see' the Holy One directly that day because all external 'stuff' had ceased to exist for us and, as a result of our hunger, thirst, and deep weariness, had ceased to matter.

"Whenever I've had deep experiences with the Holy One, my sense of the boundaries of reality have seemed fuzzy for a while. It was so much the case in this first divine encounter of mine that I have no memory of waking up from what must have been a dream. When I became aware of myself again, we were already on the move. Looking around me at my friends, my family, and my compatriots, I was filled with a deep love. I could no longer see the radiance around us, but I would never be able to deny the presence of the Holy One in our midst.

"Later that day, we finally reached the oasis and were able to eat and drink once more. While we gave thanks for our survival to the Holy One in that place, I could feel once again that 'Jehovah' was already separating from many of us. I sometimes wonder how a girl of only eleven years could understand so much, but I believe I am telling the truth. Apparently even age doesn't matter when we are in touch with the presence and movement of the Holy One. Whenever I look back, I realize that I would have liked to celebrate my experience in a public way. I might have discovered that others came through the journey with similar divine touches on their lives. But, somehow I already knew that it wasn't safe to talk about such things. With the Prophet of God at the head of the company, who would have believed me anyway? It was better to keep my own counsel. Asher, I am grateful to you for all the times you have listened to me. You help me stay rooted in my own experience."

Sarah then cocked her head to the side. "You know, Asher, I think I've figured out why I became so disheartened while we were approaching the Promised Land. I could feel Holy Awareness leaving me. I think I got caught up in the community's preoccupation with the concerns about land, property, and power - that combined with fantasies of our 'imminent' place of honor among the nations. I've believed for a long time that I could never bear the loss of the Holy One who walks with me in the wilderness. But, I'm afraid that in time I would have become just as suspicious and grasping as anyone else. It was happening to me already."

"Asher, will you promise to help me remember that the Holy One is always within and among us. It's too easy to forget. Now that we're back in the wilderness I feel better, even if we don't know where we're going."

Asher reached out to touch her arm.

"We have to find ways to keep the God of the Wilderness alive within us," she said, as much to herself as to Asher." We won't be able to survive if we lose touch with I AM in our midst."

Chapter 17

The last rocks clattered down over the mouth of the cave. Moses chest rose and fell rapidly from the exertion as he tried to keep the sound of his gasping to a minimum. He had just run the distance from the sharp turn in the path to the hidden mouth of this small space in the side of the hill. He felt the almost suffocating embrace of darkness settle around him. Even as his rasping chest began to relax, his heart continued to leap in anxiety and excitement.

The audacity of their plan amazed him. The still very present likelihood of discovery and failure dried his mouth and quickened his pulse. He found some comfort in the very careful planning they had done for his "death," so the chances of pulling off this deception remained at least measurable.

The rock upon rock noise came from the two men Eliezer had recruited to assist Moses in his part of the plan. They were not highly visible personages among the Israelites, but they were good men who had committed themselves to return to the wilderness. Eliezer had found Zuriel and Nathanel among a group of shepherds he had been training. They were young, strong, and reliable. He had some time ago recognized their propensity for daydreaming, but after selecting them for this task he found it fascinating to realize that a characteristic seen to be irresponsible in a herdsman now qualified them completely. A few well-crafted questions had rightly identified them as excellent choices. They had already accomplished the first essential job of locating just the perfect cave on Mount Nebo, because the plan could only work if Moses' disappearance happened at just the right place. Zuriel and Nathanel could not have chosen better.

They had remained on the mountain for the last few nights to make preparations for Moses' disappearance. First they had located and prepared the opening of the cave. Then they had stocked it with sufficient provisions to meet Moses' needs and with enough extra to satisfy their own during the journey ahead. Zuriel and Nathanel had agreed to accompany Moses until the time was right for the three of them to join up with the fledgling community. No one knew how long that would take. In another cave about a day's journey from Mount Nebo, they had hidden a larger cache of supplies for the journey. Already, these young men had justified Eliezer's choice.

While Moses, followed by a long parade of Israelites, was approaching the sharp bend in the path, his helpers were waiting out of sight near the cave. When they saw Moses scurrying as fast as his 120-year-old body could carry him across the twenty yards or so to the next sharp bend in the path, they were ready for action. Right around that corner and hidden from the sight of his followers Moses quickly crawled into the cave, grabbing and pulling the vine that hung down from the cave opening.

Zuriel and Nathanel had prepared the cave opening to close quickly by carefully piling rocks above the entrance and bracing them with a log. The vine Moses pulled as he dove into the cave opening was attached to the log, thus releasing the rocks. Because the cave opening was only about two feet across and two feet high, the falling pile of rocks was sufficient to cover the entrance. In the brief time they had available, the helpers immediately went to work to make the pile look like a natural part of the hillside. The log and vine were removed from sight when Moses pulled them into the cave with him. In seconds, the two young men had disappeared around an outcropping of rock and had quickly descended the mountain by another route. At the bottom, no one paid any attention when they melted into the milling crowd.

Once the rocks fell across the opening, Moses could no longer see what was happening outside, although the sounds of running and shouting filtered through to him. While he crouched just inside the cave opening, the sweat began to run down his brow and cheeks into his eyes and beard. His cloak clung damply to his back and his muscles began to stiffen as the minutes slowly passed.

Each passing moment without discovery increased the chances that the ruse would succeed. He really didn't think he would be discovered right away, because he was certain that his co-conspirators had played out their parts in the most convincing way. In all the shouting and confusion, no one would look too closely at a pile of rocks. At this very moment right outside the cave, they were looking up to the skies trying to catch a glimpse of the angels that purportedly were carrying him into the eternal presence of the Holy One. He knew, though, that everything would change once Gershom and Joshua arrived. Moses was sure that even now, the news of his disappearance was speeding down the side of Mount Nebo toward them. Those two, more than anyone else, would likely be skeptical when they heard the amazing accounts of Moses' heavenly transport. And of course they would immediately begin a thorough search of the area. Moses was sure that the priests and soldiers would not be looking at the sky. If Moses could just make it until evening without being discovered, they might actually get away with this crazy plan.

He noted with relief that his heart was no longer trying to jump out of his chest and that his breathing was returning to normal, so he decided to navigate the short distance into the main part of the cave. Because it was pitch black, Moses could orient himself only by placing his hands against the walls on either side of the cave as he crawled forward through the narrow passageway. When his hands could no longer reach both walls he knew he could stand up. Slowly, his eyes adjusted to the darkness. A faint light about five feet over his head provided a touch of illumination. His helpers had cleared a small hole in the top of the cave and had covered it loosely with large rocks so that ample air and a bit of light could filter in. Moses knew there was a lamp waiting for him in the cave, but he had been instructed not to light it until no more daylight was visible through the opening. By dark the searchers would have given up and gone back down the mountain. His brave band would be camping quite a distance away, so the chances of discovery were slim.

He knew he had some hours to wait, so he found a pile of skins and settled down to rest.

Moses must have dozed—not surprising after such an intense and exciting morning. While he slept, he thought he heard his wife rummaging around on her side of the tent. He was about to tell her to go back to bed so he could sleep, when he realized where he was and that whatever noise he was hearing could not be coming from his wife. He woke with such a start that his heart started pounding again. The noise was coming from the cave opening. It sounded like someone was kicking against the rocks. He quietly shuffled nearer to the sound and was able to hear muffled voices. Moving closer still, he was just able to make out a few words. To his horror, one of the voices sounded like Gershom. He was shouting.

"What are you doing, you fool?"

"Honored One," an unfamiliar man's voice croaked. "I stumbled over this pile of rocks and thought, since I was down here on my knees, I might as well investigate."

"Get away from there. It's Moses' body we are looking for, not snakes in a rock pile. Go join those men over there. If there's anything to find, I want it found before the sun goes down. We don't want to be stuck on this mountain when it's too dark to see."

"Right away, Honored One." Moses then heard footsteps moving away.

After a few anxious moments he was just about to lift himself up to begin moving back into the main part of the cave when he heard Gershom's voice once again. Moses froze in terror. "My father, wherever Jehovah has taken you—or will take you—I pray that he will hold your sacred soul close to his bosom." A moment later, Moses heard a rock clatter against the debris blocking the cave entrance followed by a second set of receding footsteps. Then silence.

Moses crawled back to his makeshift bed of skins. He could feel the kiss of Gershom's intended or unintended blessing wet on his face. He lay there until he fell into a deep sleep. When he opened his eyes it was pitch black around him.

He groped around in the dark until he located the lamp and then found the niche in the cave wall where his helpers had left a cache of live embers. A few puffs of breath on a small sheaf of dried grass that he had laid on the embers provided a small flame that was just enough to light the lamp. The light filled the space and gave Moses his first look at his temporary home. The main part of the cave was a round space about twelve feet across with a domed ceiling that at its highest was about half again his height above his head. He could stand up everywhere except right next to the walls. The air was dry and warm with a dusty, but not unpleasant odor to it. Soon the sputtering lamp filled his nostrils with its own pungent aroma. His supplies included some skins for sitting or sleeping on and others to pull over his body for warmth. Jugs of water and baskets of bread, cheese, and dried fruit, mostly dates, would keep him from starvation for a few days. Hopefully, he would be out of there and on his way long before the food ran out. One additional flask contained oil for the lamp.

Moses began to doze again, and well before the lamp oil ran out, he slept the sleep of the exhausted.

Just as the first light began to filter through the rock-covered hole in the ceiling, Moses was startled by a loud voice calling his name. Thinking that his rescuers had come for him, he started toward the cave opening but ran right into something solid. He recoiled from the impact and then noticed a glow surrounding whatever had stopped him.

It was a man, a being anyway, calling his name. "Moses, can you hear me?"

Moses fell back on the skins, his eyes wide with terror. "Who are you and how did you get in here?"

"I am!"

"What?"

"I am I AM!"

When the reality of what was happening finally dawned on his sleepy consciousness, Moses immediately fell on his face before this manifestation of the Holy One.

"Moses, get up! This is no time for fawning. We have a lot to consider about this situation."

Of course, it didn't happen quite that way. Moments like these never fit neatly into words. If Gershom had been around, though, he would have made it sound like Moses was receiving clear directives from Jehovah. Clear, crisp, unambiguous divine statements would find their way onto Gershom's pages;

statements that could be used to bring order to Israelite social structures and individual behavior. For Moses, though, the experience felt more like a simple conversation over a pot of warm goat's milk.

Still, words and images are all we have to work with, so in times to come, when Moses would think of this event, his memory picture would look something like this.

"Have you come here to punish me in your righteous anger because I deceived the children of Israel?"

"Actually, I thought your plan was rather clever, and well executed at that. But that's not why I am here."

"Why then, Holy One?" Moses kept his head bowed.

"Moses, you've always had good instincts even if, at times, you have been prone to misunderstand me. I must confess that the path you and the others have embarked upon intrigues me. It should be interesting to see how it turns out."

Moses looked up with a start. "You mean you don't know what will happen?"

"Well, maybe I could know if I really set my intention in that direction, but sometimes it's better not to know. It certainly is more entertaining. You humans are a fascinating brand of Divine Creativity.

"But I didn't come here to talk about that either. You know Moses, if you talked less and listened more, I wouldn't have to work so hard to get your attention."

"Yes, Holy One, I know—and I'm really sorry."

"Moses, settle down. You're not in trouble with me. I just want to address one particular piece of this new adventure of yours a little more directly."

Moses had to use all his internal strength to calm himself while he waited.

"I do know that when you emerge from this cave, you'll wonder if this conversation actually happened or if you merely dreamed it. Actually, it doesn't matter. You probably would have figured out in time what I came here to tell you. But your waking mind might not have pieced things together quickly enough, so I am making use of your dreaming mind to speed things up a bit."

Moses began to question the Presence again, but the Holy words continued as if he had not spoken at all. "It's OK for you not to know for sure if I was here at all or if this is just a dream. You will find the information useful either way. So, do I have your attention now?"

Moses looked up. His eyes blinked rapidly.

"Good! Now listen to me. You must understand that it wouldn't be a good idea for you to run right out and join your small renegade band."

"No? Why not?"

"You've been the leader of the Israelites for a very long time. This generation in particular has depended on you for everything: to lead them to food and water, to admonish them, to carry the wisdom for them, and, of course, to talk to me on their behalf. That's quite a powerful position you have held with them."

Moses nodded in agreement.

"And it appears you've enjoyed it quite a bit."

Moses opened his mouth to argue, but his companion continued on.

"Moses, remember; I know you. Yes, there have been times when you've been frustrated with these Israelites, when you've wanted more than anything to smack every one of them with your staff. But you never did. You might ask yourself why not.

"And you argued so eloquently (and so many times) on their behalf before my Holy Presence. I know it was hard, but I would venture to guess that you wouldn't have wanted it to be any other way. You loved that job!"

Moses thought on this last statement for some time before he was addressed again.

"But, Moses, now you can't have it your way any more. This brave group cannot realize its vision with you as its prophet and leader. They have to find their own way."

"Do you mean I can't go with them?"

"I didn't say that. You keep running ahead of me. Moses, you must realize that your relationship cannot ever be as it was. They have to discover how to be responsible for themselves, and they have to learn by experience that it is necessary for the well-being of the community for them to rely on their own ability rather than yours to come to me. You and Eliezer have done a good job of recruiting a group who are capable of determining their own direction and destiny. These are people who already know me or are capable of knowing me. But, you won't be alive forever, remember. If they were to depend on you too much, they wouldn't be motivated to discover their own abilities."

Moses thought about what the Holy One had said but he wasn't quite ready to embrace this new perspective. "Well, it's fortunate then that Eliezer is with them. I know he's capable of stepping into any role that I've held."

"Moses, Moses. Stop and think about what you're saying. If you take the time to consider instead of just reacting, you'll realize that you already hold two very crucial pieces of information: you've seen glimpses of the kind of community they wish to become, and you know what kind of man your second son is. Do you think for a moment that this group will want or need the kind of leader that you've been for them, even someone as obviously capable as Eliezer? Furthermore, if you give yourself a chance, you'll conclude that he will have figured that out by now. He'll never let himself be drafted into such a position."

Moses was pretty confused. He could recognize the truth in everything the Holy One was saying to him, but at the same time, he wanted to believe that Eliezer would take care of his new extended family so that he wouldn't have to worry about them himself. But then he decided that there would be plenty of time to think about Eliezer and The Community later. He had more pressing matters on his mind. "So what am I supposed to do?"

"Well, Moses, let's put it this way: When you addressed the Israelites yesterday, you explained to them why their parents would not be able to enter the Promised Land. You identified yourself with that generation and told them that you were not fit to lead them in the next phase of their journey. You were right, but I don't think you took the next logical step in your own mind."

Moses began to tremble as these holy implications took on tangible form. "So, I..."

"Yes, Moses, finally you see it. Just as you were not fit to lead the main body of Israelites across the Jordan River, you are also not qualified to lead this brave group to their Promised Land either."

Sweat once again pooled under Moses robe as he pondered this stark and difficult truth. They were silent for a long time.

Finally, Moses looked up. Even in the dim light of the cave, the lines of pain on his face stood out. "So, the joke I'm trying to play on the Israelites is actually a joke on me after all. I really do have to die!"

The next sound Moses heard was so unexpected and so inappropriate to the solemnity of the moment that he couldn't make sense of it. What's this? he thought.

Then it hit him. The Holy One was laughing—not chuckling, but was doubled over in a cave-filling belly laugh! "Oh Moses, you are too much. Here, give me the edge of your robe so I can wipe these tears from my eyes."

To say that Moses was stunned and disoriented would have been the understatement of the ages. Here he was, trying to accept with some modicum of grace his imminent sentence of death from the very mouth of the Holy One. Here he was, accepting that his vision of participating in a healthier Promised Land had just turned into so much wilderness sand. Here he was, trying to maintain some dignity in the face of this crushing disappointment, and the Holy One, yes, the Holy One, was laughing in his face.

"Die?... Die?... Hardly! Not you! What makes you think you can get out of this so easily?"

Through tears of mortification Moses sniffed. "What... are...you...talking...about?"

"Oh, Moses. I apologize for laughing at you, but you must learn not to be so melodramatic about everything. You sound like Gershom sometimes."

Wiping his own eyes, Moses tried again. "Please, I don't understand. If I can't lead them to this other Promised Land, what else could my fate be but death?"

"Well, first of all, you have to stop being so literal and one-sided. I thought you had already decided that was Gershom's problem. If you can restrain yourself from being so self-centered for a moment, you'll realize that there is more going on here than simply how to determine your next job-title. Think about your visions. It appears to me that you saw them pretty clearly. So, remember back: did you see yourself as part of the community?"

"Most of the time, yes, I did."

"And did it seem to you that you were the leader of this community or their prophet?"

Moses closed his eyes and recreated the lovely image in his mind's eye. He opened his eyes, bowed his head and looked down at his feet. "No"

"So, you were not the leader, but you were there. Right?"

"Yes, that's right."

"So Moses, look again and identify who the leader is."

Again, Moses looked inward. In a moment his face began to flush in embarrassment. He heaved a deep sigh. "There is no leader."

"No leader? You're sure?"

"No leader. Just a group of people who seem to respect each other very much."

"Right, Moses. That's right. You see, your demise is not the only possible outcome. The good news is that you are going to live quite a bit longer. The bad news is that it's not going to be easy for you to learn how to be 'one among many.'"

Moses questioning look invited more explanation.

"You were thinking that you and your helpers would get off this mountain in a day or two and wait out in the wilderness for your group to catch up to you. In just a few weeks, you would be happily ensconced in their warm and appreciative embrace, prepared to live happily ever after. Am I right?"

"Something like that, I guess."

"Well, it can't work that way. They need some time without you, and you certainly need some time without them. So, here's what you'll do. You'll leave this mountain in a day or two with Nathanel and Zuriel as planned. You'll travel into the wilderness, but you will take care to remove yourself from the likely path of the group you refer to as The Community of Promise. You'll keep yourself hidden until they pass. They will, of course, wonder where you are, but they know they have to get far enough away so that Gershom and Joshua won't be tempted to chase after them. Oh by the way, don't worry about them too much. Already, many of them are open to Holy Presence. They'll figure out the wisdom of this plan just as you have.

"And remember, you know how to take care of yourself in the wilderness well enough, so you and I will have plenty of time to spend with each other. I rather look forward to it."

Moses was so relieved that he must have fainted, because when a noise woke him up, Zuriel and Nathanel were standing over him.

The two men practically wept in relief as they helped Moses to his feet. "We thought you must have died. We didn't hear anything as we dug through the rocks," Nathanel said.

"I guess I was tired."

"Well, no time for that now! We have to get moving." Zuriel began packing up their supplies.

"How long have I been in here anyway?"

"Since yesterday mid-day."

"It doesn't seem that long. I must have slept a lot."

Nathanel now took charge "Everything is ready, we have to get going."

Moses took one last look over his shoulder at this womb-like space. As he was about to turn toward the light, he thought he saw someone in the corner, smiling. But when he blinked his eyes, no one was there. He looked again and then shrugged his shoulders. He was ready to head for the Wilderness. He would find communion again with Holy One when he got there.

Chapter 18

Sarah emerged from her tent to find Asher already tending the fire so that they could break their fast. She stretched like a cat, greedily taking in the fresh morning air. So much was wonderful about life. She felt such relief now that they were about to move away from the land of Canaan. Her sleep had been increasingly troubled in the days and weeks before these amazing events on Mount Nebo changed everything.

Asher greeted her warmly. The thrill of seeing her flourish in this setting shone in his eyes. Before Mount Nebo he had worried about her a lot, but no longer. This was the Sarah he knew and loved. He offered her some of the food that he had just prepared.

"I'm not very hungry. A small piece of bread and cheese will keep me while I go to the gathering. Are you coming?"

"I'll follow you as soon as I finish eating."

She took the food that he had just handed her and responded with a smile. She then headed across the makeshift camp toward the gathering.

Sarah found her place and looked around while those still arriving settled down to sit or recline. None of them knew what to expect, but they were all invested in the outcome. Those who came first sat in the inner circle while the rest filled in around the outside. Eliezer and Milcah sat near the center talking together quietly. In time the crowd quieted and all attention found its way to Eliezer. He seemed not to notice.

"So, Eliezer, what are we supposed to do?" came a voice out of the crowd.

"What do you want to do?" was Eliezer's response.

At that, people looked at Eliezer in confusion.

"Shall I tell you what to do? Is that what you want?" Again people turned to one another, and the buzz of conversation began to fill the space.

"It appears to me that right now you want to talk to each other. So talk!"

"But aren't you our leader?" someone shouted while others echoed the same question.

"Is that what you want? A leader? Me as your leader?"

The man who had been asking the questions finally stood and walked to the center of the circle, facing Eliezer. "I don't know what you are trying to do, but Moses has always been our leader and we—I assumed that you would take his place now that he is gone."

Eliezer stood, walked over to the man, and put his arm companionably around his shoulder. "I'm afraid I don't know your name, friend."

The man stiffened and looked wary, but then he saw the kindness in Eliezer's face. "My name is Kenan, Honored One."

"Kenan, my name is Eliezer, simply Eliezer. My name bears no honorifics. I am glad to meet you." Then Eliezer turned to the crowd while he kept his hand on the man's shoulder. He turned him around in a circle and said, "This is my new friend, Kenan. I hope you all get to know him. Now my friend, you had a question for me."

"You are Moses' son. Shouldn't you lead us in his stead?"

"Kenan, is that what you want?" Kenan just looked confused as if he had never imagined that anyone would ever ask him such a question.

"Kenan, why don't you take a seat? I think you've raised a question that is in the minds of many who are here." Eliezer then addressed the gathering. "I ask you the same question that I have just asked Kenan. Are you thinking that you want me to assume leadership of this group in place of my father, Moses, who is not presently with us?"

A murmuring rose in the crowd.

"But before you answer I want you to consider if that's even the most important question to address, because I believe there's another lying behind it. Kenan asked if I would assume the position of leader. That question assumes that this small band will do things like they have been done for the last forty or more years. So my question to you is not about whether or not I will lead. First, you'll have to decide if that's the kind of leadership you really want."

Then Eliezer sat down and began to talk quietly with Milcah. Over the next few minutes, people began gathering into small groups trying to make some sense of what Eliezer had asked. After a time, Kenan again walked to the center of the circle and said to those gathered, "This was my question, but I don't have a good answer and I know I need some help in figuring it out. It would help me to know what you're all saying to each other. Could we decide to speak in turn so we can all hear and learn?"

Other voices chimed in: "I, too, want to hear." "Let's figure this out together." And, "Yes, I'd like that, too." Many nods and grunts of assent accompanied the words.

A woman stood so she could be heard, "Is there anyone who even knows how to lead a group like this? I can raise a tent, find enough food in the wilderness for my family to survive, and I can walk a long way, but I wouldn't know how to take care of a whole group."

Then a man added, "I know Moses kept us safe, but there have been times when I wanted to go in a different direction. Not that anyone cared about my opinion."

Kenan scowled. "If it were only a matter of finding our way through the wilderness, any of us could lead. We've wandered out here all our lives. Who among us couldn't find travel routes and oases practically with our eyes closed, but what about battle? What if we run into someone who wants to fight? Don't we need a general?"

Sarah found herself on her feet before the gathering. Her heart pounded as she weighed her words. After a moment, she found her voice "Why do we always have to fight, anyway? The orders to go to battle always came from Joshua, through Gershom I presume. He probably claimed that Jehovah had instructed Moses to take us into battle. With all I've been hearing about Moses and Gershom, I'm not convinced that the Holy One wanted any such thing!"

She was sure that people would be horrified and offended by what she had just said, so she prepared herself to be shouted down. Now I've done it. Why can't I just keep my mouth shut?

When she looked up, she saw concerned but open, perhaps thoughtful, faces looking back at her. After a period of deep silence, a voice rang out. "What are you trying to tell us?"

Sarah took a moment to gather her thoughts. The words that she had rehearsed in her heart so many times before were waiting for her. When she spoke, she was a bit surprised by the strength of the voice that came out of her mouth. "One time in my youth, I foolishly wandered away from the camp. When the sun grew hot in the middle of the day, I found a shady place behind some rocks to rest and wait for the cool of the evening. The next thing I knew, I was awakened by shouting and the crashing sound of metal on metal. Apparently while I had slept through the night, a part of our Hebrew army had moved into position to engage in battle with an enemy. They were very close to the rocks where I lay. My vantage point was close enough to the battle so I could see the sweaty arms and blood-streaked faces of the combatants. But the soldiers were all too intent on their combat to notice me and I was too fascinated to feel any fear as I watched. Even more than the horror of blood, gore, and severed limbs, of men killing and dying, I remember how all the faces, Hebrew and enemy alike, looked the same. They all projected a combination of perverse satisfaction and abject terror.

"In time, the Hebrew army gained the upper hand and the enemy soldiers threw down their arms and surrendered. I could hear them pleading for mercy. Then I saw Joshua. The hatred I saw in his face chilled me to the bone. I couldn't believe it when he ordered the soldiers to slaughter every last man among the enemy. The soldiers followed orders, but without the intensity of battle, I could see that they were disgusted with what they had to do. Many fainted or emptied their stomachs during this cold-hearted slaughter. I also watched the eyes of those about to die. I saw their shame as their bowels released, and I could feel their complete confusion, though they made a brave attempt to face imminent death. Mostly I saw how young they were, killers and victims alike, strangely paired up in a bizarre and macabre dance.

"I was very young when I saw this, so I don't know whether this battle could have been avoided—perhaps not. But I hated to see what the experience did to these fine young men. All I could think was that there had to be another way. I was told later that the order to fight and then to annihilate this enemy had come from the Holy One. I didn't know what to think, but I couldn't imagine that the Holy One, whom I had already come to know in so many tender ways, could want such a thing. I still wonder to this day."

A man jumped up. He was shouting and his red face was contorted. He stormed into the center of the gathering. "What do you know about it, female? What if the god of the enemy had ordered that we be killed off? What would you say then?"

Sarah wanted nothing but to run away from this attack, but somehow she stood her ground. "I have no answer for you. I only have this question that I've carried unanswered, unexpressed even, for many years. If I can't ask it here, then perhaps I was mistaken to join this group. Without the freedom to raise my questions, I might just as well leave and cross the Jordan with the others." She looked right at the man as she spoke.

Again, he began shouting. "You women know nothing of war and battle. You should leave such things to men!"

"You're right. I don't know anything about war and battle." Sarah could hardly breathe, but she found enough air to continue. "I do wonder, however, if it's always wise to leave the decisions in the hands of you men who seem to know no other solution to problems than violent conflict. Still, I don't presume to have any answers. I have only this question." Sarah slowly turned, returned to her seat, and began examining in earnest the lacings on her leg coverings. When she looked up again, she saw that Kenan had moved back into the center of the circle.

Kenan's anger was about to boil over. As he was approaching the man Sarah wondered if he could keep from hitting him. But then he met Sarah's eyes. She watched in wonder as he regained his inner balance. By the time he reached the center of the circle and began speaking, his words came out with warmth. "My friend—I trust I can call you my friend, though we have never met. Is there something you want us to know…?

"She shouldn't even be talking about things she doesn't know anything about."

"…about yourself? What is important about you, not about Sarah, that you would like us to know? And to begin with, would you like to tell us your name?"

The man looked a bit wide-eyed. Finally, he appeared to master his own emotions and then bowed slightly. "I am known as Enosh."

"And I'm Kenan, Enosh. Clearly, you have strong feelings, but I'm mostly interested in who you are." He swept his arm around to indicate the gathered people. "Perhaps others would like to know you as well."

At the nods from the people, Kenan went back to his seat. Enosh swallowed and began to speak. "My father was a soldier. He was killed in a battle against the enemies of the Israelites. He was still a young man and I was only a year old when he died. I don't remember him at all. My uncle took me in, raised me like his own son, and taught me to be a soldier. I have done my duty to the best of my ability, and I'm offended that someone who has no experience of the life of a soldier would presume to judge me."

Kenan continued to address Enosh from his seat. "Surely, there will be plenty of opportunities for battle in the Promised Land. I can't help but wonder why you have come here with us instead of going with Joshua and the others."

"Do you want me to leave? Is that what you are saying?" Enosh's face got red again.

"Not at all. It was just a question. No offense or judgment was meant. I'd simply like to know why you made the choice to join this unusual gathering."

Enosh looked around. Sarah thought he was prepared to see angry and challenging faces, but all he found were looks of compassion and interest. He took a deep breath, looked directly at Kenan and continued. "I'm a good soldier. In fact, I'm a very good soldier. I've worked hard and I've always obeyed orders. And I am proud that I've always been able to bring my men home alive. I'd hoped that someday my talents would've been recognized, but my family has little influence with the leaders in the Army who have the power to make such decisions. The ones who get promoted to positions of real responsibility are always the sons of powerful families. I had been led to believe that Joshua was at last ready to recognize me, but someone apparently bribed him. Rumor has it that Eliezer's brother makes all the real decisions, so I suppose he is the one who's managed to keep me in my place."

Enosh then strode across the circle to stand towering over Eliezer. "Your brother is a snake. If I find out that you're at all like him, I surely will go back across the Jordan. At least I know how that snake works."

Eliezer didn't even look up. Enosh waited for the man at his feet to speak. "I am not my brother. I hope that as you get to know me, you'll find that I'm telling you the truth. Then you can decide. For now, I am glad to meet you Enosh.

"We're in a dangerous situation. Maybe we don't even know how dangerous it really is. Anyway, we need all the help we can get. One more thing, Enosh, just remember that this gathering is not the main body of the Israelites, and our Promised Land is likely to be very different than theirs. I suggest you spend some time in conversation with Sarah. I believe you'll find her perspectives to be useful to a soldier who values the lives of his men."

Enosh shot a look across the circle at Sarah. It seemed that he was about to say something, but he simply bowed his head to her and returned to his seat. The gathered community let out a collective sigh of relief.

Kenan rose to speak again. "I've been trying to think about Eliezer's earlier question: What do we want? With all due respect to Eliezer, I think it's the wrong question. It's dangerous in the wilderness to make decisions based on what we want. I think we have to determine what we need instead."

Again, a buzz of conversation arose in response to Kenan's words. Finally, another man stood. "I think we need some kind of leadership, but maybe not vested in just one person."

Then a woman: "I heard a rumor that we'd have a council of about fifteen people. Why don't we do that?"

People began tossing out the ideas of what they wanted or about what made sense to them. They were getting nowhere.

Kenan got up again. "We're still thinking about what we want rather than what we need. Whatever we decide to do we won't have to do it forever, so let's start someplace."

"I agree with Kenan." Milcah had stood up to speak. The crowd got quiet and shifted their attention to her. "What we need is some organization," Milcah went on. "We already know that investing power in a single person is too much like the old way, and spreading authority too thinly will make it too difficult to focus on our immediate challenges. I suggest we form a leadership council of three people. I've been thinking about this since you all were recruited to join this group. When each of you agreed to join, I made note of your skills and abilities, as much as I was able. So here is my suggestion. The first person I would recommend is Kenan. I wasn't at all surprised that he was the first to take leadership today. He sees clearly and is passionate for our success." Kenan dropped his head and blushed.

"My second recommendation goes to a person who is no less clear and passionate, but who represents a somewhat different way of looking at things. You've already experienced Sarah's courage and her ability to give voice to important, if unpopular, issues."

When she heard Milcah voice her name, Sarah almost fell over. Her pounding heart after her earlier speech had just barely calmed down and now it was going again like a rabbit running from a lion.

"My third recommendation is that you consider none other than our capable soldier, Enosh." She turned and spoke directly to him. "Enosh, my father served with you before his death in battle a few years ago. He spoke of you as one who had natural leadership ability and more importantly as one who had an uncommon tendency to employ lots of common sense. He had expected you to rise through the ranks very quickly. Had he lived, I know he would have been upset at how Joshua has treated you."

Sarah half expected Enosh to fall over in astonishment.

Milcah walked all the way around the circle so she could look directly at all the gathered people. "I invite you to affirm these three as your temporary leaders. Once we are on the move and have found what kind of organization works for us, they will step aside for whatever leadership scheme emerges. Six cycles of the moon should be more than enough time to accomplish this. Now, are there any among us who would not support this temporary plan?"

No one rose to speak against Milcah and all she saw were smiles and nods.

Then, a voice, "Are you three willing to serve?"

Kenan, Sarah, and Enosh looked at one another, then stood. Enosh spoke first. "I would be honored."

Kenan followed. "As would I."

Sarah thought for a moment with her head bowed. Finally, she looked up and said, "I will serve on one condition." The crowd waited for her to continue. "My condition is that we put off a final decision until tomorrow. It's important to me to know that the Holy One participates in the decisions that affect our community. I will, in my own way, open myself to the Holy One. And I invite all of you to do likewise. Once you have done so, if by tomorrow at this time you still wish us to serve, I will serve gladly. If it is your "knowing" from the Holy One for one or more of us to step aside, I, for one, will step aside just as gladly." Then she turned to face Kenan and Enosh. "Will you agree to my condition?"

They looked at each other and then at Sarah. They both nodded their agreement.

Kenan then reached out his hands toward Sarah. "You demonstrate your leadership already." At that, the gathering dispersed and the people returned to their tents.

After all had left, only Eliezer and Milcah remained. Eliezer's eyes were closed and tears squeezed out from between his eyelids. "May the Holy One always show us such caring," was all he said.

Chapter 19

The wilderness: such emptiness, such beauty, such danger, such promise. Moses blinked as the sun shone in his eyes. After his many hours in the darkness of the cave, it took a few minutes for his eyes to adjust. I'm an old man, he thought as he looked out from his place on the mountain over the dry and rough emptiness. How can it be that I feel like a newborn baby? I was so sure that the time of my death had come, but here I am alive. Then again, for all I know, maybe I did die in there. Perhaps that's why everything seems so fresh and new.

Zuriel's voice broke his reverie. "Moses, with all due respect, we have to get you off this mountain. If you are discovered many bad things are likely to happen to all of us, including those who remain here to mourn your supposed death. Come on, let's go." Moses was just about to take issue with the younger man's less than respectful tone when in his mind's eye he saw the Holy One doubled up with laughter. Chuckling to himself he nodded gravely and began his journey into new life.

It did not take them long to get off the mountain. It was so early in the morning that the camp of "mourners" was not even stirring. Zuriel and Nathanel had planned their escape route with care so they encountered no one.

Once they were on the plain, they set their feet toward the agreed-upon rendezvous point, but Moses stopped them. In answer to the puzzled looks on their faces, Moses explained, "I know the plan was to go to the meeting place, but I have been told—uh—I have decided that I cannot join The Community right away. I am no longer their leader."

Nathanel's voice was filled with horror. "But Moses, you have always been our leader. We have no one else!"

"They have the best leader of all. The Holy One will lead them. It is a very different Promised Land that we seek where things will transpire in ways that none of us could even have imagined just a short time ago. If I am truly to be one of them, they need some time without me, and I need some time alone."

"Well, obviously you can't go out into the wilderness all by yourself." Nathanel looked at Zuriel for confirmation. When Zuriel nodded vigorously, Nathanel continued. "We'll go with you. It'll be an honor for both of us to serve you."

Though Moses was moved by their devotion he put his hands on their shoulders and said, "You, Nathanel, and you, Zuriel, are fine young men. It would be my honor if you were to accompany me. But it cannot be. I have to go alone."

"But it's dangerous out there!"

"Don't I know it! You must remember, however, that I learned to survive in this wilderness long before either of you were born. It has become home to me. I'll make out just fine. Now, it's important that we figure out what you two will say when you rejoin the company."

The three men walked in silence for several hours, each lost in his own thoughts. They were only dimly aware of the heat of the sun, the breezes that kicked up as the day wore on, or the rhythmic crunching of the arid ground under their feet. They came to a small oasis late in the day where they set up their camp. After they had passed around some dried food, Nathanel asked, "Where will you go Moses?"

"I'll go where my feet and the Holy One take me. Truthfully, the 'where' is not as significant as the 'why'. I've carried the mantle of authority on my shoulders for forty years. I think I need some time to get used to being without it. What I really want is to know the man whose essential identity has been obscured, even from me, by the demands of leadership. You might say that I want to spend some time with the Holy One without worries, troubles, or problems from the people."

Nathanel and Zuriel pondered Moses' words for a long time. The crackling of their small fire was the only sound to break the stillness of the night. Finally, Zuriel said, "Moses, I was going to ask what we should say when we see our people again, but right now, I'm convinced that Nathanel and I will think of something."

Moses chuckled. "Perhaps the Holy One guides your tongues as well as your feet."

Soon each of them fell into deep sleep.

When Nathanel and Zuriel awoke early, they discovered that Moses had gone.

"Nathanel, we should follow him at a distance to see that no harm comes to him."

"I was thinking the same thing."

They quickly packed their gear and looked for signs that might indicate which way Moses had gone. As they suspected, Moses apparently had continued to walk in the same direction as they had been traveling. As long as Moses' footprints were found in the soft sand, the young men could follow. But when they came to a dried-out wadi, they could find no more signs that Moses had passed there.

"Let's go up on that hill over there. Maybe we can see him," Nathanel said.

So they climbed up a nearby hillock and peered with their young and strong eyes in every direction. But no matter where they looked, they saw no sign of Moses.

"Now what?" asked Zuriel.

Nathanel thought for a moment, then said, "We've done our best. It's clear that Moses doesn't want to be found or followed. All we can do now is go and join the others."

Zuriel looked in all directions one more time and then muttered, mostly to himself, "May the Holy One go with you, Father Moses."

"Amen."

Chapter 20

Enosh had never been a quiet person. He had lived his whole life around soldiers and battle, so he knew little about the Holy One. Oh, it was true that he had attended the gatherings whenever the Israelites were instructed about the law, but for him it was just another set of directives from a higher authority. He was a good soldier who knew how to obey orders. As for direct contacts with the Holy One, the closest experience he could identify was tied up in his anger, resentment, and fear that somehow the Holy One had something to do with his father's death.

Enosh was sitting in front of his tent, idly nibbling on a piece of bread. He was not, however, thinking of the Holy One. He was disturbed by the question Kenan had asked him: Why *was* he here? The answer he had given during the gathering seemed to satisfy the others, but he wasn't sure he believed it himself. To his own ears, he sounded like a petulant brat with hurt feelings who had run away from home. Was that really it? He wasn't sure.

This renegade gathering represented very unfamiliar territory for him. His whole life had revolved around orders and action. What did he expect to find here? Everything that had happened so far was already entirely different from anything he could have imagined.

Enosh thought back to when Jethro had recruited him to join this group. He had known Jethro for a long time. They were cousins, after all. But, he didn't even like Jethro. So, what then possessed him to stay and listen?

Jethro had been waiting for him at his tent when he had returned from his drills." Greetings cousin. How goes the battle?" Jethro had chuckled at his lame attempt at a joke, but Enosh had not found it funny.

"What brings you here, Jethro? I didn't think you even spoke to people like me."

"Truly, our paths seldom cross, but I think you're wrong in your assessment of my motives."

Enosh's eyebrow twitched, but he said nothing and waited for Jethro to elaborate.

"I heard that you were passed over for promotion again. I'm sorry to hear it. My father always spoke highly of your competent leadership."

This was the last thing Enosh thought he would ever hear from Jethro and he had no idea how to respond.

Jethro just kept talking anyway. "May I be allowed to ask you a few questions?"

Enosh nodded.

"I've been talking with some of my friends about what we might encounter when we cross the Jordan. None of us is a soldier, but we'd welcome your perspectives anyway."

Enosh did not think of himself as a big picture kind of person, but he had felt moved by Jethro's apparent sincerity, so he took a moment to think about his answer. "Well, I've heard from the scouts that the land across the Jordan is heavily occupied. Armies defending their land from intruders always fight tenaciously, so many will die on both sides. Still, Joshua says that Jehovah has given this land to us and that means we should win. I can't help worrying, though, about the toll the next few years will take on both sides."

"Enosh, if you were in charge, how would you proceed?"

Enosh flushed crimson. "What are you trying to do, get me killed? Who sent you here anyway?"

"Please forgive me, cousin. You're right to be suspicious of that question, but let me assure you that my presence and my questions do not come from Gershom or Joshua or any in that company. I actually have a request to make and I was very clumsy in my attempts to be subtle. I really just wanted to find out if you think we're taking the best approach."

Enosh's mouth fell open and he was about to reply when Jethro continued. "Before you answer, you deserve to know where this question originates. You have, of course, heard the rumors about Moses."

"Hasn't everyone?"

"There'll be a hundred families that will be chosen to stay on Mount Nebo to celebrate Moses' life and to mourn his departure. I am asking you to stand among those families. It will be possible for you to rejoin the army later. I'm sure they'll already be across the Jordan before our sacred rituals are completed."

"So you want me to desert?"

"Not at all. Gershom himself has authorized it. You'll have full permission." After a pause Jethro continued. "I would hope that you have a place in your heart that follows Moses."

Enosh's head started to hurt. He knew he was a good man with a good mind. Unfortunately, his military career had not given him enough opportunity to use it. He concluded that he liked things to be clear and he was sure he wasn't very smart, although that wasn't really true. But, thinking took effort. Still, something within was leading him to consider this odd request. He was still reeling from Jethro's earlier question. How could he have suspected that Enosh saw the conquest of the land across the Jordan as a foolish and costly plan?

And then, what was that about a place in his heart that follows Moses? Enosh wasn't so sure about that part. He never knew much about what his heart was up to. Then he remembered the dream.

As a soldier he had never paid too much attention to dreams. The only purpose of sleep was to rest. He took care of himself so he could perform as a good soldier needed to, nothing more. But now he remembered that dream from the night before. He wasn't sure but he might even have dreamt it several times over a long period of time. All he remembered was being in a peaceful place where he was walking with Jethro. There were others around and all seemed content. Perhaps he even saw Moses there. The most noticeable part of the dream, though, was his feeling. In the dream he had no worries at all about promotions! That was significant. He always worried about promotions. And lately, since he had been passed over once again, his worry had been hardening into resentment.

Though his mind couldn't quite make the connections, he had then decided it was no accident for Jethro to be here with his curious request.

Why not? he thought. It can't hurt to play along.

"Enosh! So what do you say?"

Enosh realized that his attention had wandered and now Jethro was speaking to him. "What? Oh, sorry. I was thinking. Yes. Yes, I'll do it. You're right. I can catch up to the army later. Nothing to lose by doing this. Moses has led us well, after all. He deserves a good send-off."

So here he was. And now things had become really interesting. Not only was he a part of this unusual company, ready to desert with them, no less, but incredibly they had tapped him to be one of their leaders. This was too much. He should pack right now and retreat immediately to more familiar surroundings.

If he decided to stay with them he would be violating every principle he had followed for a lifetime. Now that he thought about it, his duty was to inform Joshua without further delay. Besides, that whole business about Moses' journey to be with Jehovah had a funny stink to it. Enosh wondered if he was really dead.

Suddenly, a chill rose up through his body and made the back of his neck tingle. He found himself reflexively reaching for his sword. As soon as his hand touched the hilt, he felt foolish and pushed it away again. Then, he noticed that he had broken out into a sweat, but he had no idea what could have caused such a reaction. Enosh remembered similar feelings that had often alerted him to unknown dangers on the battlefield. He had decided early on always to take those feelings seriously and that decision had saved his life and the lives his men many times. But why feel it here? What was the danger? He was not in battle—except with himself.

If he were on the battlefield he would know what to do. He'd be able to tell friend from foe. But, who was the enemy in this place? He had to figure out what path held the greatest danger: remaining or returning across the Jordan? He was sure he had never faced a more difficult decision.

What had Sarah said? It was something about opening herself to the Holy One, whatever that meant. And she had suggested that everyone else do the same before deciding on their choice of leadership. Maybe I could do that, too. But how?

Before these thoughts had a chance to get him totally confused, he decided he could use some exercise. He strapped on his footwear and picked up his sword. After walking a short distance from camp, he came upon a flat piece of ground that was protected on two sides by steep embankments. He took off his shirt and began to work through his soldier's conditioning drills. He lifted his weapon and swung it in a circle above his head several times. Then he began carving large figure eights in the air. On each down stroke he used extra force. At the same time he ran back and forth, jumping high in the air each time he turned around. After a while he transferred the weapon to his other hand and repeated the entire exercise. Finally, exhausted, he wiped the sweat off his body, put on his shirt, and sat to catch his breath.

Maybe he dozed off, maybe not. Suddenly, he sat up with a start. Someone was there! Enosh reached for his sword but it wasn't where he was certain he had left it. Strangely though, he wasn't concerned. Whoever was here represented no danger.

"Look at me, Enosh. Do you recognize me?"

Now Enosh started to tremble in earnest. He did know who this was, but it wasn't humanly possible for him to be here. Enosh had only been an infant when his father had been killed in battle and he had no recollection of him at all. But, impossible as it was, this was surely his father.

"Father?"

"It's good to see you, my son."

"How can you be here? You're dead."

"Enosh, I can't answer your question in any way that would make sense to you. Let's just say that the boundary between the realm of the living and (what shall I call it?) 'the rest' is not always as clear and identifiable as it usually appears from your side of things. Let it suffice that I am surely here."

"If you are really standing before me, and I can't deny what I see with my own eyes, then why here and why now? I've invoked your name countless times before and you never appeared then."

"Enosh, I'm sad to hear you say that. I've always been with you, especially when you've called for me."

Enosh had never been more stunned. No blow on the battlefield had ever rendered him more senseless. He could think of nothing to say.

"Perhaps, my son, there's a more useful, and perhaps more answerable, question: How can it be that you actually are seeing me this time?"

It astonished Enosh when he realized that he knew the answer. "Father, there have been many times when I've wanted you to rescue me or ease the loneliness I always felt in the army. I know now that those were frivolous requests."

"I did my best to respond to them anyway."

"Maybe so, but the question at hand is about me, not you."

Enosh thought he saw his father nod. "I think my real battle is with myself. Father, it may be that you're the only one who can understand what a dangerous battle it is. A part of me wants to run back to Joshua and my place in the army. I know it's a hard life in a way. But it requires only skill and obedience without imagination. I'm a good soldier. Perhaps I could be a General, but suddenly it troubles me that I could so easily perform and obey without ever having to become a person.

"I have a great temptation before me. If I return and tell Joshua and Gershom what I've come to know about this gathering, I know they'll reward me handsomely. I'll receive the acclaim I've always coveted. My future will be assured—but I can't seem to do it.

"It makes no sense to me at all that I can even be considering going out into the wilderness with this rag-tag bunch. They don't know what they're doing, and apparently they don't want to select another prophet like Moses to be Jehovah's spokesman. They're doomed. They'll wander out there until there's nothing left of them." Enosh shook his head. "How can it be that I am actually entertaining the possibility of going with them? If I had any sense at all, I'd run to Joshua right now!"

"So, what are you waiting for then, son? If you're so sure, just go. You know, you can leave right after dark. No one will even miss you—until tomorrow, that is."

"Tomorrow?"

"Yes, tomorrow, when the people gather to affirm their new leaders."

"Oh, that tomorrow."

"What's the problem? Joshua will take care of them in no time. These people don't need you because they won't be going into the wilderness anyway. He'll probably just execute them on the spot."

The color drained out of Enosh's face and he thought he was going to faint. Images of Eliezer and Milcah, Kenan and Sarah, and the rest being slaughtered by Joshua's henchman assaulted him from all sides. He could hear their screams as macabre accompaniment to the crunch of metal on sinew; and the all too familiar stench of spilled blood and split entrails made him want to vomit. He had never reacted like this in battle. He prided himself on his strong stomach when he was doing whatever soldiers were required to do to the enemy.

"That's just it. I can't find an enemy among them." A wave of emotion welled up from the depths of his gut, emerging in hot salty tears that rolled of his cheeks to mingle with the sweat on his chest.

"It seems that you are faced with a dilemma."

Enosh barely heard his father's words through his sobbing, but they spoke to his heart. "Those courageous people who hardly know me saw something in my character that the army will never, ever, see, much less value. They have chosen to trust me, not for my ability to take orders, but for something else. I don't know what they see in me, but I know I have to find out what it is."

Enosh turned to tell his father that he had made a decision, but no one was there. "Father," he shouted as he ran out into the open. "Where are you?" But the only answer he heard was the sound of his own voice.

Slowly, he found his way back to where his shirt lay in a heap on the ground. Picking it up, he wiped the tears off his face and the sweat off his neck and chest. Without his really thinking about where he was going, his feet found their way back to his tent where he fell onto his mat and slept a dreamless sleep until morning.

Chapter 21

Moses glanced up at the desert sun. It was approaching its zenith and its strong rays beat down on the old prophet's head and back. He decided it was finally safe to stop walking so he looked for a place to sit down. The ass that carried Moses' provisions snuffled in the wadi looking for any green plant growing up through the cracks of the drying stream bed. Moses was exhausted, likely because he had not slept at all the night before. He had left Nathanel and Zuriel as soon as he had been sure they were asleep. With one of the beasts of burden in tow, he had headed for the nearby wadi, knowing that its rocky bed would obscure all traces of his passing. He stopped long enough to find and pick up an old branch that had been deposited by the last flow of water through the wadi. It wasn't quite the right length, and it didn't have the familiar feel of his old staff, but he needed something and this would have to do. He couldn't use it right away because he didn't want to leave any tell-tale marks in the bed of the wadi. He'd use it soon enough.

By the time the young men awoke, Moses was far away. Just in case they had noticed his absence in the night and decided to follow, he had continued walking as far and as fast as he could.

Safely alone at last, he allowed himself to register the fatigue that went all the way into his bones. At times like this he felt as old as he really was, older than he could even imagine, and after his strenuous overnight hike the years weighed heavy. The morning had passed quickly, but then, time had a different rhythm in his beloved wilderness. He had already been away from it too long. It was great to be back. On the surface, his surroundings displayed a dry and inhospitable appearance, but after forty years he was not fooled. Even in its sparseness, the wilderness could always provide, if you knew where to look.

His instincts for survival had been honed in the wilderness, so he readily located a small hillside next to the wadi that would protect him from wind and sun. Finding water was always a challenge, but Moses could practically smell it. A less skilled traveler would never think to look here for water. The bed of the wadi was dried and cracked. It had seen no water for some time. Moses wasn't sure if he had visited this exact place before, but he knew what he would find. There was surely water here.

He grasped his walking stick with both hands and used the end to break up the dry earth under his feet. Then he pulled up several clods of the loosened dirt before kneeling down to dig through the sand with his bare hands. After he had removed about a hand's breath of dirt, he felt the moistness. Another hand's breadth down and his hands were suddenly wet. When he lifted a finger to his lips, he tasted sweet water.

Moses felt a twinge of shame when he remembered the first time he had demonstrated this technique to the Israelites. He could never convince them that it was the result of simple observation and experience, not a miracle. Oh, well, he thought, nothing to be done about it now. Before resting, Moses managed to fill all his water skins, so he would be ready for his next foray into the desert.

Moses always slept well in the wilderness. Its expansiveness conveyed the same sense of security that city dwellers enjoyed in their hard-walled homes. And Moses loved how present the Holy One always seemed to be in this desiccated openness. As he surrendered himself to sleep, the Holy One was as close and intimate as the rising and falling tides of each brand new breath.

He awoke refreshed just as the first light tinted the horizon with its faint blush. He splashed cooling moistness onto his face from his hand-dug washbasin in the floor of the wadi, then rummaged around in his sack until he found a piece of dried bread to chew on. After eating, he repacked his gear. Then he climbed to higher ground. He looked around, trying to decide where to go next.

Which way should he go? He couldn't go west; he had just come from there. He could conceivably go north, but he had no idea what lay that way, nor did he feel any northward pull. To the south lay his old friend, the wilderness; that was always a possibility. He remembered that The Community would be traveling east first and then perhaps to the south toward the Sinai wilderness, and then realized with a start that he had no way of knowing where that larger company might go after they left their agreed upon rendezvous point. Whatever their plan, in no way did he want to lose touch with them.

After a short while, he decided. He would travel near enough to the rendezvous location so he could shadow the movements of the company. From there he would keep an eye on the larger group while he remained hidden himself. Then, when the time was right, he would either join them or go away by himself. That was a decision he was not yet prepared to make. But at least he knew what to do next. Filled with sufficient purpose and hope, if not answers, he turned toward the rising sun and began to walk, and inevitably to muse.

It delighted him that he now had the time and space to think about his holy visions. He had enjoyed (or suffered through) so many of them. It struck him as curious that only the mountaintop experiences seemed to interest most people. Those were always intense, to say the least. They were as perilous as being caught by a torrent of water exploding through a dry wadi. No one could stand before such raw power. At the same time they were infinitely complex. Each such experience promised to occupy him for the rest of his days, and even then, he didn't expect to be able to understand them fully. He'd be content simply to find suitable words to describe them. When he (or Gershom) finally did find words, he discovered that the clearer the telling became, the less truth it could carry. So many times he had tried to explain that to Gershom, but his son never understood. Gershom was convinced that Jehovah would never engage Moses in any way that could not be captured in concrete terms and communicated clearly to all the people. What kind of god would provide experiences or make demands that humans couldn't grasp completely? Gershom insisted that Jehovah gave him the words to describe Moses' experiences and that was that.

Moses agreed that the people needed to hear about his experiences but he remained troubled that in all the official accounts Gershom consistently slanted the meaning the same way. Oh well, he couldn't do anything about that now, either.

The mountaintop wasn't the only place for mystical experiences and it wasn't always the best place either. Actually Moses had come to believe that the Holy One occupied no particular location anyway. Holy Presence was no greater on the mountain than could be found on the flat desert, at an oasis, or, for that matter, even in the cities of Egypt. Human awareness and perhaps human expectations actually made the greatest difference in direct experiences of the mystical realm. He had tried to explain this to Gershom, too, but, as usual, Gershom was only able to grasp the details while entirely missing the central point of the visions.

It occurred to Moses that it was Gershom's idea to locate Jehovah's presence in a tent. Gershom argued that Jehovah had directed him to identify that particular Holy Location. Moses supposed that locating the Holy One in a particular place did have its advantages. For one thing, it allowed people the comfort of putting some distance between themselves and soul-assaulting divine power. He just wished they didn't insist on being so literal all the time, particularly when it came to the Holy One.

"The Holy One ..." Moses rolled that description around in his mind. Even those words didn't quite capture the full meaning. He had overheard some of the priests arguing about what this divine designation "really" meant. It appeared to Moses that their minds went into a paralyzing spasm over the word "One." Where was this "One?" Why was God not called the Holy "Two?" or "Three?" or "Ten?" Moses spat. Gershom and his priests persisted in nailing everything down. They insisted on being right and consequently they treated dissenters with scorn if not violence.

Walking created a spaciousness in Moses' mind where he played with divine words and ideas. Instead of the Holy One, what if we referred to the divine as the "Holy Everything?" "The Holy All-There-Is-or-Ever-Could-Be?" or "The Holy

Everything-In-One-And-One-In-Everything?" And furthermore, what about the word "Holy?" Gershom loves that word. Moses let his mind drift for a while, accompanied only by the slap of his sandals on the hard-packed desert floor. If the Holy One is truly Holy, then where does one find the unholy? Are the gods of the Amalekites unholy? Or what about the Canaanites who are about to be slaughtered by Joshua; are their gods unholy? Is holiness or unholiness really about gods at all? Though he couldn't quite put it into words, he wondered if holiness might more properly refer to a quality of relationship. Moses tried to sum up where he was in his thinking: "The Holy/Unholy One/Everything Relationship among humans, gods, and all creation." He felt that this better described the actuality, but it would be awful trying to get those awkward words into a beautiful and satisfying ritual of worship. Oh, well…

Moses thought more about the experience of Holy Presence. It seemed bigger on the mountain, but easier in the open wilderness. The connection seemed less intense out here, but everything was so delightfully quiet—no interruptions like those from the busyness and noise of the city. When he was walking in the open, he felt the Presence in every step, every breath, every heartbeat.

This day, he found himself settling into that state of mind and body where human and divine inter-penetrated. Given the choice he could remain like this forever.

So Moses, he asked himself, is life in the wilderness what you want? You could choose right now, you know. You could turn south and simply vanish into the Sinai. It's big enough and empty enough to swallow you. You could remain in this blissful state until your days run out. But again, is that what you really want?

Moses found the question troubling. Why would he choose such a life? Maybe he had always been a loner. For sure he had never quite fit in Pharaoh's court. Of course, he eventually found out why that was so.

Maybe he just liked being alone. He'd never really thought about it before. What about those early years with Zipporah when they lived in the shadow of the Holy Mountain? The hours and days spent alone while he tended the flocks had been glorious.

That all changed, of course, when he returned to Egypt and became the leader of a freed people. That led to a life of extremes. Everyone saw him as the Prophet of God, so he was either in demand to fix their problems, or he was left utterly alone—left without any real intimate connection with the people. His father-in-law, Jethro, was the closest friend he had ever had. Moses still felt sad that Jethro had not lived very long after joining up with the Israelites. Moses had been taken by surprise at the intensity of his grief when Jethro died.

Other than that one person (and a Midianite at that!), the Holy One had been the only constant in his life. He had long appreciated the presence of the Holy One, but since his "dream" and since his recent connection with Eliezer, a new sense of the divine had begun to emerge in Moses' consciousness. He had felt its first glimmerings with Eliezer. It was certainly not new to him to experience the Presence both within his being and around him in the natural world. But when he was with Eliezer, he found a particularly strong sense of the Presence in their human being to human being connection. That same Holy Love had washed over him again when he sat with those young people in Eliezer's tent to plan their escape and his 'death.'

Remembering such holy moments led Moses to discover an emotion in himself that he had never noticed before, and it shook him to the very foundation of his being. He finally admitted that he had mostly been profoundly lonely. He wondered if he had always been so. He wasn't sure.

How could he be lonely when so many people needed him? Moses had always accepted the situation as the natural order. People needed him and he, in turn, needed the Holy One. But now, in a remarkably short time that familiar formula had turned itself upside down. He needed the people, too.

Moses was shocked to think his next thought. "Does that mean that the Holy One might need me in some way as well?"

His mind and heart naturally went back in time to that first encounter on the mountain. Holy Love had suffused him. In those moments when Moses had discovered his love for the

Israelites in their bondage, he had fallen in love with the Holy One, too. None of that was new to Moses.

Something new was stirring in him now, though. Little by little it came to him that love always moves in both directions at the same time. His connection with Eliezer offered the clearest example, but the more he looked, the more obvious the pattern became. He guessed it had always been present, but who knew even to look for such mutuality.

The faces of so many significant people crowded into his consciousness: the mother who raised him, his birth mother whom he met later in life, Zipporah and Jethro, Eliezer and Milcah, his siblings, Miriam and Aaron, and even Gershom in a strange way.

Moses had not noticed the mutual flow of love in those relationships, but he saw it now. And he felt its absence here in the open solitude of the wilderness. The loneliness was so palpably heavy that he could no longer stand. He was driven to his knees. He wept until he fell asleep, visited by those very ghosts in his dreams.

Moses awoke a few hours later. The sun had passed its zenith and was beginning its slide toward the horizon, making the shadows lengthen around him. With the edge of his sleeve, Moses wiped the sand and dried tears from his face. Moving into the cool shadow of a boulder he drank some water and chewed on a piece of dried lamb. His chest still hurt from his sobbing. He couldn't remember the last time he had ventured so deeply into his own feelings. In forty years he had never indulged himself so. After all, during that entire time he had shouldered the responsibility for the safety and survival of this people. They were never easy to lead, so he always had his hands full. There was no time or space to think (or feel) much beyond the demands of simple survival from one day to the next. That generation of slaves had been so thoroughly unprepared for the wilderness that Moses had felt like he was almost literally tending a flock of sheep.

There was so much to think about. His mind skipped about attempting to think about everything at once. Then Gershom's face emerged from the eddy of his thoughts. For what narrow purpose had he translated Moses' mystical experiences into a concrete set of laws? Still, Moses had to be fair. Even though his experiences were never that clear and definite, he had seen the utilitarian value in Gershom's approach. Unfortunately, once Moses had allowed the oversimplified version to be used as a control mechanism, Gershom took his assent as blanket validation to use the same approach with all divine communications.

A wave of sadness hit him at the thought of his elder son. They had never seen life from the same perspective, but Moses felt no moral judgment toward his intelligent, though myopic, offspring. He was convinced that his son wasn't a bad man. Gershom was simply faithful to what he believed. It was only because he was so sure of being right, (or afraid of being wrong,) that he imposed his views on others with such a vengeance. The tragedy of Gershom was in the narrowness of his view. There was always just one way to see anything, no matter how complex or ambiguous its hidden truths. Gershom had a two-point plan: Salvation depended upon clarity of direction from Jehovah, and then on human obedience to those instructions. That, of course, was the heart of the problem, and it represented the very reason that Moses had not been able to go with Gershom into the Promised Land.

In all honesty, Moses had to admit that without the imposition of Gershom's legalistic structure, that group of institutionalized slaves probably would have been hard pressed to survive those first years in the wilderness.

Moses sighed. He felt a deep love for his son and an even deeper sadness at their inevitable alienation from each other. Oh well, he thought, I can't spend the rest of my life consumed with haunting visions of what might have been. At the moment he had bigger problems. What was he to do, now that he had left the main body of the Israelites? And, having left that life behind, what preparation would be required of him before he was ready to enter this new community.

Against what might have been his better judgment (had he thought to consult it years ago), Moses had agreed to lead according to Gershom's version of the law of Jehovah. Without doubt, Moses would now have to change his understanding of leadership. His new family had already demonstrated a level of awareness and maturity that was beyond legalism. Was there more he could teach them about divine relationship from what he had learned on the mountain?

To attempt an answer, he decided to think about the law he had received for the people. Moses had heard the priests recite The Ten Laws so many times that he had to concentrate hard to remember what had been transmitted to him in the original experience. He would have to clarify his own understanding before he could tell others what he really believed. He speculated that the version according to Gershom would not be a sufficient religious resource for this new community.[12]

Gershom actually did a pretty good job with the "Laws," Moses thought. Idolatry was perhaps the most significant barrier to any relationship with the Holy One, though Gershom consistently misread the reasons: Jehovah would have to be a jealous god. Why else would "He" take issue with other gods? Moses knew better, however. In each of the mystical experiences he had entered into with the Holy One, there had never been the slightest hint of that only-too-human emotion of jealousy. The Holy One emanated pure invitation. Creation mattered so much to the Holy One, so the divine message always reflected that love. Humans just needed to discover and learn what was most healthy for them: that which could sustain the integrity of individuals, families, tribes, and nations. When humans worshiped idols, whether of other gods or even of the Holy One, the human/divine relationships became crassly manipulative in nature. Humans seemed to suffer under the ever-present temptation to create a god who was predictable, if not controllable.

Gershom had succumbed to that temptation years ago. He believed in a discrete god who had definite expectations for humans. As long as humans obeyed the rules, Jehovah would guarantee the desired result. According to Moses' experience of the Holy One, Gershom's perspective was exactly the kind of idolatry that was most damaging.

Unfortunately, once Gershom decided he was right, he became inured to anything that might contradict his understanding. He couldn't imagine that ideas about the Holy One could be even more idolatrous than golden statues. At least with a statue you knew it was a statue, but Moses could see that simple human ideas could easily (and diabolically) masquerade as absolute divine truth.

Moses perceived another dilemma. There were some people (Gershom was certainly not alone) who naturally saw things in concrete terms. Was there ever a non-idolatrous, non-manipulative way to hold definite images of the Holy One? Chances were good that at least a few of The Community saw reality in this way. Moses would have to think long and hard on that question. For now he merely accepted the reality of the situation. He still wondered, though, how to nudge people away from the vision of the Holy One as a separate entity. The Divine always inhabited the relationships among people and creation. This dilemma would take more thought, too.

Moses was tiring from all that deep pondering, but he wanted to clarify his experience of these laws, so he continued thinking and walking.

The second law had to do with making "wrong use" of God's name. As Moses saw it Gershom violated this law when he began calling the Holy One by the name, "Jehovah." Gershom used "Jehovah" as exactly the same kind of name as "Moses" or "Gershom," "Sarah" or "Jethro." Moses had seen that no single name could capture the essence of this god. The Holy One was Relationship, Being Itself, and the Process of Becoming, all at the same time. No name, picture, or idol could contain this reality. Or, said differently, any name, picture, or idol served to communicate too much about what was not-god while crowding out the relational essence of the Holy Presence. In a sense, the second law was a restatement of the first. Any use of a name that "idolized" even the Holy One constituted wrong use.

Moses thought that Gershom was on the right path when he described "Sabbath" but, as usual, he made it become more than it could be and less than it was. I tried to tell him, Moses thought, that humans needed Sabbath for two reasons: for rest and as an opportunity for reflection on the All That Is Holy. It was essential to set aside time where humans could be freed from toil and distraction. Moses had suggested setting aside one out of every seven days when people could enjoy total permission and affirmation to rest without any guilt or blame. But Gershom, being Gershom, turned opportunity into requirement. He demanded that the people avoid anything not clearly rest: not the same thing at all. People then had to worry about 'proper' rest instead of simply resting: a gross misinterpretation. Moses hoped people could appreciate the holiness of every thing (and every day) from a restful perspective. Furthermore, by referring to Sabbath as "Holy," Gershom made other days intrinsically less holy.

Moses was a bit surprised at these thoughts. They weren't exactly new, but he had never before taken the time to clarify his honest understanding of these Divine Messages. He sighed in regret that he had ceded so much power to Gershom, but then he felt a wave of defensiveness. When did I ever have the time to think these concepts through? he reasoned with himself. My life was consumed with leading and providing for the safety of an undisciplined and contentious crowd. I might as well have been trying to herd Egyptian cats, he argued.

Before long though, he chuckled at his adolescent attempts to justify himself. He knew that assigning or deflecting blame didn't change anything. Besides, right now, on his own in his familiar wilderness, he did have the time and even the ethical obligation to think through the implications of Holy Presence. He didn't have to be the leader or carry a Prophet's Mantle in order to contribute to the new community. It was simply true that his experiences gave him a measure of wisdom. Beating himself up for not having become this wise a lot sooner would get him nowhere.

Moses stopped to rest when he saw a place that offered respite from sun and wind. First, he inspected and re-secured his supplies on the ass. He pulled out his cache of food and a skin of water and then sat. In that instant nothing was more pleasing than the wetness of water and the salty tang of dried lamb. He felt like the most pampered ruler in Egypt.

He had been following the meanderings of a wadi for several hours now, so it didn't take him long to sniff out a likely site to dig down and replenish his water skins. Once he had eaten and refreshed himself he resumed his journey.

Before long his thoughts returned to The Ten Laws. Moses felt disturbed by how much he had taken for granted. It was too easy to see the value of a particular position or statement and never even think to see the other side of it.

He thought now about the law requiring people to honor father and mother. What might that look like from the other side? On the face of it, to honor one's parents made perfect sense. Parents bring their children into the world and care for them, supporting their growth to adulthood. What's not to honor? In the world according to Gershom, however, honor implied status, and status conferred power over others. However, Moses concluded, power over others soon results in a sense of ownership and entitlement.

A particular social structure naturally followed Gershom's approach. Obviously, Jehovah deserved the most honor, so Jehovah must have the most power. All creatures should tremble before "his" Holy Authority. Next came the Prophet, of course also male, who deserved to be honored and obeyed by everyone else. The heads of the twelve tribes and Gershom with his priests came next, and on down the line. At the bottom of this pyramid of power were the women and children. They were required to honor everyone who occupied a place above them. Furthermore, no one honored them. This assigned women and children the same status as the goats and donkeys. Moses felt sick to his stomach when he saw the implications of this hierarchy upon the women and the children.

He supposed he had missed noticing these disturbing implications for so long because they didn't stand out as much in the wilderness. A natural and necessary equality among all people worked best in the wilderness. All people were honored and valued because all people had to work together for the survival of the tribe. That beautiful mutual respect fell apart, however, when property and booty were on the line.

Is this what the Holy One had told him? He was reasonably sure that the notion of honoring parents was part of the message, but wasn't there more? The Holy presence was the fullness of relationship. Love and mutuality were the foundational qualities of all divine participation. Another of the laws said it more directly: love the Holy Lover, and love one another with the same Divine Love you yourselves have received. Every other law can be adequately understood only from the perspective of that most basic principle.

So Moses, he asked himself, how much have you honored this law of mutual love? His stomach turned in shame when he saw his own hypocrisy in service to any number of much more superficial and mundane pressures. Fear (including his own) had the uncanny knack of redefining love as cheap and dangerous sentimentality. Love always appeared to be so impractical. He now saw with heart-piercing clarity that every time he failed to base his life and decisions on love, someone else paid a burdensome price. Most often, those "someones" turned out to be the women and children. When he considered how those wonderful women and children of the wilderness would be crushed and virtually enslaved in the so-called Promised Land, his heart broke, releasing torrents of pain, sadness, and regret. He found he was weeping again.

What has happened to me? He thought. I've cried more in the last few weeks than I have in the whole rest of my life put together. Still, crying didn't feel bad. It actually felt surprisingly holy. But it wore him out. Well, he reasoned, perhaps I needed a nap anyway. Before long, he was snoring peacefully in the shade of a boulder.

Moses dreamed of salty seas whose waves washed over him without respite. In the midst of the dream he wondered if Pharaoh's charioteers had felt the same when the waters had flowed back over them, annihilating their entire company. Somehow he knew, though, that these were not seas of annihilation; they were seas of cleansing. He watched as if floating beside himself while a century of dirt and grime, guilt and shame, failure and superficial compromise loosened and washed away from his body to be reclaimed by the salty waters. Bit by bit his clothes tore away, cut to shreds by the penetrating currents. The last article of his clothing still clinging tenaciously to his body was a heavy mantle across his shoulders, and of course, he still held his old familiar staff. A sudden shift in the undercurrents twisted the staff out of his hand, and his stomach dropped as he watched it borne away by the water. He was bereft of his staff and now almost totally naked, but he was most terrified of losing his mantle. Without it he knew he would be more exposed than he had been even before the first blanket was wrapped around him at his birth. He knew this mantle more intimately than he knew his own name. It was even more essential than his staff. It was the mantle of holy responsibility: the mantle of the Prophet of God. His observing self in the dream was shocked to discover that

Moses had carried the identity of the Prophet since long before his encounter with the Holy One on the mountain.

The surging currents pulled at his mantle while Moses hung onto it with all the strength his desperation could muster. Letting go meant dying to every shred of identity he had ever known.

"So this is what it is to die," his observing self noted dispassionately.

Moses' strength was running out, but still he held on. From the corner of his eye he saw something spinning towards him. It was the staff. He reached out to reclaim it, but instead it rapped against his knuckles causing the last shred of the mantle to fly from his cramping fingers. It was over.

"Now what?" the Observer inquired as if giving voice to the distress of an audience grieving the loss of its protagonist.

"New life in the Community of Promise!" rang out the holy answer. Then Moses awoke from his dream and sat up blinking.

Chapter 22

Sarah and Asher sat in silence by the small fire near their tent. After all their years together going back to childhood, they were still one another's best friends. Asher couldn't keep his eyes off Sarah and she fairly glowed under his gaze. Her eyes were open but focused on some far away image, whether outside of herself or deep in her inner being was not obvious. They had spent a delightful afternoon together, walking and talking.

Asher had made a habit of telling Sarah how much he enjoyed watching her. The looks of excitement that played childhood games across her face always brought a smile to his. They had been talking about the morning's events. He couldn't stop himself from reflecting back to her his delight at watching her during the meeting. He had observed her nose crinkle up as she alternately felt joy at being recognized and awe at the weight of responsibility that was about to come onto her shoulders. She found comfort in how he tracked her emotions. He rode with her through the swell of delight and the shadows of her concern and even fear.

They shared a feeling of wonder at the miraculous gift from the Holy One that allowed them to observe and support one another through the joys and challenges of life. Sarah particularly appreciated how much he respected her.

They had both seen other men react in fear and recrimination when their women had emerged in their own right. When love turned to resentment in them, they ached along with those women in their suffering. How confusing it was that so many men could not even see, much less accept, what a Holy gift was exploding into full flower before their very eyes.

They were horrified at the recent change in a majority (Asher estimated) of men, who became even more grasping and demanding toward their women during the final approach to the Promised Land. How fortunate they were to find themselves in a group that moved in a radically different direction. It was still an open question, though, whether some of the men even in this company would become hurt and resentful when their women inevitably emerged into leadership roles. Well, time would tell.

Sarah came back from her deep musings.

He noticed the wrinkle in her brow. "What is it?" he asked.

"Asher, I need you to help me understand something."

"If I can."

"I was thinking about the request I put before the people this morning. You know, that they consult with the Holy One before affirming a leadership group."

"What about it?"

"Well, I know how I do it, but without really knowing how (or even if) other people do it, doesn't that make my request unfair somehow?"

Asher smiled. It was so typical of Sarah to think beyond her own experience. "I don't know. I guess that's possible."

"If I am going to be a part of the team, I think I need to know more about others. It has never occurred to me even to ask you how you connect with the Holy One. I assume you have your own way."

"I suppose I do. What do you want to know, exactly?"

"Well, did you respond to my request?" she asked.

"I did."

"So, what happened?" Sarah shifted on the skins, trying to get more comfortable, though the discomfort was really inside her.

"Let me think about it for a minute," he said, and then laughed out loud.

"What's so funny?" she snapped, almost ready to take offense.

"Relax, it's not about you. I just said I had to think about it. That's how I do it—in my mind. It's always running, you know. I suppose I can think for days about things that other people don't even notice.

Now he was uncomfortable, so he reached out for the water skin and took a drink. Then he stood, paced a bit, and finally began speaking. "I don't think I trust people very easily, except for you, of course. So, I try to figure out all the possibilities and eliminate as many risks as I can.

"To be honest, I even had problems trusting Moses. I've admired him from the first, but sometimes I wondered if he always knew what he was doing. Still, what choice was there but to follow the Prophet of God? All the divine wisdom came through him. Somehow, relying on Moses like that pushed me too far away from the Holy One. I just wanted to hear the divine directives for myself, not through other people who always have their own issues and interpretations."

"I think I feel some of that, too."

"What has surprised me recently is how much I seem to be trusting in our new group. The Holy One appears to be very—how shall I say it—available."

Sarah nodded and grunted her recognition.

"I loved it when you stood and named the divine movement in the group this morning. I kind of heard something." Asher looked like he was trying to recapture the moment and the voice. "I had no distrust at that moment and all I could seem to think was 'I AM with you.'"

Sarah's hand flew to her mouth. "You heard that, too?"

"I did. And somehow, I knew none in this group would have the right, the responsibility, or perhaps even the inclination to insist on a selfish path. And I think it helped that you let us know how much our own wisdom, experience, and connection with the Holy One would matter. I was really surprised, but I loved it. And if it's even possible, I loved you more than ever."

Sarah had the good grace to blush.

"You know that I've had 'experiences' since childhood, even if you haven't known the details. But we could never talk about them or share them with the community. I remember trying to tell my father about one. He just got angry. Now I understand that he was afraid, for good reason, I might add, and he was just trying to protect me. What I'm getting at is this:

our experiences of the Holy One are not challenges to the power of the religious leadership. They are divine gifts, given for our collective benefit."

"I think I've always believed that. But it's nice to be able to talk about it," she said.

"You took a chance, even with this extraordinary group. It's always harder to be specific about holy encounters than it is to affirm them in general, particularly for a woman. I think you took a bigger risk than even Eliezer did. And I admire you for it. You are a remarkable woman," he said with pride and awe.

"Asher, I appreciate your saying that, but don't get carried away. I'm just one person among many remarkable people."

"You're right," he said, even more to himself than to Sarah. "I just said that I had a hard time trusting others, even Moses, but I know I need to take the next step."

"What step is that?"

"It's not enough for me to admire you, though admire you I certainly do. I have to claim my own right, no, make that my responsibility, to contribute to the collective wisdom."

"Wow, I hope others think that way, too."

"But, that's where I'm stuck," he confessed.

"What do you mean?"

"I've been trying to do as you suggested ... to consult the Holy One and not leave all the responsibility to others (even to people as obviously competent as Kenan, Enosh, and your most wonderful self). Anyway, I haven't gotten very far. It seems that something is missing."

"Like what?"

"I'm not sure. I've always been able to have profound conversations with myself—almost like I was talking with another person. But I couldn't do it this time."

"Perhaps you could choose to invite someone else into your thoughts."

"Are you volunteering?" Asher asked with an odd smile.

"Are you inviting me?" Sarah met Asher's smile with one of her own.

"I guess we could try." He took a deep breath, looked around at the nearby tents, closed his eyes only to open them a moment later, wrinkled his forehead, opened his mouth as if to speak, but then, feeling foolish, closed it; then he examined the dirt under his fingernails, began counting the pebbles beneath his feet, and tried to release a kink in his neck.

Sarah waited patiently, but then after several minutes, "What is troubling you, Asher?"

"I'm not sure I know." Asher sighed again and then gave it another try. "When Eliezer first approached me about our coming here, he was vague about where this would lead, but I heard a note of hopeful promise in his invitation. You and I had just been talking about our misgivings regarding the move into the Promised Land. I—we were hopeful that some other outcome might be possible. While I could identify my discomfort with Joshua's plan, I haven't been able to imagine what any alternative could possibly look like. I think I know what I don't want, but I have no idea what I do want. Do you think that's strange? Is there something wrong with me?"

Sarah took a moment before responding to Asher's question. "Do you think you're supposed to know?"

Asher focused his attention inward. Finally he spoke again. "When I think of how Moses has been with us, it's always seemed to me that he had a long term plan—like he could see into the future. When I try to look ahead, all I see is dust and smoke. There seem to be two possible explanations: either my picture of a far-seeing Moses was pure fantasy, or else something fundamental has changed in the way the Holy One relates to us so that we can only see as far as the next decision." Then after a long pause, "I guess there is a third possibility."

"What's that?"

"Maybe it's me. Maybe others can see far, but I'm the short-sighted one." Asher looked painfully distressed.

Sarah took her time before she responded. "I understand your concern. But I'm pretty sure that no one knows where we're going or what it will look like when we get there. The danger of long-range visions is that they get in the way of the ongoing relationship with the Holy One. That's what was happening as we approached the Promised Land. The vision of a homeland and its military and political necessities may have obscured the possibility of a more current awareness of Holy Presence among us. Whatever we human beings harden into a 'divine plan' actually inhibits the holy relationship."

Asher pondered those last words, then responded, "You mean that I have been looking in the wrong place for the wrong thing?"

"It's possible."

"So rather than trying to discern where we are going, I might have more success in discerning where we are."

"Well, it's worth a try." Sarah reached out to put her hand on Asher's arm.

Asher smiled as he put his other hand over hers. "One thing I know for sure. Our Community of Promise cannot help but benefit from the leadership you are already bringing to them. If I've picked up nothing else from the Holy One, that much has come clear to me. The support I would give you anyway as your husband has been divinely ratified." Then after a pause, "One more thing—May I ask for your help again when I find myself in another woolly-headed state?"

Sarah just smiled.

Chapter 23

So much had happened in the last few days that Kenan hardly knew where he was. Along with Sarah and Enosh, he had been selected and confirmed as part of a temporary leadership team. They had started meeting right away, but at Sarah's encouragement their meetings included a new and surprising element: anyone could attend. At times they would solicit other perspectives and information from the attendees. They also saw right away that it would serve them well to delegate as many specific responsibilities as possible to others. Most of the time they were able to find willing designees right at hand from the gathered spectators.

It didn't take them long to discover what a diamond in the rough Enosh was turning out to be. He convinced them that Joshua and Gershom would have set spies in the surrounding area to ensure the proper behavior of the mourners. Based on his military experience, he predicted exactly where those spies were most likely to be deployed. Armed with that information, they easily rounded up the spies, and thankfully, the element of surprise prevented the shedding of even one drop of blood. Naturally, the spies were terrified, but their well-being and their release at the proper time were guaranteed.

Their first challenge was to figure our how to remove themselves from Mount Nebo undetected. And then they would still have to decide on their route back into the wilderness. Meanwhile, how were they going to find Moses? They began by consulting with Eliezer so he could fill them in on Moses' escape plan, including the roles that Nathanel and Zuriel played in the plot. Until that moment none of them, including Eliezer, had any direct knowledge about what had happened to Moses. Eliezer promptly told them about the plan to rendezvous with Moses at a predetermined location well to the east of Mount Nebo.

There was one problem, however and it involved Moses.

"A group of us met with Moses to plan his 'death' and subsequent escape..." Eliezer explained.

"So Father," Eliezer had asked, "How will we find you in this vast wilderness?"

"Go to the oasis next to the mountain where we shared our last encounter with the Holy One. I'll find you there."

All had agreed that this was a fine plan until Moses face had darkened, suffused with a strange and faraway look.

"What is it, Father?"

"Don't wait for me for more than ten days. If Gershom and Joshua discover what has happened, they will surely come in pursuit. You cannot allow them to catch up to you."

"But Father, we can't go on without you!"

Everyone present had expressed horror at the thought.

Moses only chuckled. "I'm touched by your loyalty, but calm down and think for a moment. It's much easier for one person to hide from Gershom and Joshua than for many to hide. Also, it will be easier for one of me to find many of you than for you to find me. And finally—something could go wrong. Remember, my life is much more expendable than all of yours."

There was dead quiet among them as each of them digested the import of Moses' words.

"Father, you've always been present in my visions. I expect to see you again."

"That's what I wish, too. But visions have a habit of being somewhat less than precise. So, we'd better be prepared to respond to any eventuality."

No one had been able to refute Moses' wisdom.

Kenan was relieved to learn how much good planning had already been done and to know that Moses was in good hands. As long as all had gone as planned (and it was unimaginable to think otherwise), Moses had by now been taken off the mountain and was safe (at least as safe as anyone could be) out in the wilderness.

Relieved that they still had time to decide their ultimate direction, they turned their attention to more current challenges. How do you move a hundred families down and off the mountain, and then travel across an open wilderness area to a specific oasis without raising suspicion? The removal of Joshua's spies helped immensely, but who could be sure that all of them had been found, and who could guarantee that a stray traveler wouldn't notice them and innocently reveal their location to the main body of the Israelites.

Once again, Enosh proved his value with his genius. He quickly orchestrated a simple but brilliant plan. Good soldiers and especially good commanders always paid careful attention to the surrounding landscape. The difference between survival and slaughter often depended solely on having an escape route. Enosh had noticed the terrain around the well-trodden path that the Israelites had followed to the banks of the Jordan. He knew that the easiest routes became the most traveled roads and he had noticed that the road was limned on both sides by relatively high ground. It was not so high as to be unreachable, but it was just difficult enough that practically no one ever used it. After the initial climb from the road to the high ground, however, it was relatively easy going. Some time ago, Enosh had climbed up to see for himself what possibilities presented themselves on the high ground. When he came to the crest, he discovered an ancient wadi that ran parallel to the road just on the other side and below the crest. He found a similar wadi when he explored the other side of the road.

Enosh proposed that the company break up into ten smaller groups. Each night two groups would depart from Mount Nebo and climb up into the wadi, one group on each side of the road. Each group would be small enough to minimize the chances of detection. They would travel only at night, hiding deep in the wadi by day. Fortunately, Eliezer had instructed each family to bring provisions sufficient for a thirty-day stay on Mount Nebo so there would be plenty of food and water.

Enosh calculated that these small, and therefore agile groups would be able to arrive at the rendezvous point after six nights of travel. The last two groups would leave four days after the first so the entire company would make the journey within ten days.

Enosh reasoned that after six days of travel away from the main body, the chances of travelers associating them with the Israelites were minimal. It would then be safe enough to travel together because they would look just like any other small nomadic tribe. Once they had reassembled and had collected Moses, then they could decide on their next steps. Kenan and Sarah had a few questions for Enosh to help them understand the plan in sufficient detail, but both found that placing their trust in this very capable man was delightfully easy.

Could it be that this grand scheme might actually work? With hopeful visions of their nascent community now nudging against the edges of their minds, each of them returned to their respective tents to rest and prepare for departure. The next few days promised to be full—to say the least.

Chapter 24

The transition from daylight to darkness dragged on interminably. Soon, Kenan and the last two of the ten groups could take leave from Mount Nebo. About twenty families had made the journey during each of the last four nights. Tonight they would make their way down the mountain, cross the open area where the much-traveled road lay, and then climb up into the high ground and the old wadis that paralleled the road on either side. Enosh had led the first group. Sarah and Asher had accompanied the fifth and sixth groups. And Kenan with his family would be moving this night along with the last two groups of The Community. The four days since the first group left had seemed unending. Kenan had faith in their purpose and he trusted Enosh's plan, but he knew he would rest easier once they had put more distance between themselves and the main body of the Israelites.

Finally it was dark enough for them to depart. Kenan took one last look around to see if they had left any incriminating evidence behind, and to fix in his memory this holy place where their lives had experienced such a remarkable transformation. Even though they were returning in the direction of the wilderness, Kenan felt like they were crossing a metaphorical Jordan River to enter their own Promised Land filled with hope and divine possibility.

They picked their way carefully down the mountain trail past the place where Moses had "disappeared." Nathanel and Zuriel had done a thorough job of obscuring the cave mouth, so none of them even noticed it as they passed. Many of the members of the party, however, stopped momentarily, their shoulders hunched in prayer while their eyes briefly scanned the skies, half expecting to catch a glimpse of Moses. By now, most of them had heard about Moses' escape, but they couldn't quite shake the image of the Prophet being taken up into the clouds to reside with the Holy One.

After a couple of hours, they found themselves at the bottom of the mountain, near where the Prophet had given his final address to the people. Soon, they reached the road. Travelers were not generally on the road at this hour, but they still needed to be careful. They did not want to stumble into the camp of any other travelers. Kenan stretched out his senses, alert for the dimmest glow of a fire, the slightest whiff of smoke, or any discernible human or animal sound. Just as they were crossing the road, Kenan smelled something burning. He ordered the party to stop even though they stood in an exposed location. If he was going to keep his charges safe he had to locate that fire. He lifted his face, trying to sense any movement of night air on his cheeks. Finally, there it was! A faint breeze was blowing from his left. The camp had to be in that direction. He dispersed the party into the shadow of some nearby rocks while he crept up a low rise in the direction of the smoky smell. As he neared the crest, he began crawling on his belly, all the while listening carefully for any sounds of life. He thought he saw the glow of a fire a distance away. That was good news. Now that he knew where they were, he could take his band by a route that would avoid contact.

He was just standing up when he found himself face-to-face with a man brandishing a sword. "Would you be spying?" He lifted the sword to point at Kenan's belly.

"No, of course not!" Then he considered what his presence must look like, so he decided to modify his response. "Well, to be honest my friend, in a way I was. Would you allow me to explain?" Kenan sent a prayer to the Holy One as he waited for an answer. The sword-wielding man thought about it, then nodded. "I'm traveling with my extended family. We're camped not far away. I was awakened by the smell of your fire and didn't know if it spelled danger for us, so I came to investigate. I was prepared to move them to a farther-away location if need be. I'm not armed, and I don't want any trouble."

"Hold out your arms to the side." Kenan did as he was told. "Even in this light, I can see that you are poor and not worth robbing, even if that were my wish, though it is not. And, by the way, if you are lying to me and you actually are a thief, be assured that we are well guarded and well armed. Take your family and depart. If we find you here by first light, I cannot guarantee your safety."

Kenan realized that he had stopped breathing. "It will be as you say. I'm grateful for your forbearance."

He backed away and then ran to join the others.

"What took you so long?"

"Well, it was good that I checked. We could easily have stumbled into the camp of an armed band. Then, I was accosted by the sword of one of them, but I presume he was reluctant to awaken his band. For some unknown reason he wasn't impressed with my size or wealth. As you can see, he released me, but we have to leave right away."

Kenan led them around the armed camp, and before the first hint of dawn, they had climbed safely to the high ground and into the protection of the wadi. When they had gone a short distance, they reached a stretch that had a high eastern bank. After spreading their cloaks on the dry wadi bed, they huddled in the shade and slept.

For each of the next several days, they spent afternoon and evening hours eating, conversing, and quietly contemplating their new direction in life. They traveled only in darkness and slept wherever they could find shade in the morning and early afternoon hours. They restricted their diet to the dried food each of them carried so they would not signal their presence with smoke from cooking fires. Each day melted seamlessly into the next until the wadi that served as their highway spilled them back into the embrace of the larger group. Their fledgling community was whole once more.

Chapter 25

From his carefully chosen location in the hills above the rendezvous point, Moses watched as The Community of Promise grew to its full size. He had wondered what had gone wrong when only about twenty families had shown up. The temptation to rush down into their midst to hear news of the apparent disaster was great, but he was not yet ready to lose his solitude. His anxiety abated some when a second group appeared one day later. By the time the third group arrived, Moses had figured out their plan and was pleased and perhaps even proud at their ingenuity.

Still, he remained in hiding, watching with interest now that all of the groups had arrived. Very soon he would join them, he told himself. He just needed a few more days to be alone. This was a much smaller group awaiting him than the nation he had escaped from, but still he was wary of the potential for any new demands being put on him.

Though the Prophet's Mantle had been torn away in his dream, he still could feel his shoulders sag under its imaginary weight. He feared that in spite of their new relationship, it would only take one small crisis to tempt him (with their complicit encouragement) to resume his leadership role. He was enjoying his retirement, but he would have to join them soon. Maybe tomorrow he'd be ready to receive their welcoming embraces… but not today.

Slowly and carefully he moved away from his hidden observation point and returned to the cave where he kept his belongings and where he could rest in safety. He looked forward to a meal of dried meat and fresh water, and then a good night's sleep.

The quality of his sleep had changed so much in the last few days. While he still dreamed vividly every night, he was sleeping more soundly than any other time in his whole life. He awoke rested after each untroubled night. Mornings for Moses still began with a feeling of confusion before it dawned on him that no Israelite troubles awaited his awakening. There were no command decisions to make and there was a delightful absence of occasions requiring mediation between the people and the Holy One.

He no longer felt any compulsion to go to the Holy One. There was no Ark of the Covenant, no tent, no priests, and no rituals—only a quiet and reliable Holy Presence... and so much time to think. It was wonderful. With few tangible supplies to encumber him, he thought himself blessedly fortunate. Moses had confessed to himself that, at least in part, he yearned to keep it that way.

Maybe he could make just a brief appearance with the small band that awaited him. He would let them know that he had survived the journey, but had decided to go his own way wanting to die in peace at the right time in his beloved wilderness. "Why couldn't I just do that?" he asked aloud. But all he heard in answer was the echo of his own voice as it bounced off the walls of the cave.

"I could! I could!" But, why did that internal declaration sound so hollow? Then he remembered. The Holy One apparently expected him to take his place as an equal participant in The Community of Promise. "Well, that takes care of that." Moses scowled. "I'll join them tomorrow. Although, I must say, I'm much less content with the idea than I thought I would be." Though he seemed to have made the decision, his mind continued to replay the arguments on both sides as he fell, this time, into a disturbed sleep.

No matter how deep and restful his sleep nor how vivid and compelling his dreams, Moses was still a creature of the wilderness. He had long ago developed the habit of leaving a small part of his mind on semi-conscious sentry duty. Thus at some level of perpetual awareness he heard the footsteps. His olfactory glands registered the strange fishy odor, his hand found and grasped his staff and his awakening mind figured out that someone was speaking near by. The dialect was unusual, but Moses was able to understand well enough. There were at least two of them. They seemed to be wondering aloud about his cave.

"There's someone in there, I tell you."

"Maybe it's just an animal."

"I think we should look."

Moses lay deathly still in his corner of the cave. It was possible that they might overlook him. But he had forgotten about the pile of gear he had left just inside the cave opening.

"I don't know any animals that are supplied like this."

"There he is… over in the corner."

The next thing Moses knew, drawn swords hung in the air before him. One of the men growled, "So, who are you?"

Encouraged by the proximity of the sharp swords, Moses figured that his imitation of death might just hasten it, so he chose to release his grip on the staff and to reply. "Just a traveler taking his rest."

"You're kind of old to be wandering out here by yourself without protection. You're liable to run into trouble. In fact, it looks like you have!" The man laughed loudly at his own joke. Moses just looked at him.

"Get up old man and move out here into the light so we can get a good look at you." The second man waggled his sword at Moses

Moses rose up slowly and carefully, in part due to his advanced age, but mostly in response to the swords that remained perilously close to his chest. Followed by the men, he shuffled out into the early morning light. All Moses could think of was the proximity of The Community's camp. It would be devastating if they were discovered, so Moses started to plan a way to send these men in the other direction. The main body of their tribe (or whatever they were) could not be too far away. He would use every resource at his disposal, even his own life if it came to that, to protect his people from harm. These two were emboldened by their swords, but they had no authority. Moses was secure in the knowledge that authority could neutralize swords every time. And if he possessed nothing else, he had authority, and to spare.

"So, who are you to disturb an old man's rest? Do your superiors know how foolishly you conduct yourselves?"

The sword tips wavered as Moses' commanding voice assailed their courage. One of them, noticing the sword in his hand, poked it at Moses and squeaked, "This sword is all the authority I need. Remember, you have no sword at all." He put on his bravest face and looked to his partner for support.

"Oh, put those things away before you hurt yourselves." Moses quickly reached out and pushed the two blades away. The men jumped back as if they had stepped on live coals.

Moses decided to try to keep the men off balance. "You have three choices, as I see it. You can let me go. No one will ever know you had so clumsily stumbled into my rest." Moses paused, calculating that he had to stay with them so he could impel them away from The Community. "Of course, you have no idea what I will do with my freedom.

"Your second choice is to kill me, if you even have the nerve, but sooner or later news of my death will come to your superiors. I am certain that they will know whom you have killed even if you don't. I guarantee you that they will not be pleased with your actions.

"So, your only viable choice is to escort me to your superiors and receive their accolades for my capture." Without waiting for their slow minds to comprehend his true reasoning, Moses decided for them. "Well, what are we waiting for?" Moses began walking south, away from The Community's encampment. I can always catch up with them later, he mused to himself. I am sorry for their inevitable worry about me, but there is no other choice.

Before they had gone very far, one of the men moved ahead of Moses to lead them. He had finally figured out that Moses, though he was striding purposefully, did not know where they were going. Moses could see that the man in front of him had put away his sword and he suspected that the same fate had befallen the sword behind him as well.

About two hours later, as they came around a ridge line, a sprawling camp lay before them. At first, Moses thought this was their army, so he immediately considered the peril to his kinsmen. Then, as they drew nearer to the camp and he could see more clearly, his fear turned to horror. This was no army. It was a slave encampment. They were probably rounding up slaves to row the boats on the Red Sea. His stomach turned over as he thought about the Israelite slaves he had led out of Egypt. It would be a terribly crushing irony if their brave journey for more than four decades were to return even this small sample of Israelites to slavery. It was unthinkable. Well, he would have to be very careful to ensure that no such thing would happen. He would do all in his power to protect them from discovery or capture.

Moses knew that The Community would not break camp for at least ten days, but when they did, it was likely that they would march directly into the grip of these slavers. He would have to make sure that the slave camp had moved away long before the Israelites arrived.

Moses had seen much in his accumulation of years. He had seen life from the top and from the bottom. He was inured to most of its horrors, but he had never been able to abide slavery. Even from his position of high favor in Pharaoh's court, he had been troubled by slavery: all those people who no longer had lives that they could call their own. So when he walked through the slave camp, Moses couldn't take his eyes off the scores of men, women, and even children who huddled there together in fear and disbelief. Moses wanted to stop and talk with each one. He wanted to know where they had come from and where they were going. He wanted to hear about their dreams and their gods.

He hadn't really thought about it before, but his loathing of slavery had helped motivate his decision to return to Egypt on behalf of the enslaved Israelites. He had never been a slave himself, but he realized with cold dread, how easily that could change, and very soon at that. He decided he wouldn't think about that unpleasant possibility right now. Saving his friends was the only matter of significance. Whatever happened to him would happen.

Chapter 26

Massoud had a headache. The commander's day had begun badly and had worsened by the hour. He had not even begun to break his fast when word came that a group of his new slaves had escaped. Of course, his men would recapture them, but some slaves and perhaps a few of his men would surely die in the process. Then he would be forced to make an example of the escapees in front of the rest. More would have to die to show the others the futility of escape; it would be a messy business at best. He knew he was embroiled in a cruel profession, but he was not by nature a cruel man. Practicality sometimes demanded death, though he took no pleasure in it.

While they had captured many new slaves, they were nowhere near reaching the quota the Sea Prince had set for them. And time was running short. If that wasn't enough to upset his day, one of the raiding parties had returned prematurely with too few new slaves, because an old man had convinced them that he was someone of importance. What were they thinking? Slaves are slaves, he thought, as he slammed his fist down on the table before him.

Well, he would know their reasons soon enough as they were even now bringing this ancient to him. None of the food that sat before him appealed, so he simply finished his watered wine hoping for some internal fortification.

Moses strode toward the commander's tent looking not at all like a captive. His steps were remarkably long and strong given his age, and the way his robes swirled around him contributed to his air of authority. Several of his "captors" followed in his wake, having to exert themselves to keep up with this vigorous old man.

The two men who had found him in the cave had delivered him to the captain of their raiding party. As soon as they had arrived Moses had handily nullified the captain's predictable orders to confine him. Before anyone even realized what had happened, Moses had convinced the captain that the only reasonable course of action was to bring him to his commander. Even though the raiding party was nowhere near filling its quota of new slaves, they found themselves packing up and returning to the base camp, not quite knowing why they had decided to do so, but not able to imagine having chosen any other alternative.

As soon as Moses strode into the tent, the force of his presence caused Massoud to jump to his feet as if the Sea Prince himself had entered without prior notice. To reestablish his authority, Massoud spoke first without looking at the captive. "Who is this old man who interrupts my breakfast?"

"Two of our party found him hiding in a cave and felt compelled to bring him to me," the captain reported.

"Why, then, was this man not secured with the others while you completed your quota?" Massoud growled.

The Captain was obviously embarrassed and it showed in the timidity with which he answered. "With all due respect, sir, this is no ordinary captive. I feared risking your greater displeasure if I did not bring him to you immediately. Perhaps you will understand when you question him yourself."

This was not the answer that Massoud wanted to hear, but he decided to ignore the captain. He turned and looked over his venerable captive. Moses met the commander's gaze and held it.

"What is your name, old man?"

"Moses. And may I also know who asks?"

The commander blanched at Moses' effrontery, but answered in spite of himself. "I am Massoud, commander of this encampment." Again, attempting to maintain his tenuous hold on his authority, he went on. "So tell me, Moses, what brought you to be in that cave where my men captured you?"

As he spoke, he leaned on the word "captured" to remind Moses of his lack of status in this inquisition.

Moses seemed not to notice. "Does my name, then, mean nothing to you?" He added Massoud's title of "Commander" with such a note of disdain that he could just as easily have been referring to the dust under his feet.

The Commander flinched at the insult, but chose to ignore it for the moment. "I have heard of one by that name who wandered, apparently aimlessly, in the wilderness for countless years. My spies report that his horde of followers has removed themselves far to the north, so what could they have to do with an old man like you?" Moses said nothing. "Now, answer my question, how did you come to be in that cave?"

Moses smiled. "I have, shall we call it, resigned my commission and retired. I have been surviving alone in the wilderness for the last several weeks. I was just napping when your goons so rudely interrupted my sleep."

Massoud was intrigued. "Do you mean to say you've lead your people for years and they just let you wander off alone? I think there must be more to this story, Moses."

"Now I understand why they have made you a commander. You are quite right. There is more." Massoud waited, but looked interested. "I had to die first!"

At this, Massoud jumped back as if Moses had thrown poisonous snakes at his feet. Involuntarily his mouth invoked the protection of his gods while his hands surreptitiously made the signs to ward off evil. "Take him to the stockade and triple the guard. If he escapes, every last one of you will pay with your lives!"

Just before they led him out through the tent flap, Moses caught Massoud's eye, smiled an enigmatic smile and bowed imperceptibly toward the commander who, as soon as they had left, promptly collapsed onto his sleeping skins.

"What was that?" Massoud asked out loud to the now empty tent. "And, more than that, what am I to do with it?" He hunched over and buried his head in his hands. All he could do was rub his temples in response to his worsening headache.

He forced himself to think around the pain. What should he do? He couldn't kill a man who had already died. He really couldn't spare the men necessary to guard Moses properly.

And he dreaded the thought of returning to the Sea Prince with fewer than his quota of new slaves. He was faced with two impossible choices. He even contemplated deserting his post, though he concluded immediately that he could never do that. "Only two options remained then: suicide now or death by order of the Sea Prince. What a choice?" He felt as if he held a desert lion by the tail. He had captured the lion; he just could never let it go.

Massoud rummaged for a skin of unwatered wine in his stores and shook as the pungent liquid burned his throat. "No, this won't do either!" And he threw the skin across the room to smack against the side of the tent. He stood there and stared at the runnels of amber liquid sliding down the wall.

After a few moments, when the commander in him finally regained control, he summoned his aide. "Send messengers to all the absent raiding parties that we depart for the coast in two days. Then mobilize the camp for travel. Anyone not ready in time will be left as food for the desert beasts. But first, summon the healer to me. My head feels ready to fall off."

Meanwhile word of Moses, the walking dead man, saturated the camp like water through dry sand. Many came to stand guard around him and all exuded a potent combination of curiosity and fear. Moses found that all he had to do was scratch his chin and all of them would flinch in concert. Inside, he was delighted. He felt confident about Massoud's likely response and he couldn't have been more pleased with it.

Chapter 27

"So, where is he?" Kenan inquired, looking around the tent. "Where is Moses?" Sarah and her husband, Asher, Eliezer with Milcah, and Enosh all looked sourly at Kenan. Eliezer looked from face to depressed face. "There's been no sign of him. We've scouted the area as much as we dare, but to no avail."

"What about Nathanel and Zuriel, have they been able to shed any light on Moses' disappearance?"

"They arrived here two days ago. It appears that Moses snuck away from their company one night and went off on his own. They tried to follow him, but that wily old fox had covered his tracks too well. Apparently, Moses had given them the impression that he could take care of himself just fine. They think he intends to join the group at some point, but they can't be certain."

Kenan looked as perplexed as the rest. "So what do we do now? How long do we wait?"

Enosh replied, "Moses knew it wouldn't be safe for us to remain here very long. I think we should depart immediately."

Sarah, who had been listening intently, added, "I have been circulating among the people. Virtually all of them now believe that Moses is alive and will join us soon. If we leave without Moses, they may resist, perhaps strongly."

"Didn't they empower us to lead them?" Enosh rejoined.

"Well, yes, but only to a point. I think this is too significant a decision for us to make on their behalf. We can recommend and present our reasons, but I think the final decision will have to belong to the people."

Enosh opened his mouth to argue, but then closed it again. Each of them pondered Sarah's words in silence. They had all grown to respect her profoundly. Finally, after a long silence, Milcah spoke. "You three, Sarah, Kenan, and Enosh are going to have to determine how to handle such an important decision, but I want you to know that I support Sarah's perspective. We are, among other things, learning how we will exist together, how we will decide, and how we will act—as a whole people. Leadership, as vital as it is, should never disrespect the integrity of the people. I have great hope that the quality of their response will mirror your capable leadership."

Sarah and Kenan nodded their assent, but Enosh looked disturbed so the rest braced themselves for his next argumentative outburst. When Enosh had sufficiently clarified his thoughts and formulated his words, he spoke. To their surprise, rather than having to endure a tirade, they heard quiet words of conviction, passion, and yes, even of humility. "I've been a soldier for all my days. In the army, orders are given and must be followed through discipline and obedience. This is how armies work. Recently, I have been learning that there may be other ways—even better ways—to function. Perhaps there are times when my military experience can be useful, but maybe that will be more the exception than the rule." And then, turning to Sarah, he said, "Sarah, I defer to your wisdom."

They sat in silence for a time while they took in the significance of their passionate General's words. Then Eliezer addressed them, speaking mostly to Enosh. "Over the years as a result of my dreams and other forms of contact with the Holy One, I've come to believe that a community of faithful people can embody the depth, power, and diversity of the divine. In such a community, disagreements, opposing perspectives, and variations in style may function more as strengths than weaknesses. The vision of community I carry welcomes a level of conflict that would be considered insubordinate in the army. I'm sure it'll take some time for us to learn this new way of being."

Then Asher chimed in, "Deference to authority isn't limited to the army. We've all looked to Moses to command us in keeping with Jehovah's wishes and we've been surrounded by priests who were empowered to enforce our compliance with those wishes. I tremble in old fear even now as I express my opinions in the company of this small group. I welcome the day when I can relax and be myself without fear of censure, reprisal, or even death."

Each of them could hear and feel the wisdom in Asher's words and they all could identify with his feelings.

Suddenly, Kenan disturbed their meditative atmosphere. "We don't have any priests! Who will instruct the people and judge whether their behavior is acceptable to the Holy One? Who will perform the rituals? I admit to you that I've often chafed under the heavy-handed authority of the priests, but now I wonder, don't we need them?"

Eliezer responded, "These are important questions. We'll need to address them over time. But let me tell you why we have no priests. It was purely a practical decision. It wasn't about religion or authority. The truth is, I didn't dare recruit anyone who would have felt obligated to bring this group to Gershom's attention. Naturally, this whole venture is highly risky, but recruiting priests was much too dangerous." Then Eliezer smiled. "We did take some risks however. And you, Enosh, were among the riskiest."

Enosh was about to take offense when he looked around at the smiling faces and understood the joke. His face split into a wide grin as he bowed in mock solemnity to each of them.

Sarah picked up Eliezer's theme. "Not one of us would be here if we hadn't had some personal experience with divine guidance. This whole venture is a collective response to a new revelation that we hope to embody in a totally original way. I don't know if it's even possible for priests to exist in such a community without destroying the revelations of the many for the sake of the powerful few. As long as we support the right and responsibility of every person to communicate with the Holy One, I believe our community will be able to decide if and when it needs priests."

"There'll be plenty of time and opportunity for us to address and respond to these questions," noted Kenan. "But, we have a more pressing concern."

"You're right, Kenan," Sarah added. "How will we discern the community's will regarding Moses, regarding departure, and regarding the direction we will go next?"

Once they got over their collective experience of being stunned, (they still were not used to being so respectfully consulted) the gathered community readily embraced the wisdom of an early departure. Eliezer had shared with them Moses' assessment that one person, particularly one familiar with the wilderness, could track down a relatively large group with ease. They really had no choice but to trust in Moses, though many still feared for his safety.

One among their company recounted a vivid dream she had been having for the last several nights. In her dream, the company was traveling with the sea to their right side. Following her detailed description of the scene, several others remembered similar images from their own dreams. In this way, they chose to travel to the Red Sea and follow its east bank as they made their way to the south. Without what they interpreted as a clear sign, they never would have dared enter such totally unknown territory.

They waited three more days to see if Moses would appear, then reluctantly they packed up their families and provisions and took their boldest steps yet toward an unknown, but promising future.

For the next several days, The Community and the slavers moved along parallel tracks with less than a day's journey separating them. At the tip of the easternmost horn of the Red Sea the slavers followed the western shoreline while the smaller group of seekers hugged the eastern one.

Whenever he had the opportunity, Moses' eyes scoured the horizon, hoping beyond hope not to see signs of his beloved Israelite remnant. A few miles away the Israelites travelers, also hoping beyond hope, looked longingly for Moses to appear.

Chapter 28

Captivity itself didn't bother Moses too much, but the level of noise and the intrusive attention of his many guards were most annoying. Internally, Moses found no peaceful respite either. He worried terribly about the well-being of his new family. All his arguments to himself about their competence and their obvious connection to the Holy One could not quiet his growing dread that something bad would happen to them.

Guilt and remorse crushed him. Why had he been so selfish? If only he had come out of his hiding place a day sooner. Underneath those obvious feelings lay a profound sense of loss and deep sadness. He had only met a few of the remnant tribe, and he had known those only briefly, but he still felt like he had lost everything that had ever mattered. At the center of his remembrance floated the face of his son. Moses and Eliezer had forged a powerful bond when they had gone out to seek communion and guidance from the Holy One. Eliezer was such a fine man. Moses regretted deeply that his busy life as Prophet to the people had left so little room even to come to know his own son. It was such a waste.

When he was by himself in the wilderness, he seldom felt lonely, but now surrounded by so many people, his loneliness was palpable. Even beneath his heavy sadness, Moses knew he felt more. He was angry and he felt betrayed. Why had the Holy One shown him such a hopeful vision and then separated him from its fulfillment? Moses didn't deny his capacity for self-delusion. He had misunderstood the leadings of the Holy One many times before. But this time his path had seemed so clear. He was certain that his decision to leave Nathanel and Zuriel was in response to Divine leading. How could the Holy One be so cruel: to entice him toward real community and then slam the metaphorical tent flap in his face? Step after painful step Moses alternately grieved, raged, questioned, and hoped. Confusion became his only consistent companion.

At the end of the day's march, the slavers made camp. Most of the slaves and their captors slept on the ground, but widespread fear put Moses in a tent for the night. Though guards surrounded his tent, Moses experienced a welcome solitude inside. He found himself locked in prayer. His guilt, grief, and confusion served to deplete him, but his anger forged an uneasy bond between Moses and the spirit of the Holy One. Though exhausted, Moses stood in the middle of the tent with his face toward the ceiling and his arms cast out to either side. By closing his eyes, he could imagine himself standing alone in the vastness of the wilderness. He could almost feel the hot desert air moving across his face. Great salty tears flowed from his eyes, leaving muddy streaks in his dusty cheeks. He wept silently for a long time and eventually he came out from behind the wall of his anger, climbed up out of the valley of his grief, passed through the scrabbly hills of guilt and remorse, and emerged through the mists of his confusion.

Bereft of his defenses, he stood naked and unguarded before the Holy Presence. Moses noted a random anxious thought that his nakedness would offend the Holy One, but then recognized it as the residue of Gershom's fear-based religion. Without fanfare or struggle the thought dissolved.

To any observer, Moses would have resembled a madman as he attempted with utter futility to form his thoughts and feelings into words. He wept, rocked, and spun around, sat down, only to jump up again. His arms waved and his hands clenched while his mouth worked furiously in useless attempts to speak. But all he could do was groan.

Far above him, the lights in the heavens danced inexorably toward the dawn. One last time he sat and this time could find no strength to rise again. Only infinite darkness remained.

Someone was shouting and Moses felt a sharp pain as a stick poked him in the ribs. The tent had been removed from the spot where Moses lay, his nostrils filling with dust from the dry ground. "Up old man! Get up. No, you're not dead yet," Massoud yelled as one of the guards poked at Moses with the scabbard of his sword. Not by temperament or nature a superstitious man, the commander apparently had mastered his earlier fright. Watching Moses from a distance had convinced him that this strange old man was no member of the walking dead. No, he was very much alive. Massoud still had many questions about Moses, but he now felt confident about his decision to bring him to the Sea Prince.

"Give him some food and water." And then to Moses, "We have a long way to go today. You will need all your strength. Perhaps later you will choose to tell me who you really are."

Moses looked at Massoud blankly as if some other voice commanded his attention instead.

As soon as he had consumed a few strips of dried meat and a skin of goat's milk, Moses was ordered to his feet and the day's march began. While able to put one foot in front of the other, Moses moved as if in a trance. He looked neither right nor left, but kept his eyes focused on some impossibly distant image. To Moses, there was nothing to be seen at all. His ears, however, were on fire. "Moses, you are a slave. Moses, you are a slave," reverberated all around and through his being. The words sang like a bad song with only one verse: no refrain and no ending. Over and over the words assaulted him until a very personal image began to form before his mind's eye.

Night after night during the years of wandering in the wilderness, the people had recounted stories of their ancestors. While he walked, Moses pictured a gathering of Israelites who were listening to a storyteller. They heard the marvelous account of how Joseph came to Egypt, then later invited Jacob, his father, and all of his kin to settle in the land of Goshen. The storyteller spoke with obvious pride about how they had flourished in this new land. The famine that had brought them there in the first place was still crippling the known world, but Joseph's foresight as one of the most powerful men in Egypt had amassed a prodigious store of grain. While he let Egyptians go hungry, Joseph insisted that his own family be fed. And thus they prospered under his care.

The picture in Moses' mind transformed from the storyteller to the story. Impossibly, Moses saw himself among the Hebrews (as the Egyptians called them). He could taste the food and the image was so vivid that he felt his stomach distend, so full did it become. Moses observed as Joseph turned the Egyptians into slaves of Pharaoh by making them pay for the food of their survival with their riches and their lands. Everything that he gained he turned over to Pharaoh. Moses watched in some horror as, one by one, Egyptian families lost their hopes, their dreams, their dignity, and their civic pride. Meanwhile, the family of Israel grew strong, rich, prosperous, and numerous. He could feel the resentment grow as it was planted in the hearts and minds of Pharaoh's Egyptian slaves.[13]

In the generations since Abraham, experiences of contact with the Divine were usually acknowledged in tangible ways—most often by the construction of stone shrines. Abraham had come to know a new God, one who exuded power but who did not require human sacrifices like some other gods did—sometimes even of children—for propitiation. Relationships of trust developed as this new god took the initiative to provide the necessary elements for faithful relationships and a thriving community life. Moses saw how, from the beginning, men—yes, men—were tempted by power and wealth. What they received by means of divine love they hoarded and fought over, because they were not able to imagine a God of sufficient abundance to care for them. Jealousy, envy, and fear brought out the worst in them. Those who remembered the Holy One at all responded with fear rather than love and it was always more tempting to manipulate than trust. What those Israelites in Goshen trusted in the most was their prosperity and their power. And so they became slaves to it in spirit, long before any Pharaoh would make them slaves in body.

Moses was horrified to see himself in the midst of them. He was worshiping power and authority and he was exhibiting as much fear of being without it as any of them. He knew, in that moment, that he was truly a slave. It had never before occurred to him that his abhorrence of slavery was actually a deep reaction to his own internal enslavement.

His vision shifted abruptly to that critical time with the Israelites in the wilderness when he first understood why the present generation would never have the capacity to experience true freedom and when he concluded that the present generation had to die in the wilderness before their children could enter the Promised Land.

Moses had never denied that he belonged to that generation of slaves, but now he recognized that his own exodus from bondage was not yet complete. At the first sign of crisis he had automatically resorted to his old friend, authority, and now he saw where it had gotten him: into this state of physical slavery. He thought he had been transformed sufficiently when he dreamed of losing the Prophet's Mantle, but obviously he had been mistaken. There had been more to lose. He shuddered at the possibility that his losses were not yet complete. In his entire life he had never felt so hopeless.

They were no longer moving. Guards were scurrying about making camp. Once again they erected a tent for him. Before they had a chance to throw him inside, however, Massoud appeared.

"Old man, tomorrow we come before the Sea Prince. Then we will see what to do with you. I suggest you get some rest."

Moses didn't need to be told twice. He immediately moved into the tent, where he lay down in a corner, wept quietly, and fell into a deep and dreamless sleep.

Chapter 29

Day after day and week after week The Community of Promise journeyed southward. At a size of not more than four hundred, counting men, women, and children, they were vulnerable to any larger tribes or marauding armies they might encounter. Enosh had recruited a group of scouts to be deployed before and behind their main body. Whenever word came of other perhaps larger and stronger tribes or armies approaching, they would melt into the shelter of higher ground to the east and wait until the danger passed. This simple tactic allowed them to travel in relative safety. Each night as they gathered to eat before sleeping, the conversation most often touched on the wonders of the Sea. They, of course, had seen the Sea before. Wandering in the wilderness of the Sinai for all those years, they had occasionally come to the shores of one or the other of the "Horns" of the Red Sea. As impressed as they had been by the vast expanse of water before them, none could have imagined how vast it really was. Now, traveling along its eastern shore, they wondered if it had any limit at all. Whenever the road brought them near enough to it, they would peer across, straining to see if they could discern a western shore, but none was ever visible.

In addition to marveling at the vastness of the Sea, they couldn't help but speculate about their final destination. Some of them wondered if they would continue to exist as a nomadic tribe, surviving as they had in the wilderness by traveling from oasis to oasis—always on the move, never able to call one place home. As nomads now, each time they set up camp, they would eye their surroundings wondering if home might look something like this. But they knew in their hearts that their journey was not yet ready to come to an end. For some, this was simply a fact to be endured, if not understood. For others, the length of the journey and the inhospitable nature of the surroundings opened opportunities for doubt and fear to grow. Bit by bit conversation sprang up around their questions. Were they lost? Were they foolish? Was it a mistake to join this breakaway community? Should they have followed Joshua across the Jordan instead?

Sarah, Enosh, and Kenan were troubled by the growing level of unrest in the group. One of their first activities had been to set up a communications network so that everyone would have ready access to their thinking and decisions, and so the three of them could remain current with the mood and concerns of all their compatriots. Still, discontent was bubbling beneath the surface and rumors filled with inaccuracies were starting to propagate.

"What's this all about?" Kenan began. "You'd think we were behaving like slave masters."

"How do they twist things around so? I thought they trusted us. You know, until now I found it easy to trust them, too." Sarah added.

She and Kenan couldn't have been more surprised when Enosh started chuckling.

With her forehead turning red, she turned on him. "I don't see any humor in this; we have a serious problem here!"

"Sarah, Sarah, relax. I'm not the enemy and I have no intention of belittling you or the seriousness of the situation."

"So," interrupted Kenan. "Don't leave us wandering in the wilderness. Where's the oasis?"

"Well, first of all, what's happening is no surprise. I'm sure that if Moses were here, he would recognize the pattern right away. Apparently it happens in all organized groups. I learned of it when I became an officer in the army. One of the perversities, if I can call it that, of human beings is expressed by means of a kind of dilemma. Most people in a group prefer to cede the responsibility for significant decisions to someone else. When we were empowered to act as a leadership team, did you hear even one other person clamoring for the job?

Kenan and Sarah shrugged in response.

"The perversity comes out when they begin to question the very decisions they have empowered us to make. While they say they trust their leaders, and honestly believe their trust to be well placed, they just can't sustain it. Believe me when I tell you, this is nothing personal. They are not accusing us of being untrustworthy. It's just that real trust can only come from an accumulation of experience. It's much harder than you would think for people simply to decide to trust. So, what do you think? Are you following me so far?"

Sarah and Kenan still looked confused so Enosh went on. "Let me give you an example from my own experience. When I was still relatively new to the army, I was put in charge of a group of soldiers. I had been taught very well by my uncle who, in his day, had earned the respect and trust both of the soldiers he commanded and of his superiors. My young squadron knew of his reputation and knew that he had been my primary teacher. From the first day, they bragged about their good fortune at having me as their leader.

"As soon as we marched out toward our first battle, all the accolades, pride, and trust seemed to evaporate. I could tell that they resisted every order I gave them and whenever I would catch them whispering to each other, they would cease immediately as if nothing were amiss. Of course I took it very personally. I was hurt and angry, and frankly, I began to entertain doubts about my ability to lead them. I had just about decided to offer my resignation to my commander when we engaged the enemy. I no longer had the luxury of idle speculation. It was time for action.

"In the midst of the battle, my squadron was nearly surrounded by the enemy and I know many of us were expecting to die. But my uncle had taught me always to observe the landscape and I remembered an outcropping of rocks nearby that might provide some shelter and perhaps help us regain the advantage. I brought my troops to a weak place in the enemy line where we broke through and then ran for cover. The enemy, thinking we were routed and retreating, gave pursuit. As soon as we reached the rocks, I gave the command for them to turn and attack. We prevailed with no loss of life. Fortunately, in spite of their doubts, when their lives were on the line, they chose to follow me. After that, the grumbling and doubts diminished greatly, but not completely, of course. At least now they could hold on to a tangible experience that gave them some real evidence of my leadership. That actual event helped them learn to trust me."

Sarah sighed deeply and then smiled warmly at Enosh. "And you continue to give us tangible reasons to trust you as well. I can see that we don't have to take this grumbling personally, but we still have to figure out some appropriate response. Any ideas?"

After a long discussion, they decided it would be wise to gather the larger group together to review where they were now, where they were going, and to encourage any and all expressions of feeling. Beyond that, they decided to have no expectations that the meeting would help in any measurable way. Sarah and Kenan understood the wisdom in Enosh's assertion that only experience could engender real trust. Before long, the three leaders did notice, and were grateful for it, that at least the passing of rumors had decreased to a mere trickle. The journey continued.

Chapter 30

Moses awoke at the first hint of dawn, still shaken to the core by the previous day's revelations. He had been so certain of himself—so sure that he could bluff his way through what he had hoped would be a brief detour before he could return to his new friends. His vision had taken him deeper, though, to an experience of captivity that he now realized had dogged him for years. His physical captivity at the hands of the Sea Prince's minions represented reality at one level, but his enslavement to his own power and authority troubled him much more deeply. He now realized how often he had lost patience with the Israelites—whenever their faith in the Holy One had wavered. Moses had become furious when they obviously preferred reliance on their own powers, ideas, and even in their ability to wheedle and cajole. His face flushed as he allowed himself to take in the height, breadth, and depth of his hypocrisy.

It remained to be seen how he would face his next opportunity. Did he or did he not trust in the Holy One? Had the Divine Presence ever failed him before? He couldn't think of even one time. He felt humbled when he realized how difficult it was to trust—even when faced with overwhelming supportive evidence. Moses' head bowed in tribute to all those brave people who had followed him into the wilderness. How much he regretted those times when self-righteousness and arrogance had ruled his behavior towards them.

But right now he had a more pressing problem. What was he going to say and how would he comport himself when he came before the Sea Prince? Well, he was about to find out, because the guards had just appeared to escort him to his prince-captor.

During his long life Moses had never seen a collection of tents that looked more like a palace than those he was about to enter. The dwelling of the Sea Prince had been constructed on a bluff overlooking the northeastern arm of the Red Sea. When he glanced off to the East and across the water, Moses had to squint from the brightness of the still-low sun as it glinted and sparkled on the waves.

It took his eyes a few moments to adjust to the relative darkness of the tent after the brilliance of the morning sun. Moses was brought before his captor, who sat on a dais piled with soft skins. Moses began by making obeisance as he had been instructed. He waited for what seemed like forever for the order to rise. He felt surprisingly calm for one whose fate rested so precariously in the hands of another. He had somehow stepped beyond the temptations of arrogance and authority and so he carried his honesty as his only resource.

Finally, the Sea Prince commanded him to rise and look at him. Moses saw a man of indeterminate years whose power shone more through his eyes and the carriage of his shoulders than from any royal accouterments. Though Moses had no way of knowing if he had been born to his position or if he was simply a successful pirate who had usurped the title of Sea Prince as a mark of his nefarious accomplishments, to say nothing of his vanity, Moses realized with a start that didn't matter much. In this place, the Sea Prince had all the power and Moses was his captive.

"So, who is this ancient who has managed to divert my reapers from their harvest?" His voice was so loud and deep that Moses was tempted to tremble, but somehow he managed not to show his discomfort.

Moses was grateful that during his wilderness years he had gained at least a smattering of the languages and dialects that were spoken in the region. He was able to understand well enough, though he was not certain whether the Sea Prince wanted him to answer or whether he was addressing Massoud who stood nearby. Moses remained silent.

The Sea Prince's brow creased as he boomed again, "Answer me old man!"

All doubt having been removed, the once-Prophet of God replied quietly, "My name is Moses."

The prince leaned forward to scrutinize Moses. "So… Massoud has told me an intriguing story about you. You claim to be the Moses who commanded a band known variously as Hebrews or Israelites. That apparently aimless, wandering tribe in the Sinai has now settled in the north and presumably you have 'died' in order to retire in solitude into the wilderness once more. Is that about it, Moses?"

"That is substantially correct. Will you allow me to modify one small detail?"

The Sea Prince flicked his wrist in assent.

"Well, the truth is that they just *think* I'm dead."

At this, his great voice exploded in laughter. When his chuckles finally subsided he waved at Moses, "Go on, I can't wait to hear how you did that."

"Suffice it to say, I had help." One corner of the Sea Prince's mouth betrayed his inclination to laugh again; instead he waited for Moses to explain further.

Moses chose his next words carefully, for in spite of his decision simply to be honest, he didn't want to say anything that would imperil The Community. "In the wilderness my people developed a strong practical reliance on their god. Because they saw me as the Prophet of that god, much of their reliance fell on me. Regarding my departure, if they had come to believe, no matter how valid my reasons, that I was abandoning them, my defection would have been too damaging to their developing faith. I reasoned that only my natural death could extract me from their dependence. A few friends and a small measure of sleight of hand proved sufficient. The details are unnecessary. Let me say only that I was just beginning to enjoy my retirement when I was captured." Moses thought for a moment, and then added, "And I do sincerely apologize for any inconvenience I may have caused you, however inadvertently."

For the first time since the beginning of the interview, the Sea Prince appeared uncomfortable. Obviously, Massoud's briefing had led him to expect the same bluster and bravado that Moses had demonstrated previously, but this simple, quiet honesty had changed everything. Moses could tell that the Sea

Prince had been prepared to humiliate him, to expose the lies in his story, and then to punish him appropriately.

It took some effort for Moses not to laugh at his captor's apparent discomfort, but mostly he was relieved to see that the Sea Prince actually believed him. Moses wondered what would happen next.

After a few moments, the Sea Prince raised his hand as if to dismiss Moses but then put it down. "Moses, I don't know whether to believe you or not," he lied. "But, just for the sake of my curiosity, tell me how you had planned to live out your remaining days."

Before he gave his answer, Moses considered again just how honest he wanted to be. He decided that a partial, perhaps intermediate, answer would suffice. "I have considered two possibilities, but before I share them with you, allow me to give you a glimpse into the life of a Prophet of God."

The Sea Prince nodded, so Moses continued. "For the last forty years, I have not had even one day to myself. Each waking moment, and for that matter even in my dreams, I have concerned myself with the well-being of my people. At times they were able to exhibit a delightful level of maturity, but too often they behaved like cranky, demanding, and thoroughly unruly children. Perhaps you know what I mean?"

In spite of himself, the Sea Prince smiled.

"Finally, I just didn't want to do it anymore. I was completely worn out so I decided I had to get away. Some men find relief from their responsibilities through death, but for reasons that are beyond me, I have been granted an extraordinary longevity that shows no sign of abating. So, as I said, I had two choices. Because I have come to love the wilderness and can survive perfectly well in it, I planned to spend the rest of my days in blissful solitude, needing only to commune with my surroundings and my God. Then, one day in the indefinite future, the journey would be over and I would die.

"More recently, a second choice has occurred to me." And here, Moses reminded himself to be careful. "I began thinking that perhaps I might encounter a group of desert tribesmen who share my god's requirements of hospitality to strangers. In my fantasy, they would welcome an old man, not a Prophet of God, and I would live out my remaining days in their company. But as fate would have it, here I am instead in captivity before you. So, I must conclude that some other outcome awaits me." Moses bowed his head to emphasize his honest recognition of his plight.

The Sea Prince had been listening carefully, almost respectfully. Then, his face clouded and Moses knew that the interview was about to end. "Take him away. I will decide about him when I am ready."

As Moses left the tent, he heard his prime captor dismissing the rest of his court. He smiled to himself with a feeling of appreciation and understanding for the Sea Prince's obvious need for solitude at this moment. Well, Moses thought as he was returned to his rough quarters, I wonder what the Holy One will do with all this?

Chapter 31

For two days, Moses waited for the inevitable summons that would call him once again before the Sea Prince. In spite of all his efforts to pray and to remain open to Holy Presence, nothing remarkable happened; there were no dreams, no visions; not even an intuitive hunch. Finally he stopped trying and instead started paying attention to learning whatever he could about his captors.

Whenever the guards came to give him food or a bit of exercise, he would engage them in conversation and listen carefully for clues. While asking directly might have gleaned him more information, Moses did not want to raise their suspicions about him any further. The walls of the tent allowed some sound to pass through, so he would eavesdrop on the conversations among the guards or among any others who haphazardly passed within hearing distance.

Eventually he learned that the Sea Prince was in fact from a royal line, but was considered a renegade. Apparently he thought of himself as a merchant who owned a large fleet of trading vessels. His ships carried varying cargoes among ports bordering the Red Sea, but not only among those. His ships also traversed the eastern coast of Africa to the south and as far as India to the east. While he engaged in the trade of many goods, his most lucrative trade was in slaves and many of his vessels carried nothing else. He had discovered that the demand for slaves never ceased to grow and consequently the price he received remained delightfully high. Always the opportunist, if the chance arose, he was not above engaging in acts of piracy against any other merchant vessels that sailed these same waters. While his royal family did not formally approve of his activities, the Sea Prince made sure they benefited enough from his activities that they largely left him alone.

Moses shuddered when he considered his life-long abhorrence of slavery and the odds that he might live out his last days as a slave. He couldn't remember for sure, but he suspected that sometime during the Israelite's years of wandering in the wilderness his army had probably engaged the Sea Prince's slave hunters in battle. If the Sea Prince ever made the connection, he could find himself in big trouble, indeed.

Moses had to remind himself many times about the presence of the Holy One and of that vision of community that had originally urged his return to the wilderness. Though he couldn't imagine how he could possibly be rescued, he tried to believe that the Holy One would not abandon him.

On the morning of the third day, Moses was dozing after his morning meal.

"Moses, get up and brush yourself off. The Sea Prince awaits you." Moses looked up at the guard who towered over him. Moses had been treated relatively well, but that didn't stop his guards from taking every opportunity to remind him that they had all the power and he had none.

A short time later, having once again performed his obeisance, Moses stood before the Sea Prince.

"Old man, I must confess that you have caused me more concern than any other captive I have ever taken. Usually one of your advanced age would simply be abandoned or, shall we say, otherwise disposed of. Young slaves who grow old may continue to be useful to their masters, but one such as yourself who is already ancient is not likely to take well to the training. At this point it would be most efficient to release you back into the wilds to fend for yourself. You'd just love that, wouldn't you, Moses?" the Sea Prince added in response to Moses' hopeful look.

"Unfortunately for you though, Moses, I just can't do it that way. You see, I do believe that you are who you say you are, and therein lies the problem. As I am sure you have figured out by now, we are not really strangers to one another at all, now are we?"

Moses blanched. He knew where this was going. He was really in for it now.

"More than once, your army has prevented me from doing my job. Your interference has resulted in significant losses in trade and, yes, Moses, in some casualties as well. If I just let you go, word of my soft heart would surely get around. So you can see why I cannot let that happen.

"On the other hand, it seems I can't just kill you either. Even in retirement, as you so eloquently put it, you are still a prophet of your god. And while it may be argued that the gods do not approve of my chosen line of work, so far anyway, they seem to have left me alone. I don't choose to do anything to you that is likely to invite the wrath of your god or of any of your followers either. As I said, word gets around. And, quite frankly, I prefer to be left alone to attend to my business.

"I am faced therefore with a dilemma. I can't just release you, I can't kill you, and you are quite worthless as a slave. Fortunately for me, I have had considerable experience in dealing with difficult situations, so I have come up with a solution. I believe it is brilliant, if I do say so myself." He looked around to receive the fawning looks of his courtiers.

"So, Moses, here's what we're going to do. While you may not be very adept at it, you will, nevertheless, be given as a slave to the captain of one of my boats who will use your limited talents as he sees fit. Who knows, perhaps he will tire of you and dispose of you at some point if that is his pleasure."

The Sea Prince sat back and watched as Moses recoiled at the idea of being a slave. His captive's distress obviously delighted him. "And I expect you to be grateful to me that I don't throw caution to the wind and just kill you right now." And then, before Moses could even begin to formulate any appeal, the Sea Prince stood and barked to his guards. "Take him away!"

As Moses was being led away, the feeling in his bowels was like falling off a cliff. It wasn't bad enough that he was about to be a slave. It was much worse that he was also leaving his beloved wilderness, his home. Must everything that matters to me be removed?

At that instant in his mind's eye he saw himself standing with the Israelites just after they had crossed the sea to escape the Egyptians. In his vision, however, he was not leading them into the wilderness; he was among those being led. He realized then that they must have experienced the same kind of sinking feeling that he suffered now. Moses' face flushed with shame as he remembered his angry and judgmental response to their questioning fear. He realized that just now he had been thinking the very same angry thoughts that they had expressed. And then, in an echo of their exclamations of hopelessness he prayed, "Holy One, is this why you led me back into the wilderness, so I could die as a slave on some boat?"

Moses wondered if he had the faith or fortitude to be the recipient of the same admonishment that he had given to the Israelites: "O you of little faith. How much more proof do you need from the Holy One than what you have already received?" Well, Moses sighed, I guess I have no choice but to find out.

He was taken directly to the small harbor where a collection of small ships bobbed in the shallow water near the shore. They were kept in place by ropes fastened to rocks that were either thrown up on the beach or dropped into the water like anchors.

His captors waded out with him to the side of a medium-sized boat. Heavy cloth stretched across the bow fashioned sleeping quarters for the small crew. A cage had been constructed in the middle. The tiller and single sail were at the rear. Moses looked around at the nearby boats and quickly figured out that the cages were designed to carry human cargo. Moses cringed in horror at the thought of being put behind those bars. To his surprise and relief, just after he had been lifted into the boat, the captain ordered him to sit on the deck forward of the cage.

Soon after, about twenty shackled male slaves were secured in the cage by their armed guards. It appeared to Moses that the crew consisted only of the captain, two guards, and perhaps himself. After they had pushed off from the shore, the captain took the tiller while the others paddled them into deeper water. Soon they raised the sail in time to catch the late morning breeze.

Then the captain addressed Moses loudly enough for all on the boat, crew and 'cargo' alike, to hear. "Moses, just because you are not held in the cage with these other slaves means nothing. You are just as much a slave as they are." He indicated those in the cage with a calloused thumb. He then kicked a wooden pot toward Moses. "This is your equipment. You'll notice that it is just the right size to pass through the opening in the cage. It's your job to collect their wastes and throw them overboard and to bring them just enough food and water so they don't starve. We only have so much that we can spare for the likes of this lot." The captain then pointed to a pile of dried meat and an open cask of water.

"With just the one pot?" The horror of the situation made it difficult for Moses to breathe.

The Captain's grin exposed his few remaining blackened teeth. "You'd better clean it well in between, then." At his crude joke, the captain and his crew laughed derisively.

Moses tried with all his strength not to think about what he had just been ordered to do. Instead, he looked up and noticed that the breeze was freshening and filling the sail. Then, he turned to look back at the receding land. With tears in his eyes he said his final goodbye to the wilderness that had been his home for more than forty years.

Chapter 32

How much sea could there be? The Community had been moving south for weeks now, but no matter how far they went, the Sea continued to be their constant companion to the west. At no point so far had they been able see to its other side. None of them had any clear idea about how long they would have to travel before reaching a suitable place to settle, but they were beginning to wonder if they would ever get there.

They had been traveling on what appeared to be a trade route, and while they no longer feared pursuit by Joshua and Gershom, they were still careful to avoid too much human contact. They continued to deploy scouts before and behind so, with enough notice, their company could find sanctuary in the hills whenever any potentially menacing group approached. So far they had traveled without serious incident.

They had seen just a few small collections of dwelling places, including some coastal villages where fishing was the main activity. The villagers typically utilized a handful of small boats to catch fish in nets. The fish was then dried in the sun and sold to passing caravans. Gratefully, the members of the community were able to trade with the villagers for a supply of fish and although the taste was unusual to them, such fare provided a welcome supplement to their diet. The villagers told them stories about a land that lay beyond the Sea, but because their boats were so small, none of them had ever gone there. They had heard from the caravan traders that many weeks' travel farther south, the land across the sea lay close enough to be reached by boat.

Equipped with this vital information, the leaders called for a gathering of the whole Community to plan the next leg of their journey. They noted to the gathered families that they had found a few places in the coastal mountains that could possibly be habitable, but either they were too obvious to passers-by or they were not sufficiently defensible. As they talked more with one another about the future, it became increasingly clear to them that having to invest great resources into the defense of their community and to be forced to engage regularly in other forms of violence did not fit their vision. So, their only remaining choice was to continue on southward, and perhaps to try to cross the sea—if that even turned out to be possible.

During their journey and with the full knowledge and blessing of the leaders, Eliezer and Milcah set about encouraging people to get to know each other. They encouraged the ancient practice of storytelling in the early evening. For as long as they could remember, the people had used the storytelling times to share news and to remember and then pass on the lore of the tribe to their children. Eliezer and Milcah made the rounds of these smaller gatherings and when the ancient stories were done for the evening, they invited people to tell their own more current stories and to share with one another their fears, their hopes, and their dreams for the future. Not only did the people learn about each other, but the very process of relating their own experience to others helped them to understand themselves better, too.

Enosh, Sarah, and Kenan were celebrating the unexpected bonus they had received from the community. Encouraging people to share directly with one another had cut down the traffic in rumors dramatically. People learned that if they had any concerns or questions at all, they had only to ask someone. In the wilderness when they had been with the larger group, even innocent questions were often interpreted as criticism or complaining, so the people had learned to keep their mouths shut. There had been less visible controversy then, but no less worry or turmoil.

The three leaders discovered that the longer the people journeyed together, the less work was required of them. Occasionally they would be consulted over some small dispute, but for the most part the people got along and functioned quite well. Before long everyone had learned what was required for each day of the journey, so they simply did it without much fuss.

Enosh had organized the scouts and was considered their commander, but each one of them appreciated the importance of the function so much that they just did their jobs with a minimum of supervision. The scouts continued to bring valuable information to the larger group. Their accurate observations made it possible for the people to trade for their necessities with some of the caravans and with the occasional fishing village that they passed. With each new encounter the people would inquire with care and diplomacy about the existence of that land across the Sea. And they never stopped wondering if they should try to cross or whether it would be better to continue south as far as they could go?

All the information that came to the leaders was promptly passed on to the larger group. They did not yet have to make a decision about crossing the Sea, so they had ample time to prepare the ground necessary to achieve a group consensus.

Little by little, The Community figured out that they were looking for a homeland that was not occupied too densely. They did not want to have to fight to inhabit it. They speculated that it would be convenient to be located near a trade route, but they wanted to be remote enough so the main body could stay largely hidden. And of course, the land had to be arable. Like the larger body of Israelites that had crossed the Jordan, this smaller group was also looking for a place to settle down. They had been nomads long enough.

During the journey, they developed and practiced their religious rituals. They still rested on the seventh day and periodically they recalled in detail the rescue of their people from captivity in Egypt. They also began to develop a ritual of their own to commemorate their departure from Mount Nebo. Whenever they prayed to the Holy One, they always asked that Moses be cared for. They worried about him and grieved his absence from their company.

They fell into the habit of gathering together on the day of rest. They exercised no formal ritual, but they shared with the larger group whatever contact they as individuals had experienced with the Holy One. They described the dreams, visions, and ideas that had come to them during the preceding six days. Little by little, a picture of their potential homeland began to emerge. They discovered that the process of their shared deliberations and the ultimate character of their community belonged to all of them. Even though they were apparently far away from their ultimate destination, they were already beginning to experience the essence of home in the quality of their relationships. When at some point in the future they actually settled down in a new land, there would be huge and varied challenges, but intuitively they knew they were already developing the tools and social foundation that would make those challenges manageable.

After several months, having traveled the entire west coast of the Arabian Peninsula, their Community of Promise finally arrived at a small but thriving town. They wondered if this would turn out to be the place where they might decide to cross the water. Together they had made many small decisions along the way, but none of their company could have been adequately prepared for how difficult this one would turn out to be. The town came into view just as they were completing their day's journey. The Sabbath began at dusk and they were grateful to have the next day to rest and think before considering this potential change of direction in their journey that would transform their lives forever.

Chapter 33

The small boat that was Moses' new home had sailed to the south after leaving the Sea Prince's encampment on the western shore of the Gulf of Aqaba. They followed close to the coast, never losing sight of land. The boat was surprisingly agile and fast, but cargo and crew alike were often tossed about unmercifully.

Moses was so sick for the first few days that more than once he was tempted to throw himself over the side just to be free of the suffering. He had hoped that his voyage on this sea would have been more like his time on the placid barges of his childhood that had glided him up and down the Nile. But this was no barge and the Red Sea, even near the shore, was no Nile River.

After an interminable week he was able to gain enough stability to stand up. When he did, he saw that their human cargo had fared no better than he had. The cage was an unholy mess. All he could do was pull up bucket after bucket of seawater to sluice the deck under the cage. Then, he required each of the slaves to come near to the bars so he could pour water over them. After many hours of this backbreaking work the cage, while not actually clean, at least was no longer smeared with vomit and feces. Some of the slaves seemed to have adjusted to the incessant pitching of the boat, but others looked like their seasickness might be a permanent condition.

During each subsequent day Moses was kept so busy feeding and washing the slaves and their cage and then emptying the slops that he hardly had a moment to think. Each night he fell into the fitful sleep of exhaustion.

Though the labor was mind-numbing, Moses tried to remain aware of the characteristics of the coastline. He was able to orient himself by sun, moon, and stars so he recognized when they came to the southern tip of the Sinai Peninsula and then turned west across the rough waters at the mouth of the Gulf of Suez. He was never more afraid than during that next night. What could be more unnatural than trying to sleep in the middle of the Sea? Prior to that, they had always anchored near the shore to sleep. Moses felt thoroughly helpless. It was bad enough being a slave, but the threats of the deep sea struck terror into his heart, especially on this moonless night when he could see nothing. He might as well have been floating amidst the stars.

Finally, the western shore appeared and the small boat turned south once again. By this time Moses had adjusted to his routine but he felt surprisingly lonely. The crew wouldn't talk to him except to deride him or give orders, and the slaves were afraid to talk at all.

One morning he had a terrifying thought: what if the Holy One actually belongs to the land we have left behind? In all the time he had been on the boat, he had experienced no sense of Divine Presence. Without the Holy One, he thought, I might as well jump into the Sea.

Now that Moses had established a routine for his duties, he had more time to think. For the first few days his seasickness had made thinking, well, unthinkable. He hadn't even been able to muster the strength to cry out to the Holy One. Besides, when he wasn't sick, he was terrified. He had believed that terror could provide the energy needed to call out for help, but his experience now taught him that a different kind of energy would be required, energy that would enable him to be open to the possibility of an answer.

Once again his attention went back to the Israelites during their first months in the wilderness. They had had plenty of energy to cry for help. In fact, it seemed like they never stopped crying out. Moses, though, had not been afraid. He had traveled that particular wilderness before. He knew where they were, where they were going, and he knew how they would be able to survive. He wasn't stupid—he was aware of the enormity and the attendant dangers of their journey, but at no time was terror his companion. Not so the Israelites: they had been taken away from the only life they knew. It was true that they had suffered in their slavery, but at least their life in slavery had been predictable. It humbled Moses to discover that here, on this small boat, his own terror was as all-consuming as theirs had been, and it was blocking out his faith. He needed to find a way to calm down, to center himself, so he could once again become open to Divine Presence. He was horrified though, to discover how hard it was to be calm, much less faith-filled, when every element of one's surroundings screamed out danger signals.

Of course the children of Israel couldn't have faith just because I told them to, he reminded himself. They were too preoccupied with simply breathing, standing, and walking. That they were able to do even that much was commendable under the circumstances.

With his stomach pitching in fear as much as the deck pitched under his feet, a new idea hit him like a blow to the head: Gershom wasn't the only one who had exploited the image of a fearful God. For some time now, Moses had carried a deep resentment toward Gershom for his depiction of the Holy One as an angry and demanding god. But now he realized an embarrassing truth: he was every bit as much to blame as Gershom.

Moses thought back to the time with the Israelites when he had gone up into Mount Sinai to be with the Holy One. Could he, so very many years later, reconstruct with any semblance of accuracy his memory of that event? He remembered how the people had run from him when he first returned to them from the mountain. They told him he had become different—changed somehow. The looks on their faces and their efforts to avoid being near him made him feel like a monster. It had been his first-born son, Gershom, who had come to his side and had guided him (or was it carried him) into the tent. For days Moses had tried to express what he had experienced with the Holy One. While he talked, Gershom wrote. In time, Moses had fallen into a deep and dreamless sleep. When he woke, Gershom showed him all that he had written.

Did it really happen that way? Were those really the words of the Holy One? As he thought about it now, he realized with a considerable start that he couldn't be sure. But Gershom had comforted him and assured him that he had recorded Moses' descriptions faithfully. Whatever anger and threat surrounded and penetrated the words, Gershom ascribed to the divine voice! I don't remember the anger, Moses confessed to himself. But I chose to believe Gershom. I still don't understand why I accepted Gershom's version so readily? Even then, had I been more honest, I could have seen and perhaps corrected his gross misrepresentation of the character of the Holy One.

Was I afraid that he was right? Was I afraid that the people wouldn't believe me, and that they wouldn't be willing to follow a god of love and compassion? Moses dropped to his knees when he realized that his motivation didn't matter. The truth is, he confessed, it was my own lack of faith that made Gershom's version so attractive. It is obvious to me now that I lacked faith in the Holy One, but even worse, I lacked faith in the people, so I misinterpreted their legitimate fear as immaturity and willfulness. And then I made matters worse by punishing them for it in the name of Jehovah so they wouldn't see *my* fear or recognize *my* lack of faith.

Moses was filled with remorse. He found himself fighting another impulse to jump overboard, not to escape this time, but to expunge his evil self from the world. However, when he tried to rise, a weight like a hand on his shoulder held him in place. Even now, I want to run away, but truly there is nowhere to run or hide. I have to face myself and, perhaps for the first time in my life, face the Holy One as a man.

Again he allowed his old memories to emerge. He saw himself holding the stone tablets he had brought down from the mountain. Arrayed before him were the Israelites. They were dancing, reveling, bowing down before Hathor (yes, I recognized that gentle god of the Egyptians). I was furious with them. How could they do this to me? I mean how could they be so unfaithful to the God who had rescued them?

Wait, wait, Moses! Back up. What did you just say?

Moses gulped as he heard his inner thought replaying in his mind: *How could they do this to me!*

So, he thought, there it is: the truth, at last. O Moses, you stupid, selfish, childish man! He began to sob.

"Moses, get up and do your job!" The captain kicked him in the ribs. "You'd better quit that sniveling and get used to it; you belong to us now."

Moses was just about to snap back, but then thought better of it, picked up his bowl and began his daily duties. For the rest of that day he moved like a man in a trance. When he wasn't working, he just stood at the rail, his eyes searching for some unknown reality in the mists of the Sea. He continued to look out even as the darkness of evening came upon them.

Moses then had the sense that someone was behind him so he braced himself for another kick or cuff. "Moses, relax," he heard a light and musical voice say. Turning around, he saw someone standing there who was completely swaddled in desert garb. Moses couldn't see much of the person's face, only the glint of some far-away light in his, or was it her, eyes.

"Who are you and how did you get out here?" Moses heart drummed so hard that it threatened to burst through his breast.

"Moses, Moses, don't you know I'm always with you?"

At that, the color ran out of Moses' face and he fell to the deck in obeisance. The Holy One stood there.

"My dear Moses, how did you come to be so fearful? Stand up so we can talk."

Moses rose cautiously while he tried to catch a glimpse of this being. He still suspected a trick. "At least let's keep the noise down. It wouldn't be good for them to find you here."

"Are you ashamed of me, then?"

"No, but they won't be able to see you and they'll think I've completely lost my senses."

"I'm sure they already think that."

Moses wasn't sure, but he thought he heard his visitor chuckling. He blushed but didn't know what to say.

"So, my old friend, I get the impression that your understanding has been developing in some interesting ways."

"How did you know that?"

"Didn't you hear me a moment ago? I told you, I'm always with you. I know what you know—maybe even before you know it."

Moses reddened even more. It was one thing to encounter the Holy One on the mountain, or be visited in a dream, but he had never thought of the relationship as being so personal, so intimate, so revealing. But if the Holy One knew everything anyway, what did he have to lose.

"I've been feeling pretty ashamed of myself. I see now how unfairly I've treated the Israelites." He didn't want to say the next thing, but he couldn't stop himself from speaking. "If you were so close all the time, couldn't you have stopped me? Or at least warned me?"

"Those are legitimate questions. Of course they come with complex answers."

"I was afraid of that."

"You humans have a bad habit of identifying your strongest or most obvious characteristics, increasing their amplitude, and then ascribing them to me. For example, if you have a need to control people, you assume that my need is even greater, and for some reason you think that I will go to any extreme to get my way."

Moses was about to argue and disassociate himself from the judgment, but his visitor went on. "Be honest now, Moses. You said yourself that you used Gershom's image of an angry god to keep the people in line. But remember, I'm not here to judge or condemn you. This is a process, see? You were simply the way you were. And now you're learning that there are other possibilities. You might never have learned these things without your recent experiences. What you have been going through has given you a new perspective that you didn't have before. Actually, it wasn't even possible for you to see these things until now. Of course, you always have the power to reject any new learning and to continue to see, think, and function as before. Or you can choose to try something new: to see what life looks like from this new vantage point. You can always make fresh choices based on new information.

"This is how all people learn and grow. But I'm sure that from your own experiences you'll understand what I mean when I say that it's not easy to stand back—to resist interfering that is—when those you care about make original and unexpected choices."

At that, Moses' mouth dropped open.

"That's right, Moses. You heard correctly. I don't know what choices people will make. I can make some pretty educated guesses about where the various options lead, but I always have to leave room for freedom of choice. Allow me to remind you why I offered you the opportunity to go to Egypt in the first place: so my people (and that includes you) could be free. Yes, Moses, I share your concern. Sometimes, free choices result in pain and loss—for all involved, I might add.

"You might not be able to see it yet, but you, Moses, are more free today than you have ever been before. And, let me commend you. You've exercised your freedom marvelously."

Moses shook his head, opening his mouth to argue, but then closed it again and waited for his guest to continue.

"You freely chose to lead your captors away from The Community of Promise, as you call them, even though you must have guessed it would lead to your own captivity. Among several available options, you picked the only one that you could live with. With that choice, you exercised your freedom. As courageous and selfless as that decision might appear, it is practically insignificant compared to what you have done most recently."

Hearing this, Moses was completely baffled.

"The two most difficult choices in human existence are, first, to affirm life in the face of apparent hopelessness. And the second is to learn from your experiences by adopting a new, and therefore unpredictable, perspective. When you take responsibility like that, you exercise hope—as distinct from wishful thinking."

Suddenly, Moses was worried.

"No, Moses, I don't know how this will turn out. And, no, I don't know if you will ever be reunited with your new friends. All I can tell you—and it is a great deal—is that all possibilities remain open. Those possibilities will be affected by your choices, but there's more to it than that. You're not the only one who has to face decision-making opportunities. Only time will tell whether and how the myriad of choices will converge into a particular reality. Meanwhile, don't be so hard on yourself. Too much self-judging and recrimination actually gets in the way of learning and growth. Whenever that happens, I call it a tragedy.

"And, if nothing else, keep in mind this one thing: you will always affect those around you with your attitudes and with your decisions. And so as you make them, remember to consult your humility, your wisdom, and your love. True freedom finds root in these."

Moses became aware of the rocking of the deck under him. The eastern sky showed its first blush and the salt air blew fresh in his nostrils. A wave of gratitude filled him as he rose to begin his freest day ever.

Chapter 34

The Day of Rest had come to be a welcome diversion from the rigors of travel. Movement required focused attention and focused attention made conversation difficult. It was only in the evenings and on the Sabbath that stories were told and relationships celebrated. This particular Sabbath was ordinary in the quantity of talk, but far from ordinary in the high anxiety that was crackling through the camp. Everyone knew that they would probably cross the Sea at some point, but the time for decision had now come. Soon their lives would be so different that they would hardly be able to recognize themselves.

Sarah and Asher sat by their tent with Enosh, Kenan, Nathanel, and a few others. They were trying, without much success, to share a quiet meal. Sarah was so angry she could hardly look at anyone, particularly Enosh. Though he sat quietly, the flush on his cheeks betrayed the depth of his discomfort. Over the last few days while they had been approaching their decision point, Enosh and Kenan had attempted to convince Sarah that their plan was the only viable one. But she just didn't want to accept it. They knew that a delegation had to go into town to negotiate passage if The Community decided to cross the Sea. Sarah had argued that she had contributed as much leadership as anyone and insisted that she be part of the delegation.

"No one underestimates your contribution or your value to us," Kenan now said as warmly and gently as he could.

"So why are you excluding me, then?"

"There is no way to know for sure how the villagers regard women as leaders, though it's possible that it wouldn't be any problem at all."

Enosh picked up the thread of their argument. "Every village we've passed by, every caravan, and every traveling band so far has been led by men. Chances are that this one will be no different."

"Well, that shouldn't matter. We are who we are. They'll just have to accept it and respect me!"

"And if they don't," Kenan wondered, "Then what?"

Sarah considered several answers to the thorny question, but expressed none of them. Abruptly she got up and went toward her tent. Asher saw the look on her face as she came near him and made sure he was occupied with his food as she stormed by him and went inside. She had hardly spoken to him since yesterday's meeting and showed no indication that she was going to break her cold silence now.

Finally, Asher said, "I am worried."

All of them, save Sarah, erupted with some version of "Well, who isn't?"

"No, I don't mean about crossing the Sea, at least not directly."

"What, then?" Enosh asked.

"I've been hearing rumblings in the camp. I can't be sure I heard right, but it seems that there's a growing division between those who favor crossing and those who may not want to go."

Even Sarah roused from her silence and came out of the tent when she heard Asher's concern. "How can that be after we've come so far? I think the only ones who want to stay are just afraid of the unknown across the sea."

"How can you be so certain, Sarah?" Asher spoke quietly because he was still treading carefully around her.

"When we left Mount Nebo and turned away from the Promised Land, we made a commitment to this community."

"That's true," Kenan added, "And our commitment was to be a community, not a slave camp—though I must confess that it never occurred to me that we would encounter any challenge big enough to break us apart after we had separated ourselves from our Israelite kin."

It was evident that none among them had entertained such a possibility. They sat in silence for some time, each one of them considering the potential implications of even a small defection, much less, unthinkably, a larger one.

Finally, Kenan broke the heavy silence. "We haven't had to face such a possibility as this 'til now because we had no choice but to go in the same direction. We were all responding to the vision Eliezer offered us." And then after another thoughtful pause, "Perhaps not everyone sees the vision in the same way."

Nathanel, who had been following the conversation intently, finally spoke up. "I don't get what you mean, Kenan. Can you explain it to me?"

Kenan stared off into space as if he hadn't even heard Nathanel, but he was just collecting his thoughts. The rest of them waited patiently. They had seen Kenan do this before. Finally, he turned to look at Nathanel. "It appears that I have the same question as you, Nathanel. I'm not sure I get it either. But let me try to be more clear, as much for my own understanding as for yours."

Kenan shifted in his seat to get more comfortable and then began to think out loud. "It's easy to answer your question in general terms. There are countless times I could point to in the past when Moses has spoken to the assembled Israelites. When he was finished, the people usually talked with each other a lot because they weren't always clear about what Moses had said. Invariably, people had heard different things. Sometimes they heard what they wanted to hear. Different people heard different levels of meaning in Moses' words. And some folk were just plain confused. So, even if Eliezer had been crystal clear in his offer of a new vision to us, each of us who heard him would have taken away something uniquely different.

"But he wasn't even that clear. When he recruited me, he was purposefully vague. Apparently he was waiting to see if I was predisposed to follow. Of course, at that time none of us were told that there was a chance we'd be leaving. I think we just felt that some important thing was about to happen that might offer some new, if still vague, hope.

"Then, on Mount Nebo, we heard about the plan to return to the wilderness to seek some other manifestation of the

Promised Land. If I remember correctly, Eliezer didn't even know himself what it was going to look like.

"And now, here we are. We've been traveling for a long time with no fixed destination. How could we assume that everyone would carry the same idea of where we would end up or what it would look like when we got there?"

"What about the Holy One?" Asher interjected. "Isn't the Holy One leading us?"

"Yeah, what about that, Kenan?" Nathanel asked. "Eliezer said we would follow the Holy One."

"Once again, the situation makes sense if you look at it from the right angle." Kenan said these words as if singing the refrain to his own private song.

The rest looked at him agape.

"Don't you see? Now it's become a reality."

Sarah was looking more agitated by the minute. Finally she broke into the conversation with the loudest voice she had used for some time. "Hah! We've all missed the point!"

At the stunned look on the faces of the men, she continued more quietly. "Yes, me, too. I've been so angry and focused on what I thought was unfair to me that I forgot to use the skills that put me on this leadership team in the first place.

"I forgot that we're still in the process of becoming a community. Just because we committed ourselves to this joint venture doesn't mean that we've arrived. We still have so much to experience and so much to learn before we can possibly attain our Promised Land."

The men still looked confused. "Don't you see? Our Promised Land is not a place. It's a brand new way of being together. Even the idea that more than one leader can be the conduit for the will of the Holy One is brand new." She looked into each of their faces before continuing. "What if the Holy One doesn't care at all where we end up?"

The men suddenly came to life, all trying to speak at once. "But how will we know which way to go?" And, "What do you mean the Holy One doesn't care?" "Without the Holy One to direct us, we're really lost!" These panicky questions exploded like a fireworks finale for several minutes until Sarah couldn't stand it anymore. Her eyes got wide, her cheeks flushed, and she looked like she was holding her breath to the point of bursting. And burst she did—into knee-weakening guffaws. She laughed until she fell over and rolled on the ground. She laughed until no one could tell if she were crying or crazy.

The men just watched her in the stunned silence of masculine incredulity.

When she could catch her breath again, she looked up from her prone position at the red faces of the men. She almost laughed again, but she knew that they already thought she had taken leave of every sense she had ever possessed. So, she took a deep breath and said, "Don't you see it? Can't you see how funny we must seem to the Holy One? No, I guess you don't. Well, don't feel bad. I didn't get it myself either until just a few moments ago."

"What, Sarah, what? What are you talking about?" Enosh had stood up to tower over her, his hands on his hips.

"I think I get it," Nathanel said. "Zuriel and I didn't understand why Moses left us to go alone into the wilderness rather than joining the group right away. It didn't matter at all to him which direction he took. He just had to get to a place where he could, shall we say, get his new assignment from the Holy One. He expected the Holy One to help him prepare for a new way of being."

"Ah, I get it, Nathanel," Kenan added. "The Holy One is helping us prepare, too. It really doesn't matter whether we cross the Sea, head east, or even return where we came from. We are, our very selves, becoming the embodiment of the Promised Land. If we learn to be a community, the Promised Land will always be with us no matter where in the world we decide to settle."

"Right," Sarah said. "We've been looking for the wrong kind of Divine Leadership. What we have to do now is help our company stay connected to one another in the face of a major crisis. We need to teach them a new way to manage their fear. When they remember how much they have grown to mean to each other, then they will be able to decide which way to go."

Asher had been quietly following the conversation. "I have a feeling, maybe even a divine premonition, that once we decide as a full community which way to go, nothing will stand in our way."

"You may well be right, Asher," Sarah went on. "But let's not get ahead of ourselves. Right now we need to think about how to help our people shift their sights so they can be open in a new way to the calling of the Holy One. It wouldn't surprise me at all to discover that the people already possess a wealth of divine inspiration that they haven't been able to acknowledge, much less use. We can get them all together tomorrow, so let's figure out how to do this."

As they looked around at each other they could feel their hopes rising and their fears diminishing, though none of them expected the large gathering to go on without conflict or at least some surprises. Still, that was nothing new. What mattered was that they now knew they would get through this.

Chapter 35

Even though they were not conversing very much, the waiting group sparked with anticipation and uncertainty. By this time everyone knew that they were living in a divided camp. No one could see an easy path to resolution, either. Most of them stood or sat with those of like mind, so the sense of division, already palpable, was magnified even more by their physical arrangement.

Sarah, Enosh, and Kenan were among the last to arrive. They looked around at the assembly with a combination of trepidation and interest. According to their plan, Sarah stood to speak first.

"As you know, we have reached a point where we have some major decisions to make regarding our next steps and directions. All of us have had ample experience with someone else (mostly Moses) telling us what to do and where to go. Our reactions to those directives were varied, but every one of us knew that we would obey, like it or not.

"It is also true that we have had too little experience deciding for ourselves, but now that we have left the main body, we're all the leadership that we have. We have no one over us to give directions. So whatever we do, we will be the ones to decide what our next steps will be. And that's why we have come together today."

Sarah paused to make sure that everyone was following her. Most people were listening intently, and while the level of anxiety in the group was palpable, it didn't have a hostile feel to it. The leadership team had decided that each of them would simply maintain their own calm presence because everyone knew how easily anxiety could spill over into angry panic, given the right provocation.

Sarah sat down and nodded to Kenan. He stood and slowly walked to the center. "We've come a long way since our first gatherings on Mount Nebo. The enormity of the distance we have traveled is obvious. What might not be so obvious is how far we have traveled in becoming a community. I invite you to look around at each other. Remember the experiences you have shared with each other and how much you have learned about the similarities and differences of your respective lives. Remember why you decided to travel in this direction from Mount Nebo. Remember the vision of a new community that you carry in your hearts.

"Over the last weeks, you have shared these visions with each other, and so you have a deepening understanding that as a community you are participating in a common journey and your goals are congruent. Is there anyone among you who doesn't see the truth in my words?" Kenan waited to see if anyone would speak. No one did. "If truly we are led by a shared vision, then our differences will only be found in the details. Ultimately, it probably doesn't matter which way we decide to go. There will be challenges waiting for us no matter what path we take. In fact, even if we don't all decide to go the same way, I think we'll be all right."

At those words the level of anxiety in the group swelled. People began to mutter and talk to those closest to them. Clearly this was a new idea to them and it was not sitting well. "Please, hear me out. There will be plenty of room for conversation in a few moments." Kenan waited for the noise to die down before resuming. "Without question, this is the greatest challenge we have faced on our journey. It's the first real test of the vision that we adopted on Mount Nebo and that we have carried—together—for the last few months.

"But, until now, we haven't had to make active use of our vision. That is no longer the case. We stand at a crossroads. We have to decide which way to go and it seems that a great deal, if not everything, rests on the choice we make. Who wouldn't feel anxious under the circumstances?" Kenan waited to see if the crowd would react to his words. Then he nodded to Enosh and sat.

When he stood up, Sarah and Kenan could see that Enosh was uncharacteristically nervous. Earlier he had confessed to them that addressing this group was harder than leading soldiers into battle. He looked over at Sarah right then and seeing her helped him gather his courage. He walked around in a circle, making eye contact with as many people as he could. Then he smiled broadly before speaking. "You might be wondering right now what is so amusing about these serious matters. Well, I just had an image flash before my eyes. I imagined Joshua on the eve of a battle calling the entire army into consultation in order to formulate the strategy for the next day. Wouldn't that have been something?" When Enosh began to laugh, he saw a few eyes crinkle and a few corners of mouths rise as they pictured the scene along with him.

"Friends, that's exactly what we're going to do! We carry this vision together and furthermore we all have equal rights and responsibility before the Holy One. There's no other way but for us to decide our immediate future in concert. I, for one, have come to trust us and to trust the spirit of the Holy One in us. Now, do any of you have questions?"

"How do we know this will work?" someone asked.

Sarah caught Enosh's eye and then rose to respond. "In a way we don't know. But, I think a different question would serve us better. I don't know what particular outcome would tell us that we have succeeded, but I'm sure we can at least attend to the health of the process itself. Then, no matter how things turn out, we should be able to embrace and carry out our decisions gladly."

Sarah looked straight at the person who had asked the question and took the answering nod as affirmation to continue. "As your leadership team, we have thought carefully about how to proceed."

Enosh, Kenan, and Sarah had outlined an approach that they thought would bring people together, one that would help them move toward a decision. They also knew any approach would be risky if for no other reason than they had never done it before. It had been Sarah's idea (in a way) to use four elements in the process. She had seen them in a dream: Vision, Holy One, Options, and Choice. She explained it this way: "We all need to participate fully in this process and I think the only way to accomplish that is by having the opportunity to talk to just a few people at a time."

They had used this method before, so people started to look around for a few individuals they might feel comfortable with, but she wasn't quite finished yet. "Before you start to move, I have one more suggestion."

People stopped moving and turned toward her. "Because we are really all in this together, please consider talking with some people whom you don't already know well. Or talk with people you think (or assume) might want to go in a different direction than you do."

At first there was an uneasy silence followed by another round of anxious muttering. "People, relax! It was a suggestion—just consider it. No one is giving orders here. And now, let me finish describing the process to you.

"I want to remind you again that this is just a suggestion. If it doesn't work for you then do something else that works better. Please, hear me out. This process may take some time, but we think it will move us in a good direction. First, share with each other your understanding of the vision you chose to follow on Mount Nebo. After a time we'll ask you to describe to the full gathering the visions from the smaller groups. This will work best if you make sure to listen carefully, for what you hear may complement your own vision.

"Then we'll share intimately once again, this time talking about how the spirit of the Holy One has been speaking to you recently. After we bring those ideas to the larger gathering, we will then start to identify the available options. Next we'll try to choose what we want to do. Finally, we'll see if a consensus choice emerges from the groups. Any questions?"

No one had any questions and soon they were milling about and then sitting and talking in small knots. As far as Sarah, Kenan, and Enosh could tell many of them actually chose to meet with others of a different future persuasion. The groups worked all day, moving from smaller to larger gatherings and then back. At times they were animated, threatening to erupt into battles, then they quieted down again as they disciplined themselves to listen even more closely than they had just a moment before.

At first, the gathered participants found some discrepancies in the particular manifestation of the vision, but all were surprised and pleased to discover most of the elements to be in broad agreement. As they added their individual experiences of Holy Presence, most of the differences slowly melted away. Then they were amazed to discover that they had many more choices than they had dreamed possible. Initially, some feared that an increase in the number of choices would cause increased dissension, but their earlier practice at careful listening had a transforming effect. They discovered a strong motivation to make a final choice that would benefit the whole community. Their vision of the Promised Land, as it turned out to Sarah's satisfaction, had more to do with the integrity of their community than it had to do with finding a particular location. Staying together was more important than getting one's own way. When they had sorted through the choices, all of the identified options, save one, turned out to have relatively predictable outcomes and pretty severe limitations. The last choice: crossing the Sea, had plenty of perils and a shortage of guarantees, but the possibilities for a successful outcome were endless. And that's what they—all of them together—decided to do.

By the end of the day, they joined together to celebrate their wonderful community, relieved and a bit amazed at how much contention they had worked through, and just happy to be together. It had worked out like Sarah, Enosh, and Kenan had hoped, but none of them had been able to admit until it was over how fearful they had been about the chances of a disastrous outcome.

They were now truly a community. The perils of the Sea and the unknown remained before them but by tacit agreement no one would think of those until the next day.

Chapter 36

Moses thought he had already learned well enough never to take anything for granted. Life had been unpredictable for the last forty years, so he was used to unpredictability. In the wilderness, survival depended on the ability to pay attention, because the smallest variation in the surroundings, or even in the air, could signal a major, perhaps life-threatening (or saving) situation.

He was not, however, prepared for just how routine a sea journey could be. As a consequence, maybe he had become less vigilant now that he was no longer in charge. His sense of freedom from responsibility coupled with the unrelenting sameness of each day left Moses in a persistent somnambulistic state. He didn't worry. He didn't think much. He took naps! Moses had not indulged himself with a nap since childhood. At night, he slept like a baby without a care in the world. Well, he had one care that popped into consciousness from time to time, though it seemed to be fading: his Community of Promise. What had become of them?

He did his work (in between naps, of course) and occasionally exchanged a few words with the slaves, having picked up a rudimentary familiarity with their language. Each day replicated the one before and presaged the day to come. Day after day, night after night, nap after nap, time (and shoreline) passed.

Weeks before, Moses had stopped noticing the shoreline. Each place they landed looked just like the one from the night before. He might not have been so shocked today if he had been paying more attention to the gradual changes in the land as they had passed by. He might have anticipated some changes if he had allowed himself to consider the likely fate of his charges in the cage on the boat. But, he hadn't let himself think about that.

So now, Moses stood on the shore of the Red Sea watching his most recent home disappear into the distance. And he was not alone.

"Come along, old man. You belong to us now." The man on his left grabbed his arm.

"Perhaps the gods know what we'll do with you though," the other man said. "But, if we don't want to donate our heads to the Sea Prince, we'd better figure something out."

Moses felt more at sea now than at any time while actually riding the waves. It had happened so abruptly. He had failed to notice the day before that they had sailed away from the shoreline, so he had no way of knowing that he now stood on an island. All he knew was that they had moored the boat in this place just like they had so many other times. Moses had slept soundly, expecting to rise to one more in a succession of identical days, a day he thought would have nothing to distinguish it from any other. Then two men had arrived: the very men who escorted him now. Even that hadn't alarmed him though, for the sudden appearance of strangers had also become routine. Sometimes men brought supplies, and at other times they just huddled for a time with the captain and then vanished as abruptly as they had appeared.

These men had done both. After placing several sacks of supplies on the boat, they had moved a distance away with the captain, crouched down on their haunches, and began a conversation that seemed to Moses to be just like any other. He continued to attend to his work until he heard the raised voices. Moses couldn't hear everything, but his ears perked up at the sound of his own name being spoken. Well, this is different, Moses had thought. No one had spoken his name for weeks. He almost didn't connect it with himself. And then he heard it again. The men had stood up and were shouting and gesturing wildly at one another.

Moses could tell that in the end, the captain had succeeded in convincing the others that his wishes would have to be followed. As Moses pieced it out, the Sea Prince had decreed that he be set ashore at this place, though he could not at the moment imagine why. The captain and the men had then lifted Moses off the boat and just as quickly it was gone.

Now, as Moses walked between the men, he tried to shake the woolliness from his mind. He had not thought directly about his own fate for some time. Frankly, he had expected that at some unspecified moment, the captain or one of his crew would simply have put a blade between his ribs or slit his throat. It would be over—just like that. He had been feeling so powerless for so long that he could no longer find the energy to worry about it, though now he was surprised to discover that living did, in fact, still seem to matter to him. He flinched when it occurred to him that his death still might be mere moments away, but somehow he didn't think so. He vowed to remain awake and aware to see what would transpire next.

The Holy One! Where was the Holy One? Moses felt panic rising up in him as he cast about inwardly wanting to grasp at divine security. Then he remembered. There would be no miraculous rescue. His fate rested in his own hands and depended on his own choices. What he did would have the most effect on the outcome, or so the Holy One had told him. He called to mind their last encounter and felt a twinge of hope in his wilderness of woolly confusion. For now, his job was simply to pay attention to everything that would happen around him. Whenever moments of choice might appear in his future, he vowed to be ready.

Moses hadn't used his voice very much during his time on the boat, so when he spoke, the sound was thin and raspy. "Who are you, and what place is this?"

The two men just looked at him, so Moses wondered if they understood his language. Finally, the shorter man broke the silence. "So, the slave speaks."

The second man shot a wicked frown at the first. "Pay no mind to him. He's a backward clod who forgets his manners."

"But, I *am* a slave."

"Well, you were a slave. But now, I am the one who is forgetting manners. I am called Cabrun. And that oaf on your other side is Herno."

"I am Moses, but I guess you already knew that. So, what is this place?" While he was interrogating the men, Moses was reclaiming his lifetime habit of noticing the details of his surroundings. They were walking along a well-trodden path that disappeared from view at the base of a ridge of foothills. On either side, he saw unbroken stretches of gravelly beach that melted away as the shoreline curved in the distance. It was a forlorn-looking place. Even the hillsides that he could see seemed to be covered with hardscrabble. He thought he could make out some vegetation nearer to the top, but from this distance it was hard to tell for sure.

Cabrun answered. "I assume you already know that you're near the western shore of the Red Sea." Moses nodded. "You're on Kebir, an island not far from the Sea's southern end."

"An island? How did I get on an island?"

The two men didn't know how to answer him, but Moses was already figuring it out himself. He wished he had been paying more attention over the last few days. He surmised that the boat must have recently crossed the opening between the mainland and the island. Oh well, he couldn't have done anything about it anyway, and now it wasn't going to do him any good to complain. He was where he was and that was that.

"Does the name have a meaning?" Moses wanted to know.

"Kebir means 'large' for this is the largest island among several near here," Cabrun said. "But only this one is inhabited. Our village is at the end of this path. We'll pass through an opening in the hills to get there."

"Do you have a leader?" Moses inquired.

"Our island is small enough to do without much governing." Cabrun replied. "We do pay some tribute to the Sea Prince, but if we pay on time and don't go against his wishes, mostly we're left alone."

Moses blanched at the reference to the Sea Prince. He wondered if the Sea Prince had ordered his abrupt relocation from boat to land. He chose not to ask right now, but to wait for his companions to volunteer more information.

And then it hit him... an island! They said he was on an island! Well, that settles that, he thought, gloomily. Visions of the people of The Community swam before his inner eye. He thought of the last actual glimpse he had had of them while looking down on their encampment at the rendezvous point. Besides Eliezer and Milcah and the few who had planned his escape from the main body of Israelites, he hardly knew any of them personally. Still, thinking of them now, he was filled with a stabbing grief for every last one of them as if he had known them forever. He hadn't, of course, but now there was no chance he ever would. Sudden hot tears sprung to his eyes, so he raised his hand to his face as if wiping away the grit of blowing sand.

What choice could he possibly have made since his last encounter with the Holy Presence sufficient to eliminate the possibility of ever seeing The Community again? He couldn't think of anything. And right at this moment, he could barely stand, much less walk for the pain of loss.

Even in the depths of his grief, Moses' mind was still working, and already some things were coming clear. He realized the perverse wisdom in the Sea Prince's plan. It was the perfect solution. Moses represented too much of a threat, so of course he had to be removed, but he was too well known to be executed. The Sea Prince had said as much. So, his cleverness was obvious now: put Moses on an island where he can live out his days in obscurity. And as that conclusion set in, he ventured a guess with his companions.

"I get the impression that I am no longer a slave, but that you have been asked, make that commanded, to keep me here as your permanent guest. Is that about the size of it?"

Clearly amazed at Moses' perspicacity, they nodded. And the quiet one mumbled, "You got it... lucky us!"

"So, what am I supposed to do as a guest around here?"

"Well, we grow some things. And we have some animals that need tending. Our sheep are shorn each year. They have a very coarse fleece that we make into a heavy thread that is then woven into material for rope and sails. If you choose, you can help with any of those tasks. It's not hard work but it gives us something to do."

Moses' mind was now working furiously. All his confusion had vanished. Maybe he could find a way off the island if he paid attention carefully enough. Only one thing mattered: he wasn't ready to give up hope of reuniting with his newfound Community.

They showed him to a small cave next to the village where he would live. It was roomy and dry enough, and he'd slept in much worse places. He volunteered to tend the sheep and soon discovered that he loved it as much now as he had forty years before—but not so much that he would want to do it forever. Little by little he learned about the island, how self-sufficient they were, and what things needed to be supplied from other places by the boats that occasionally put in to the island's several harbors.

There were a few villages on this island that turned out to be much larger than Moses had first thought. He considered escaping first to one of the other villages, and then making his way to the mainland somehow, but he soon surmised that the Sea Prince would never allow that. These people would keep him away from the boats to remove any hope of leaving the island. He was also pretty sure that at least parts of this island were used to support the slave trade, so there were likely to be guards everywhere to prevent escapes.

He decided to wait, watch, and, if possible, not worry. The way would appear in time. Before long Moses settled into the routine of the island, but he always kept his eyes open for anything that might facilitate an escape. He noted the comings and goings of the villagers and soon could determine with a good degree of accuracy when boats were landing to take on supplies. Sometimes Cabrun and Herno would be gone for days and Moses concluded that they were probably escorting slaves to an encampment somewhere else on the island.

While on the boat, Moses had missed his early morning walks. He had been walking at dawn just about every day since his youth. One day, shortly after his arrival on the island, he scrounged around in a stand of trees until he found a branch to serve as a walking stick. His first replacement still lay in the cave where he had been abducted. He tried several new ones, but not one felt right. His old staff, the one that Joshua now carried, had felt like part of his body. His fingers ached to hold it again. In frustration, he chose the least offensive replacement and went for his walk.

Walking alone enabled him to sort through his thoughts and experiences. These days, however, his walks had taken on a different purpose. He now spent his time observing and learning about the island. Each time he left the village, he walked farther and farther away. Some days he would be gone until the time of the evening meal, but no one paid much attention. Everyone knew there was no way he could get off the island, so he could pretty much do whatever he wanted.

Moses had always had an affinity for high places, and so it was natural for him to explore every hill. Besides enjoying the altitude for its own mind-clearing properties, he also found this an efficient way to explore the island. From some of the hills he could see long stretches of island coastline and he made sure to note the location of any villages and harbors. On the clearest of days he thought he could see the mainland to the west, a thin brown ribbon floating on the Sea.

One day while sitting at the top of one of the island's highest hills, his gaze fell on a small irregularity in the island's southern shoreline. All the villages on the island were built near harbors, but it was just possible that not all the harbors had villages. He suspected that there was a harbor there and he was pretty sure that no village attended it, so he determined to take his next long walk in that direction.

Moses had recently been enjoying the opportunity to tend sheep, but fortunately he was not required to be a shepherd. The other shepherds hardly noticed when he stopped showing up. As long as his overseers saw him at the end of the day, all was well.

He woke with excitement on the day he was to explore the hoped-for harbor. He took sufficient food and water to last the whole day and he tied a long cloak around his waist in the event of inclement weather. The two-hour walk to the edge of the sea was a mere stroll after half a lifetime of nomadic wandering. Moses found himself standing on a bluff overlooking a small harbor that was well protected from wind and tide. He surmised that the water was quite shallow and unsuited to cargo-laden vessels. He guessed that no one ever came here. He carefully picked his way down the long embankment until he stood with his feet at the edge of the gently lapping waves. The only features that broke up the smoothly curving beach were pieces of driftwood of all sizes and shapes. Moses didn't need a visitation by the Holy One to begin formulating his audacious plan.

Islands were wonderfully secure places, especially when proper attention was paid to the only known ways onto and away from the island. Such security made other kinds of vigilance unnecessary, so Moses had an easy time appropriating the necessary materials for his escape.

It was no problem at all to find enough braided wool rope. Rope was everywhere. Stealing a piece of sailcloth during the dark of the night required only slightly more effort. He was making regular trips to the harbor now with lengths of rope wound around his middle. Each day he would leave some of his food at the harbor in a hole covered by a large flat rock. He could barely move it into place, so he felt sure his stash would be safe from any nosy animals. On the day he put the sailcloth in his sack, he didn't worry about packing any food. He had accumulated more than enough under the rock.

Moses worked at the harbor under an overhang in the bluff, so anyone wandering about (and there was little chance of that) would not be able to see the raft he was fashioning out of driftwood. Over time, the sea breezes had created a dune of sand between his workspace and the water, so he was invisible from that direction as well. No one would see him unless they were within twenty feet of him. He felt quite secure.

Moses started waking up earlier and earlier so he could begin his walk in the dark. He always showed up in the village at dusk to share a skin of goat's milk and conversation with his overseers. He made sure they knew about his observance of the Sabbath so that on every seventh day he would be able stay away from the village for an extra day. Moses planned to use the extra time to advantage.

When the construction of the raft was completed, Moses decided to test it. He would not be able to give it enough of a test within the harbor. He needed to see if it really could be seaworthy. If he made use of his Sabbath, he would have two full days for his shakedown cruise. He left his cave just after full dark and padded out of the village. He arrived at the harbor with time for a few hours of sleep before sun-up. His years of overseeing building projects in Egypt had served him well. He had constructed a sturdy craft that could be moved with very little effort by placing rounded pieces of driftwood underneath and rolling it. Even a man of his advanced years could get it to the water.

There was never any breeze in the harbor this early in the morning, so the water was smooth as a mirror. Even though he was pretty sure it would float, he was relieved when the raft actually proved itself to be buoyant. He was tempted to giggle when it didn't sink to the bottom as soon as he climbed aboard. Moses had rigged the tiller so he could move the raft through the water by swinging it from side to side. It took only about an hour to reach the mouth of the harbor where the waves were much higher and the breezes fresher.

Had he thought to look back at the land, he might have noticed a lone figure watching from the top of the bluff. After a short time, the figure vanished. But Moses had not looked. He was too occupied with his new craft. By means of an ingenious arrangement of ropes, he was able to raise the sail. He made a note in his mind to learn all he could about the prevailing winds during this practice run. His wilderness experience served him well once again because though the wind patterns were different on water, they were still patterns that could be observed and were probably predictable.

As soon as he put up the sail, his ungainly, but lightweight craft moved rapidly away from the harbor, pushed by a strong offshore breeze. If the Sea was anything like the wilderness, these winds should make some sort of shift in the middle of the day and blow in a different direction for several hours. This possibility was vital to his plan.

Though he could harness the power of the wind and steer in a rudimentary way, he still had to depend largely on the direction of the wind. Moses surmised that if he didn't sail too far, he could ride the afternoon onshore winds back to the harbor. He felt confident that he could steer that much, anyway. At about the midpoint between dawn and noon, Moses lowered the sail and allowed himself to drift in order to test the current. As long as he kept tabs on the hill that rose in line with the harbor, he would be able to find his way back.

He ventured to stand up and look north and south in an attempt to estimate how far he had crossed. Because this was no becalmed harbor, he had to pull himself up hand over hand on the rugged mast that supported the sail. Fortunately he only needed a glance to take his bearings and he felt much more secure once he sat back down. According to his estimate he was about a third of the way across. Theoretically, if he allowed the morning waves to blow him as far as they would to the south, he should be able to pick up an onshore breeze in the afternoon that would bring him safely to the mainland.

As he sat calculating, he thought of the Holy One. Since their last encounter, Moses had not sought nor received any more divine appearances. He now trusted that he could never outrun the Holy Presence. What surprised him was how calm he felt and how ready he was to face any conceivable, or even inconceivable, outcome. Anything could happen. Perhaps his plan wouldn't succeed, and he would be left stranded on the island. Perhaps he would get caught in the turbulence of wind and water in the center of the Sea, only to die of exposure. Or perhaps he would actually reach the mainland. At this moment, it didn't matter. All that mattered was that he had made his choice to try.

An hour or two after the sun reached its highest point overhead, Moses felt a new breeze emerging out of the noonday calm—and it was blowing north just as he had predicted. He raised the sail and took hold of the tiller. The trip back to his harbor invigorated him. He had learned a great deal this day and soon he would attempt the crossing. He was grateful that his trip back was surprisingly uneventful. Because he was not expected to return until the next evening, he was able to sleep for a few hours before walking back in the dead of night to reach his cave before first light.

He was too excited to sleep anymore. Now that he had gained confidence in the viability of his plan, he had to think about what provisions to gather for the trip. He would need more than the minimum required for the crossing because he was certain that no one would have a ready-made bed or food awaiting his arrival. At dusk Moses left the cave and walked to the village for his regular conversation with Cabrun and Herno over goat's milk, dates, and cheese. Though, had he known about the conversation they were having just then, Moses would not have felt so at ease.

Cabrun was saying to Herno, "I have been following Moses as he goes out on his frequent walks. I think he might be up to something."

"Where does he go?"

"Well, it's quite strange. He's been going up into the hills where he sits and looks."

"What do you think he's looking at?"

"It's a little hard to tell, but I think he must be watching the slave encampment on the east end of the island," Cabrun said smoothly.

"Why would he do that, do you suppose?"

"I don't know, but I'm worried. Yesterday he managed to go down from the mountain and get himself right next to the compound without being seen. After he conversed with several of the slaves for a long time he then retreated once again without arousing the interest of the guards."

"What should we do?"

"Well, I've been thinking about that." Cabrun scratched his beard. "I think he means to start a slave revolt. Maybe he thinks he can get away in one of the boats in the confusion."

"I wondered how long it would take him to try something. So, what should we do?"

"I'm glad you asked. I've been formulating a plan. Pay attention now, Herno. I'll continue to follow him for the next few days, while you take all our men to the compound where you can make sure the boats are well guarded. When he makes his move, we will catch him between us."

"Ya, that is a good plan. I will go and organize the men." Herno got up to leave.

"Sit down, you fool. Moses will be here shortly expecting to see us both here. We don't want to make him suspicious."

Herno sat.

"I'll walk him to his cave tonight and ask him how he's settling in. Perhaps he'll betray something in his answer."

"Ya, good," Herno reached for another handful of goat cheese.

Later that night Cabrun escorted Moses back to the cave. "Moses, I know what you're up to."

Moses heart leapt up into his throat, but he managed to mask his panic. "What?"

"I know what you are doing. I've been following you."

"Well, I hope you've enjoyed walking all those miles to watch me sit on a hilltop." Moses hoped that his bluff would work.

Cabrun just smiled. "That's quite the seaworthy raft you've built. I'm impressed."

Moses was stunned. He had been certain that no one cared about his movements. He'd been very careful besides. "I don't know what you're talking about." Moses hoped that Cabrun was the one who was bluffing.

"Moses, calm down. I'm not going to turn you in—actually, I'm going to go with you."

Moses just stared, unable to believe what he was hearing.

"You must be wondering what's in it for me."

Moses could only nod.

"You're not the only prisoner on this island—I am, too, in a way. It doesn't matter why, but I've been wanting to leave for a very long time. The problem is that I've never had the means. Now I do."

Moses finally found his voice. "It appears I have no choice but to trust your good intentions, but I think the weight of two men will make the raft go too slow. We'll never make it."

"I must disagree. By the way, I've already figured out your plan. It won't work, you know. The distance is too far."

Moses gasped.

"Settle down, Moses. I know another way that has a much better chance of succeeding. Of course, sea travel always includes peril, but my way is at least possible." Now Moses was intrigued. "A bit more to the east and south from the direction you sailed there is an uninhabited island. If we stop at the island, the journey to the mainland can be accomplished in two parts. And by the way—before you even ask the question that I know is on your mind, here is the answer: If I don't go, no one goes!"

At that moment, Moses remembered the Holy One's emphasis on choices. Here was one now. Moses closed his eyes and sighed. "Very well, we will sail together and perhaps we will even succeed."

And so they set to planning.

Chapter 37

Eliezer was devastated. He had never given up hope that Moses would catch up to them eventually. But once they crossed the Sea, all hope of a reunion with his father would be gone.

He sat by himself some distance away from the camp. Most people were so relieved at having achieved a consensus decision that they had created an impromptu celebration. Some were eating, some dancing, and there were knots of people catching up on one another's news and making up for the estrangement among them that had lasted far too long.

He pulled his cloak tight around his head and shoulders, attempting to blot out any disturbing sounds of happiness. Eliezer was grieving.

He heard no telltale sound, but sensed that someone was standing near him. Without looking, he knew it was Milcah, and he knew that she understood what he was feeling.

"May I join you?

"Of course. Please sit down." He shook the cowl of his cloak off his head and turned to Milcah. "I wonder if anyone besides me thinks of Moses."

"I know they do, Eliezer, but perhaps not in the same way that a son thinks of his father. Besides, they're just now discovering the power of their adulthood. In a way, we've all been children of Moses for our entire lives. After a while, such a father becomes burdensome, no matter how competent and caring he may be. In their own time they will grieve, too. I promise you."

"But my grief is now. You know, it would have been easier if we hadn't discovered ourselves to be kindred spirits, Moses and I. I'd just found him when I lost him again."

"Are you certain he is lost to you?"

"I can't imagine how he could ever find us once we get across the Sea."

"I think I understand what you're saying, but perhaps there's another way to look at this."

Eliezer's face showed his confusion.

"Think of it this way. All we know is that we don't know where Moses is, right?"

"Right."

"So, how can we know which choice will bring us closer to or remove us farther away from him?"

Eliezer scratched his beard.

Then she said, "You've been assuming that he must be following us, haven't you?" Eliezer nodded. "Well, it seems to me that one man traveling alone could easily have caught up to us. Moses said as much. So, something must have happened back there. If Moses is still alive he could be absolutely anywhere."

Eliezer thought about her reasoning. "I think I would feel it in this son's heart if he were dead. My heart says he lives, so perhaps you're right. All we can do is make our most honest choices, I suppose." Then he smiled and reached out to touch her face. "I am so glad I haven't lost you."

"Me, too. Now, let's go celebrate what this marvelous group has achieved today."

"Yes, let's." He took her arm and guided her toward the sounds of revelry.

Chapter 38

As it turned out, the most difficult part of The Community's crossing of the sea had simply been making the decision. The town, due to its prime location, already had a history of engaging in trade and of dealing with diverse peoples. Riding in the harbor were two fleets of boats: one fleet equipped to carry goods on long voyages for trade and the other equipped for more local fishing. Kenan, Enosh, Eliezer, and Sarah formed the delegation that had negotiated their passage. Sarah's gender was relegated to a non-issue once they realized that "Money is spoken here."

They had approached the traders first, but because they recognized an increased peril for their people as a result of the slave trade, they decided to try the fishing fleet instead. Fortunately, they had arrived during the poorest fishing season, and so two boats and crews were readily placed at their disposal—and for a reasonable cost at that. Each boat could transport about ten people at a time. The travelers sold most of their livestock for a good price, but kept a few of the best animals for breeding stock. It would take about forty trips to get them all across the one-day passage to the other side.

After only forty-five days, The Community of Promise, complete with goods and livestock, found itself in Africa.

From the moment that the first group had sailed under Kenan's supervision until the last trip with Enosh on board, Sarah and Asher had positioned themselves on the beach next to the loading ramp. In a sense, they attended to this momentous crossing as a priestly embodiment of the presence of the Holy One. They stood there as a reminder that this community held together better when individuals nurtured their connections to the Divine. And they stood as a sign that Holy Presence rode in each and every boat. Furthermore, they gave ritual expression to a perpetual blessing.

Many townspeople gathered day after day to watch the departures. Though they didn't understand the religious beliefs of this traveling band, they were impressed with the caring presence clearly represented by Asher and Sarah.

After Enosh had seen to the loading of the last boat, he helped the two "priests" to gather up their belongings and occupy the last two places. This wasn't the Jordan River, but their crossing held every bit as much promise for new life in a new land as that other crossing had for the main body of the Israelites. That each of the crossings went relatively smoothly, and the fact that all of them were deposited safely on the African shore would, over the generations, grow into a legend of miraculous proportions. And maybe it was exactly that.

After the last boat had deposited Enosh, Asher, and Sarah on land, the whole people feasted and celebrated their boundless gratitude, as much for the community they had become as for their safe passage. Each and every person was relieved and delighted to sense that the presence of the Holy One was still with them even on this side of the Sea. No one had actually doubted that that would be so, but the actual experience was sweet, indeed.

It didn't take them long to find a suitable place to set up their camp on the other side. With relish and trust this time, the gathered Community began the familiar process of deciding which way to go next. They still had to locate the land that would support their promise.

Chapter 39

While Herno escorted the able men to the slave camp, Cabrun was supposed to be keeping an eye on Moses. According to plan, as soon as he had moved out of sight of the village, Moses waited for his new partner to catch up. Moses was nervous because he had never worked like this before. Either he had been the leader or he had been by himself. Collaboration with an equal felt awkward and uncontrollable. Moses had always held his destiny (and the destiny of others, if need be) in his own hands. But he had no real choice this time, so he did his best to learn this new skill.

Because they expected the trip to the mainland to take just two days, they didn't need to take very much with them. Lamb was a staple on the island, and Moses had accumulated enough for one person to survive on for a few days. It hadn't been too difficult to slip an extra piece into his robe at each meal. So now, strings of lamb were drying on a rack near the beach, surrounded by the protective fence that Moses had built out of driftwood and thorny brush. The meat wouldn't last as long as properly dried lamb but it would serve.

When Moses shared his concern about their limited supply, Cabrun laughed at him. He had been preparing for his own escape for years and always had a stash available in the event that an opportunity presented itself. Combining their stores, they would have more than enough to eat. Stockpiled water and dried bread completed their menu.

Both men knew that sooner or later Herno would get suspicious, so they had to make their last minute preparations hastily. They agreed to leave the village that very night and sail with the early morning offshore breeze.

Moses still wasn't positive that the raft would even float carrying the weight of two men. But, they were committed now. There was no going back. If they didn't stay afloat, their escape attempt would sink with the raft. Of longer-term concern was Moses' certainty that the raft would be harder to steer with the extra weight. He hoped they would be able to navigate at least well enough to reach their small half-way-point island. If they missed the island and got caught up in the currents of the open sea, they might never reach land.

When Moses told Cabrun about his concern, his fellow escapee frowned in a way that wrinkled up his whole face. Moses' fear rose up into his throat.

Cabrun looked like a man with indigestion. "I've never personally been on this part of the Sea, but I have always listened with great interest and care whenever the captains have related their experiences—the wonderful and the frightful. I've learned more than enough about the Sea and its navigation by listening. At this time of year the currents run from east to west. In order to reach the island we will first sail to the east along our coast. The current is weaker close to land; sometimes it actually flows in the opposite direction. When we've sailed almost to the harbor of the slave camp we will then be far enough to the east so that when we turn toward our long and narrow island the current and the wind should help us hit its broad side. With a small bit of luck we'll run right into the middle of it."

Moses felt sick to his stomach. Give him a barren desert any day. He could survive for years. He had survived for years. But he had no way of knowing if Cabrun was telling the truth or even if he really knew what he was talking about. It seemed to Moses that, in spite of Cabrun's assurances, they were about to navigate a truly treacherous body of water. Then again, did he have any choice? That got him thinking about this and other choices he had made so far. In his mind, he desperately cast about for other options, but no alternative course of action presented itself.

With a start he realized that Cabrun was still talking—now about the second leg of their sea voyage. "We must hope we don't land too far to the west because our point of departure the next morning will have to be the southeastern-most tip of the island. The westerly current is even stronger there."

Moses wasn't convinced. "How can you be so sure this is the best approach? Do your boats use our life-saving island for their voyages?"

"Well, not exactly." Cabrun seemed averse to giving Moses any more information, but finally, under the heat of Moses relentless stare, he reluctantly added one more tidbit. "The boat captains use that little island as a navigational aid. If they're going to the mainland, they sail east and south of the island and then pick up the prevailing winds that help to counteract the strong westerly sea current. If their objective is to travel farther to the west, then they sail along the north side of the island."

Moses grimaced. "So you're telling me that there will be slaving boats all around us?"

"Well, it's not quite as bad as that. If we sail on time and our trip goes as planned, the slavers will always be behind us. That's why we have to leave so early: to be in position to turn south as soon as the morning offshore winds pick up." Then, Cabrun smiled and said lightly, "You didn't think our little escapade would be completely devoid of peril, now did you? What kind of a story would that make?"

In that instant, Moses was reminded of the times that he had known the laughter of the Holy One. It always tended to put things into a healthier perspective.

Now that he thought he understood the magnitude of their impending risk, Moses wondered if they should abort the plan. When he offered that possibility to Cabrun, the other man's face darkened. "I'm afraid we can't do that now. Herno expects you to be up to no good. Things can never go back to the way they were. Besides, this is my opportunity for escape, too and I've already waited for it far too long. There'll be none better in the future."

Moses sighed. For most of his life, he had been the one with the strongest commitment to action in the face of peril. It was strange to be on the receiving end, but then, nothing in his present situation was remotely like the rest of his life. Then, before he could lose heart, he clapped Cabrun on the shoulder. "Very well then. Let's do it!"

Cabrun let out a relieved laugh. "Everything is ready. We only have a few hours until we depart. We'll benefit later from getting some rest now."

Moses lay in the shelter of the overhanging bluff. In the dim light he could see the shadowy form of the raft that would serve as home for the next two days (only two! he hoped). He wasn't sleepy, but he felt remarkably relaxed. Because he had made his choice, his anxiety had now dissipated.

As illogical as it seemed, the decision to go south onto the African mainland had the feel of the right way. Could it be possible that The Community might also get there someday? If so, he wondered if he would live to see them. He felt the tears well up in his eyes as he pictured Eliezer and Milcah surrounded by the others, those he already knew and those he had yet to meet. They were his family and he longed to be with them again. Though he took responsibility for his choice, he recognized the truth that he had no power to bring about the final outcome. Many others were also making significant choices. Finally, his fatigue caught up with him and he slept.

Chapter 40

Just before The Community members had begun their crossing, Kenan, Sarah, and Enosh had arranged an informal meeting with some traders from the land across the sea. In exchange for some gold, an Israelite meal, and a few entertaining stories, the traders offered a wealth of practical information about their land and its environs.

They learned that a trade route ran to the north along the coast, but it was only lightly used because the main trade route went by sea. Some goods were exchanged in a growing village port about three hundred miles to the north, but the general area was not heavily populated. Encouraged by this information, the assembly was hopeful as they camped between the beach they had landed on and the road. A few people had advocated that they settle down right away once they had crossed the Sea. But others, remembering the variety of environments they had passed through in their years of wandering, wanted to consider other options before making a final decision. They wanted to know that they were making a real choice. The others were open to persuasion so, fortunately, this didn't develop into a serious conflict.

The whole company had learned that the land to the south soon turned into ocean, and that traveling due west would put them back into a relatively inhospitable wilderness again. They had had enough in their past years and recent months of wandering. They were truly ready to settle down.

The only real option left was to head north for a time, all the while gathering more information about likely places for settlement. Largely as a result of Sarah's encouragement, they determined to maintain their individual and collective openness to the Holy Presence. No one could explain just how it worked, but as a group they seemed to function better when they allowed Holy Presence to support their human relationships and decisions. In this case the idea of traveling north ultimately appealed to everyone. They soon embarked with a growing trust in their ability to steer an appropriate course for themselves.

They felt no urgency to hurry. There were certainly no armies chasing them, and on this side of the sea they encountered even fewer travelers than on the other. Furthermore, most of those they did meet traveled in bands smaller than theirs. The terrain was quite flat so it was an easy traverse. Or it would have been had they not traveled so far south from where they began their bold journey. It was beastly hot here—uncomfortably hot. It was true that they had lived for years in heat, but at least in their old familiar wilderness it had been a dry heat.

Sarah was amazed when she thought of how far they had come. At first she thought of the immense distances they had traveled and the physical challenges they had faced. Without even considering the extraordinary perils of bandits and oceans, she marveled that a group such as theirs could simply have found enough food and safe places to sleep.

She thought about how their numbers had fluctuated. A few adults and children had become ill along the way, more than once necessitating a hiatus in travel as those people died and had to be buried and mourned. Even if the ill ones survived, they still caused the whole company to wait as they recovered and became able to travel once again. Several babies had been born, too. Some of the women had already been pregnant when the journey began and many more had conceived since. Sarah wondered if the new promise inherent in their company might be responsible for this apparent increase in fertility. She thought, too, about how most of these new parents still carried on the old custom of removing the foreskin from the male infants a few days after birth.

As a whole group they represented a wide array of talents: scouting, trading, military maneuvers, healing and midwifery, food preservation and preparation to name a few.

The most incredible part of their journey had been their transformation into a highly respectful and functional community. Sarah could not stop marveling and rejoicing at the most recent developments. Often their community gatherings took place on days when they rested and did not have to travel. Yesterday had been such a day.

The term of service for Sarah, Kenan, and Enosh as leaders had come to an end. When the community gathered to replace them, the most extraordinary things happened. First, Eliezer rose to reprise the question that had stunned them all back on Mount Nebo. "What kind of leadership do you want? Clearly, no one wanted to revert to investing authority in another Prophet of God. Someone then asked Sarah and her colleagues to report on their experiences of leadership over the last six months. Back when they had been selected, each one of them had expected to have to make wise decisions on behalf of the whole community. But, to everyone's surprise the need almost never arose.

Sarah stood to give her report. "It never felt right to tell any of you what to do, though we spent long stretches of time analyzing situations and considering options. In each case, however, the whole community made the final decision."

Then Kenan spoke up. "Sometimes we acted as representatives of the community, but usually we pulled in some other people whom we thought to be essential to the successful outcome of the particular situation."

And then Enosh added his insights. "Mostly we thought about how to help the community come to decisions that everyone could live with. It often didn't end up the way I would have predicted or even wanted, but as I look back, each decision turned out to be a good one. It scares me to think about what could have happened if I had insisted on making decisions for you." Then he sat down, smiling crookedly.

"But you directed us well many times," a man said.

"In small ways, I did, but the directions I gave dealt with execution, not policy. And there have been many, if not most of you, who have used your own skills to do just as much for the community."

Sarah had another thought. "I wonder if we still need to have a leadership team. Couldn't we function just as well without one?"

In response, Jethro stood to speak. He had been one of the most useful people in the whole company. Most of them had by that time heard the story of Jethro's contribution to planning Moses' faked death. His natural propensity for clear and wise thinking had helped then and it had helped many times since. "We could simply redefine leadership," he said, "without having to eliminate it. In some ways we're all leaders, living and deciding our next steps based on our integrity. Still, it's useful to set aside a small number of persons who can pay attention to what's happening, much as our retiring leaders have done. They've raised the necessary questions and have helped us to address them. Besides, they've respected us so much that our respect for each other has increased proportionately. They've also reminded us to stay open to the collective wisdom of our experiences of the Holy One. Without actually directing us they've enabled us to have direction. I, for one, am deeply appreciative."

At that, many in the gathering echoed their agreement with nods and words of thanks.

Kenan rose to speak once more. "If this body decides to continue to ordain individuals for this special type of leadership (and I'm guessing you will), you'd do well to include Jethro on the team."

In response to the validating noise of the crowd, Jethro nodded with an attempt at solemnity, but his obvious pleasure at their affirmation shone brightly in his face. The gathering quickly agreed that their leaders would continue to emulate the direction set by Sarah, Enosh, and Kenan. They would pay attention to the events in the community. And they would consider and then offer approaches to aid the community in their collective decision-making process. Furthermore, they would continue to encourage everyone among them to maintain their openness to the Holy One.

Along with Jethro, Tirzah (Eliezer's sister-in-law) and one of the midwives named Tamar were ordained as leaders for the next half-year. In one of their first recommendations, they asked the group to set Asher and Sarah aside for a special task.

They had all been so moved by the couple's blessing of the sea-crossing that they wanted Sarah and Asher to create and oversee the development of the community's Sabbath (for that is what they called their day of rest) rituals. There would be no specific requirements around the rituals; they would simply be offered as opportunities. Deeply humbled, and honored at the same time by their selection and affirmation, they accepted.

Enosh continued to advise the scouts while Kenan began sharing the tent of a woman whose husband had died along the way. He informed the gathering that he did not wish any other responsibilities right then besides getting better acquainted with his new wife.

In high spirits, the company resumed its northward journey, open to any stirrings or hints that might lead them toward their new home.

Chapter 41

The stars shone brightly and the moon hung low behind them in the western sky as Moses and Cabrun used make-shift paddles to wend their way along, but just offshore the coast of the main island. They traveled in silence during the dark hours until the eastern sky began to pink before them. As soon as there was enough light, Cabrun scanned the shore to verify their location. "Good. We've come far enough. Now if the offshore breeze will just kiss us a bit more passionately, we can begin our run for freedom."

Every few minutes he would stand and face the land, hoping to feel the freshening breeze on his face. Then finally it was time. "Get ready, Moses, here it comes. Prepare to turn south when I raise the sail."

In a few seconds they felt the raft lurch forward. The farther they got from land, the more they felt the strong current pushing them to the west. "Keep trying to steer into the current a bit more. That'll help." Cabrun had to yell to be heard over the sound of the wind and waves.

By mid-morning, Moses' arms and shoulders were knotted with pain from pushing on the tiller. "Cabrun, I'm getting too old for this. Can we change places for a while? I think I can handle the sail well enough. I learned quite a bit during my long journey to your island."

Cabrun looked skeptical, but then shrugged and handed the rope to Moses while taking hold of the tiller.

So far they had seen no other boats and now the island was in sight. As they came closer, Cabrun yelled, "The current is moving us too far to the west. If we don't fight it we'll miss the island altogether!"

"What do you want me to do?" Moses hollered back.

"We have to start paddling." Cabrun lashed the tiller to keep them pointing at the island. "Here, take this!" He handed Moses one of their rudely constructed paddles and took the other one himself.

Both men paddled as if their lives depended on it, for of course, they did.

Armed with just hearsay knowledge, Cabrun had never heard about how much faster the current flowed near to the island. No matter how hard they paddled, the island continued to slip by them at alarming speed. Even so, with a bit of luck they could still make it.

"Over there! Paddle for those rocks at the end of the island. If we can get in among them, we can wade to shore. Don't let go of the rope when we go in."

Moses shifted around so he could secure the sail rope in the crook of his arm while he still paddled furiously. Just as it looked like they would make it, the wind abruptly died leaving them at the mercy of the strong current. They watched helplessly as the tip of the island slid by and then receded into the distance behind them.

Neither man spoke for a long time. Finally, Cabrun stood, and while holding onto their crude mast, looked carefully in every direction.

"What are you doing?"

"Maybe it's crazy, but I'm trying to figure out the direction of the wind and current. I'd like to think that we could still hit some piece of land before we starve. If the current takes us too far north, there's no hope of that, unless of course some boat sees us and rescues us."

Moses scowled. "I have the distinct impression that most of the boats around here are slavers. That wouldn't improve our lot very much."

Cabrun's face fell, but he kept a hopeful note in his voice. "Well, a few of them are bound to be fishing boats. Let's hope we'll be rescued by one of those."

"And if we're carried toward shore?"

"There is a very large bay, not very far to the west of here. It's possible that the currents moving into it might help us. But it's so vast that we might still find ourselves impossibly far from land." Cabrun thought for a moment and then made his recommendation. "I think it's worth trying to aim in that direction. The sun's beginning its downward slide, so we should be able to navigate by it. Let's set the sail and tiller to point us as much as possible to the south. Maybe that'll improve our luck."

And so their little raft fought wind and current as it bobbed like a cork in the open sea.

Though Cabrun and Moses would never find out, at just that time, a fleet of slaver boats and men had just left the harbor by the colony. They were heading for the small island that had been left in the raft's wake. Herno had become suspicious of Cabrun and had taken a party to look for them. By chance they had spied the raft in the shallow water just as Moses and Cabrun had raised its sail. Herno had sat with Cabrun many times listening to the same boat captains while they described their sea voyages. Herno was not as ignorant as he acted, so it had not taken him long to guess at Cabrun's plan. He hurried back to the harbor at the colony, where he persuaded several of the captains to sail to the small island. He assured them that they would find the escapees camped out there that evening. Herno would be in big trouble when no runaways were found on the island.

Moses was exhausted by the time the sun sank into the waves. In moments, he was asleep. He dreamed of mountains, caves, and the desert wilderness. Walls of water threatened everything. In each scene, Moses stood with his staff raised, trying to hold off the floods. In his dream his arms ached and he didn't know if he could persevere any longer. He was strongly tempted to lay down his staff and his body so that the waters would carry him into oblivion.

At long last, he decided to give up, but he found he couldn't lower his arms. It was as if some unknown power held them up.

Then he knew. The power was not unknown and he was not alone. He had never been alone. No conversation took place in his dream, but he would awaken with new knowledge as if a conversation like this had transpired:

"My arms are not tired, but I think yours are, Moses."

"How long have you been there? I wasn't aware of you before now."

"Long enough."

"I don't think I can do this anymore. Are we at the end?"

"Do you want it to be the end, Moses?"

"I'm so very tired. I think it'd be easy to stop striving."

"Is that what you want, Moses?"

"I'm not sure. Actually, I'm very confused about my present situation."

"That's understandable."

"I still have this very strong sense that I made the right choice by sailing with Cabrun—that somehow he would lead me to Eliezer and the others. But, now it seems unlikely we can succeed. Perhaps I was wrong in my choice."

"Moses, you have become so wise in so many ways through your long life, but apparently some personality traits die hard."

"What do you mean?"

"You always think you're supposed to know how things will turn out. This is not the first time we have had a conversation about a situation like this. Do you remember, Moses?"

"Yes. Sometimes it's very hard to trust."

"Well, to your credit, you usually get there eventually."

"So, if I am getting your drift, there may still be hope, right? ...Right? ...RIGHT?

"What's right, Moses? Wake up! What's right?" Cabrun was shaking Moses' shoulder.

"Huh? What's the sun doing there? I thought it had set some time ago."

"It's morning, Moses. You were crying out in your sleep. Now tell me, what's right?"

"Oh, just a dream... Right." Moses rubbed his eyes and then stood up to stretch. "I don't remember exactly, but somehow I think there's hope."

"Of course there is, Moses. Look!" Cabrun was pointing to the south. "Look, land!"

Moses shaded his eyes from the sun with his left hand and squinted through the pearly mist. There, ahead, a rocky finger of land pointed right at them. Just to the left was a beach, and with the aid of current and breeze they couldn't miss it.

Chapter 42

"Don't worry, I'll find you," Eliezer was saying.

"How can you be so sure?" Jethro's question sounded like a complaint. "We can't bear to lose you, and we can't wait here forever to see if you return."

Eliezer smiled affectionately. "You are such a good man, Jethro. And there are so many men and women as good as you in this company. The risk to you isn't very great. You'll do fine with or without me."

Jethro's brows furrowed as he searched for another argument, but Eliezer cut him off. "I have to do this. I had a dream. I have to go and see for myself."

"We'll go with you, then."

"No. I don't know why, but I think it would be more dangerous for everyone if you came with me. I'm not even taking Milcah, but I have every intention of seeing her, and you, soon enough. Now go, take the people up into the highland to the west. Find our new home and I promise I will join you there."

The next morning when The Community was about to resume the journey, Eliezer embraced Milcah. Then he took hold of the rope attached to the neck of the solitary goat that carried his supplies. After one more glance at his friends, he headed north.

Such a dream it had been—so vivid—almost like he was observing reality from a strange angle. He didn't dream about Moses often, but such dreams couldn't be called unusual. Most of the time in the dream world he saw Moses at some distance away from him and try as he might, he could never close the gap between them. Sometimes his father seemed to be well and at peace and at other times Eliezer had the impression that Moses was in some kind of trouble.

But this dream—he still couldn't get over how real it was. He and Moses were sitting by the same fire eating a delicious meat stew. In the dream, they sat in a clearing near to, but just hidden from the main path. Eliezer kept reaching out to touch his father's sleeve, hand, shoulder, and beard as if to make sure he was actually there. He couldn't remember what they had said, but everything else was so real: trees, plants, rocks.

Each day now as he walked alone, Eliezer replayed the dream in his imagination. He couldn't get enough of it. And then, there it was. He had stepped off the path to relieve himself when he saw it. Every rock, tree, and plant was exactly as in the dream.

He removed his pack from the goat and spread two skins out on the ground. Then he slept. In the morning, Eliezer rose and laid a fire. When it was burning evenly, he rinsed the dust and ash off his face and hands. He took a piece of cord from his pack and then laid the goat on its side so he could bind its feet. With one flick of his razor-sharp knife, he cut through the large artery in the goat's neck and then hung the dying animal from a tree by its back legs so the blood pooled around the roots.

He set about cutting several slabs of succulent goat flesh into small pieces and then he placed them in a new skin that he had half-filled with water. After he had added some spices, grains, and a few edible plants he had found along the way, he hung the skin over the fire.

Then he sat and waited as if in a trance.

Chapter 43

Cabrun had no intention of remaining with old and slow Moses once they were on dry land. He hastily gathered up his supplies before he ran off leaving Moses alone. He practically kicked up his heels in glee as he bounded off toward his freedom.

Moses wasn't sure what to do next. He pulled his pack off the raft and spread its contents on some large rocks. He had no idea where he was or how far he would need to travel before he could replenish his supplies. He kept what little food and water remained along with his cloak, his extra sandals, and his still-inadequate staff, but the rest he left behind.

Moses decided to follow what seemed to be a much-traveled path going south. He would orient himself by keeping the Sea on his right. He saw a few signs that others had walked this road before him, but he encountered no people. By the second morning, he had eaten all his food. Fortunately, he periodically came upon small streams and springs, so he had plenty of water. Without anything to break his fast, his stomach growled as he took up his pack to start walking again.

Moses always had the most interesting experiences when he walked. He could practically take a walking nap without falling over. Sometimes in this meditative state he would relive events from the past that were incredibly vivid. It was as if they were happening right before his eyes. He could engage in long conversations and, when he was hungry he could conjure up whole meals in such detail that he was sure he could actually smell the aroma of the food.

Like now…!

Oh, that smells good. His mouth watered and he wondered if he had ever before been able to create such a realistic, though imaginary, culinary experience.

When the smell started to fade, he stopped abruptly, turned around, and retraced his steps. The intensity of the aroma increased again! Meat, a stew …Oh, that smells so good.

He never even stopped to think that he could be walking in on bandits or slavers. Moses just left the path to follow the savory aroma. As soon as he walked into the clearing, he saw it. There was the fire with the stew bubbling in a skin suspended over it. A man sat staring into the fire with his back to Moses. Just as Moses was about to signal his presence, the man stood and turned to face him.

Chapter 44

They stood on a ridge overlooking a lush green valley. A river wound its way through it from end to end. On the slopes below, Moses and Eliezer saw trees bearing strange, but clearly edible fruit. The valley teemed with life. About half way down on a wide terrace of land, they saw tents, men, women, children, and a few sheep and goats.

A lovely sound landed lightly on their ears. It was the sound of singing. The breeze shifted and they caught the words: "The Promised Land is within us and among us."

They had found the valley that would contain and nurture their Community of Divine Promise.

They were home.

Eliezer

My father was so overwhelmed when he saw me in the clearing that his knees buckled and he fell to the ground. For one horrible moment, I feared the ultimate irony that after our respective astounding journeys, the shock of our even more astounding meeting had killed him. But then he opened his eyes wide and reached out to touch my face. Neither of us could speak. All we could do was look and touch – hands, sleeves, faces, heads, over and over again.

We cried for the longest time, but then with a twinkle in his eye he said, "Are you going to keep all that stew for yourself, or are you going to give me some before I expire for real?" We laughed together when simultaneously we pictured that other inarticulate meal after our shared vision quest.

We ate our fill. Then I walked over to the tree where the carcass of the goat still hung. A beautifully smoothed and carved staff leaned against it. I had carried that staff since we left the oasis next to our vision hill. I had planned to give it to Moses at the occasion of our rendezvous to replace the one he had ceded to Joshua, but of course, that had never transpired.

That staff had become my symbolic Moses. Little by little I stripped its bark and oiled it to make its surface, and particularly its handle, perfectly smooth. Into its length I carved symbolic representations of our journey and our challenges. I cried over it and caressed it during the many nights when I feared that my father was lost to us forever. For me, it was Moses, and after I gave it to him, it became for him the sign of the community he had long craved and since came to love.

He told me that from the first time his hand grasped its girth, he knew he belonged to it, and belonging to the staff, he knew he was at last ready to belong to the community. He lived with us for a few precious years after we settled our Community of Promise in this lovely valley, but now he's gone and we have only this staff to help us keep his memory alive.

Moses wanted his people to know the Holy One as intimately as he did, so he never tired of hearing us tell him how we grew into that relationship. And we never tired of hearing how much he had learned from his time in slavery. The staff attended all our stories, so now that he has died (for real this time), we will use it as our "talking stick." It will be at the center whenever we meet for stories or for business. Just like our Promised Land, it will forever remain within and among us.

Notes

Resources

and

Study Guide

General Notes

The book that you hold in your hand is a work of fiction. While I have made use of many of the Biblical stories involving Moses and the Israelites. I have most often given them an interpretation that fits with the novel's plot. I have tried to write Moses' story in a way that it could have happened, but there is no evidence that it ever did happen this way.

I encourage you to read the "official account" in the Torah. You will find portions of it in the books of Exodus, Numbers, Leviticus, and Deuteronomy. There are also several references in the Book of Joshua. It is very difficult from these sources to create a clear time-line of events. In the pages that follow, I have included a few references to particular Biblical passages that have inspired some of the events and ideas in the story

My novel is not a work of theology. It is simply a playful experiment that I hope will raise social, political, economic, and theological questions and will generate meaningful dialogue. After the notes you will find a Study Guide to stimulate group discussion.

Endnotes

1. The Biblical story of Moses is found in portions of Exodus, Leviticus, Numbers, and Deuteronomy in the Hebrew Bible.

2. The Israelites in Moses' time would not have used Gershom's divine designation, "Jehovah," in the concrete manner ascribed in my novel to Moses' elder son and his followers. Such usage is a more modern practice when people (predominately non-Jewish people) use it (and the name, "God," for that matter) like a proper name for the divine.

   I am grateful to Rabbi Mimi Baitch for explaining to me that "Jehovah" comes from adding the vowel sounds of another divine designation, "Adonai" to the unpronounceable tetragrammaton (YHWH) that Moses received on Mount Sinai while next to the burning bush.

3. See Exodus 3: 1—4: 19

4. See Exodus 4: 20—15: 21

5. See Exodus 15: 20—25

6. See Numbers 20: 1-13 for an account of the event that caused God to prohibit Moses from entering the Promised Land. It has always seemed like a pretty flimsy excuse to me, so I decided that it was appropriate my story for Moses to use a variation of the Biblical event as his explanation to Gershom for not entering the Promised Land.

7. For the story of Zelophehad and his daughters, see Numbers 26: 33; Numbers 27: 1-11; Numbers 36: 1-11; and Joshua 17:3.

8. See Numbers 14 for an explanation of why the first generation of freed Israelites could not enter the Promised Land.

9. For the Biblical account of Moses' final discourse, see Deuteronomy 29 – 34.

10. Legend has it that Moses was taken up directly to God and did not die. Could something like my story be the source of the legend?

11. See Exodus 32.

12. See Exodus 20.

13. See Genesis 47 for a description of how Joseph turned the Egyptian people into Pharaoh's slaves. This chapter also provides a possible motive for the Egyptian priests' enmity toward the Israelites.

Study Guide for *Community of Promise*

Community of Promise is a work of fiction that deals with many social, religious, economic, political, and theological/ spiritual issues. It is not presented as a challenge to the traditional Biblical texts. Rather, by means of the author's imagination, readers are invited to look at the traditional story from a different perspective. The novel has been used for a number of book study groups in congregations, though readers need not have a religious background to find this story of Moses interesting and thought provoking. After all, much of the framework for Western civilization has been informed and shaped by Biblical themes.

There is no correct way for a group to organize its study of the novel. Some groups have agreed to read only so many chapters between sessions in order to focus the themes of that particular discussion. Other groups have chosen to read at their own speed and have scheduled as many group sessions as desired for a thorough discussion. Your group should determine its own course.

The questions that follow are offered simply as a resource to stimulate discussion. Of course, your study group may choose to rely on its own questions. For that matter, the questions can be useful for individual readers, too.

The text of the novel contains a few footnotes, mostly to identify the Biblical references to themes and stories included in the novel. Some people find it useful to read the Biblical accounts indicated in the notes as a further resource for participation in a Study Group.

Enjoy!

Eliezer, Prologue, and Chapter 1

1. Eliezer, Moses' younger son, tells the story of his father from a very personal perspective. What might your interest be in exploring Moses' more personal thoughts about his role and objectives as the "Prophet of God?"

2. Some people believe that humans and God find a point of contact in the depths of the human unconscious. The *Prologue* describes the inner journey of a new, but confusing idea that comes to Moses through the remnant of a dream. Have you gained new insights, perspectives or wisdom through your dreams? And do you believe that others can experience similar "revelations" in this way?

3. Eliezer claims that there are other ways to tell Moses' story. Some people believe that there can be no particular bias in biblical stories if God is the "author." So we might wonder: is the Bible essentially a biased human story about relationship with God, or is it essentially God's unbiased story about humans?

4. The idea of attaining the Promised Land in the future has been the singular goal for the Israelites during their time in the wilderness. In Chapter 1, Moses reflects on how the Israelites' practical expectations for the Promised Land have been changing, becoming more materialistic, as they have come closer to their goal. Are fear, greed, and violence unavoidable for the Israelites and by extension for all of humanity?

Chapters 2—4

1. In his dream, Eliezer discovers divine presence and leading in human being-to-human being relationships, where the authority for relating to the divine is shared by the whole community. What do you think life would be like if we were able to rely on our human relationships as a way to experience divine relationship and direction?

2. Gershom wants to use military force under Joshua's command to enforce compliance with the letter of divine law. Can you identify other times in history, including the present, when religious ends are used to justify forceful means?

3. Given that Gershom wants to use force to keep people in proper relationship with God, how does Moses see the nature of that relationship differently?

Eliezer, Chapters 5–6

1. Moses tries to describe his history of mystical experiences. What are some of the ways you think people have mystical experiences? What kinds of mystical experiences have you had? And what was it like when you tried to describe in words the experience and any message contained in it?

2. Read the account in Exodus 3–4. What do you think of how Moses' first time on the mountain with God is recorded there? How would you compare the official version with Eliezer's version?

3. The author makes the assumption that mystical experiences can be interpreted in a variety of ways and that the expectations and presuppositions of the mystic (or the "stenographer") affect how the story is subsequently told. How might your pre-conceived ideas about God and life affect your understanding of a personal mystical experience?

4. On page 40, Moses learns that rescuing the Israelites not only benefits those who are being rescued, but also benefits the "Egyptian Collective Soul." We live in a world that tries to assign God's favor to one side of a conflict or the other. What do you think of the idea that a divinely guided activity could benefit both sides?

5. On pages 44–45, Moses knows where to look for sweet water, but the Israelites see his action as a miracle. What

levels of understanding become available to you about this event if the miracle in Exodus 15: 20—25 can be "explained?" Does the story then necessarily lose its meaning?

Eliezer, Chapter 7

1. Two brothers grow up in the shadow of the same great man. What explanation could you imagine for why they turned out to be so different?

Chapters 8—9

1. Perhaps many of the Israelites had the capacity to be mystics, but only Moses was considered the "Prophet of God." What problems and possibilities might be associated with a shared community-wide responsibility for communication with the divine?

2. When modern people say that God has spoken to them or in some way given them a message, we might consider sending them to a psychiatrist. How can we ascertain if a message is of healthy (or divine) origin rather than simply a product of psychosis?

3. As Moses and Eliezer share their mystical perspectives, they seem to validate one another. Do you think that the validity of mystical revelation increases as more people are involved in the sharing?

4. The Promised Land has traditionally been thought of as a particular place. Moses and Eliezer learn from their shared vision that while place is an optional condition, other characteristics are more important in defining the Promised Land. At this point in the story, what other characteristics have you identified? What other characteristics would you include in your description of a divine Promised Land?

5. Moses is toying with the idea that God's name (I AM) when looked at from another angle must include divine and human love. Do you think this is too much of a "stretch?" Might there be connections between being/creation and love?

6. A new vision begins to emerge for Moses and Eliezer. It compels them to consider a radical change in their direction and even their purpose. What is your experience of being motivated to unexpected actions and directions when your sense of "calling" has changed? What barriers or challenges inhibited the change for you? And what factors or conditions helped you embrace the new vision?

Chapters 10—13

1. What do you think of the story of Milcah and her sisters? Could an experience like theirs motivate some kind of radical change or activism for you? Think about times when you have experienced or even observed injustice based on some characteristic like gender, race, class, or disability? What factors affected your response to the situation?

2. Moses, Eliezer, and Milcah share the concern that proximity to the Promised Land has demoted the status of women from valuable community partners to chattel or property. Do you think that crises like those in the wilderness create more or less human equality? What leads you to your conclusions?

3. On Page 100, Gershom decides that God is testing him to see if he will offer Moses' life as evidence of his commitment. What are some examples (ancient and modern) when the lives of others are offered in the service of some political, economic, or religious purpose?

Chapters 14—15

1. In the Biblical account, (Deuteronomy 29—34) Moses' final discourse before his death is mostly about divine directions and detailed laws. In the novel, Moses addresses two issues: the necessity for people to develop mature individual freedom so that they can exist as a faithful community; and, secondly, love as the necessary perspective from which all law must be interpreted. How do you see freedom and love affecting the quality of your participation in your community of faith and in your life?

2. The people who gathered to mourn Moses' passing now discover that there is another possible route for them to take in their search for The Promised Land. When in your life has the inevitability of a death (either literal or figurative) turned into new possibilities or a new vision for your life's path?

Eliezer, Sarah, and, Chapter 16

1. Sarah identifies a shift in the understanding of the Promised Land held by the new group. She says that the Promised Land has become "an eternal direction" instead of a geographical destination. Furthermore, she notes the paradoxical idea that they are already in it, but they will also continue seeking it. How easy or hard is it for you to live with such a paradoxical understanding?

2. If you could embrace the above paradox, how might that change your personal objectives and your relationships?

3. Sarah is not the first character to be concerned about the idea of having to take over the Promised Land by force. What do you think about that idea?

4. In the modern world, the phrase, "the rule of law," is often used to protect the wealth that the rich may have unfairly obtained from the poor. Sarah is concerned about what she

terms "The Stuff Laws." She thinks that many social ills are perpetuated by the inequalities of personal ownership. For the sake of argument, what do you think a community might look like and how might its constituents behave if personal wealth were less important?

5. Sarah's mother tells a story about her experience when Moses received the law on Mt. Sinai, and about the response by the Israelites of creating the Golden Calf. In her version, they were not being unfaithful to Jehovah; rather they were trying to help Moses survive against a God that they found to be incredibly powerful and perhaps dangerous. Short of determining the best or correct interpretation, what do you think about interpreting stories like this from the Bible using a variety of perspectives and possibilities?

6. Discuss the trust issue between Moses and the people. What factors might have motivated the people to have more or less trust in Moses?

7. Sarah recounts a mystical experience that has made The Holy One very real to her. Have you ever experienced anything like that? When someone tells or writes about a mystical experience, how ready are you to accept the validity of their account?

8. Most of the mystical experiences described in the novel take place in the wilderness. Do you think that being in some kind of "wilderness" is necessary for a mystical experience to happen?

Chapter 17

1. Moses and Gershom have a complex relationship. Does Gershom think that Moses did not actually die, but is within hearing distance? If so, what would motivate him to let Moses get away?

2. During Moses' encounter with the Holy One in the cave, the reader is left with the possibility that Moses has dreamed it

all. Does it matter whether or not this was a dream? Would the answer to that question affect the sacredness or meaningfulness of the experience?

3. How do you think it would be for Moses to be required to develop a new way of relating to a community? Have you ever had to change your status within a group? What was it like for you?

Chapter 18

1. Clearly, The Community is filled with both anxiety and hope as they consider the issue of leadership. What other models of leadership do you think they might have developed? Particularly identify those models that are different from Gershom's hierarchical structure.

2. How do you think an intentional openness to divine guidance like Sarah recommends might influence the functioning of groups to which you already belong?

Chapter 19

1. Moses is about to embark on a kind of sabbatical leave from a lifetime of responsibility. What are some of the questions you might have if you were in Moses' shoes?

Chapter 20

1. Enosh, the career soldier, has made a somewhat impulsive decision to join The Community. And much to his surprise he has even been selected for one of the leadership positions. How do you think he assesses his ability to serve in this capacity? And how does he resolve the conflict between a lifetime of duty and this practically treasonous decision?

Chapter 21

1. Now that he has the spaciousness of retirement, Moses begins reflecting on the experience and meaning of his

mystical contacts with The Holy One. What examples can you find from your own history where it took the perspective of time for you to plumb the depths of your own past and its various meanings? What understandings have emerged from your reflection on such events?

2. Moses struggles with putting his understanding of The Holy One into words. Do you think there is a correct way to understand God? If (as Moses believes) there is a built-in limitation to how accurately we can understand or articulate the essence of God, how might that affect the practice of a God-based religion?

3. Moses identifies Gershom's two-point plan for salvation: Understand "Jehovah's" clear directions and then obey them. Do you think we possess a clear divine plan? And, do you think that obedience is the primary measure of faith? If not, what other measures would you identify?

4. Moses discovers that he has been profoundly lonely for most of his life. Do you think loneliness is an inevitable consequence of having a position of authority in a community? What are some appropriate ways to mitigate that loneliness? What dangers might be inherent in being "lonely at the top?"

5. Moses struggles with the apparent usefulness of a legalistic structure early in the development of a group. There are many legalistic communities and organizations in our modern world. How can a community be encouraged to outgrow its need for such a structure? Is it even possible?

6. Using Moses' ponderings on the potential meaning(s) of the Ten Commandments, what is your understanding of idolatry?

7. Do you agree with Moses that the idolatry of words and ideas can be even more destructive than physical representations (i.e. idols) of divine characteristics?

8. Moses sees physical idolatry and improper use of God's "name" as two versions of the same problem. What examples of idolatry and using the name of God in vain do you find in the present?

9. Moses identifies "the Sabbath Day" as a way to ensure rest and divine reflection. What meaning does Sabbath have for you, and how do you make use of it? What helps or hinders your experience of Sabbath?

10. The Commandment about honoring mother and father has been confusing to many people, particularly if they have grown up in an abusive home. Moses notes that whenever this commandment is exercised in a hierarchical manner the people at the bottom, particularly the women and children, suffer. What do you think honoring father and mother means?

11. Moses dreams about losing his prophet's mantle of authority. He fears that if he loses it, he will lose his entire identity. At what times in your life has a change in title, profession, or status threatened your understanding of your identity and/or purpose? One common example is the challenge of retirement.

Chapters 22—24

1. Sarah has invited The Community to consult with The Holy One regarding their organizational structure and the selection of the leadership team. She worries that others might not know how to invite divine contact and she wonders about the variety of approaches to mystical connection. In what ways do you think mystical experiences happen? Do you think her process is the same as prayer?

2. Asher worries that he cannot see into the future, but then concludes that his mystical experiences might confine themselves to the present. Do you think mystics are able to see into the future? If so, does that mean that the future is foreordained?

3. Think about how you feel whenever you embark on a new direction in your life, particularly when you realize that you can't know how things are likely to work out.

"Moses" Chapters 25, 26, 28, 30, 31

1. Moses has been contemplating his readiness to join The Community. Suddenly he is captured and the choice he must now make stands in a succession of life-changing choices. What examples can you give of times when you (or others you know) have been required to make previously unthinkable choices? What factors do you think influence such choices?

2. Moses confronts his abhorrence of slavery. While the evils of slavery are obvious, it is still prevalent in the world. What issues associated with slavery can you identify? Try to include factors besides money that might encourage people to engage in slave trade. Do any of those factors play out in social situations and roles that might not be identified as slavery per se?

3. Moses wonders why his life has taken such a radical turn. It had seemed that everything was moving in the direction of his uniting with The Community, but now that seems impossible. Often, humans question what God is up to when lives take a radical turn. How do you think God participates in the course and direction of human lives?

4. Moses begins to identify with the slaves he had led out of their bondage in Egypt, and he ponders how they had become slaves in the first place. He notes that his ancestor, Joseph, had used his position of great authority to turn most of the Egyptians into slaves of Pharaoh. Moses concludes that the resulting Egyptian resentment became the seeds for the eventual slavery of the Israelites. What historical examples can you identify where the overuse of power and authority eventually transforms into its opposite?

5. What do you think of Moses' idea that people can become slaves in spirit even before they become slaves in body?

6. When Moses thinks he has lost everything, there is still more to lose. Do you think that profound loss is necessary for spiritual transformation? Have you experienced anything like this?

7. Moses discovers how difficult it is to trust even when there is evidence for a positive outcome. He realizes that he had been unfair in his frustration with the fear-filled Israelites. Have you experienced times when you have tried to reassure someone else in their difficult time or when someone else has tried to reassure you? How did that approach work?

8. Moses reaches a new depth of understanding of the fear the Israelites, who could not imagine any hope for themselves in the wilderness. What has been your experience of apparent hopelessness, and how did you come through it?

"Community" Chapters 27, 29, 32

1. When Moses doesn't appear at the expected rendezvous site, The Community and its new leadership team face their first opportunity to make a major decision. Have you had experience with leaders who facilitate the larger group in coming to a decision rather than making the decision for them? How did it work?

2. Do you think a group has sufficient collective wisdom to determine the best direction or course of action? Some believe that relying on the opinions of the masses results in inferior decisions. What do you think?

3. The team wonders if they need priests to "instruct the people and judge whether their behavior is acceptable to the Holy One?" Is it necessary for a community to have

someone specifically trained or "called" to perform that priestly function?

4. Can dreams, particularly those experienced by several people in a group be a reliable guide for establishing direction?

5. The leadership team discovers that the people both want to trust their leaders and resist trusting at the same time. What do you think about Enosh's explanation that trust cannot take root without experiencing some evidence of trust-worthiness?

Chapter 33

1. Moses realizes that he has relied on Gershom's image of "the angry God" to control the Israelites more than he previously was able to admit. At this moment he takes his own responsibility for it. What times can you identify in your own life when you have empowered someone else to perform a task that is fundamentally abhorrent to you? One extreme example of this is taking a stand for peace while still paying the taxes that fund armed conflict.

2. On the slave boat, Moses plumbs the depths of his inner motivations and his hypocrisy. He concludes that his own fear-tinged egotism has restricted his compassion and has magnified his self-righteous anger for years. To his credit he faces himself and prepares to face the Holy One. How much do you think the presence of power, influence, and apparent freedom might have on the ability of humans to make an honest confession? Do you think such a confession is valuable, or would you recommend that we let the past simply remain in the past?

3. The Holy One helps Moses face his past compassionately. Some would hold that such an admission of guilt should be met with at least a measure of scorn, if not outright punishment. Do you think the Holy One is being too easy on Moses? Can you imagine having such a conversation

with God about your life and decisions? What do you think God might say to you?

4. The Holy One states: "The two most difficult choices in human existence are, first, to affirm life in the face of apparent hopelessness. And the second is to learn from your experiences by adopting a new, and therefore unpredictable, perspective. When you take responsibility like that, you exercise hope—as distinct from wishful thinking."
   Do you agree that these are the most difficult choices for humans? Do you see current situations where the ability to affirm life and exercise hope might be useful or even necessary?

5. In your understanding of God, do you think it is necessary for God to know how everything will turn out? If it were your choice, would you prefer a god who knew the future or one who did not, but was always with you in the present?

Chapters 34—35

1. The Leadership Team concludes that the development of the larger group as a community is more important than any particular decision they might ultimately make? How hard is it for you to live without the promise of finding the "right" thing to do in a given situation? What other ways are there to evaluate decisions besides whether or not they result in a particular outcome?

2. How hard do you think it is for a group of any size to stay connected and functional in the face of a major crisis? In your experience, what helps or hinders the process?

3. Sarah encourages the members of The Community to work with people who might hold differing opinions. Why do you think she suggested that approach? And what do you think might be gained by listening respectfully to conflicting positions?

4. A difficulty for many groups arises when too many individuals are pressing to get their own way. The Community members discover that it is more important to stay together than to get their individual ways. What do you think is gained or lost by such a position?

"Moses" Chapters 36, 39, 41

1. Moses experiences a moment of panic when he realizes that the Holy One will not rescue him. Have you ever experienced a situation when you realized that you would just have to face it, that there would be no rescue?

2. What do you think it was like for Moses to have to follow Cabrun's plan rather than be the one with the power to determine their course?

3. Moses is very anxious until he makes his decision to go ahead with the escape plans. How have your feelings changed once you have finally made significant decisions in your life? What do you think this means?

4. Moses makes a choice, recognizing that he has no power to make things turn out the way he wants. How hard is it for you to decide what to do when you can't guarantee the outcome?

5. It appears that just when Moses is ready to give up completely, a new and hopeful possibility appears. What have been your experiences of giving up in a difficult situation only to discover new possibilities?

"Community" Chapters 37, 38, 40

1. Through the activities of Sarah and Asher, The Community has the experience of a new kind of priesthood. Do you think this "priesthood" is necessary for The Community? If so, how would you like to see them function?

2. How would you assess the effectiveness of The Community's leadership model? What modifications would you make?

Chapters 42—44, *Eliezer*

1. Eliezer gets a hint that he could actually meet up with Moses if he follows a specific plan from one of his dreams. Do you think people sometimes come to discover directions or truths about their lives from dreams? Have you ever experienced anything like this?

2. How do you feel when Moses and Eliezer are reunited with each other and with The Community?

3. What do you imagine Moses' life is like during his last years with The Community?

4. What problems do you think The Community will encounter now that they are settled?

5. How would you communicate to the next generation the wisdom that The Community has gained?

Bonus Question
What do you think might happen with The Community in the sequel to this novel?

Thank you for making use of this Study Guide. I hope it has encouraged and aided your journey toward your own *Community of Promise.*